HANGMAN'S KNOT

"I was sent here by the President of the United States to restore the rule of law in a lawless land, and as God is my creator, that is what I am going to do. If my ways seem harsh, then so be it." Hangin' Judge Parker paused. "James Sundance," he said, "I hereby find you guilty of murder. The sentence of this court is that you be taken from this place to a place of execution, on the morning of March 16, 1887, and there hanged by the neck until you are dead, and may the Lord have mercy on your soul."

APACHE WAR

Sundance felt his energy draining away, as he and the Apache fenced with their long, thick knife blades. Victorio jumped with his right leg forward, thrusting with his right hand at the same time. The point came in straight and true but Sundance was already moving back and the knife just pricked his stomach. He slashed down hard and cut Victorio across the back of the wrist. Victorio's knife fell to the ground. The Apache straightened up with blood dripping from his hands.

SUNDANCE

HANGMAN'S KNOT

APACHE WAR

PETER McCURTIN

LEISURE BOOKS NEW YORK CITY

A LEISURE BOOK®

July 1999

Published by

Dorchester Publishing Co., Inc.
276 Fifth Avenue
New York, NY 10001

ISBN 0-8439-4561-3

SUNDANCE

HANGMAN'S KNOT

APACHE WAR

HANGMAN'S KNOT

CHAPTER 1

When Sundance woke up there was nothing but blackness in front of his eyes. The blackness was as thick as the stink. The stink was a mixture of many things, piss and sweat and things worse than either. Mostly it was the stink of fear.

It wasn't completely dark in the dungeon; light glimmered faintly from an air hole set high in the wall. The air vent was about the size of a shoe box; a cat could have crawled through it, but never a man. Sundance reached up and put his hand in front of the aperture cut into the solid stone and felt no movement of air. It was the size of a shoe box and yet it was barred.

His skull throbbed with pain and he sat on the greasy floor of the dungeon. Blood was caked on the back of his head and there was a soft, soggy place where he had been struck. The door of the dungeon was of solid iron, as solid as the walls, and after he ran his hands over it, he could find no peephole. But even through the massive iron door he heard the sound of moaning out there in the darkness. In the darkness, waking up in utter darkness, it was hard to think. Then his brain cleared and he remembered the fight, the argument, and the killing that ended it.

Pictures jerked through his mind like stereo slides; they dropped behind his eyes, one after another. The main street of Fort Smith. A crowded saloon. Behind the bar a fat bartender pulling a beer. Then a man with a Texas accent saying as how he hated red nigger halfbreeds. The man was drunk. Sundance finished most of his beer. Tried to walk out. His back was turned when the first shot came. The bullet clipped a strand of buckskin from his coat. The man was steadying his gun when Sundance turned and put a bullet in his head. A movement behind him then, too late to turn. His head exploded. . . .

He knew he was underground; the air vent probably slanted down from street level. Feeling his way around the moisture-sweating walls, he found that he was alone. In the darkness there was nothing but darkness and stink. He reached down to see if they had missed the thin-bladed knife strapped to his leg. They hadn't. They had even taken his belt so he couldn't hang himself from the bars of the vent.

It had been self-defense. He had tried to walk away. There had been twenty-five or thirty people in the big saloon on Governor Murphy Street. Some of the witnesses would be gone by now, but the two bartenders were still there. So was the faro dealer and the lookout with the sawed-off shotgun watching the game from a high stool. That should do it, that ought to be enough. Outside, boots thumped on a stone floor, and more than one man was coming. The door crashed open on its hinges and a dark lantern knifed through the gloom of the cell. The beam of light hit him in the face, blinding him.

"Walk out, you," a rough voice said.

Two big men with round silver badges on their chests were with the jailer. The jailer held the dark lantern and he got out of the way when Sundance came out. The two deputies jumped him, wrestled his hands behind his back, and locked on wrist-irons. Iron door lined the stone-floored hallway, and the only light there came from a hanging lantern turned low. The far end of the hallway was dark and the moaning came from down there. In the hallway the stink wasn't as bad as in the cell.

"What's the matter with old Hankins?" one of the deputies asked the jailer.

The jailer said, "What do you think's the matter with him? He don't want to hang."

The other deputy laughed. "Imagine that!" he said. "Old Hanky don't like to climb steps."

Sundance's lips were salty and dry. "You got any water in this jail?"

Instead of giving an answer, the first deputy punched him in the stomach and he nearly went down. They lifted him and slammed against the wall.

"I'll give you water," the deputy said.

The deputy who laughed was still laughing. "Save your strength, Gruber," he said. "It's a hot day. Besides, he ain't been convicted yet."

"He will be," Gruber said. "One look I know he's guilty. He's guilty as hell. They're all guilty."

"For Christ's sake, Gruber, give the man a drink of water," the jailer said, slamming the door of the cell.

They pushed and kicked Sundance up stone steps to a bare dirty room with deep zinc basins set along the wall. At the far end of the room there was an iron cage and in it were piled boots, gun, saddles, hats of every shape and make. Topping the pile was a black silk skullcap; a Chinaman had passed this way. Above the sinks iron cups were chained to pins driven into the spaces between the block of stone.

11

"Drink and get yourself cleaned up," Gruber said. "Only do it fast. The judge don't like to be kept waiting by a man that's due for trial."

Sundance gulped down four cups of water and was trying to fill a fifth when Gruber knocked the cup out of his hand. The chained cup clanged against the wall. It made a sound like a bell. Sundance turned.

"What trial?" he said.

"For murder," the second deputy said. The second deputy looked mean, but the meanness in him hadn't gone as deep as it had in Gruber.

"So now you're a lawyer, is that it, Mullins? Stick to what you do, let the judge take care of the rest. Start washing, halfbreed."

Gruber pulled Sundance away from the sink and shoved a faded floursack at him. It was dirty and so old that the letters on it were almost completely faded. Sundance dried his face and combed back his long yellow hair with his fingers. With water in his belly and some of the dirt washed away he didn't feel too bad.

Mulling pointed. "Out that way."

More stone steps took them up to another level of the building. The room they were in now was big and had criss-crossed bars on the high narrow windows. The windows looked like the high, narrow windows in a cotton mill. The windows had been painted over with light gray paint so that not much light came through. At the far end of the room was an iron cage. The cage had two iron-slatted doors, one to let the prisoners in, another to pass them through to some other part of the building. Sundance guessed the courtroom. Past the second door there was another door; this one was made of wood.

In the cage there were seven men of ages from seventeen to sixty-five. Three of them were Indians and one was a halfbreed of mixed Indian and Negro blood. The youngest prisoner, a pale-faced farm boy with matted black and patched overalls, had his face in his hands. From the cage came the stink of fear; fear seemed to have seeped into the walls of the big stone building.

Some of the prisoners looked at Sundance when Gruber unlocked the door and pushed him inside. Most ignored him, lost in their own troubles. A long bench was bolted to the wall and beyond the farm boy there was a place to sit. The boy looked at Sundance and put his face back in his hands. Sundance was so close he felt him shaking. The boy had been crying and there were streaks on his dirty chinless face.

The halfbreed spoke first. "What you in for, friend?" The black Indian had an easy smile and a slow way of talking. "They got me for making a little withdrawl from a bank over there in the west. Me and a few friends. My friends got away with their savings, I got caught. My old black daddy always told me never trust banks."

"They're charging me with murder," Sundance said.

"And naturally you didn't do it," the halfbreed said.

"That's right," Sundance said. "A whole saloon can tell the way it happened."

"You'd be a stranger then," the halfbreed said. "I mean the way you're talking you must be a stranger."

"Meaning wht?" Sundance said.

"This and that," the halfbreed said. "Mostly meaning you can't know much about the Honorable Judge Isaac Parker, otherwise known as the hanging judge. Listen to me, my friend, don't set too much store by these witnesses when you get out there and face the judge. The judge listens to as much evidence as he wants to listen to, then come hell or high water the judge makes up his own mind. He won't laugh at you if you try to make an appeal. The people in the court will laugh

13

at you, and that's a fact. Oh sure, you can try to make an appeal and the judge won't try to stop you. The only problem is you'll be dead before the lawyers finish arguing."

Sundance looked at the black Indian, a big, wide-shouldered man with grayish skin and a bush of wiry black hair turning no special color. Maybe he was trying to mask his fear with smooth talk. Maybe he wasn't. May be he was as tough as he looked. He looked like a man with a quick mind and a quicker gunhand.

"If I'm found guilty," Sundance said.

"Don't mean to distress you, friend," the halfbreed said. "But I'm afraid that's how it's going to be. The judge upholds the law by dropping citizens through the trap."

One of the other prisoners, a middle-aged man with one eye and a scarred face, had been glaring at the halfbreed. "You talk real smart, Sugar, but you ain't smart a-tall. You can't be smart or you wouldn't be in here. Joe Buck and the other boys got away, but you're in here. I'll bet they're spending your share of the bank money right this minute."

Sugar smiled. "Thank you for the kind and thoughtful words, Brother Conklin. I appreciate them, 'deed I do. Yawl are so right about me not bein' smart. Eby-body know a nappy-headed nigger Cherokee caint be smart. As for this Joe Buck. If you-all talkin' about de no-two-ree-us outlaw, Ah hab to confess Ah hab nevah made dat gennum's ack-kwayn-tence."

Conklin said, "You don't fool me with that minstrel talk, Sugar. Everybody in the Territory knows you ride with Buck. Did ride with him. Makes no difference you did or not, Parker's going to hang you."

"It looks like that, don't it," Sugar said. "But like the man said, you never know."

14

"Know my backside," Conklin said.

"That'd take a lot of knowing," Sugar said. "Big ass! Take a lot of knowing. Get it? It's a joke, son." Sugar smiled at Conklin.

Nobody smiled except Sugar.

Conklin said, "You won't be making jokes when they take you out."

"Oh, I don't know about that," Sugar said. "I just now recalled a pretty fair joke. This joke is going to chase away all your sorrowful thoughts, Brother Conklin. See, there was this feller and he was standing on the trapdoor with the rope around his neck and just before they let him go the hangman sez, 'You got any last words, son?' So there they were, him on the trap and the hangman with his hand on the lever and this feller thought and thought and thought. Finally, after all that deep thinking, he sez to the hangman, 'You know, sir. This is going to be a pretty good lesson for me.' "

"You lousy son of a bitch!" Conklin said. "I still say you won't be joking when Maledon drops the noose over your head."

"No doubt you're right, Brother Conklin," Sugar said. "But I *know* I'll take it better than you."

Sundance heard the boy whispering to him. "What are you saying, boy? I can't hear you."

Not wanting the others to hear, the boy didn't raise his voice very much. Close to Sundance his breath smelled sweetish as if he had been eating spoonfuls of jam. "I just stole some horses," he said. "They won't hang me for that, will they?"

"You kill anybody?"

"I wounded one of the riders that came after me. I heard later it was just a flesh wound in his arm. I wouldn't have shot him if he hadn't been shooting at

15

me. Nobody was killed, so how can they hang me?"

"I don't know," Sundance said. "It doesn't seem likely, this being a federal court. You'll have to wait and find out. I'm not the one to ask about this."

Sundance hadn't given the boy any encouragement. The boy said, "It makes me feel better you saying that about this being a federal court. Be different if the stockmen caught me. They'd hang me sure. This can't be the same as that, can it?"

"I told you I don't know," Sundance said.

"What's Judge Parker like?" Sundance asked Sugar, who seemed to know a lot about everything.

Sugar displayed all his teeth in a mirthless grin. "Not being a personal friend of the judge I can't say first hand. Maybe you ought to ask me what he's not like. Judge Isaac Parker, among other things, is the Wrath of God. The Sword of the Almighty! He smites the wicked wherever he finds them. There must be a whole lot of wickedness in these here parts because the old Judge he never stops that smiting. He's part showman and part saint. He doesn't talk just to the President, he talks to God, and he don't take any guff from either of them high mucky-mucks. He's nothing if not a religious man, for he prays to the Lord with all his might for those he sends his way in such a goddamned hurry."

"Why don't you shut up," Conklin said.

"Just answering the man's question," Sugar said. "You think you can tell it better? Course you can't. As I was telling my friend here, Judge Parker just knows the Lord is squarely on his side, so anything he does is all right. Now we have to give the man credit, don't we? Cause from the law and order point of view he's doing one hell of a job. He's a fair man, they tell me. He'll hang a rich man as fast as a poor man. Last year that state senator's rascally son up and stabbed that whore for something or another. Wasn't giving him the special satisfaction he craved. Old Buford, his daddy, hired the smartest law talker in Little Rock, pulled all kind of strings behind the judge's back, even got somebody to whisper in the President's ear. Didn't do him one bit of good. The boy got hung in company with four two-bit desperados. Does that answer you question, my friend?''

"It'll do," Sundance said.

The door from the courtroom opened, then the gate to the cage. Gruber's ugly red face had a solemn look. "Benjamin Woodhouse," he called.

CHAPTER 2

It didn't take long.

The tall, barred windows of the courtroom were open and the air coming through smelled good after the stink of the cage. All the benches were packed and men were standing in the back. Heads turned as the tall copper-skinned halfbreed with the shoulder-length yellow hair walked to the spike-topped box where prisoners had to stand while their cases were being heard. Even though Fort Smith was on the edge of Indian Territory, there was a murmur of surprise at his appearance. Then Judge Isaac Parker, the most feared judge in the West, brought down his gavel with a crash, and Sundance got his first look at the man who was to send him to his doom.

Parker was tall and thin and though his voice was almost gentle it reached to every corner of the courtroom; in its very gentleness there was more menace than in a display of rage. He struck the gavel pad only once and there was absolute silence. His beard was silky and light brown and his eyes were the kind of washed out blue that comes up white in photographs. He looked a little like John Brown in those last pictures made before he was hanged, but instead of being wild

Parker's eyes were mild and his light hair was smooth instead of spiky. He wore a black frock coat and a stand-up collar and a black cravat was tied high on his thin neck. He sat erect in a high-backed chair and his eyes bored into Sundance as he took his place in the prisoner's box.

"Read the charge, Chief Deputy," Judge Parker said.

A big barrel bodied man with a scarred eyelid and a grizzled mustache got up and said the charge was murder. Said James Sundance, of no permanent abode, had murdered one Elijah Nickerson in Quigley's Saloon on the previous day, April 14, 1887. Principal witness for the prosecution was Deputy Marshal John Henry Gruber who happened to walk into Quigley's Saloon at the moment the murder took place. Deputy Marshal Gruber was present in the court and would testify as to the facts in the case. . . .

Judge Parker leaned forward in his chair. "How do you plead?" he asked Sundance.

"Not guilty by reason of self-defense," Sundance said. "There are witnesses."

Parker ignored him. "Call Deputy Marshal Gruber," he ordered.

Gruber was used to giving evidence and he kept it short. "I witnessed the killing," he said, "and immediately arrested the accused, James Sundance."

Judge Parker waved Gruber away and told Sundance he could speak. Sundance told it exactly as it happened and when he finished he asked the court's permission to call witnesses. Parker nodded but no one came forward.

Sundance tried to say something but Parker shut him up. He leaned forward and placed both hands, palms down, on the bench. "I think this court has heard enough," he said. "The facts in this case speak for themselves. What is your occupation, Mr. Sundance?"

He interrupted Sundance before he finished explaining. "Enough. That will do! Do you deny that you are a professional gunman?"

"Not in the way you mean," Sundance said.

"Don't quibble, Mr. Sundance," Parker said. "By your own admission you are a man who makes his living with a gun. No matter what you think you are, to this court you are a gunman and a killer. But I think it is safe to say that you have killed your last man. The man you killed in Quigley's Saloon was not a gunfighter of any kind. Elijah Nickerson, the deceased, was a well-known horse breeder."

"He fired a bullet at my back," Sundance said. "He was trying for a second shot."

Parker said, "That is beside the point. You are a gunman—a professional killer—and you killed a man here.

"Your very presence in this town, in any law abiding town, is an affront to its citizens. Men of your loathsome profession bring violence and death wherever you go. There would be little violence if men like you did not exist, and I might say, Mr. Sundance, that your name is not unknown to me. For years you have broken the law in your pursuit of what you call justice. If injustice exists it is for the courts to decide. Men like you have no place in decent society and, by God, it is my intention to make sure that you break no more of its laws. Do you have any further to say before sentence is pronounced?"

"I guess you like hanging better than women," Sundance said.

For an instant Parker looked ready to lose his temper, but he gripped the edge of the bench and forced himself to be calm and his voice remained steady.

"For all of you listening," he said quietly, "I will say now what I have said so many times before in this courtroom. This is a nation of laws and they must be obeyed because without law we might as well be beasts of the field. I was sent here by the President of the United States to restore the rule of law in a lawless land and as God is my Creator that is what I am going to do. If my ways seem harsh, then so be it, for to me the horse thief of today is the murderer of tomorrow. To me whiskey runner is as guilty—indeed, even more guilty—than the Indians who commit atrocities under the influence of liquor."

The judge paused. "James Sundance," he said. "I hereby find you guilty of murder. The sentence of this court is that you be taken from this place to a place of execution, on the morning of March 16, 1887, and there hanged by the neck until you are dead, and may the Lord have mercy on your soul."

As Sundance was led away he heard the judge calling the next case.

It was still early morning when they put him back in the cell, but after the door was slammed and locked it was hard to tell night from day. A few hours later they brought him a plate of beans and a cup of bitter coffee. The beans were cold and stale but he ate hungrily and thought about the time he had to live. Maybe less than twenty hours; after that it would be all over. Death had been a long time coming, and now here it was. After all the trails he'd ridden, it was all going to end in a town he was just passing through. A drunk with a gun and a hate for Indians, and a judge who saw himself as the Angel of Death. No matter. If it wasn't that it would be something else.

He had to face the truth: there was no way out. He had faced death many times and always he had hoped that his death would come swiftly in the roar of gunfire. He had hoped to die as he had lived; the rope had never figured much in his thoughts. But now, after all the years, all the danger, the rope was out there waiting for him. The rope and the crook-backed German hangman, the silent, legal killer they called Maledon.

Waiting for death in the darkness, he felt no emotion as he decided that he would try to make them kill him before he reached the gallows. If he got lucky he would grab for a gun and they would shoot him down. He would try for a quick death when they came to tie his hands behind him. If he didn't die then he would have to take the long walk.

Hours passed and he knew it was night when he stood up and looked at the air vent in the wall. The light was gone. He guessed it was close to midnight. Down the hall the man they called Old Hankins was still moaning. Except for the moaning it was very quiet.

He could have slept but he didn't because sleep wasted time when he could think. But no matter how many times he went over it, he knew there was no way to escape. The jail was a fortress, a stone machine that carried men along to their deaths.

Air glimmered in the vent and he knew it was morning. First light came early in April. How long had he left? Maybe an hour, unless they started before the sun was full up in the sky. What he had to do was to face Gruber when he grabbed at Mullins' gun. If he showed his back, Gruber would knock him on the skull and they would carry him out unconscious. He had no special reason for wanting to kill either of the deputies, though Gruber looked like a man who needed killing.

It must have been about eight when he heard them

22

coming. He stood up and waited. The door swung back and there was Doolin with a stubby shotgun pointed at his middle. It wasn't a regular double-barrel cut down for close work. It was one of the new, specially made short guns they used in jails.

"Step lively," Gruber ordered.

Sundance's eyes jumped to Mullin's holster. It was empty. So was Gruber's. Gruber saw the look and laughed.

"You don't get off that easy," he said. "You'll get it in the legs if you try anything, then we'll hang you sitting in a chair. It's been done."

Mullins tied his hands with a strip of rawhide that cut into the flesh. The jailer, with his big ring of keys, looked on without interest. Mullins didn't say anything.

"Up you go," Gruber said.

Down the hall Old Hankins was yelling that he had money stashed away. Enough to buy his way out. The jailer went down and kicked the door.

They marched Sundance upstairs to the room where the cage was. At this hour the cage was empty. Mullins held the iron cup and let him take two drinks of water. He turned to face them.

"Not just yet," Gruber said. "The Judge wants to see you."

Judge Parker lived on the top floor of the federal building; a circular stairway went up to his door. Gruber knocked then Parker opened the door and let them in. The chief marshal was by the window looking out. He wore a gray hopsack coat with a bulge under the left armpit made by a shoulder holster. A pot of coffee steamed over an alcohol lamp on the desk. There was a flag and paintings of Presidents and an engraving of John Marshall, Chief Justice of the Supreme Court. By itself on another wall was a picture of an English judge with a sour face in a wig.

"Leave us," Parker told Gruber. "Stand outside."

Sunlight washed through the big barred windows of the judge's chambers, glistening on the oiled backs of lawbooks in oak bookcases that went from floor to ceiling. The steam from the coffee pot was yellow in the sunlight, and there was the smell of wax and old books.

"You haven't got long," Parker said. "Do you follow any religion? Do you want to see a clergyman?"

"I'd like some of that coffee," Sundance said.

"Show some respect," the chief deputy said without looking away from the window.

Parker took Sundance by the arm and led him over to the window. "We'll see about the coffee," he said. "First, I want you to see something."

The ten-man gallows stood in a little grassy square directly below Parker's window. The grass was well-watered and neatly trimmed and there were bright flowerbeds along the edges. An old black man had finished watering the grass and now he was dragging the hose back to the building. Drops of water on the grass glittered in the sunlight, and people were already gathered in front of the gallows. In the crowd were more men than women, but there were some women, and even some children. One man was carrying a small boy with long curls on his shoulders.

While Sundance watched, a line of condemned men came out of the basement of the building with shotgun-toting deputy marshals guarding them on all sides. The hangman, an old hump-backed man with a ragged beard, was already up on the gallows putting his weight on the ropes. The men to be hanged were halfway across the square when the executioner pulled the big lever and dropped all ten traps at the same time. The traps dropped with the sound of thunder and the line of condemned men faltered and almost broke until it was shaped up again by shotguns and curses, and then it went on. Sundance saw the farm boy and the man called Conklin; Sugar, the black Indian, wasn't there. A fat minister with a round collar and a book in his hands ran to catch up with the men who were about to die.

Sundance counted nine men. "You're a man short," he said.

"Pay attention," Parker said.

The stubby minister found his place in the book and prayed for the prisoners all the way to the foot of the gallows. He prayed as they were being led up, one by one, some stumbling, some rigid with fear or one last display of pride, and he kept on praying after they were all up and standing on the traps. The minister went up after them and took his place well away from the traps, and though the Bible or the book of prayers was open in his hands, he didn't need to look at it, and his mouth seemed to move by itself.

The farm boy was doing all right, and he stood up straight while the bent-backed hangman put the hood over his head and adjusted the noose so the fist-sized knot was in the hollow behind the left ear. One of the men collapsed and began to strangle on the rope though the trap had not yet been sprung. The hangman dragged him to his feet with thick powerful arms, but the man collapsed again, and his pants were wet with piss, and the hangman left him sitting on the trap while he went to the great lever at the end of the platform and looked up at Parker's window.

The minister finished praying at the last man and got out of the way. Sun sparkled on wet grass and an early morning breeze stirred the leaves of the elm trees that bordered the little square, and the hangman and the crowd waited for Parker's nod.

Before he gave it, he turned to Sundance. "That could be you out there." Then he nodded, a single grave nod of his head, and the hangman hauled back on the lever. The traps clattered downward with a crash and the ropes jerked tight and some men died instantly and some jerked and spun at the end of the ropes. The small boy with the curly hair was clapping his hands and jumping up and down on his father's shoulders. Now the bodies hung motionless on the ropes except for the body of one skinny man which continued to jerk and twitch. The hangman scuttled down the steps and under the gallows and swung on the man's legs until the twitching stopped. The crowd began to disperse.

Sundance saw that Parker, the murderous son of a bitch, was praying. The chief deputy chewed on a gold toothpick with no more interest on his face than if he had been looking at a hog-slaughter. His name was Doolin and he was fat and geting fatter all the time in the man-catching business. Sundance looked back to the square and it was deserted except for the nine dead men stirring in the breeze at the end of the ropes, a strange crop of fruit already starting to go bad in the hot sunshine.

Judge Parker rubbed his thin hands together to make a papery sound, a movement that signified that one job of work was done and done well, quickly and efficiently. The dead men had been put out of his mind. Parker's eyes were bright and clear, the eyes of a man who slept well and never doubted himself for a minute, and, standing there, Sundance wondered what the hell he was up to. Parker had treated him to some early morning entertainment, and there had to be a reason.

Parker sat behind his desk and poured a cup of coffee. "You still want coffee?" he asked Sundance. "You think you can hold it down after what you've seen?"

Doolin helped himself to coffee. "This may be a mistake," he said. "If it goes wrong it won't look so good for you. Don't mind me saying this, Judge, but if you do this it won't look so good for me. People will say I wasn't able to do the job I'm paid for. Give me a little more time and I guarantee I'll bring him in. Him and the rest of the gang. Dead or alive, I'll bring them in."

There was no reproach in Parker's voice. "But you haven't brought them in, Virgil. They're still out there robbing and killing. The last time you went after them they caught you in an ambush. You nearly lost an eye."

Virgil Doolin raised his hand to his scarred eyelid. "We came close to getting them when they robbed the bank in Idabel. Only trouble they got to town just before we did. We didn't have a chance to get set."

"Coming close didn't get it done, Virgil. You say people will talk. They're already talking and that crank Gately even ran an editorial about it. You want me to read it for you?"

"I know what it said," Virgil Doolin said. "Seems to me you ought to charge Gately with contempt, something like that."

"Why should I? Gately's right. What did he say? The Honorable Judge Parker continues to hang elderly whiskey runners while the real desperados run wild from one end of the Territory to the other."

"Why does it have to be this man?" Gruber said, jerking his thumb at Sundance.

Parker said, "Nothing's decided, Virgil. First, we'll talk. Untie his hands and give him coffee."

Sundance rubbed his wrists after the rawhide thongs were removed. The rawhide had dug in and at first there was pain as the blood began to flow freely.

"Sit down," Parker said. "Sit down and listen. Speak when I tell you to speak.

The judge made good coffee. So far that was the only

decision Sundance had reached. When he sat in a chair facing the judge's desk he could no longer see the gallows.

"In an hour those men out there will be buried in a lime pit," Parker said. "No bodies are turned over to relatives, not in my jurisdiction. In my opinion, a comdemned criminal does not deserve a normal burial. This is not because of any enmity for the dead. It is simply a way of demonstrating the absolute will of this court. You may think this is arbitrary. It is not. I say this because I know you are an intelligent man, a man gone bad, but still intelligent. I take no pleasure in the power of giving life or death. What I do must be done because, at this time and in this place, there is no other way. I can raise my finger, nod my head, and you will be dead in less than ten minutes."

The judge paused to sip his coffee. "Or I can let you live. It's up to you which way you want it to be."

Sundance held out his empty cup and Parker filled it.

"What do you want me to do?" Sundance said.

"I want you to bring in Joe Buck," Parker said.

CHAPTER 3

There was a long silence and then Parker said, "You aren't surprised?"

A bluefly came in the window and buzzed noisily against the sun-warmed glass. Doolin rolled up a newspaper and went after the fly. He killed it on the third try. Sundance and Parker waited.

"I'm not surprised about Joe Buck," Sundance said. "I met Sugar in the cage. He talked about the bank, so did Doolin here. Not hard to put it together. What's the deal?"

"No deal, not yet. Any deals to be made I make them. You just listen. I knew who you were as soon as I heard your name, read it on the court docket. So I did some checking. Mr. Doolin sent some telegraph messages to Washington, other places you're known and not liked. You know Rufus—Joe—Buck, don't you?"

"Maybe," Sundance said.

"You know him," Parker said. "My information is you knew him five or six years ago before he went completely wild. Is that correct?"

"What's the deal?" Sundance said. "No deal, no talk."

Parker turned to Doolin. "Take him out, Virgil. Tell

29

Maledon there's one more. That's all, Mr. Sundance."

Sundance didn't move even when Doolin came close holding the strip of rawhide.

"I changed my mind," Sundance said.

"Good," Parker said as if nothing had happened. "Was it five or six years ago?"

"Five. Like you say, Joe was just getting started. Nothing too serious. Running off a few stray cows, a few horses. No killing at that time."

"How did you get to know him?"

"I was after some whiskey runners out in No Man's Land. Joe was after them too because some of his people went blind and some died drinking rotgut."

"What happened to the whiskey runners?"

"We killed them. Killed them and burned their wagons."

"That part is true," Doolin said. "We found the wagons and the bodies, what was left of them. They did a good job."

Parker held up his hand. "It was murder," he said. "You were friendly with Buck?"

"More or less," Sundance said. "We're both halfbreeds, if that's what you're driving at."

"That's what I'm driving at," Parker said. "You didn't stay with the gang?"

"I wasn't part of any gang. Anyway, it wasn't much of a gang. Joe helped me nail the whiskey runners. Maybe I helped him. The job got done."

"How long did it take?"

"About five weeks. They knew the country as well as we did, so it took some doing."

"You were with Buck for five weeks, that says you were part of the gang.

"Six of one," Sundance said. "I rode with Buck for five weeks, then we split up."

"You mean you quarreled?"

"Not what you'd call a quarrel. Killing the whiskey runners was Joe's first taste of blood. He liked it. I could tell he liked it by the way he talked. The whiskey runners were all white. Joe hated whites. More so now, I guess. After we killed the whiskey runners he wanted me to stay on. We'd pay back the whites for what they had done to the Indians and get rich at the same time. Joe had it all figured out. I said no. I said I worked alone."

"You mean Buck let you ride out?"

"Finally he did. I thought I'd have to shoot my way out or die trying, but it did't come to that. It came close to killing but stopped short of that."

"Then you parted friends?"

"Something like that. Least we shook hands and Joe said I could always come back if I changed my mind."

"He's just talking for his life, Judge," Doolin said.

"No better reason I can think of," Parker said.

"What's the deal?" Sundance asked again.

Parker spoke slowly. "Your life for Joe Buck's. I don't like what I'm doing, but I can't see any other way. I won't mince words. If I could do this any other way, you would be hanging out there with the rest of those men. I despise men of your kind, insolent, swaggering killers."

Sundance tried to remember the last time he had done any swaggering. It couldn't have been lately because nothing came to mind.

"Bring Joe Buck in and you go free," Parker said. "Just remember this. The death sentence remains in force. Officially you are a dead man until you bring Buck in for trial."

"Suppose I have to kill him?"

Parker slammed his hand on the desk. "No! I don't want that. Joe Buck must hang. If you kill him he will

31

become a legend like the James brothers and the Daltons and the rest of that scum. Bring Joe Buck to me! It's hard to be a legend when you're executed with horse thieves and store robbers. If you have to kill Buck, bring back his head."

"You don't ask for much, Judge."

"You've done worse things than cut off a dead man's head."

"How do you know this man won't just ride out and keep on going?" Doolin said. "Who's to stop him, what's to stop him?"

"I'll stop him," Parker said. "He may make a run for it, but I'll stop him. I'll bring the full might of the federal government down on top of him, if I have to. Every federal marshal in this country will be looking for him. He can run but he can't hide. And just so there is no misunderstanding, I will personally post a reward of $10,000 for his capture. But not dead. Definitely. Not a penny will be paid if he's brought in dead. You hear me. Mr. Sundance?"

"I hear you, Judge."

"Forget about Mexico, Mr. Sundance. Canada, too. Run and I will have you brought back in irons. And when they bring you back I will hang you myself."

"What about Sugar, the halfbreed I met in the cage?" Sundance said.

"What about him? He's due to be hanged tomorrow."

"That's fine. How soon do I start?"

Parker stood up and opened a closet and handed Sundance his weapons belt, his rifle and bow. He watched while Sundance buckled on the belt and checked the loads in the long-barreled .44 Colt and strapped the thin-bladed knife to his leg.

"A question," Sundance said. "How did I get out of your jail?"

"You escaped," Parker said. "The first escape ever. The deputies who brought you in missed the knife on your leg. You put the knife to Doolin's throat and walked out."

Sundance nodded. "It's thin but it will have to do. One more thing. Nobody follows me. Doolin, nobody. It won't work if I'm followed."

"Listen, you," Doolin said.

"He's right," Parker said. "You followed that mulatto you sent in last January. You got him tortured and killed. This time you stay in Fort Smith."

Sundance picked up the Winchester and Parker said, "How soon will I hear from you?"

"When you see me. If you don't see me you'll know I'm dead."

"You'll be no loss to the world, whenever you die."

Sundance smiled at the silky-bearded fanatic. "The same goes for you, Judge."

Parker turned away. "You heard what I said. Bring in Buck—or bring in his head. Nothing else will do."

Eagle whinnied when he saw his master standing in the shadows of the stone archway at the top of the steps that came up from the underground cells. It was early evening and dark and Gruber watched while he swung into the saddle and rode away. At the end of the street, under the leafy elms that shaded the street, he looked back and Doolin was gone. The cold air and the trees smelled good and his pulse raced with the joy of freedom. Once again he had cheated death, if only for a while. For how long he had no way of knowing. Death lay ahead, as it always did for him, for now he was alive, with his life-blood flowing through his veins and clean air in his lungs. Conklin and the farm boy were already rotting in the mass grave, and he wondered if the man they called Old Hankins had been among the nine men hanged that morning. There was no way to tell. He had never seen Old Hankins.

He rode downstream from the ferry and swam Eagle across the river. He crossed on a slant and it took thirty minutes to get to the other shore. Up where the ferry was there were lights, but there were no sounds except for the sounds of the river washing up into the reeds that lined the western bank. The river was wide and dark and the reflection of the moon was bent into the ripples on the water. Lights from Fort Smith winked from across the water.

Oklahoma spread out in front of him, dark and limitless, the prairies of the east rolling out to meet the western hills. In this year of 1887, Oklahoma was the most lawless territory in the Southwest. It was home to good people and the scum of six states and territories. Parker's handful of deputies was the only law for hundreds of miles, so for the most part the killers and deserters and whiskey runners ran free and wild as the land itself. Wildest of all was the western section known as No Man's Land, and to ride in there without an invitation was to ask for death. They called it No Man's Land, but for now it belonged to Joe Buck, christened Rufus, and his gang of half-wild renegades. In a few years, Joe's notoriety had spread far beyond Oklahoma, and he was feared even in Texas. Sundance knew all the stories about Joe couldn't be true. But some of them had to be true, and they were all bad. Stories of torture and rape, of lonely settlements burned in the dead of night.

Sundance smiled. Bring Joe Buck in, Parker said. Made it sound like just another job. It would take more than nerve to deliver old Joe to the hangman. But he had to give it his best try. He knew Parker wasn't bluffing. The silky-bearded fanatic with the soft voice would dog him till his dying day if he tried to duck out, and that wasn't how he wanted to live the rest of his life. There was still too much work to be done—the Indian Ring was stronger than ever—and time was too precious to waste in dodging and hiding, always looking over his shoulder, always sleeping with a gun in his hand.

Sundance rode on into the night, putting distance between himself and Fort Smith, not sure that Doolin wouldn't try to follow him, wouldn't try to backshoot him and leave him to rot. He was caught between enemies, and yet there wasn't much he could do but see it through to the end.

Late that night he made camp beside a creek but didn't light a fire. Doolin had sent him off with a good supply of canned goods and bacon. He threw the bacon away, not knowing that it might not be poisoned. He ate a can of cold beans and rolled himself in his blankets and slept for three hours. Then it was dawn and he rolled out and when he did Eagle was already drinking at the creek. He rubbed Eagle's nose and the big stallion whinnied with pleasure. He smiled when the stallion sniffed at his clothes.

"You're right, I stink," Sundance said.

He stripped off and washed the jail stink from his clothes and laid them on the bank to dry in the sun. Then he waded into the creek, still cold at that hour, and scrubbed his body with handfuls of clean yellow sand. He scrubbed himself until his tall, lean body, crisscrossed with old puckered scars, tingled and felt good. The place on his head where he had been hit still hurt when he touched it. It would be sore for a while but the sun would heal it fast. Willows and reeds grew all over the creek and it was quiet and peaceful in the early morning. Though he was a man who lived with violence, and would always live with it, he wondered, as he did so often, why life had to be the way it was. But then, as always, he found no answers, and knew he never would.

His clothes were still damp when he dressed and mounted up. He didn't know the Territory as well as he knew Texas but he knew it well enough. Joe Buck had hit the bank in Idabel but that didn't mean the gang was back in No Man's Land. Joe was not a predictable man, one of the many reasons he was so hard to kill. A lot of men had died trying to outguess Joe. Years on the run had taught him to trust nothing and no one and there wasn't a sneaky trick he didn't know. He knew all the tricks and had added a few of his own. He turned up in places he wasn't supposed, and when he was rumored to be somewhere else he wasn't, and so it had gone for years.

The place to start looking was Idabel because Joe had been known to rob the same bank twice in a short period of time. He would start in Idabel: if nothing turned up there, he would have to keep on looking. Sooner or later, if he kept riding long enough, he would find Joe. After that it was all up to chance.

Idabel was a town run by the descendants of Scotch-Indians from Georgia. Idabel was the county seat of McCurtain County and the Scotch-Indians ran the county along with the town and thought they were better than anybody else, white or Indian or half and half. Years before he had passed through Idabel, a neat trim town with three streets and a Presbyterian church and a white-painted hall where the Grangers and the Woodsmen of the World met to talk about what was best for the town and the new strain of wheat everybody was so enthusiastic about.

A wind blew in mist and then it started to rain, cold, heavy, bone-chilling rain. Twice during the long wet day he stopped to water Eagle and to drink himself. In front of him, stretching away into the gray mist of the horizon, the prairie seemed limitless, as if it ran all the way across the continent to the sea. Now and then he passed a farmhouse and people came out to stare at him, for this was a land where any man was an enemy until he proved not to be, and even then he was not completely trusted, and when he left people were glad he was gone.

From time to time he checked his back trail, searching for signs of Doolin and his men. He didn't see anything, but that didn't mean they weren't there. Doolin made his living hunting other men and would know how it was done. At one point, when there was good cover, Sundance lay in a grove of trees on a low hill and glassed the country behind him with binoculars. He lay there for an hour and still saw nothing. It was starting to get dark when he moved on. The rain stopped.

That night he made another cold camp and was on his way again before first light. Another day's ride would take him close to Idabel. He looked up at the sun. It was about eight o'clock. Another line of men stumbling toward the gallows. It was good to be alive with the hot sun in his face and the wind blowing through his hair.

During the day there was nothing to see but prairie, and then more prairie. On the road he passed two Indians and their women in farm wagons. The tame farm Indians stared at him as if he belonged to another race, a wild free race to which they had once belonged themselves. He saw no one else for the rest of the day. And there was still no sign of Doolin.

Now it was noon the next day and only a ripple of bare, brown hills stood between him and Idabel. On the far side of the hills the prairie rolled on again. He crossed the wrinkle of hills and when he was still on high ground he could see the town about ten miles away, the church, the tallest building, standing up tall in the scatter of houses and streets. Past the town, about twenty miles away, was another line of hills. Joe Buck could still be there, watching the fat little town, or he could be five days' ride away.

An hour later, Sundance rode into town and the men who came out to watch him had rifles in their hands. The town had grown an extra street since the last time he was there. Other than that, it looked the same. Two halfbreeds on tall ladders were giving one wall of the grange hall a new coat of paint. They climbed down when they saw him ride in, and when they got down they dropped their paint brushes and picked up rifles and walked down the street to where a crowd of armed men had gathered in front of the bank.

Sundance kept riding until a dark-faced halfbreed with a constable's badge on his shirt help up his hand. The other men crowded in after the constable as he came forward with a rifle in his hand.

"Good day to you," the constable said.

Sundance nodded. "Where can I get something to eat?"

"There may be a place where you can eat," the constable said. "First, you mind saying who you are and what your business is?"

"Not a bit," Sundance said. "I'm on my way to Texas and my only business here is a steak, if you got it."

"We got it," the constable said, bringing up the rifle. Other rifles came up and pointed at Sundance.

"What the hell is going on here?" Sundance said. "I never saw a town so scared of one man."

"Not scared, just careful," the constable.. "Not meaning to give offense, nor you to take any, why don't you get rid of your weapons while you have a go at that steak. Be more comfortable and so forth. You could be one man and you could be the scout for a lot of men."

"You're crazy," Sundance said, "but I want that steak." He unbuckled his weapons belt and one of the Indians took it.

"That's the only way you're going to get it," the constable said. "Mind if I come along and drink coffee with you?"

"Suit yourself," Sundance said.

CHAPTER 4

There were wanted posters for Joe Buck all over the town of Idabel. The constable had overdone his job: A picture of Joe stared down from beside the coffee urn in the Chinaman's place where Sundance ate a tough steak and the Indian badge-toter drank coffee. After the moldy beans and water of the Fort Smith jail, the steak and coffee tasted great.

The Chinaman's place was called John's Place and there was nothing on the card except meat and potatoes, ham and eggs, three kinds of beans, and peach and apple pie. On the wall, Joe Buck's face was as sour as if he had drunk some of the Chinaman's coffee. In real life Joe smiled a lot, but a drooping eyelid, from some childhood disease, gave his smiles a sinister look. Joe's face was the color of a smoke-cured ham, a ham with holes for eyes, nose, and mouth. His short black Indian hair was parted in the middle, slicked down with grease, and his little ears stuck out like handles on a cup.

Behind the counter the Chinaman bustled about, fighting a losing battle with the flies. The Chinaman was just a Chinaman a long way from home.

"I guess you won't be staying long in town," the Indian policeman said.

"Not long," Sundance said.

"There's nothing here for a stranger."

Sundance told the Chinaman to bring more coffee. The Chinaman had been adding pecan pie to the card, a cracked slate blackboard. He made several attempts to spell pecan and finally got it wrong. He brought the coffee and went back to his writing.

"That's Joe Buck up there," the Indian constable said, and went on to tell about the bank robbery. "We got one of them, the worst of the lot after Joe himself. I dropped him with three shots in the legs."

"That's the way to do it," Sundance said, thinking that Sugar's legs had looked fine a few days earlier.

"Judge Parker'll take care of him," the Indian constable said. "I guess he's dead by this time. Joe Buck'll get the same if he comes back to this town."

"All ready for him, are you?" Sundance said.

The constable was suddenly suspicious. "Let me say it this way. If somebody was to ride in here to get the lay of the town for Joe, I'd like for him to tell Joe when he sees it's suicide to try it again. Every man and boy is going armed in this town. Joe has better shooters but we have more guns. One thing you can say for a town on the prairie, you can't get at it so easy."

Sundance spooned rough brown sugar into his coffee to kill the taste. "He wouldn't have a chance," he said.

"But let him come if he has a mind to," the lying Indian said. "We'll gun him down like the mad dog he is. I'd like him to know that." The wedge-faced Indian leaned across the table and got confidential and Sundance knew he'd been having a few nips.

"This town is lucky to have a man like me lawing it," the Indian constable said. "You know this is the only town Joe ever robbed a bank in and lost a man. I did that. No help, just me. I been all over though. Arkan-

41

sas. Texas. All over. Joe Buck's going to be one sorry man if he tangles with me. Hell! I wish Joe would come. It gets dead in this town, no women, no saloons, not like in Old Mexico. I was there once with a horse herd. I speak Spanish good as any greaser. *Chinga* is the Mex word for skunk, which is what Joe Buck is. You speak the lingo?''

"Never got the hang of it," Sundance said. It was time to move on.

"What in hell is going on out there!" the Indian said. He knocked over is chair and ran out to the street. Sundance went after him. The Chinaman, bland and skinny, didn't move from the blackboard.

In the middle of the street a wagon was drawn up with an Indian woman and a halfbreed on the seat. The Indian woman's face looked odd under a faded poke bonnet; blood soaked the shirt of the man beside her. The side of the wagon was splintered with bullet holes. Dirt and sweat streaked the face of the halfbreed driver and he was shaking with excitement.

"Joe Buck is coming!" he yelled. "Joe and the whole gang!"

Two other wagons, a long way back, were entering the long main street. The mules pulling them were worn and old.

The Indian constable hiked up his plain leather gunbelt over his fat stomach. Men and boys with rifles and shotguns were gathering.

"What's this talk?" the constable said with sudden sweat on his jowly brown face.

"They jumped us back in the hills," the halfbreed said. "Shot up the wagons, shot me, killed another man, took the young girls. Took the few dollars we had. I swear I was as close to Joe as I am to you. He said to give the constable a message. Joe says he's coming into

42

rob the bank and nail your hide to a door. You catched or killed one of his boys and he's going to do you for that. That's the message and Joe said I didn't believe it he'd be coming after me. Us, we just want supplies and we're gone from this town."

The halfbreed leaned out from the wagon seat and yelled back to the two other wagons, still moving slowly. "Get on with it! You want us to be caught here when Joe comes!"

The constable gripped the butt of his gun, but didn't do anything else. One of the men in the crowd, a skinny old halfbreed with wispy white whiskers and a frock coat and rubber collar, looked like the town's leading citizen.

"How soon will he come?" the old man said.

The halfbreed got excited again. "How do I know? Soon as he feels like coming. You folks better get set, set as you can."

The other wagons got closer and the halfbreed cursed the drivers for being so slow. Driving the fast wagon was an old Indian with a white man's features set in a buff-colored face. On the seat of the second wagon was a boy no more than thirteen. The first wagon pulled up ahead of the halfbreed's wagon, the other stayed behind. There were bullet holes in the canvas of both wagons.

"Come on," the old man in the frock coat said, taking a tighter grip on a .50 Sharps rifle.

"What's the hurry?" Joe Buck said as the canvas of the second wagon rolled back. He didn't aim when he shot the constable. He just pegged a shot and the constable dropped dead. The bullet had gone in just below his badge.

Fifteen rifles pointed at them from two wagons. Beside the halfbreed the old Indian woman in the bonnet remained motionless, staring straight ahead. The halfbreed opened his bloody shirt and drew a lady's .32 caliber pistol from his belt and threw the shirt in the street.

Sundance knew that Joe had seen him standing in back of the crowd. "No need anybody else has to get shot," Joe said. The two men who were painting the hall were still up on tall ladders. Grinning, Joe Buck took a rifle from one of his men, snapped it to his shoulder and shot a hole in a paint bucket. One of the men fell off the ladder, the other started to come down.

"A man is a bigger target than a bucket," Joe said. "Pile the guns in the street. My friends, fellow Indians, that means every gun in this town. I catch a man hiding a gun he will go quick to the Happy Hunting Grounds. It is what they call martial law. All we want is your money.

"Put them in the church and guard them," Joe told the halfbreed, who was tucking in a fairly clean shirt. "You—banker—you stay with me. Don't look so mad, old man. You have my promise this is the last time we will rob your bank—this year."

The halfbreed had another gun now, a new single-action Colt .45, and he pointed it at Sundance. "Go with the others," he said.

Sundance looked at Joe Buck, and didn't move.

"Move or get shot," the halfbreed said, cocking the big revolver.

"Hold up, Brindar," Joe Buck said. He came close with no expression on his dark red face. "This one looks like a bad one. Some of the boys think so too."

All Joe's men were staring at Sundance. He recognized some of them, but the halfbreed, Brindar, was a new face. Joe Buck was smiling.

"I don't like him," Brindar said.

44

"You'll hate him when you get to know him better," Joe said. "I'm good and mad at this man. Mad as hell!"

"You know him?"

Smiling, Joe said, "He promised to write but he never did."

"What!" Brindar said.

"When did you ever read anything but wanted posters, Joe?" Sundance said.

Joe said, "I like what they write, but they ought to get a better picture of me. Next time I'm in a real town I'm going to have one made and send it to Ike Parker. How in hell are you, Sundance?"

They shook hands warily. Now the street was empty except for the bandits, the people with the wagons, and the frock-coated banker.

"Pretty good," Sundance said. "I liked that part about the Happy Hunting Grounds."

"So did I," Joe said. He went through the banker's pockets and found a well stuffed wallet and a fat gold watch. The Indian woman on the wagon seat didn't turn her head as he thrust the money and the watch into her hands. "That will buy you a farm, missus. You tell people Joe Buck didn't kill a one of your folks. You tell them Joe treated you decent 'cause you're Indian just like him. No need to thank me, missus. You help yourself to what you need and put it on my bill."

The Indian woman didn't turn her head. "We don't want anything from you. Let us go is all we want from you."

"Fill your wagons with food and supplies, or I'll shoot the boy," he said. "First the boy, then the old man. Go on now and count your self lucky you met with Joe Buck. You throw the food away and I'll know about it. You'll be sorry if I hear about it."

Joe turned back to Sundance. "You have to push

people hard if you want to do a good deed," he said. "It's good to see you. I think it's good to see you. Walk along now and we'll go on down to the bank and make a withdrawal."

Sundance had to match his long stride to Joe's shorter legs. "That's what Sugar called it."

Joe stopped abruptly. So did the banker. "You know Sugar?"

"I met him. Big man, black Indian. Judge Parker was getting ready to hang him the last time I saw him."

They went on again in the sunlight of the silent street. "You were in the Fort Smith jail?" Joe said.

"Parker was fixing to hang me too, but I broke out."

"You broke out of Parker's jail."

"They had me in jail for killing a drunk in a saloon. He shot first. The noise of the guns, I didn't hear that deputy marshal coming up behind me. I woke up in a cell."

"But you got out?"

"Still had a knife when they came to take me to the hangman. I guess that deputy didn't want to die. Like I said, I got out."

They weren't far from the bank, a brick building with white doors and window frames. "This deputy you took the gun from, he must be a dumb deputy."

"Been hanging men for too long, I guess you can get careless," Sundance said. "This one did."

It didn't sound like too much of a story, and he knew Joe would check it back. Joe had eyes and ears, even in Fort Smith, and he paid well for the information he got. But maybe a thin story was better than a story that had been worked out too carefully. By now there would be wanted posters printed up. JIM SUNDANCE/WANTED FOR MURDER AND JAILBREAK. He wondered how much Judge Parker would offer to get him, dead or alive.

Joe said, "No man has ever escaped from the Fort Smith jail. Up to now. That's going to make Ike awful mad. I would like to meet Ike one of these days. But not in court." Joe laughed. "How did Sugar take it."

"All right. He talked a lot."

"He was a good man, the best. He joined up with me a couple of years after you ran out on me."

"You going to start that again, Joe? We had that out years ago."

"Any other man tried to run out on me, I'd have shot him. After you were gone I got so mad I thought about going after you. I didn't find another good man to side me till Sugar came along. Old Sugarboy robbed and murdered pretty good in Texas before they chased him up here. All that time, never took a bullet. Smart too."

"He sounds all right," Sundance said.

"Was a good man, you mean. Was a good man, though I could get sick of that smart nigger talk when I put my mind to it. But maybe Sugarboy wasn't all that smart. He got caught."

"That's what one of the prisoners in the jail said."

"What prisoner?"

"An oldtimer, Conklin. Did some murders and got caught."

"That old fool," Joe said. "For the life, I don't know why he wasn't hung long since."

"He's hung now."

The banker opened the big Leydecker safe built into the wall and got out of the way. Joe went in and kicked a sack of silver dollars. He opened the sack to make sure what was in it.

"Sometimes they fill these things with washers," he said. "One of the first banks I robbed cheated me like that. Damn! I thought I was rich. Got some paper money but I was counting on all that silver. Took me a long time to live that down. You can bet I was good and mad. A wet hen wasn't madder'n I was. First off, still mad, I thought why don't I go on back to that bank and show them what a real joke is like. They wouldn't like my kind of jokes. Then I said no, they cheated me fair and square, and I'd do the same thing, was I them.''

Joe looked at the banker. ''Go on down to the church, moneybags, and lock yourself in.''

''Coin can be an awful bother if you're in a hurry,'' Joe said. ''It's hell to leave it behind, hurry or not, but that's what you have to do. I tell you, Sundance, there's more to robbing banks that just walking in with a gun. A lot of things you have to figure, if you want to make a go of it. Picking the right town is one part of it.''

Sundance knew Joe was hiding his suspicion behind a lot of talk. But Joe always was a talky man. Indians were silent only with white men.

''Never rob a town with a lot of Irishmen in it,'' Joe said. ''Bastards always mix in. A friend of mine, sort of a friend, Jimmy Flax, got himself murdered by a mob of Irish lead miners in Colorado. Jimmy killed three of the clodhoppers before they beat Jimmy and his boys to death with anything that was handy.''

Brindar, the halfbreed, came in and began to scoop the money out of the drawers. He stared at Sundance and Sundance knew that he had been talking to the other men.

''Everybody quiet?'' Joe Buck said.

''Not a peep,'' Brindar said. Another man came in and helped him to drag out the money sacks. In the sacks the silver dollars clinked.

''I like that sound,'' Joe said. ''I like it better than the sound a woman makes when she's lighting off. Both sounds, makes you feel good, sort of proud of what you

48

just done. You never did much bank robbing, did you?"

"None that I recall."

Joe laughed. "You'd probably remember, if you did it. Why, I tell you, there's nothing like it in this world. Everything else you can think of is all complicated. You have to do this and that before you get folding money, spending money, in your hand. Steal horses and you got to find a buyer that won't ask questions, won't talk. It's not like you can put a notice in the newspaper saying horses for sale, then sit on the hotel porch and let the buyers come to you waving money. You have to feed the buggers before you can sell them. I stole a horse herd one time and had to keep them so long half the bastards took sick and died on me. No, sir, give me bank robbing every time. A bank is like a store that stocks money. You want to buy out the whole store, you do it. Nothing to be fed or traded later, and the nice thing is just about every damn town, small or not, has a bank. For a man that knows how to do it right, it's Christmas the whole year."

"I figured I'd join up with you," Sundance said. "I'm wanted for murder. Parker won't let go of it."

"Not likely, knowing Parker," Joe said. "A dog with a bone, that crazy man is. But I never did figure you for a bank robber. You said it one time, before you ran out on me. You call it what you like. I call it running out. I figured we'd do some nice work together, but you ran out. You sure you want to join up? Sure they got you down for murder, and anybody hears the telling of it will know it wasn't a real murder. Not a man around doesn't know what Ike Parker is like. I don't see them hounding you just for killing a drunk in a saloon. Just talking it out, you understand. Texas is that way! You could go there, go clear to Old Mexico."

Sundance said, "Parker won't cross it off the books. I'll still be a murderer. Self-defense or not, it will stay on the books as murder. The hell with that! If they got me pegged as a bad one, that's what I'll be. As bad as you, if I have to be."

Joe grinned. "Nobody's as bad as me, and you know it. Seems to me you're making too much out of this. Your business. 'Course they'll have you down for bank robbing too. After today they will. You came in to look the town over, then we happened right along. You're a bad one all right."

"Do I get to join?"

"For now you do. You know what I mean. You don't just waltz back after five years and say sorry, Joe, I had to sit it out because I got dizzy. You got to explain a few things, what you been doing all this time."

"Doing what I could for the Indians. Been a lot of places. Texas. California. Canada. Mexico."

"How are the Indians doing these days?" Joe said. "I know how *this* Indian is doing. How about the rest?"

"Not so good."

"You don't help them the right way. When I was a kid my old man always said the best hope for the Indians was to be farmers. Do everything the white way. Learn to speak American, and so forth. You know something I wouldn't want to get around? I even tried farming for a while. I didn't like it. You plant corn so you get to eat corn. I don't like corn. Now I'm a Robin Hood instead of a farmer."

Sundance smiled at Joe's ugly red-brown face, the greasy black hair sticking out from under his hat, the drooping eyelid.

"You're a funny looking Robin Hood."

Joe wasn't offended. "That ain't such a nice thing to

say. You're no prize yourself. Sugar told me the story of Robin Hood. I sort of think the red nigger—God rest his soul—was trying to kid me. No matter, I liked the story. 'Course I don't give it all away, and I don't just rob from the rich. I'll rob a storekeeper when I'm short on banks. You still as shy of killing people as you used to be? Was a time you'd hold back. In my business that can be risky, and even when not risky killing tells people what you're like, gets them to remember. The word gets around, people do what you want them to do. Without the usual fuss.''

"I won't kill for no reason," Sundance said.

"Didn't I just give you one reason? What the hell! I got to get myself something to drink. Come on now and we'll talk some more. Does me good to see a man that doesn't just grunt back. Poor old Sugarboy! I'm going to miss that smooth-talking nigger. It's not so bad though. You'll be around. Boy! Didn't we have a time we went after those whiskey runners? After we shot the first bunch the ones we drug out of the brush kept begging for their stinking lives. You said no, they'd be back in the rotgut business in a week. You decided they had to die and you did the killing. Lord! How they hollered when you brought out that Colt!''

"You're not in much of a hurry today," Sundance said.

"Nothing to hurry about," Joe said. "Not a cavalry patrol inside two days ride. I got my boys posted on all the roads and trails. We'll be long gone if they start this way. I like not having to do things in a hurry. I tell you, leather face, we are going to plunder this territory from one end to the other.''

CHAPTER 5

The Chinaman found whiskey and brought it to the table. Then Joe Buck sent Brindar to the banker's house to bring back some good steak. There was no one in the restaurant but Sundance, Joe Buck and the Chinaman.

"Bankers always eat good grub," Joe said, pouring a drink. "I like to rob bankers. All that money they have I never figure why they have to look so skinny and miserable. Even when they're fat they look miserable. I sometimes think they must have ugly wives. On the other hand, with all that money, why would they have ugly wives?"

The Chinaman made fresh coffee that tasted just as bad as the first batch.

"You see that Chinaman over there?" Joe said, pointing. "That Chinaman isn't afraid of me. You know why?"

"Why, Joe?"

"Because I haven't eaten his lousy food," Joe said. "If you don't do me dirt, I won't do you. Not usually."

Joe rolled the whiskey around in his mouth. "I think this must be Chinaman whiskey. See, take a look at the Chinaman. He heard what I said about his whiskey and now he's scared. He thinks I don't like his whiskey. I like it fine but he doesn't know that, so he's afraid. That's what you have to do, keep people nervous. I learned that as I went along."

"I'm not nervous," Sundance said.

"You're not a Chinaman. Most people are like that Chinaman over there. You don't even have to threaten them to make them want to do you favors."

"Is that how it works?"

"The way it works," Joe said, "is I do anything I feel like doing. When I was a poor ugly Indian dirt-farming kid with a gimpy eye I couldn't do anything, so now I do everything. I kill people, or I let them live. I like the feeling of being able to do that. See now, I'm going to cheer up that Chinaman."

Joe raised his glass and made smacking sounds with his lips. The Chinaman smiled nervously. "Good whiskey, Charley," Joe Buck said.

Behind the counter the skinny Chinaman's head bobbed up and down and he said, "Thank you! Thank you!"

Joe said, "See how easy it is? The Chinaman likes me now. Wasn't no special reason to scare the yellow bastard. A man has to stay in practice."

"What you're saying is that you can kill me as easily as you scared the Chinaman?"

"You, an old friend? Why, as the saying goes, we practically ate off the same plate in the old days. Even so, that's what I can do any time I feel like it."

"Do you?"

"God no!" Joe said. "You're talking foolish, is what you're doing. Didn't I just tell you we're going to put every bank in the territory out of business? Before we get through they'll be turning banks into general stores. Not a thing to stop us. We'll hit the banks the way the Sioux hit Custer. You and me, we'll make the Jameses and the Daltons look like chicken thieves. Few years back when things were getting hot for Jesse there was talk he was thinking about doing some work here in the Territory. Now me, I'm nowhere as famous as Jesse—not yet—but he knew who Joe Buck was. When I heard what he was planning to do, I got word back to him that if he wandered up here I'd do what the Pinkertons hadn't been able to do, not that the Pinkertons wanted to cut off his balls and make him eat them. That's what *I* said I'd do. Jesse, dumb in some ways, not in others, took the hint."

Joe filled his glass again. "I won't have outsiders robbing my banks. "Is this the Indian Territory, or isn't it? Damn right it is. I'm an Indian, you're an Indian, and don't you forget it."

Joe was getting drunk. Sundance said, "They never let us forget it." He needed a little more than the wanted posters and the story about breaking out of the Fort Smith jail.

Joe said, "It took you long enough to get that through your head, all these years you been palling around with the whites. You may be smarter than me, leather face, but I could tell you plenty about whites. You think you're better'n the rest of us, 'cause your father—whatever he was—made you different. Bullshit! Your so-called white friends think you're dirt. Now you're running from the law, so you're double dirt. Dirt, like me."

"You feel better now?" Sundance said.

"About time somebody gave it to you straight. Time you learned where you're at. You're at where you rightfully belong. Ain't never going to get better for the Indian. Never. Not a chance. Your so-called friends can mouth off till kingdom come. Nothing's going to change for the Indian. All my old man ever had was that stinking so-called farm. It was shit to me. The old man loved it. You know what happened? The soldiers ran him off. That wasn't what they called what they did. They did it just the same, even paid the poor old son of a bitch. Some money anyhow. What the hell did money mean to my old man? You know why the bastard drove him off? Some white son of a bitch thought there was oil on the land. What the hell is oil for? There was no oil, and my old man died in a neighbor's house."

"You don't have to convince me, not now," Sundance said.

"You can't back out this time," Joe said.

"It's different this time."

"I'm just telling you. This time you don't run out."

"How long are you going to keep saying that? I can get out now, if you like."

"You can't do that either," Joe said. "Asking if you can join is the same as joining. Same rules."

"You sure are cranky today."

Joe smiled as if he liked the idea. "I guess I am. Seeing you again made me mad. The whiskey brought it out. That's over. It's going to be all right, leather face."

"Sure it is, droopy eye."

"I don't like that name," Joe said.

"I could do without leather face," Sundance said.

"By God! It's good to have you back. Nobody talks to me the way you do. Too bad you don't drink, we'd do a few things to this town before we call it quits. You know what we're going to do when we leave this town?"

"You tell me."

"Damn right I will. We're going to find a town—with two banks! Now that's what I call a real town. There are towns with even three banks. Wouldn't it be something to rob three banks in one town in one day? They'd be still talking about it twenty years from now. Three banks wouldn't be that easy."

"More like hard," Sundance said.

"I'd still like to do three banks," Joe said, warming up to the idea. "Three banks at the same time, the same day. I was in Little Rock one time. That was before I took to robbing banks. The time I was there I didn't think to count the banks. How many do you figure?"

"Little Rock's more like a city," Sundance said. "Anyway, more than three banks. Could even be four or five."

Joe considered the banks in Little Rock. "Too many," he said. Joe was thinking hard, and suddenly a smile spread across his battered face. "Fort Smith, that's it! How many banks in Fort Smith?"

"I don't know," Sundance said.

"You should have counted them," Joe said. "Makes no difference. I can find out. But there's got to be three banks in Fort Smith. Maybe nobody ever robbed even one bank in Fort Smith. Ike Parker's town! The Hanging Judge's town! We'll do it, Sundance. It'll take time and planning, but we'll do it, rob the banks, make the judge look sick. You know what they're going to say when it's done? They're going to laugh the judge out of town. They're going to say if the murdering son of a bitch can't keep the law in his own town, how in hell is he going to keep it in the Territory?"

Joe drank more whiskey. "You're going to bring me luck. Why I never thought of hitting the Fort Smith banks is something I'll never know. We get enough men together, we'll hang old Ike on his own gallows. Ike and all his deputies, that hunchback German. And I ain't forgetting that Bible-thumper neither."

Sundance said, "All that's going to take some doing."

"Well, I know that," Joe said. "At the mission

56

school I was drug to years ago, there was this old maid teacher, an old prune of a white woman, she used to say, 'If something is worth doing, it's worth doing right.' Damn! That old cow was right. We'll do it just right, everything planned ahead. I guess there's no way to burn that jail of Ike's. We'll dynamite the bitching thing.''

"We'll need a safe place after we do it," Sundance said. "Especially if we hang Parker. You'll see more soldiers than you ever saw before."

"No need to tell me that. We'll see the soldiers, they won't see us. The safe place? I know a place they'll never find us. We'll lay up there long as we like, then we'll start hitting again. We will, if that's what we want to do. That's what I like about being an outlaw and a killer. You're already a dead man, so there is nothing to lose. If you win, you win big. If you lose . . . you have to die sometime."

"How soon do you figure Fort Smith?"

"You'll know when I start planning. It will get done, just like I said. I'm going to do it, if I never do another goddamned thing in my life. Ike's been hunting me for years. Up and down this country he's had his deputies after me. Not let up, not a minute, not an hour his murdering deputies aren't after me. There's no sporting blood in that man. You'd think I raped his mother, the way he keeps dogging me. I've had men after me besides Ike but not personal like. Sometimes I think Ike is a worse killer than I am. You'd think a judge would have more respect for the law. No, sir, he breaks every law in the book and feels holy while he's doing it. That old weasel has sent every kind of man against me: spies, sneaks, hired killers paid for out of his own pocket, Indians claiming me for a brother."

Joe finished the whiskey and corked the bottle, a sure

sign that he was drunk. "They're all dead now," he said. "I smelled them out, every damn one. Not a one of them died an easy death. If Ike doesn't want to play fair, that's what happens. Their blood is on his hands, not that blood bothers him much." Joe grinned. "Me neither."

"Good whiskey, Charley," he said as they went out.

Joe was drunk but they rode all night and by morning he was red-eyed and sober. They crossed the low brown hills to the west of Idabel and made camp in a dry wash. Joe squinted in the morning sunlight and pulled his hat down over his eyes. Steak cooked in skillets and the wind blew the smoke away before it changed and then blew the other way. In the wash there was sunlight and long yellow grass and brush growing along the sides.

Four men had known Sundance in the old days: Dancer, Horn, Murphy, and Silva. Dancer, Horn, and Murphy were halfbreeds; Silva was a renegade Kiowa who had drifted up from Texas. Dancer, a wiry man with a sneering mouth, would make the most trouble. There was no special reason for Dancer's bitter hatred. It was a fact to be faced. The others didn't like him because they knew he was different and therefore someone not to be trusted.

Joe sat with his back against a rock and rubbed his eyeballs. "I knew I was right about that whiskey the first time. We made good time though. We'll make better time soon as I get a few hours sleep. Ought to be at the hideout day after tomorrow. A fine hideout, a fine woman waiting for me. I didn't tell you about my new woman?"

"You were busy with the banking business," Sundance said.

"Wait till you see her," Joe said. "Hair like wheat on a sunny day, eyes so goddamned blue, and the rest of her! That says she's white. Me, I don't have a thing against white women. It's their men folk, so-called, I can't stand. I like Indian women when there's nothing else to be had. Lack of spirit is the main things wrong with them. I don't mind nigger women buy you don't meet hardly any out this way. But you take this particular white woman! All piss and vinegar! Lord! Does she get mad. I'm going to have to break her of some of that. Most of the time I kind of like it. Then I get tired, have to give her a few licks to let her know who's got the pants on. When I'm with her I have to watch there aren't any knives laying around. Things like that. She cooks my grub but I make her eat some before I do. You'll like her, Sundance."

"You got any more women there?"

"Only my woman. We had a good-looking white girl, real young, but she ran away and fell down a hole. Out here a lot of white women are poor grade beef. Not my woman. I captured her in a place called Danforth's Crossing down near the Texas line. Must be the best part of two months ago. It's taking her a time to get used to my ways, but this one is worth the extra trouble."

Sundance knew Brindar, the halfbreed, would side with Dancer and the others. As yet, the rest of the gang didn't give a damn. There were not white men in the gang, though one man, hardly more than a boy, could have passed for white if he cut his hair and wore farmer or range clothes.

Aside from Joe, there were sixteen men. Brindar was a sort of second in command. That meant he was good with a gun. In Joe's kind of army they didn't break a man back to the ranks if he didn't measure up. He got shot, a sensible way to handle a difficult situation.

It was too soon to make any plans. Time for that when they got to the hideout. He wondered about the white woman. No ordinary farm or ranch woman, from what Joe had said. Any woman who stood up for Joe couldn't be ordinary. Maybe it would be good to have her around. Maybe not. If Joe got edgy it could go two ways. Joe would be watching him all the time. The warning in the Chinaman's place was unmistakable. All it would take was one slip to get him killed. Joe was the same and he was different. He was worse. Years of out-thinking and outfighting the law and the cavalry had driven him a little crazy. It showed in the way he talked. Sundance had seen that happen to other outlaws, men who started out thinking they had been wronged, wanting to get back at the world, and after a while the wrongs and rights didn't matter any more.

He knew they wouldn't try to kill him while he slept, not unless Joe had already given the order. He had no doubt that they would try later. The least they would was try to turn Joe against him. That would be Brindar's job. Brindar wasn't dumb. Vicious but never dumb. Joe might listen, or he might tell Brindar to go to hell. It all depended how Joe felt at the time.

Sundance decided that the Fort Smith idea was going to keep him alive. If Joe came up with a plan, he would come up with a better one. His orders were to bring Joe back to be hanged, but first there were sixteen men to get rid of. He didn't think Joe was going to decide against the Fort Smith idea. He hated Parker too much. He hated the silky-bearded fanatic he called Ike. They were both crazy, Joe and the judge. Two men with a lot in common, both killers in their own way. Both justified what they did, the usual way of killers. Sundance had never yet met a killer, even the worst of them, who didn't explain it all away.

He slept for a few hours. Joe was still asleep when he woke up and got coffee from the pot steaming at the fire. He saw Brindar watching him. Silva was watching too, with sullen Indian hatred. Silva was the one to look out for right now. Brindar knew better than to kill without orders. Silva wouldn't think about the consequences. Silva was a killer so vicious that even the Comanches had driven him out, banished him from Texas. After all the years with the gang, he spoke no more than a few words of English. He had no friends in the gang, no friends anywhere. Silva, above all, was the one to watch.

Silva was an Indian and that made him more dangerous than the others. He knew the things Sundance knew, some of them, and he knew how to kill silently. Sundance knew that Silva would come at him with a knife. Silva carried two pistols and a tube-loading rifle, but he would use the knife, for it was the weapon he knew best, the one he liked best. How soon it would come, Sundance had no way of knowing. It wouldn't come during the day and not with Joe around. Once again, not unless Joe gave the order. It was hard to figure what Joe would do, because Joe might not know himself, and that was going to be the hardest part to get around: knowing what Joe would do. A man who wasn't crazy could be outguessed. Not Joe.

Joe woke up and pushed his hat out of his eyes. "I dreamt that I died and went to Heaven and Heaven was the biggest bank in the world. Mount up, you sons of bitches—we're going home."

CHAPTER 6

They crossed another line of hills and after that there were mountains ahead. Over the top of the mountains mist looked like smoke. On toward night they reached a fast-flowing river and they followed it until it got dark. Then they made camp beside the river and started again in the morning. The past day had taken them far out of settled country. People had seen them, a few Indian farmers, but if the army came to ask questions, nobody had seen them. Joe said he had never been caught because he had Indian friends all over the Territory, and if he didn't exactly have friends, an awful lot of people were afraid of him. But good information was more important than anything, Joe said, and so he paid good money to people who got it for him.

"They just think I'm top-heavy with good luck," Joe said when supper was over and they were lying in their blankets by the edge of the river. In the dark riverbed the water ran fast and it looked like a good fishing river to Sundance. The fire was packed down with green wood and dirt to make enough smoke to keep away the mosquitoes.

"Sure, luck is a part of it," Joe said, "but it's reliable information that keeps me fat and happy. I pay people in two ways, money and protection. And never go back on my word less absolutely necessary. In wild country like this protection can mean more than money. You got every kind of bad man coming into the Territory, whites as well as mean Indians like that Silva over there. Most of them don't rightly know what they want. Everything is spur of the moment with them. But I won't have them bothering my Indians and halfbreeds. Lately I been passing word around the old days here are done with. I'm king in this Territory. Sugarboy was telling me about a man name of John Murrell down on the old Natchez Trace got himself the idea of whipping and coaxing all the bad men thereabouts into joining up with him. One big army of bandits. You ever hear of this man, Sundance?"

"Used to be well-known," Sundance said. "More than forty years ago. Murrell. Talked the hard cases into coming in with him. Tried to make a real business out of it. Made deals all over the state, some with the politicians, some with the sheriffs. At one time he had five hundred men he could call out if he needed them. Doing fine until he had a falling out with the politicians."

"That's what Sugarboy said. I'm going to take it slower than Murrell. Slow but steady. Sugarboy said Murrell never got the people behind him, didn't want to share his ill-gotten gains. I can see wanting to hold onto what you fight for, risk your neck for, but you have to be smart enough to let some of it go."

Joe rolled up in his blankets and pulled his hat down over his eyes. The mosquitoes buzzed trying to get through the smokescreen. "This time tomorrow night we'll be home," Joe said. "And I'll be bedded down with my woman. Wait'll you see her. You got to grab yourself a woman next time we hit some town. Last time I hit a bank over in Centerville there was this nice-looking sort of a Swede woman dealing out money in the cage. If I didn't have the other one back home I'd have took her like a shot. Maybe I should have, come to think of it. Might teach the one back home she ain't the only fish."

"What's her name?" Sundance said.

"The one in the bank? How in hell would I know a thing like that?"

"Not that one."

"Never did get to hear it. Fought me so hard, never did get a chance to enquire, so much fire in her I started calling her 'Sparky.' What do you think of it?"

"I think it's a lousy name for a good-looking woman, which you say she is."

"That's what she is. She didn't like the name neither. You think maybe I ought to stop calling her that?"

"It would be a start."

"I might," Joe said, already half asleep. "If I feel like it, if she behaves better. You'd think we were married, the way we fight."

All the next day they followed the river until it grew wider and deeper. The river cut through the mountains. Confined by rock walls it roared and frothed. The rock walls gave way to a small sandy beach of white sand and gravel and up ahead was a gorge with cliffs going up on both sides. In the gorge the water ran faster than a sluice and there was the thunder of a waterfall far into the gorge.

"That's where we're going," Joe said. "You'll see."

On the far side of the river a smaller strip of sand ran down for about a hundred feet. A man came out from under the hang of the cliff and yelled across to Joe, and it wasn't until they were right at the edge of the river that Sundance saw the ledge that went along the bottom of the cliff and into the gorge. It was just wide enough for a man and a horse and when it got into the gorge water foamed up and over it, covering it completely.

The man on the other side picked up a bow and an arrow with a light rope tied to it. The rest of the rope was coiled loosely on the sand by the edge of the water, and before he shot the arrow, the man shook the rope to make sure it would run out smoothly when the pull came. He loosed the arrow and the rope snaked across the river and the arrow buried itself in the sand. Brindar coiled up the rope and attached to the end of it was a thick rope hawser, the kind used to make riverboats fast to the landing. He hauled in the thick rope and wound it around a tree and put a hitch in it. On the other side it was wound around a rock. Brindar pulled in the rope until there was no slack in it.

"That's how we do it," Joe said. "Now and then we lose a man, usually a new man, or one that wants to get across too fast. That current is something fierce. If a man goes under the rope there's nothing can be done for him. Off he sails and over the falls. I don't know what's below the falls. Ain't never been there. River drops on down over, I guess, but how many drops and falls before it flows straight and smooth again is any man's guess. I'd just as soon not ever go down there. That ledge over yonder continues down a long way and on time I followed it a ways till it got narrow and the water got too high. I guess it could be done. Couldn't be done with a horse though. Not wide enough and damned if I ever knew a horse that couldn't spook in there, all that water rushing past and the noise of the falls coming up at you. A year or so back I gave a wiry young fella two hundred and fifty dollars, said there was another half to make an even five, if he'd be willing to follow the ledge

65

down the side of the falls and see what was down there, if there was a back way out of the hideout. The boys started laying bets on him right in front of his face, and at first he didn't want to go, then he got mad when they started doing that, so he went and that was the last we ever saw of him. Course he might have made it if he hadn't put away so much whiskey before he started out. I still think it could be done. Sugarboy says —said—some fella name of Powell, a fella with one arm, mind you, sailed down through the Grand Canyon and lived to tell the tale. Well, sir, if a man can do that a man can do anything. Look at the boys there, see how handy they get across when you know how to do it right."

The first of Joe's men had started into the river, guiding the frightened horses along the thick rope. The current pushed the horses and men hard against the rope, trying to push them under, and water boiled white against the flanks of the horses. Then the first man was across, waiting for the others to cross. The others began to come up out of the water.

"Must say I didn't find this place on my own," Joe said. "A lonesome old man told me about it. A trapper all trapped out himself, sick and old, half-dead and ready to die. Found him in a hollow, his water and food gone. No reason to shoot him though I did shoot him after I filled him with water, then whiskey so he'd go easy to the other side. Funny thing he told me he took to the mountains years back so he could kill the craving for whiskey that caused him to lose his family and business back East. Now it was forty years later, dry bone-like all the years, and all he wanted before he went out was a bottle of whiskey. Wasn't half way down the bottle before he told me the story of this place, me being so good to him and all. Said forty years back he finished off a last bottle and fell into the river miles upstream. Said he wasn't that eager to come up again when he fell in. When he came too he was washed up on that sand over there. Had a rope wound around his ribs. They'd been cracked and binding himself up with a rope was the best he could do out here. The rope was how he was able to get back to this side. Tied a rock to the end of it and kept throwing it across till it caught in a tree. Used the light rope till he got a heavy one like the one we're using."

Sundance took Eagle across and Joe followed him. "You got a good animal there," Joe said. "Usually the new horses haven't been across before we have to put ropes on."

Sundance wondered what the woman called "Sparky" was going to be like.

Joe led the way along the ledge and the white-topped water rushed and roared between the rock walls. The gorge was narrow when they started in and stayed narrow for hundreds of yards, and there was no sun for a long time, but there was sun up ahead. Sun slanted down from the top of the gorge, sparkling in the spray thrown up by the rocks. In the gorge the water looked black and very cold except where it rushed over rocks and then it looked cold and white, but always it ran fast.

For part of the way the ledge was a few inches under water. "River's in flood now," Joe said, yelling to make himself heard above the thunder of the falls they couldn't see from where they were. "Never gets any higher than it does now. A real heavy flood would maybe come up higher. Can't recall that happening but the one time. I tell you, Sundance, there is nothing like this hideout in the Territory."

After he saw how the gorge widened out after they rounded a bend in the cliff wall, Sundance knew that

Joe was right. On the way in the gorge seemed to run down high-walled and narrow all the way to the falls. Between the rock walls the river ran like a millrace, black and dangerous. It didn't get any wider where the rock walls began to curve, but past the curve the sheer cliff fell back from the water for about a hundred yards and there was white sand and caves that burrowed into the cliff. High up the east wall of the cliff was split and sun slanted down in a powerful beam that lit up the wide sandy stretch between the river and the caves. The light didn't penetrate as far as the caves, which lay in shadows. The mouth of the caves looked black in contrast to the white sand and sunlight.

Joe was very proud of his hideout. He waved his arm like the proprietor of a fine farm or a bustling business. "Got everything we need stored in the caves. Had to drag it all in, naturally. Don't ever let my stores run low. Rifles, plenty of ammunition, enough canned goods to last half a year. Got my own cave fixed up real nice. Furniture, lamps. Brought in the boards and one of the boys, used to be a carpenter till he stuck a man with a chisel, knocked it all together for me. Feel that sun coming down there. Down here we get sun a good part of the day. Don't get any sun after about four o'clock this time of year. Get enough, all we ned. It's snug here in the winter. A river that fast don't freeze so nobody can walk in on the ice. No way they can come at me from downriver. Can't get at me from above. Cliffs too high and smooth. Only way in is the way we came. If they found the ledge they could try to come in that way. First they'd have to find it, no easy thing to do even if they got this far. Then they'd have to cross the river, which is just as hard, for we'd be shooting at them all the time they were crossing. Got a man posted there day and night. We could stand them off till that river

68

ran dry, which is never going to happen. Hell! It came to that, we could dynamite the ledge and try to go out the hard way. Now where, I would like to know, is that damned woman?''

A lanky woman in Levis and a wool shirt came out of the biggest cave and stood looking at them. Her short white-blond hair was cut short and combed back over her ears.

"There she is, old Sparky," Joe said. His wild whoop enchoed in the gorge. "Come on over and meet the missus."

Joe grabbed the lanky girl so Sundance could see him doing it. Sundance liked them long and lean like that. This one was a little hard in the face and mean in the eye. He liked that too. She had no boots on, perhaps she didn't own any boots. Joe pulled her away from the mouth of the cave and into the light and her eyes were yellow when the light hit her face. She broke away from Joe and punched him in the belly and he doubled up pretending to be hurt.

"Didn't I tell you she was something?" Joe said. "You ever see a woman with such brass and nerve. A man did what she just did and he'd be laying there dead on the sand. Say hello to Sparky."

Joe looked at Sundance, then back at the girl. "What in hell *is* your name?"

"Anna Jacobson," she said. "What's yours?"

Joe whooped. "Didn't I tell you! This here is Jim Sundance, murderer and bank robber, the only man that ever broke out of the Fort Smith jail. They got poor old Sugarboy. Run of the luck, I guess."

"I'm glad they got him," Anna Jacobson. "Too bad they didn't get you too. You and this one. All of you."

Joe laughed and slapped her behind before she could dodge away from him. "How can you say a thing like that about my friend Sundance? Why, you hardly know the man."

"He can't be any good, he wouldn't be with you."

Joe grabbed at her again, but he wasn't really trying. "You miss me, you cranky Scandihoovian? Come on, 'fess up like a good girl. You been missing me something fierce, isn't that a fact now?"

"You'll be sorry you joined up with him," Anna Jacobson said.

"It looked like a good idea at the time," Sundance said. "Still does."

He still couldn't figure out what she was. She had a hard voice but it hadn't been hardened by farm work or working drunks in a saloon. The hardness in her voice, in her yellow eyes, seemed natural, as if she had been that way all of her life. She was lanky and well-muscled and her breasts were on the small side but firm as fresh fruit. The name as Swedish and so was the white-blond hair, and that was about all he knew about her. He liked her looks, even the hard voice, but didn't know what was in back of them.

"She can cook too," Joe said. "She eats like a man and never gets fat. First I thought she'd be picky and shy, no such thing. Mornings she comes out here on the sand and jumps up and down. Exercise, she calls it. Now that I'm home I guess I'll have to start washing again. I don't know as I like all that water. Some doctor, some kind of a doctor, told me one time never take a bath. He said bathing washes away all the precious oils on the skin."

Anna Jacobson said, "That whole river wouldn't be enough to get you clean."

"See how much she likes me?" Joe said. "Damn! I feel so hungry I could eat a bear. Usually I go for the other thing first, then I eat."

70

Anna Jacobson told him what he ought to do.

"I'd rather do it to you," Joe said. "Be no fun for the other man, even if possible. Rustle up some grub for me and my friend. Do it quick or I'll hold your head down in the river. Had to do that a few times. Slapping her about didn't work so I tried the river. That worked, sort of."

Sundance and Joe sat on the sunlit sand while Anna Jacobson went down to the river and hauled in an oilskin pouch at the end of a rope. A small cookstove stood near the cave and a tin chimney went partways up the cliff.

"Burns charcoal," Joe said. "No smoke, nothing to give us away in here. In the cold weaher we take the stove inside the cave and hook up the chimney again. Gets cold in here, hardly ever hot. Be it ever so humble, as old Sugarboy used to say."

"I see you're a man short," Sundance said.

Joe looked surprised. "And I now? Hadn't noticed myself." He laughed. "You wouldn't miss a thing like that. Sure. Johnny Baker had some business to tend to."

Sundance said, "Like checking back on me?"

"That's what he's doing," Joe said. "Not that I doubt you a single minute. Hell! Your word is good as a solid gold bar. Me, I'd take your word in front of the President's, only I got to look out for my boys and see they don't come to any harm, which is what could happen was I to let a stranger—not that you're exactly a stranger—come in with nothing more than his word he wasn't a spy for the judge. You see the sense of that. Johnny'll be along in a few days and til then we'll just take out ease and wait to hear what he has to say. Johnny's a pretty smart boy. Was one of Ike's best Indian deputies before he got to fretting about how low he

71

was paid. Started doing a little night work, as they say, until he knifed a man he should have made sure was dead. Only he wasn't dead and the next thing you know there were wanted posters out on Johnny. They tell me Ike has a special rope ready for him. Johnny'll check your story clear through, Sundance. His brother-in-law still works for Ike when he isn't working for me."

Joe was watching for Sundance's reaction, and got none. "You ought to be in the spy business, like the Pinkertons," Sundance said.

"What do you think I *am* in?" Joe said. "No need to worry about Johnny though. That boy's got nothing agin you. He'll tell the story straight. Now had I sent Dancer or Horn there might be something to worry about. The two just named don't love you, Sundance. The same goes for a few others."

"Brindar thinks I'm trying to take his job."

"Is that what you're trying to do? 'Course if I was to give you his job, ain't a whole lot he could do about it. He could make a face and I'd have to shoot his face off his head. I wouldn't mind having you for my second man, but that'll have to wait. Looks like the woman is about done with the grub."

Joe wanted to eat in the cave and they took their plates inside, out of the sun. A lamp hung from a hook burned low. Joe turned it up until the cave was filled with yellow light. After the sun it was cool in the cave. Two bunks, one above the other, hadn't been used for a long time. Now they were stacked with canned food, blankets, and guns. There was a clean table scrubbed with river sand and chairs against the smooth, inward curving walls of the cave. A new bed had been built across from the bunks and it had been made up, with the blankets pulled tight and tucked in at the corners. A trunk with women's clothing in it lay open.

"Used to be a sty in here before I got the woman,"

Joe said while Anna Jacobson put a cowl of salt on the table. "The woman I had before this one was dirtier than I was."

"You're still dirty," Anna Jacobson, slamming down knives and forks.

Joe ignored her. "I wasn't one bit sorry when she fell in the river and drowned."

"You threw her in," Anna Jacobson said. "You try to throw me in and I'll take you along with me. You murdered that poor woman."

"Anyway she's gone and good riddance is all I can say," Joe said, cutting his steak into bite-sized chunks. Sundance remembered that as one of Joe's peculiarities, cutting up the entire steak before he even tasted it.

"Ask your friend why he threw that woman in the river," Anna Jacobson said.

"I thought that part of the conversation was over," Joe said.

Anna Jacobson said, "Go on, ask him."

Sundance smiled in spite of himself. "Why did you throw the woman in the river, Joe?"

"He thinks it's funny," Anna Jacobson said to Joe.

"So do I," Joe said. "See how she is, Sundance? See, what did I tell you?"

Anna Jacobson turned her anger on Sundance. "What did he say about me."

"He said he captured you but you were still wild."

"You've got a hell of a nerve to say that to me. Who the hell do you think you are!"

"Hey!" Joe said. "If you want to fight, you too, go outside. I'm eating my dinner, if that's all right with you."

"I hope it chokes you," Anna Jacobson said. "Go on, Rufus! Tell him why you threw the woman in the river."

"She knows I don't like 'Rufus,' so she calls me that

73

when she gets really mad. The woman in the river? I never threw a woman in a river till that one. Not that it's such a bad idea"—he glared at Anna who glared back—"not a bad idea a-tall, when you come to think of it. Reason I threw her in, she kept after me to marry her. Day and night, she had a hold on my ear, mostly it was night in the dark, all the time whispering 'listen good, Joe, why don't we get married' and some such. 'I'll be a good little wife to you'—she must have weighed close to what I do—and it got so I was ready to run when I saw her. Hell's Bells! What do I want a wife for? When I first captured her I got to say I was sort of sweet on her and was for a time after that, so I didn't want to hurt her feelings, and so forth."

"You just murdered her," Anna Jacobson said.

"Whatever you want to call it," Joe said. "So not wanting to hurt her feelings and all, I said to her sure I want to marry you, you randy little porker, but there's no way I can get a church into this gorge."

"That's one of his favorite jokes," Anna Jacobson said to Sundance.

"Who in hell is telling this story, you or me?" Joe said. "And I told her it was too dangerous to take her on a raid. I said if anything happened to her, if she caught a bullet and such, I'd have to shoot myself, not being able to stand the grief of her passing. I thought all that would hold her for a while, and it did till one day she found out that one of the boys had been some kind of preacher in a mission church over by Tulsa. From then on not a minute's peace. I guess I could have married her and might have if she didn't press it so hard. So I threw her in the river when I couldn't stand it any longer.

"So you be a good girl," he said to Anna Jacobson,

who was chewing furiously, a lanky, brassy woman with a healthy appetite.

She looked up from her plate. "He'd kill you just as fast," she said.

CHAPTER 7

It was dark when Anna Jacobson came out of the cave and came down to the edge of the river, where Sundance was. The moon sent pale cold light into the gorge, and the thunder of the falls seemed to be a part of the silence. Full of steak and whiskey and having worn himself out with the woman, Joe lay snoring in the cave. Except for the men on guard at the river crossing and on the ledge, the rest of the gang were asleep. Broken branches sailed along in the flood-driven current and disappeared in the darkness.

Sundance had been looking at the ledge, where it jutted up again past the narrow beach and went on down to the falls. Maybe that was the way to go out, pushing Joe in front of him. They might not make it, but he knew the gang wouldn't follow. No one had ever gone down there, and maybe the ledge just stopped. If it did, there was no way out. On both sides the walls of the gorge went up smooth as a church steeple, and three times as tall. If he went down the ledge instead of going by way of the crossing, he would have to leave Eagle. Leave the big stallion for the last time. He would do it if he had to, but the thought tugged at that private part of his mind that he reserved for the few things he liked. He heard

76

her coming, her bare feet whispering in the dry sand.

She sat down and hiked up her knees and put both hands around them. There was something rangy and wild about her that reminded him of a young colt, and in the bright moonlight her eyes were very yellow. Over the years Sundance had known only three women with yellow eyes; all had been self-centered and dangerous. Anna Jacobson had cat's eyes; the other women had yellow eyes without looking like cats. Anna Jacobson looked like a long, lean cat. She didn't just look like a cat. She was a cat and she regarded him with the same distinterest. She thought he could do something for her and so now, with the initial anger gone, she came purring up to him, trying him out. If she didn't get what she wanted the claws would come out.

At the moment the claws were well-concealed. "You look different than the others," she said. "You don't mind if I say that?"

Sundance was still thinking about the gorge. "Say anything you like," he said.

"You mean you don't care what I say."

"I mean I don't mind.

Parker wanted Joe brought in, or he wanted his head. Sundance wondered what the judge would do with Joe's head, if he brought it in. Stick it on a spike in the town square, the way they did it down in Mexico? Maybe the judge would send Joe's head back East, to the wax museum they had in New York.

"Are you really a murderer?" Anna Jacobson said.

"The law says I am."

"But you think you're not?"

"It doesn't matter what I think. They'll hang me if they catch me."

"Joe said you were in Idabel."

"Did Joe send you out here to ask questions?"

77

There was a flash of anger in the narrowed yellow eyes; the claws were showing. So far just the tips.

"If you don't want to talk to me you don't have to."

"Sure. That's it."

"Why didn't you go to California or Mexico? That's what you should have done."

"Thanks," Sundance said. "Anything else I ought to know?"

"You look like an intelligent man, so I don't have to tell you. Joe—these men—don't have a chance. They're dead but they don't know it. You're dead too, if you don't get out. You'll never make it to Fort Smith, not with Joe. You may make it there but you'll die there."

"Joe told you about Fort Smith?"

"Joe tells me everything."

"That a fact? I wouldn't have figured Joe for that."

"Joe likes to brag to me. Joe thinks if he shows me what a big man he is I'll like him better."

"You think you will?"

"Joe will never be a big man. Not big enough for me."

"How big is that?"

"Maybe you're big enough."

"Joe is the hero in this melodrama, not me."

"You mean you're afraid of Joe? I don't think you are."

"Sure is a nice night," Sundance said.

Again, there was a glint of anger in her eyes. She was used to telling people what to do, even Joe.

"I don't understand why you didn't go to Mexico," she said.

"Maybe I don't like Mexico," Sundance said. "Maybe I like it here. I'm alive, with food in my belly."

"You ought to get out the first chance you get."

"Did you tell that to Joe?"

"I tell Joe what I want to tell him. I didn't tell him that. I'm telling it to you. Clear out. You don't belong here. I don't belong here, but I have nothing to say about it."

Sundance looked at her. "What did you do before this place?"

"I consider that a low, dirty, filthy remark."

"Wasn't meant to be."

Anna Jacobson said, "I was a schoolteacher."

Sundance decided that was a lie.

She knew he knew. There was defiance in her hard-edged voice. "You don't believe me?"

"If that's what you say, I do."

Anna Jacobson said, "What did you do?"

"Killed a man."

"I meant before that. That's what I meant and you know it."

Sundance told her, and maybe Joe had already told her. Anna Jacobson was a strange one and she sure as shooting was no schoolteacher. He didn't know what she was except what Joe had called her—a firecracker of a Scandahoovian.

Sundance told her about the Indian Ring and his oldest and best friend, General George Crook, known to the Indians as Three Stars. He finished telling it.

"Why don't you get this general to help you?" she said. "I know who Crook is, know his name. He could help you. Get away from here and get help from him."

"Can't do it," Sundance said. "Three Stars has too many enemies to get him mixed up in my trouble. They'd say he was protecting a killer."

"Get out anyway."

"Joe wouldn't like that. Besides, he didn't tie me and drag me in here. You don't like it but I like it fine. It must be hard for you. Different, I mean, from the life

79

of a schoolteacher.''

"Don't you sneer at me, you son of a bitch! You know I'm not a teacher.''

"Then what are you besides a conniver?''

"If you have to know, I'm a . . . It's none of your goddamned business what I am.''

Sundance was getting to like her. It wasn't easy but he was getting there. Behind the hard shell there was something trying to get out, only she didn't know how to let it loose, didn't even know how to talk about it. He guessed she had walled herself off behind lies, things she didn't want to admit to herself. But what?

She stretched out her long legs in the sand, more like a cat than ever. He hadn't seen her astride a horse, but he knew she'd be good at it. He guessed she'd be good at just about anything she did, except telling the truth. But more than anything she was easy on the eye in a campful of dirty, ugly men.

"You don't know anything about me, so how can you say I'm a conniver?'' she said.

"I think it fits you.''

"Something doesn't make sense,'' she said. "A man like you running with Joe Buck just because you shot a drunk in a saloon. You didn't shoot the President, not even the governor of Arkansas. I don't think you're telling me the truth. You're not telling Joe the truth.''

"Why don't you run and ask Joe what he thinks?''

"There's something fishy about you, Sundance,'' Anna Jacobson said. "I hear what you say—what Joe says—and it doesn't hang together. Somehow it just doesn't. I think you're up to something. Look, I don't care what you're trying to do to Joe, why you're here or what your reason. Just tell me what it is.''

"So you can tell Joe?''

"You know that's not the reason I want to know. I

just want to get out of here. You can help me do it."

"It can't be done," Sundance said. "Suppose we did get out—something I have no mind to do—Joe and the boys would be after us all the way. Not just Joe. Not a house we could beg food in they wouldn't try to shoot us in the back. Shoot me, hold you for Joe. Then there's the law. I broke Parker's jail and he won't forget that in a hurry. And think about this. How do you know I won't tell Joe what you just said? It's one thing for you wanting to escape, trying to turn one of Joe's men against him is something else."

Anna Jacobson remained calm. "If you did that I'd just tell Joe escaping was all your idea. Joe doesn't trust you, not yet anyway, and maybe he never will. He'd believe me instead of you because that's what he'd want to believe."

"Most likely," Sundance said. "Suppose we forget the whole thing? You don't talk, I don't."

For the first time there was real anger. "No," she said. "I'm going to take my chances with you. You're my choice, like it or not. Don't talk, let me. I hear what you say and I don't believe a word of it. If you want to stay alive you're going to get away from here and take me with you. I don't know how you're going to do it. That's up to you."

Sundance smiled at her, so cat-eyed and bristling with anger. Her fur was up and her claws were out.

"Why don't you go see if Joe wants anything?" he said.

Anna Jacobson called him a dirty name.

Watching her long stride as she went back to the cave, Sundance decided that he liked her better every minute.

If the girl had told Joe anything it didn't show in his

face the next morning. He rolled out late and ate a big breakfast. They were both waiting for Baker to get back, though nothing was said about it. The men avoided Sundance, even those who had nothing against him. A few might have tried to make friends, but they didn't because they knew he was a dead man until Joe said he wasn't. The girl nodded and spoke little; it was as if nothing had passed between them. It rained a lot and they were all trapped together at the bottom of the misty gorge. In a few weeks the rain would be gone and there would be nothing but long days of sunshine; for now, they set their faces against the cold, driving rain and made the best of it.

At times, carried away by his own enthusiasm, Joe would go on about the big things they were going to do together. Then suddenly he would remember the unfinished business of Baker and the conversation would trail off into silence. Sundance could almost hear Joe trying to read his mind, watching him all the time. The men watched and waited, they all waited.

There was only one thing Joe was always ready to talk about: weapons. Like Sundance, he took very good care of the tools of his trade. There were few new guns that he didn't know about; Sundance told him about the others, and only then was the tension between them forgotten. Sundance told him about the man over in Germany, Borschardt, who was trying to perfect what he called "an automatic pistol." It was loaded by a clip of bullets with a spring to push the bullets into place when one bullet was fired and another was needed.

They were sitting on the damp sand outside the cave and Sundance drew a bullet clip in the sand with the point of his knife. Joe wanted to know why that was faster than a double-action revolver and Sundance explained that it was faster because there was no cylinder to turn to put the next bullet under the firing pin. When a bullet was fired a toggle on top of the gun, in the back, snapped backward and up, and that ejected the spent cartridge and loaded a live one. The firing, ejecting, and reloading was very fast.

"How fast?" Joe said.

"Twice as fast as the fastest double-action," Sundance said. "Maybe faster than that."

"How many bullets in this clip?"

"Borschardt has one pistol that fires nine," Sundance said. "Another that shoots fifteen. If you have a long enough clip, you can fire twenty or thirty."

"Jesus Christ!" Joe said.

He was indignant when Sundance told him that Borschardt was an American, a New Englander who had been forced to take his new gun to Germany because the army or the Yankee gun manufacturers weren't interested.

"Lame-brained sons of bitches," Joe said, still looking at the drawing of the clip.

Sundance smiled. George Crook, his old friend, wasn't given to bad language, but his words had been pretty strong, that day eighteen months before, on the army testing grounds outside Washington. After beging rebuffed or ignored, Borschardt, in desperation, had written to Crook, explaining his new gun and his great hopes for it. Crook, a fine soldier and a forward-looking man, had been interested from the start.

Joe's eyes shone with excitement as Sundance told him about the test firing of the gun.

"Three Stars—that's General Crook—wasn't any more convinced than the other officers. But he's always ready to give something new a chance. I was in Washington on Indian business and Three Stars said why didn't I come along. He didn't want to look like a fool, so he made Borschardt give him a private demonstration of the gun. We went out in some woods, pinned targets on trees and started firing. Crook fired the pistol, so did I. It worked just like Borschardt said it would. Fast, accurate. Has different balance than a six-gun. The weight's in the back, so with the slender barrel it has a nice way of pointing."

"I wouldn't mind having a weapon like that," Joe said.

"We tried the three lengths of clips," Sundance said. "It jammed once when I was firing it. Borschardt said happened sometimes and he was working on it. Three Stars it was something had to be worked on all right. But he agreed with Borschardt that it was a remarkable gun, like nothing he ever saw, and should be given a chance.

"The lame-brained son of bitches!" Joe said again. "They turned it down."

"That's right," Sundance said. "But not because it jammed. It didn't jam the next day when Crook brought Borschardt and the rest of them to the firing grounds. The Assistant Secretary of War was there, so was General Miles. The test went off without a hitch. The usual thicknesses of pine board to show penetration. Everything worked fine. Borschardt showed how fast it could be reloaded, how fast it kicked out the empty shells."

"Then what?" Joe said.

"General Miles didn't like it," Sundance said. "Three Stars looked over at me and we both knew Borschardt was wasting his time. General Miles was more bothered by what he called the waste of ammunition. I thought Three Stars was going to blow up, but he's been an army man too long to buck a superior in front of strangers. Later I heard he had a big row with

84

Miles. Then and there, he just shut his mouth and let Miles talk. Miles couldn't say the gun didn't work, so he kept on about the waste of ammunition. A man armed with a Borschardt pistol would just blaze away, Miles said. Blaze away, run bullets right through that gun and never think about taking proper aim. There was no substitute for a man taking careful aim, Miles said. That's how wars were fought, how they'd always be fought. So Borschardt went to Germany. Last I heard of him he's got a whole new factory to work in. Three Stars says he's working to cut down the weight and length of the gun. He just hired a young American inventor to work with him. His name is Luger . . .''

When they didn't talk about guns they talked about knives. The knife talk got started when some of the men charcoaled a target on a sawed tree section and started throwing knives at it. Joe laughed when one of them broke a blade.

"Never saw much good in throwing knives," he said. "You know a knife it's gone from your hand and maybe you still got other fella's coming at you. Looks fancy but it's dumb. You still carry the same blade you always did?"

Sundance gave Joe his Bowie knife so he could look at it. Joe handled it almost tenderly, as he did all weapons.

"I favor a heavier, longer blade," he said, passing his own Bowie to Sundance.

Joe's Bowie was a fourteen-incher nearly two inches wide at the guard, a good looking knife, straight until it neared the saber point. Three inches from the tip, the blade curved back, ending in a razor sharp point. The front of the blade was ground so sharp that it would cut paper held loosely in the hand. On the back the knife had a three-inch ripping edge; the cutting edge on the front was just over a foot in length. The back of the knife was quarter of an inch thick and sheathed in brass; in a fight this prevented an opponent's knife from sliding down and cutting the owner's hand. The crossguard was a straight pro-pronged steel plate; the grip black walnut, and the shank of the blade went clear through the grip, ending in a knob at the bottom end.

Sundance weighed the big knife in his hand. "A mite too heavy for me," he said. "What can you do with this that you can't do with a ten-incher?"

"One chop cuts off a man's hand," Joe said. "Put enough weight behind it and it'll go through a man's arm. Used to know a fella carried a twenty-incher. He was a holy terror with that thing!"

"What happened to him?"

"Somebody shot him."

When they got through laughing Joe said, "I guess you're pretty handy with this thing." He made a few passes in the air with Sundance's knife.

"Better than most men," Sundance said.

"You mean there's somebody better than you?"

"Sure," Sundance said, "but I've been keeping out of his way."

"Like hell," Joe said. "I like the Bowie, but I like the old Arkansas Toothpick just as well. I like the feel of it in my hand. Maybe that's just me."

Joe handed Sundance his second knife, a straight-pointed blade with a double edge. It had a flat, fairly narrow crossguard with knobbed ends and a walnut horn. It was a fighting knife like the Bowie, but a lot lighter.

"I can throw it if I have to," Joe said. "But like I

86

said, I hate to have a knife leave my hand. You want to see me throw it?"

"Sure."

Joe stood up and threw the straight-bladed knife all in one motion. It flashed from his hand like a streak of silver and thunked home in the center of the target. Joe turned to grin at Sundance, then he went to get his knife.

"Why not!" Sundance said, taking the knife from Joe. He threw it fast and hard and put it in the same place. The difference was that Sundance had put so much force into the throw that Joe had to tug hard to get the blade out.

"Well now," Joe said, putting the knife away and trying to sound casual. "A throw like that could split a man's skull. You ever do that?"

Sundance said no.

Joe was grinning. "I'm going to do that sometime. Somebody I have a big hate for, I'm going to do that."

"Watch out he doesn't shoot you first," Sundance said, and they both laughed.

CHAPTER 8

Joe said he was working on a plan to rob the banks in Fort Smith, but that was all he told Sundance about it, and Sundance knew he was waiting for the man to get back after he checked the story of the jailbreak. It was spring and it rained a lot in the mountains and sometimes the top of the gorge was shrouded by mist. When it rained during the day and there was mist rainbow colors shimmered between the towering rock walls. The only constant sound was the rumble of the falls, out of sight, below the camp. At first, the men were glad to get back to camp, to sleep as late as they wanted, to loosen up after the long ride back from Idabel. But as the days passed the silence of the gorge got on their nerves. Some of the older men busied themselves, washing out their shirts and john johns, spreading the wet clothes on rocks beside the river where they could get the sun. One of the older riders, a man they called Skeeter, cooked for them and got paid for it. He was a wizened old killer who looked like a wizened old woman, and there was almost a gunfight when some of the men, the young ones, laughed and said he put lemon juice on his hands to keep them from getting red and cracked from the dishwater. Skeeter always wore a dirty canvas apron when he cooked, but always with his gunbelt buckled over it. When the shouting and the laughing started, the old man knocked the skillet off the cookstove and the steaks fell in the sand. "There goes your grub," he yelled. "You got anything else to say, you cootie-crawling sons of bitches?"

A man called Tanzy went for his gun, but before his hand got close to it, the old man's gun was out and cocked and ready to fire. There was more yelling. The old man wouldn't put up his gun until Joe came out of the cave and asked who wanted to swim over the falls.

Nobody wanted to die and the men who had egged him on to rile the cookie blamed the man who had pulled the gun. Tanzy argued and Joe knocked him down with a single punch.

"I could kick you but it's a nice day," Joe said. "Pull that gun again and I'll stick it up your funnel. If it's excitement you want you'll get it soon enough."

Anna Jacobson was watching from the mouth of cave. When she saw Sundance looking at her she went back inside. "A man has to be a fool to get the cookie mad at him," Joe said. "Worked on a horse ranch one time. Fair enough place, the food better than most. A fella there out of some meannness of his own never let the cookie be. The cookie was about the same age as Skeeter, but no hand with a gun. The foreman was too busy riding the boss's wife to pay much heed. So not a good foreman. On and on the joking went till some of the hands got sick of it and warned this fella to quit it. They sit down to eat and this fool would yell out, 'You been spitting in the stew again, Cookie?' or he'd make out he found an old sock in the coffee pot. Then one day he ate a wedge of peach pie Cookie gave him and dies an hour later. Not a man there didn't know that old Cookie had squeezed the poison out of a rattler's head into his pie. That's how you do it. My advice is, don't eat anything our friend Silva cooks for you."

Joe laughed and went back into the cave.

Sundance knew that Silva wouldn't use rattler venom. It would still be the knife. Silva watched him all the time. Silva wasn't like the others, he wasn't edgy. He could sit for hours without moving, his Indian face dark and immobile. While the others played cards or swapped stories or slept, Silva did nothing. There was hate in his eyes, but it was dull and quiet. Sundance would never know why Silva hated him. Silva knew he was of the Cheyenne; that had nothing to do with it. Silva would have found it hard to explain his reasons, if he had reasons and could explain them.

Sundance knew that Joe was using the Indian to test him. Dancer and others were dangerous, but they would hold back until they got a chance, when the time was right. Silva was different. He was Joe's probe, the point of his knife.

During the day, Sundance worked on his weapons and saw to his horse. The big stallion, accustomed to a free life, didn't like it in the gorge, and it showed in the way the great animal whinnied whenever Sundance came near. Mornings, Sundance rubbed down the stallion, grained it, and let it drink at the river. Sometimes he ate breakfast with Joe; other mornings, Joe stayed late with the woman. When Anna felt like it, she ate with them, but mostly she ate by herself, still sullen even when she had her coffee.

The men played cards all the time, some of them slapping down the cards in anger, bored with poker that had no real money in the game. Joe laid down the rules of gambling and he enforced them. He established a limit on the betting and any man caught cheating was promised a quick swim. Nobody cheated; nobody was caught at it.

"Low stakes keep them from getting too wild," Joe told Sundance.

At night Sundance slept outside under an overhang of rock that kept him dry except when the wind blew the rain in from the river. Early in the morning, he lay awake listening to the sound of the falls. He could still take a chance and go out that way with Joe. But Fort Smith looked better if Joe made up his mind to do it. What he had to do was keep Joe interested in Fort Smith, because Joe had a lot of wild ideas. They bubbled up one after the other. Sometimes he went back to talking about his plan to make all the gangs in the Territory pay tribute. Sundance wondered what Belle Starr and her husband, Henry, would think of that. Joe Buck and Belle Starr! Now there was a pair to think about. But Henry was safe because Belle was as ugly as sin, meaner than a bear with a toothache.

Anna Jacobson didn't talk much to Sundance. What had been said that night beside the river hadn't come up again. But it was there in the tension between them. And there was more than that. Sundance knew that women were attracted to him. He took no pride in it. Some women liked men like Joe Buck. There were women, the strange ones, and in a way they were all strange, who might have wondered what Silva was like.

Something wasn't right about Anna Jacobson. There was a restlessness, a feeling of discontent, of looking for something she couldn't find, that had nothing to be with being kept prisoner. She fought with Joe; they traded insults all the time. She seemed to like the danger that came with pushing him too far. She was still alive, so she hadn't pushed him too far. She kept on trying to reach some point at which Joe would turn on her for the last ime. Maybe he was making too much out of this; he didn't think so. It was possible that Joe, in his

91

way, sensed it too. Anna started the fights. Another woman would have ignored most of what Joe said; he didn't mean much by it, anyway. Joe held the power of life and death over her and the way she went back at him wasn't just the anger of a fiery women who refused to be subdued. Having her around was something new for Joe; it was obvious that she puzzled him, and when Joe couldn't understand a thing or a person he got mad. There was no doubt that Anna knew how bad Joe could be, how bad Joe really was. It didn't seem to frighten her. She seemed to like the idea of living so close to her own death.

Sundance was glad that she kept away from him. She was trouble, maybe more trouble to herself than anyone else. Danger seemed to draw her like a magnet. More men than women were like that, but there were women who broke all the rules. This one did. She sounded as if she came from somewhere in the East, was well brought up, but it was hard to know what she was, the way she talked. She outcussed Joe, always made a point of telling him how dirty and savage he was, which was nothing but the truth, but she didn't really mind it all that much. They'd have fights even in the middle of the night. One night it got so bad that the horses started to spook. Anna's yelling echoed up into the dark gorge, then it got quiet suddenly and it wasn't because Joe had punched her, because she didn't cry out and there were no marks on her that he could see when she started breakfast the next morning. It was a cold, misty morning and she was in a fretful mood, banging down the skillets and cursing the stove. Joe came out wearing only his pants and went down to the pool by the river to dip his head in the water. He yelled with high spirits and came back dripping water.

"For Christ's sake!" Anna said, turning back to stab

at the breakfast steaks with a fork.

Joe winked at Sundance.

Early in the afternoon there was yelling down by the river crossing and Joe came out of the cave buckling on his gunbelt. Sundance walked up from where the horses were in a pole pine corral. They both knew Baker was back. The men did too and they gathered behind Joe, leaving Sundance by himself. The rain had come and gone and there was bright sunlight in the gorge and high up a rock wren fluttered into its nest in a crack in the rocks. A few minutes later, Baker came along the ledge from the crossing, leading his horse. Sundance knew his life depended on how well the judge had told his story. Joe winked at Sundance and they all waited for Baker.

Baker stared at Sundance before he spoke.

"No need to hold back, we're all friends here," Joe said.

Sundance counted the men and one was missing. He knew he wasn't asleep; he knew he was pointing a rifle at his back. Joe was taking no chances: Sundance would try to kill him first if the news turned out bad.

"He told it the way it happened," Baker said. "Could've got back yesterday, but I told my brother-in-law to make sure. He got to talk to Doolin himself. Sundance broke out with a knife held on Doolin. Doolin's hopping mad about that. So is the judge. Must be to post ten thousand dollars for a jailbreak."

"Ike's feelings are hurt," Joe said. "You did good, boy. Get yourself something to eat. What about old Sugarboy?"

"They hung him. I guess they hung him. I asked the brother-in-law and he said, 'Prob'ly, you want me to check?' and I said, 'Naw, they prob'ly did,' and that was it. You didn't send me to find out about Sugar."

"Nothing to find out," Joe said.

93

"You can tell that fella to take his gun out of my back," Sundance said.

Joe laughed and raised his hand and dropped it. "You did break that goddamned jail! You long drink of water, you did break that jail."

"That's it," Sundance said, grinning back at Joe. "I broke jail."

"Ten thousand dollars! You're near as famous as I am. They don't have but twenty on me."

"You've been at it longer. You can have some of my ten if you want."

Joe sat on a rock; the men had gone away. "I been jumpy waiting for the news," Joe said. "I figured Baker would get it straight and not bend the story when he got back. Then a few times I thought Christ Almighty what if Doolin is so shame-faced he won't let on what really happened. What if he says the story is all bullshit and the judge decided to send you to the Grady prison farm instead. I wouldn't know how to think if Doolin did that."

"Doolin is a truth-telling man," Sundance said.

"Sure he is, the son of a bitch," Joe said. "I never knew Doolin to do anything but lie. What beats me is him telling the truth all of a sudden. Truth that makes him look bad. Why if I was Doolin I'd find a man that looked halfway like you, fix him up in buckskins, and hang him."

Maybe Joe was just talking out loud. "Doolin doesn't say what happens in Fort Smith," Sundance said. "Parker may be a murdering bastard, but he's no liar. If he says I escaped, Doolin has to say the same."

Joe said, "You may not know it, but you got yourself in with the judge. Damn! I'd hate to have to kill you, Sundance. I wasn't looking forward to it. You and me get along all right. You're like me. Not afraid to live, not afraid to die."

94

"Don't hurry me, Joe," Sundance said.

"I'm ready to try for Fort Smith," Joe said. "We're going to take those banks and live fast and free the way men should. You been wondering why I haven't gone over the plan with you. Sure you have. Understandable. It wasn't that I didn't trust. Not because of that. It was because I didn't altogether trust you that I kept from talking about it. Why would I want to do that if I had to kill you later?"

"Sounds practical," Sundance agreed. "You want to talk about it now?"

"I don't see it as easy," Joe said. "We have to make it easy as we can. I had the idea of doing what's been tried back East. A city gang back there broke into the banker's house early in the morning, held a gun on his wife and kids and said he'd never see them anything but dead if he didn't waltz along to the bank and empty it out. It worked fine I hear. I don't exactly like bringing women and kids into it though. I guess I'd do it if there wasn't another way. Three kidnappings is too much. Three times as much chance of something going wrong. Besides, if I have to kill the kids I'd look bad. Hell! I'd feel just as bad. So I passed on that idea. Then I thought suppose, say, five of the boys set fires all over town. I mean not in the houses, in the hotels and places like that. Draw them off. I don't mind that plan too much. A lot of fires at the same time, people running all over. What do you think?"

Sundance knew that Joe was serious. It was so wild that it could even work, if he let it happen. Joe just saw the hotels as buildings; he saw people burning to death.

"Everybody will run to the fires except the bankers," Sundance said. "They won't budge from the money."

"I know that," Joe said. "A banker wouldn't hurry to see General Grant and Robert E. Lee doing the polka. Just so everybody else runs is all I want. When

95

they do we move in nice and quiet and do our business. You don't like it."

"I didn't say I didn't like it. I just think there's an easier way. But I wouldn't go back to the wives and kids."

Joe looked cranky at having holes poked in his plans. "Why not?"

"All right. Suppose it works with two bankers out of three. You want it to work with all three, am I right?"

Joe nodded, still not liking it.

"Suppose the third banker hates his wife? And maybe he doesn't have any kids? If he has kids maybe they aren't there. What's wrong with that plan is that you have to count on them being there at the right time. You can't send a letter asking them to be there so you can walk in with guns. The morning you want to hold up the banker he's in Little Rock, urgent business that came up the night before. When that happens his assistant takes over. Only you don't know the assistant, who he is, where he lives, if he's married or not. You can't go running all over Fort Smith checking up on men who work in banks. The kidnap plan happens to you, not the other way around."

Joe gave Sundance a hard look. "Then you think up a plan. Till you do I'm gong ahead with the one I got."

Sundance knew he couldn't push his own plan too hard, when he got it finished, because for all his joking Joe was touchy if he thought someone was going against him. Having the girl there made him worse; he had to play the leader for her. The men would side with Joe, no matter what the plan was. Sundance was a halfbreed too, but they knew he wasn't like them. He was a halfbreed who had commanded respect in the white world, something they had never been able to do, and the fact that he had joined them only made that more uneasy about him. They had banded together as outcasts; he had never felt the need to ask any man for companionship or help.

But for the moment, the immediate danger has passed. It would be a long time before Joe trusted him, if he ever trusted him, but the tension had slackened. Baker's story had removed the men's fear of betrayal, something all outlaws lived with, and what he had to do now was to nudge Joe closer to Fort Smith. He had to make a good plan, one that Joe could find no fault with. There would be some resistance from Joe because it wasn't his plan. That was all right too: Joe would add a few details that weren't needed, and that would make it his plan, after all. The plan had to be good, so good that Joe would never see the catch he was going to build into it. In a way, he was lucky that Joe hated Judge Parker so much; Joe's hate would blind him to danger.

Sundance felt sure that Parker would call off the deal, if the plan went wrong and the banks really were robbed. Parker would decide that his plan of betrayal, had been turned back on himself. Sundance felt two ways about Joe and the judge; for all his murderous nature, there was more to like about the judge. Both men had their points of view, and were as fixed in their ways as any man could be. He could understand Parker's need to hang Joe; at the same time he felt sympathy for the man Joe had been and still was in some ways. But there was no use thinking about the rights and wrongs of it; no point in trying to see both sides of the long, shabby story. All you could say for Parker was that he didn't hate Indians, as Indians, yet Sundance knew that in the years to come there would be Indians, men who had once been his friends, who would shun his company because of what he was about to do. There would be no way to explain, even if he felt like explaining, for when a man bucked the tiger he was completely alone.

Anna Jacobson's attitude toward him had changed since the moment Baker rode in. Once again, now that he had survived the first test, she saw him as a way out. She tried not to show it; it was there nonetheless. Sundance wondered if Joe saw it too. It would be bad if he did. Busy with his bank plan, Joe didn't seem to notice. That meant nothing. If he had seen the sudden change in Anna, he might be putting it down to something else. So for the moment, it didn't look too bad. It looked even better when Joe said he was going to outline his plan in a few minutes. Joe grinned when he said it. Then Brindar came to the mouth of the cave and beckoned Joe outside. Brindar's brown face was as dead as always, but his eyes glittered with anticipation.

Sundance waited, facing the door.

A few minutes later, Sugar's big body blocked out the light.

CHAPTER 9

Sugar came in with Joe behind him. Brindar and the others stayed at the door. The big black Indian had a gun, but it wasn't in his hand. It stuck out of the side pocket of his dirty, ragged pants. His clothes were wet and his face streaked with mud. He looked like a man who had been on the dodge for days.

"Say hello to an old jail-mate," Joe said.

Sundance waited. He would kill Joe first, if he killed anyone: Brindar had a sawed-off shotgun at waist level.

Then Sugar smiled his great big smile and held out his hand. "You should have waited for me."

Sundance extended his hand, ready for the pull that would put him in front of the shotgun. It didn't come. Sugar pumped his hand once and let it go.

"Glad they didn't hang you," Sundance said.

Grinning, Joe pushed Sugar away so he could look at him. "I'll be damned," he roared. "I feel like I'm looking at a ghost. Between you and Sundance, this place is full of walking dead men."

"This dead man is real hungry," Sugar said. His smile was slow and easy like his voice, but his muddy eyes flicked to Sundance and then away from him.

Joe pushed him into chair and yelled at Anna to fry up a lot of meat. Sugar sucked greedily on the whiskey

Joe poured for him and held out his glass to be refilled. Joe gave him a blanket and he pulled it tight around his shoulders.

"I was all set to hang but they didn't hang me," Sugar said, his story coming out between mouthfuls of meat and sips of whiskey. "I'd hear the door banging, some of the men crying and pleading, some swearing, and every time they got close to my door I said to myself, 'Here you go, Sugarboy.' Only I didn't go. Down deep where I was, no way I could hear the trap going down, but, you know, I thought I could hear it. That went on for three days, and by then I was ready to jump out of my skin. The third day I don't know what time it was, didn't know till they took me out in the light, they walked me up to see the judge, all cool and fancy in his office."

"That bastard!" Joe said.

Sugar shook salt onto his steak with dirty hands. "They're supposed to give you a bucket in that jail. They didn't give me one. Was a stink on me you could cut. It was morning, real early in the morning when I had the talk with the judge." Sugar's eyes darted to Sundance's face. Down below the window they were hanging a bunch of men and the judge said to me, 'That could be you out there, Mr. Sloan.' Judge very polite all the time he was putting the boot to me."

Anna brought in the skillet and Joe speared another steak onto Sugar's plate.

"What did he say about me?" Joe said.

"That was it," Sugar said. "Judge didn't give a damn about me. It was you, Joe, all the time. Oh, he knew who I was, no mistake about that. But he wants you more than he wanted to hang me. So it was you mainly. It was all you. I wouldn't go free if I helped him kill you. No chance of that. I'd get sent to the prison farm down at Grady."

"You'd be better off hung than down at Grady," Joe said.

"Wrong, Joe. The way it was, Grady looked good to me. Nigger heaven. I was ready to kiss them mean guards and ass-sucking trustees. I tell you, Joe, fourteen hours a day chopping cotton or swinging a sledge didn't look so bad."

"But you got hung instead," Joe said.

Everybody laughed, even Sugar. Then he shook all over with cold and the memory of fear. "I didn't tell where you were hid, if that's what you mean. Lord! Did I want to talk, especially when that trap went down below the judge's window! One fella took a long time to die. He was light and they must've given him a short drop. He jerked on the rope something awful to see. I think the judge fixed it with the hangman so this poor bastard would die hard. I know that for a fact because the German didn't go below and swing on his legs like I hear he does when a job doesn't go smooth."

"Ike would do that sure enough," Joe said. "He wants me so bad he'd do that."

Maybe he would, Sundance thought. It didn't have the feel of Judge Parker. Yet Sugar could be telling the truth. Nothing he had said so far had given the lie to his words.

"The poor bastard finally choked to death and I felt like I was looking at myself die," Sugar went on. "Then they left the bodies there and the judge went at me again, telling me it was no good holding back because I'd talk in the end. I didn't know whether he was a judge or a preacher, the way he kept going at me. One minute it was hanging talk, the next it was get this off your conscience, Mr. Sloan. He never called me anything but Mr. Sloan."

"You must have liked that, Sugarboy. All that respect from a United States judge."

101

Suddenly, Sugar's eyes looked dead, as if turned inward, looking at his own thoughts. "I'd like to meet the judge again. Oh yes, I'd like that."

"Cheer up," Joe said. "Maybe you will. What did you say when he said he was going to send you to Grady?"

"What did I say? I didn't say a word. The judge did all the saying there was. Me, I was ready to crawl to Grady in a sack. The judge stopped asking me to tell where you were hid. That was over. He said a man like me wouldn't be able to take what happened when I got to Grady. I wasn't going to go in with the rest of the prisoners. No, sir, I was going in the a select few. The judge's words. You think you know how bad Grady is, the judge said. Well, Mr. Sloan, you have no idea how really bad."

"Ike wasn't lying," Joe said. "They keep the real bad men on some kind of an island in a swamp. Fever, rattlers as thick as your arm. When you die they don't even bury you in the lime pit with the rest of the men. You get put in the swamp."

Sugar looked up from his plate. "Made no difference to me where they sent me. I heard what the judge was saying. All I could hear was the crash of that trap. I wasn't dead— and the hell with Grady. If they put me in I'd get out. I been in a camp almost as bad and I got out. You know that, Joe."

"You got out of Leroux, Sugarboy. Leroux isn't Grady."

"I'd have got out. The judge wasn't mad at me when I didn't talk. Never got mad the whole time. You never saw a man so cool. When I was ready to talk, the judge said, all I had to do was tell the head keeper. The judge said he'd probably be hearing from me in about three months."

"He probably would have," Joe said without anger.

"I say that not to badmouth you, Sugarboy. Grady's enough to break any man. The only men it can't break are the ones with nothing to sell. You had plenty."

Sugar was offended. "I'd use a rattler first," he said.

"That's how the tired ones get out," Joe said. "That's what I'd do."

"I wasn't thinking about that," Sugar said. "The cage wagon they put me in could've been a lady's carriage, all I cared at the time. Just before we pulled out they put another man in with me. Mean looking Texas man I never saw before. Mean as hell. Cursed till I got sick of him and his carrying on. Said the judge was sending him away for five years for blinding a man with a bottle. If he'd used a gun he'd have been hung, no matter the man died or not. The first day out of Fort Smith all he did was swear. The next morning he was like to go crazy. I'm big, this fella was half as big again, and screaming and yelling he was getting the shitty part of the stick for nothing. First he kept at the bars of the cage trying to tear them loose. Hands as big as a shovel. It was like he was going to do it if he kept at it long enough. The guards were yelling and he was yelling, throwing himself from one side of the cage to the other, trying to topple the whole thing over with his weight."

"Why didn't you help him?" Joe said.

"Hell I did," Sugar said. "He wasn't going to break the bars, big man or not. I knew the guards were going to kick the shit out of him when they had enough of it. There were two guards and the one driving stopped the wagon and the other one jumped down and came around and started beating on his hands with the butt of his rifle. He pulled in his hands, but kept on yelling and shaking the wagon. Then he attacked me and I was yelling too. The second guard got down and both of them were hopping mad. The second guard, the one in charge, said they'd chain the big bastard and drag him behind."

That was how they might do it, Sundance decided.

"They were getting the door open when the wild man kicked it with his heel and got the driver in the face. The other guard fired but didn't hit him as he came out of that cage like a wildcat. I came out after him like a shot and by then he was clawing at his eyes. I picked up the driver's rifle and killed all three of them. The wild man first, then the guards."

Joe shook his head in admiration. "I can see the need for killing him," he said. "You think he was working for Ike?"

Sugar said he didn't know. "I searched him before I took a horse and lit out. Didn't find a badge, didn't think I would, couldn't take the chance he wasn't one of the judge's spies. I never did get to hear his name."

"He was too wild," Joe said. "Whoever he was. You sure you weren't followed?"

"Positive," Sugar said. "I checked by back trail all the way here. Lay up on Pike's Bluff on the other side of Minnville and scouted the whole country. Nothing. If I didn't send them here I wouldn't lead them here, Joe."

"Nobody's doubting you, Sugarboy," Joe said. "What're they saying about Sundance? I'll bet Ike is good and mad."

"The judge didn't take me into his confidence," Sugar said. "There was talk in the jail. Talk gets around even in *that* jail. I heard the driver and the guard talking about it on the way to Grady. They were laughing about the way Sundance held the knife on Doolin. I guess even his own men don't like Doolin."

Joe spat on the clean floor sand that Anna had raked free of stones and dirt. "Nobody likes Doolin. Ike will hate him for letting two prisoners break out. I tell you,

104

men, everything's going to right way. Got a good man to join up with us, got another good man back. I feel lucky. You feel lucky, Sugarboy."

"Joe," Sugar said slowly, "I feel so luckly I think I'm going to live forever."

Sugar had backed his story but Sundance didn't relax. He went over everything Sugar said, and there was nothing wrong with it. Another man might, probably would have used torture on Sugar to make him talk. But that wasn't Parker's way; with the judge everything had to be legal. Every day he broke the laws of the land in his court, but he could do that with a clear conscious because the President had given him the authority. So when he hanged a man on skimpy evidence, and after a too-speedy trail, it was all perfectly legal. Torture wasn't legal so Parker wouldn't use it, or allow it to be used. But sending a man to the island in the swamp at Grady was legal. It was as much a form of torture as flogging or starvation; even so, it was legal. The break-out sounded possible; as long as you locked men in cages, they would find a way to break out, sometimes after long planning, sometimes by chance. There was a good chance that Sugar was telling the truth. It was hard to decide because Sugar was a smooth storyteller and a smart liar.

In the end, Sundance decided that Sugar was lying; to reach that decision he had nothing working for him except his instinct. It wasn't the story: there was nothing wrong with the story. It fitted together: the ride to Grady, the wild man, the three killings. Not being able to identify the wild man as a Parker spy was a nice touch, if a touch it was, if that was what Sugar meant it to be. I made sense that the guards wouldn't want to listen to the crazy man all the way to the prison camp. That a veteran guard like the driver would put himself in the way of having a steel door smashed in his face didn't make quite as much sense as the rest of it. But maybe the guard wasn't a veteran mancatcher and keeper. If guards didn't get careless, men would never break jail.

Finally, as he did so often, Sundance relied on instinct. It had saved his life too often in the past to disregard it now. Sugar was lying. He felt sure of it—but why? If Sugar had lied about his escape, then he had to be lying about other things. But why? There was no getting around the why. If Sugar came back and said Sundance was a Parker man he would be the best-liked man in camp. He wouldn't even have to prove it; suspicion would do the rest. And, come to think of it, Sugar's story of his escape was better than his own. Sugar's story had saved his life, and he was still lying. There was no way to explain, and so he gave up trying.

When Sundance woke up he didn't move. He stayed perfectly still for an instant, watching with slitted eyes for the man who was trying to kill him. Rain fell in the darkness, splashing in the river. Then his hand reached for his gun and the figure sprang at him from the dark, the knife blade glinting dully in the faint light. The gun spun away from his hand as the attacker kicked and plunged downward with the knife. The knife flashed and he felt a cold burn along his ribs as he rolled away and came up holding his own knife. From the dark came the Indian smell of Silva.

There wasn't a sound except the rain in the river. Silva didn't seem to be breathing. Silva moved in using a knife fighter's crouch, the knife held forward and down, his feeet well apart, the right foot slightly advanced, body and head held well back, his thumb along the side of the blade.

106

A yell would have brought Joe and the others. Sundance didn't yell. Joe might decide to let Silva live. It was time to end it, time to tell Joe when it was over. Their knife blades flashed as they moved in for the kill. Sundance tried for a straight thrust and Silva parried it, quickly and easily. Then he tried for a fast downward chop, trying for the tendons in Sundance's wrist. If he had put more force into the movement he would have taken off the hand with the heavy blade. All he did was draw a thin line of blood from the side of the thumb.

Sundance drove him back with a bold, fierce thrust that came close to finishing the fight. Silva knocked the blade upward, then tried again for the hand. Sundance parried the blow and bored in, swinging his blade from side to side, trying to turn Silva so his back would be to the cliff. Silva sidestepped before he was able to do it. then he came in for another attack and Sundance drove him back.

Heard against the thunder of the falls, their clanging blades had a puny sound. They gave and regained ground, their feet sliding in the wet sand, cold rain mixing with their sweat. Once, Silva stumbled and almost fell. Sundance jumped in after him and nearly pinned him before he dodged out of the way. Silva counterattacked fiercely and their blades clanged together again. Silva kicked and Sundance felt his knife grate against bone, but the other man didn't cry out.

They fought on in utter silence, their labored breath the only sound. Now and then there was a grunt of pain or satisfaction, nothing more. Sundance was beginning to get the feel of Silva's fighting style. When he was the attacker he fought with control; anger made him careless when he was attacked. Sundance, knowing this, attacked boldly, hissing out words of insult. His hand moved like a swordsman, over and underhand slashes that backed Silva away. Sundance knew he was beginning to win and he bored in harder, driving Silva backward with a flurry of blows. He knocked Silva's blade aside and punched him in the jaw, felt the streak of pain run up his arm, felt the other man's jawbone snap. Silva moaned against the pain and tried to attack. Sundance let him come. He let Silva's hate take over, using it to his advantage. He hissed his contempt for Silva as he gave way, playing with Silva now, watching for the right moment to finish it. It would come in a minute. It came closer when Silva, still coming, jerked his head back but still took a slash across the top of his nose. Silva's thrusts were weaker and his skill was dropping away from him as he tried desperately for the kill. Sundance knew Silva wasn't going to make it. So did Silva. Sundance felt no hate for the man who was trying to kill him. He just had to kill him and have done with it. Silva expected no mercy, wouldn't ask for it, wouldn't get it if he had asked for it. They both knew that, two men who had never exchanged a word of any kind.

Silva knew he was going to die. Sundance sensed the other man's acceptance of his death. It didn't come with sudden resignation, it came in one last fierce burst of strength, a wild attack that for a moment put Sundance on the defensive. He allowed Silva to force him back, letting him wear himself out. In a minute! In another minute!

Now! Silva screamed and ran straight at Sundance. Silva screamed and ran until something hit him in the back of his head. He stumbled forward and Sundance stabbed up under his ribs. Silva didn't make a sound. Sundance pushed him off the knife and got ready to kill again.

Sugar took shape in the darkness, holding his hands

out in front of him to show he wasn't carrying a gun. Sundance didn't put away the knife. Joe came out of the cave holding the lamp. The wind blew the flame of the lamp, blackening the chimney.

"What in the name of Christ!" Joe said. He stopped when he saw the dead man lying on his face. "I'll be dirty . . ."

"He jumped me in the dark," Sundance said, still watching Sugar. "I just about had him when Sugar threw something."

"A rock," Sugar said. "Heard a yell that woke me. Knew about Silva, so I threw a rock."

Joe said, "You sound a mite peeved, Sundance."

"No," Sundance. "I'm not peeved. No cause to be. He's dead. No matter to me how he died."

Anna came out of the cave wrapped in a blanket and Joe yelled at her to go back to bed. "Goddamn that rain!" he said. "Somebody get rid of that thing."

Sugar dragged Silva to the river and dumped him in. The body sailed off in the current, rolling as the fast-flowing water carried it down to the first drop to the falls. The other men had gone back to the cave to split the dead man's belongings between them. It was starting to get light when Sugar came back from the river after washing the blood off his hands. It was still raining.

"Maybe I shouldn't have butted in like that," Sugar said, wiping his hands on his pants.

"Makes no difference," Sundance said. "It wasn't anything personal with me."

Sugar went back to the cave and Sundance went down to the pool by the river to wash the blood off the thin knife slash across his ribs. The wound burned when the water touched it; there wasn't much blood. He got an army bandage from his warbag and dried the wound before he unrolled the bandage and put it on.

Anna came out of the cave and said, "I'll do the bandaging, give it here."

She wasn't as handy with the bandage as she thought she was. Women always thought they were good as fixing up wounded men. "Go ahead, say what Joe always says."

"Say what?"

"Say it's only a scratch."

"It's a wound," Sundance said.

"You liked killing that man?"

"No. He looked for it, he got it."

"How many men have you killed, Sundance?"

"I don't recall. Some special reason you want to know?"

"You don't like me, do you?"

"You're not so bad. Sometimes I get sick of you. You're all right—you didn't tell Joe."

"You think that puts you in the clear?"

"So far. Baker says I'm clear, so does Sugar. That leaves you to say I'm not."

Anna interrupted the bandaging to look at his eyes. "Maybe you liked Joe's story about sending the woman over the falls. If I went over the falls you'd have nothing to worry about."

There was no fear in her eyes; instead, there was something that Sundance didn't like. She was excited by the thought of a violent death.

"It's not such a bad idea," Sundance said grinning.

"There's nothing funny about it," she said. "You won't get rid of me like that. All I have to do is tell Joe and you're a dead man. He'll believe me first."

"I can see where he might."

Anna flaunted her lanky figure, then got mad when

110

men looked at it. "You're a dirty sneering bastard," she said.

"You're the one keeps bringing up the subject of you and Joe," Sundance said.

"What about me?" Anna said. "Have you figured out a plan for me? You better make a plan for me. Try to back out of it and you'll never leave here alive."

Sundance said, "I'm working on a plan."

"What kind of plan?"

"So far all I've got is bits and pieces. You're part of it. When you hear what it is, maybe you won't like it."

"Tell me anyway."

"Not yet. I don't know myself, so how can I tell you?"

Anna's cat eyes glittered with sullen anger. "You're lying. You've been lying all along, to me, to Joe—everybody!"

"I guess I'm a born liar," Sundance said. "Like it or don't like it, you'll have to wait."

She tied the bandage in the wrong place, in the back. It wasn't tight enough; it would do for now. Later he would do it right when she wasn't there.

"Will Joe get killed?" she said.

There was nothing to be lost by telling her the truth. It might even shake something out of her. Something he could use.

"Joe's going to die," he said quietly. "How do you feel about that?"

For an instant, she turned her yellow eyes away from him. Then her chin tilted defiantly and her voice grew hard. "What the hell do I care what happens to Joe? I just wanted to know."

"Now you know," Sundance said. He had learned what he wanted to know, and he didn't like it.

CHAPTER 10

Clouds darkened the bottom of the gorge and soon it began to rain. It started with big cold drops of spring rain popping in the fine white sand. Then the real rain came after a strong gust of wind and water dripped at the mouth of the cave.

In the cave the lamp was turned up high and Joe went over his plan again, scratching lines and squares on the table top with a knife. Joe was proud of his plan.

"Three men dynamite the railroad depot," he said. "Place the charges under the locomotives so the boilers will blow along with the charge. That should throw the whole town into a panic. It'll sound like Judgment Day. That'll draw off the law. We'll be set and waiting to empty out all three banks. We hit them fast. Split up and hit hard. At the same time three of the boys go after Parker and the hangman. We hang them quick and make for the ferry. One of the boys is waiting to make sure the ferry is ready to go. When we get across we blow up the ferry. They'll get across but it'll take them a lot of time. By then we'll be long gone. What do you think of it?"

"Sounds like you're planning a war instead of a bank robbery," Sundance said. "Why don't you get yourself a couple of cannon and dress the boys in uniforms."

Joe grinned. "I don't give a damn what you call it. I want Ike to know what's happening. I want Ike to look out his window and see the world falling to bits. I want to hang that man, Sundance. God lets me do that I just might take up church again. Ike and the German. They tell me he sits up all night oiling his ropes. Makes them on his own spinner it's said. Ike and the German are going to get a short drop from me."

"It looks like you want Parker more than the banks."

"Maybe I do. Maybe not. I'd give every cent I ever stole to see Ike strangle. I'll take that back. I'd give a lot."

"Do it your way and a lot of the boys are going to get killed. How long since you been in Fort Smith?"

"A long time. Seven or eight years, give or take. Why are you asking?"

"Town is a lot bigger now. Must be close to four thousand people. Not like some prairie town you ride in to and take over. Not like Idabel."

"What're you saying?"

"I'm saying it can be done easy. It can be done like any other bank job. Except in Fort Smith you have to do it three times."

"How would you do it?"

"So none of the men get killed."

"Now you're worried about the men."

"I'm one of the men, Joe. So are you."

"No," Joe said. "I'm not one of the men, I'm the leader."

Sundance said, "Being boss won't stop a bullet when the shooting starts. Somebody's got to case the banks."

"Sure," Joe said, "and who's going to do it. You? Me? You want us to wear false whiskers like the Daltons did on their last job? Dust coats and false whiskers.

113

Nobody would catch on. You know what happened to the Daltons, don't you? They got shot. I got a better idea. We'll black our faces and go in to town as a minstrel show. I know nigger talk. We waltz in to the bank talking coon, saying, 'Hey there, Mistah Banker, us gennums wants to make a little dee-posit.' They'd never suspect a thing. Hell they wouldn't!"

"You got part of it right," Sundance said. "The deposit. You know anything that puts a banker off-guard faster than money?"

"A lot of money. Whose money?"

"Your money, Joe. About all you have. How much do you have? It may not be enough."

Joe didn't like the way the talk was going. "You got a way of talking that warns me to watch out or I'll be poor. The only dealings . . . for me the only dealings with banks have been the taking out and not the putting in of money. Bankers smile when they see money. So do I. A man like you that can't, won't hang on to money doesn't appreciate how another man can get attached to it. Me and the bankers agree on that point."

"How much have you got? You got five thousand in the two robberies in Idabel. That'll do in a pinch, but I'd like it better if you had more. Another thing, the deposit can't be a mess of dirty old dollar bills."

Joe was getting mad. "I'll wash it for you. That suit you? What the hell do you mean five thousand isn't enough? You hear me agreeing to give over any money, five thousand or five. I tell you putting money in banks is bad luck. Banks get robbed or didn't you know about that."

"Hear me out, Joe," Sundance said patiently. "You're the boss, you say no and we'll do it the way you say. Just listen to the way I lay out. Somebody . . ."

"Like the girl said to the bashful fella. 'If you're going to do me, take off your pants.' Who is this somebody?"

"Anna," Sundance said.

Anna sat up straight. "Me? Are you talking about me? This is crazy."

"Never thought I'd agree with something you said," Joe said.

"Who the hell asked you," Anna said looking at Sundance. Her face was angry but her eyes were bright.

"There are other ways but Anna is better than they are," Sundance said. "Will you listen! You go into town you'll be shot on sight. You already said that. Same goes for me. I don't know what posters Parker has out on Dancer, Murphy, Brindar, the others. Those are the smart ones and you can't trust the smart ones. Give Dancer or Murphy a bag of money and that's the last you'll see of them or it."

"Wrong, Sundance. I'd find them. All right! All right! We're not talking about that."

Sundance said, "Anna goes and you send two men with her. Two reasons. One, so she doesn't skip with the money, maybe run to the law. The second, the two men will be part of the plan."

"Thank you for talking like I'm not here," Anna said. "Like I don't have any say in this, no feelings. What am I supposed to be, a stick?"

Joe told her to shut up. "Then what?"

"She'll look like a lady, more so in a dress."

Anna said, "What do you mean 'look like'!"

"She may look it, but that's all," Joe said, grinning at Anna.

"She'll be dressed like a lady. She has the clothes for it, the money to back it up."

"My money," Joe said sourly.

"What she puts in the bank gets taken out again,"

115

Sundance said.

Joe smiled suddenly. "Sure, with interest. I like this better. It has a sound to it. What bothers me, why doesn't she just case the bank, forget the money? When we get her dressed up the bankers won't be looking for money. Why can't she just ask for change of maybe a hundred dollar bill, something like that."

Sundance said, "You ever get change in a bank. I mean a bank you weren't robbing."

"A few times I did."

"Did you get to meet the head banker."

"You foxy bastard," Joe said. "Say the rest of it."

"Anna's story is she's from back East. Make it Philadelphia. The bankers will like that. She asks to see the manager or the banker because she wants to deposit a big sum of money and is kind of nervous about western banks. What she read in the papers is making her nervous. There is a notorious bandit name of Joe Buck running wild so she's nervous about her money. That's why I say don't be stingy with the deposits. It has to look right. Fine Eastern lady, big Eastern money. And more to come."

Joe looked sour. "Not from me. I won't back more than one hand in this game."

"Wait," Sundance said. "Anna's story is she wants to go into the beef business. A lot of rich Easterners are doing that. Even Englishmen. Take one bank. After the banker tells her the money is perfectly safe—who'd rob a bank in Judge Parker's town—she gets a confidential. The big deposit is just the start of the money, she tells him. Then she tells him she's expecting two men from back East with another fifty thousand. They'll be arriving in Fort Smith early Sunday morning. That's when we'll do it."

"Sure," Joe said. "Sunday when the banks are closed." He spat on the floor.

"They'll open for Anna," Sundance said. "A beautiful lady with fifty thousand dollars. They'll open the banks. What's so easy about it, it's all a big secret, her going into the cattle business. That'll keep them from talking. Anna is too nervous for the banks to open on Monday. She can't wait to get her fifty thousand in the vault. If they talk about her business being a secret, then she'll just take her money, all her future business, to another bank. Depend on it, Joe, they'll be waiting for her to show up with the money on Sunday. She tells the same story to all three bankers, then Sunday morning she come a-calling. Fort Smith is a churchgoing town. Say church takes an hour, a little more. Anna drives up in her buckboard with her two men, both from the Territory, and they clean them out. While they're loading up the buckboard we'll, some of us will go in easy in case there's trouble."

"Can't let them kill my woman," Joe said.

Anna got angry. "The hell I'm your woman! If you think I'm going to get mixed up in this you're crazier than I thought. I won't do it, you hear."

"You'll do it if I tell you."

Sundance shook his head. "That way won't work so good. It'll show if the boys have to hold a gun on her. The bankers will smell it. She has to want to do this."

"I'll make her want to. When I get through with her she'll be begging to do it."

"I just said, Joe."

"How would you make her do it?"

"Let her go when the job is done, give her a fair split of the money. She'll be the one who can make it easy. Without her we'll have to go in cold."

The idea hadn't occurred to Joe. Anna glared back at him when he looked at her with new interest. "You mean you'd take stolen money?" he said.

"Hah!" Anna said.

Joe was surprised and it showed in his face. "You're no lady saying a thing like that. I had you figured different."

"You never had me figured at all."

"There are plenty of other women," Sundance said. "There's nothing that special about this one."

"I don't care what you say," Anna said. "Say what you like. Both of you say what you like. I just want to get out of here but you won't buy me with a few dollars."

Joe wasn't cut out to be a suitor; the way he tried to make sheep eyes at the girl made Sundance want to laugh.

"You don't want to leave here, Anna," Joe said. "You're just saying that to make me mad. Sundance is wrong, what he said. I don't mind you. The fact is I don't mind you a lot and I never said that to another woman in my life. You'll look at it different when we get all that money. How much you think we'll get, Sundance?"

"A lot. Fort Smith's not a one-day payroll town. From three banks I don't know how much, maybe a quarter of a million. The town's a whole clutch of saloons, gambling halls, lumber yards, hotels and eating places, all kinds of business. So it has to be a big haul."

"You heard him," Joe went on. "Enough money to last a lifetime even the way I'm going to spend it on you. I had big plans for the Territory. Nothing that can't wait or be changed. Answer up now like a good woman."

"Is it a deal or not?" Anna said.

"That's no answer," Joe said. He got up and walked to the back of the cave, then he turned slowly and the

118

sheep eyes were gone and so was the soft talk. "It's a deal."

Anna's face hardened. "How much of a deal, Joe? I want twenty-five thousand. I'll be taking the risk. If I get caught it's Parker for me."

Joe sat down and drummed his thick fingers on the table. He looked at Anna. "That's a lot of money."

Sundance knew that Joe wasn't thinking about money, but he said, "It's worth it."

"She'll get it if she does it right," Joe said. "It's still a lot of money."

Anna sneered at him. "You spend it to make it."

"Doublecross me and the boys'll kill you," Joe said. "Woman or no woman, they'll kill you. They know they don't kill you I'll kill them. That'll get it done, you bet. Just you try running out on me. People running out is one thing I don't like."

Joe glanced over at Sundance, then back at Anna.

She said, "I told you I'd do it. You want me to write it down and sign it?"

Joe's voice was flat and cold. "If this wasn't business I'd show you what I want you to do. You'd do it. I made you do it one night. Look, that's in the past, all right. You didn't like me making you do that. No more, if that's what you want. You're throwing away something good walking out on me."

Anna's hard eyes didn't waver. "Sure I am. Living like a pig with a lot of other pigs."

"It doesn't have to be like that. We don't have to stay here."

"With you in it it would still be a pigsty."

Joe jumped up so suddenly that he knocked over the chair. He bunched up his fists and took a step toward her. "You're not in Fort Smith yet, missy. Maybe you never will."

Anna came back at him, angry but a little scared. "Where will I be? At the bottom of the falls like the other woman? You're good at killing women."

Joe called her a filthy name.

"And what does that make you," Anna yelled, backing away from him. Joe sat down again.

"The Preacher would do for one of the men with Anna," Sundance said. "The older one. How well is he known in the Territory or over in Arkansas?"

"Hardly a-tall. Preacher's from Texas. Never got the whole story of it. Something. He murdered his wife, got sick of looking at her. Can't say I blame the man, women being what they are. Nothing a man does pleases them."

"How does Preacher look without the beard?"

"Never saw him any other way."

"Tell him to shave it off and trim his hair. We're going to have to stop off along the way and get him some decent clothes. He ought to do all right. Who else have you got? What about young Gates?"

Joe laughed. "You don't want him. Not a bad looking sort of a fella. Be fine except now and then something kicks up inside his head. Then he gets crazy and falls down in a fit, shaking all over, yelping like a dog. Brindar thinks I ought to shoot him, but that's not for him to say. No biting this far so why kill a good man. Gates is all wrong for what you want him."

"What about the man that guards the river? The regular guard."

Joe said, "Never thought of him. Hardly ever do. Newley is the name he goes by and I guess he's not much for the company of people. Likes that lonely job, never wants to go out on a job. Guards the river crossing, eats, sleeps, keeps to himself."

"Then he isn't known?" Sundance said.

"Nobody knows him. Never saw a poster on him. All I know is he killed a soldier over a woman, so I guess the soldiers want him. But nary a wanted poster."

"Which brings us back to the money," Sundance said.

Joe went to the back of the cave and pulled a box of rifles aside and started to dig in the sand with his hands until he uncovered the top of a brass-banded box. He yanked it out and opened it while Sundance brought the lamp close. The box was filled nearly all the way to the top with paper money and gold pieces, American and Mexican. The paper money was sorted according to the denomination of the bills and tied with thin rawhide strips.

"A lot of hard riding and killing is in that box," Joe said picking up a handful of gold and letting it clink back in the box. "Notice the nice soft sound solid gold makes. If it rings too sharp you know it's got something else in it. Got to have an ear for money. Silver is all right, but there's nothing like gold. I got the silver in another box, the watches and rings and collar studs in another. One of these days I'm going to get that stuff melted down and separated into gold bars."

Sundance didn't touch the money. "How much is there?"

"Gold and paper, about forty thousand."

"Thirty's enough, split three ways. Ten thousand a bank. That'll make them sit up and bark."

"Thanks for not taking all of it," Joe said.

With the beard gone Preacher's long face looked like a plucked chicken with some of the black pin-feathers still sticking in the skin. His face was white up to the cheekbones; the sun would take care of that. Preacher felt his bony chin and looked at himself in Anna's mirror.

"I don't know," he said doubtfully. "I just don't know."

"Preacher doesn't know who he is," Joe said. "I got to warn the boys so they won't shoot him for a stranger. You look real handsome, Preacher. The girls in Fort Smith are going to lay awake all night all sweaty thinking about you."

The Preacher's mouth was wet and toothless; little sliver of silver-colored saliva showed at the corners. "You got any store teeth?" Sundance said.

"They hurt," Preacher said. "Only use them mealtimes, then stow them away."

Sundance told him to put them in and Preacher took a small leather purse from his pocket and opened it. He put in the uppers and lowers and snapped them together. He did it again, a cick-clacking sound.

Joe roared, "Play us a tune, Preacher. Something Mexican. Smile! you old son of a bitch."

Preacher made a face like a vicious dog about to bite.

"God Almighty!" Joe said. "The bankers see that smile they're going to make for the hills."

Joe pulled his gun. "I said a smile, a real smile, you mournful old cow flop!"

Sundance said, "No need for him to smile. What's your name?"

"You know what it is."

"You're Mr. Grady Hightower," Sundance said. "Get the name right. You're Grady Hightower and you work for Mrs. James B. Torrance over there."

Anna had been drinking some whiskey. "What does the 'B' stand for?"

"Bullshit!" Joe said.

"B for Baker," Sundance said. "It's better for you to

122

be married. You're a young widow. Your late husband always wanted to come out west. Now you're doing it. Bankers are sympathetic toward people with money."

The guard from the river crossing came in, a man in his late thirties looking more white than Indian. He wore canvas pants, a faded blue shirt and a thick woollen coat fastened with leather thongs instead of buttons. He didn't look happy to be called away from the river during his watch.

"Something wrong, Joe?" he said.

Sundance looked him over. Newley was a quiet, open-faced man who could pass easily as somebody who took orders and worked hard and probably had a wife and kids.

"Don't look at me, you blasted fool," Joe said. 'Listen to what's being said.

"Your new name is Ned Crown," Sundance said. "Get used to it."

CHAPTER 11

The whole camp was buzzing with talk of the Fort Smith bank job. Nothing like it had ever been tried, not by the Jameses, not by the Daltons, not by anybody. The most money the Daltons had ever tried for was in the two banks in Coffeyville, Kansas, and it should have been an easy job for old bank robbers like them. Coffeyville was in the middle of the farm country. It wasn't one of the wild cowtowns where everybody joined in when the shooting started: the principal reason why wild towns like Abilene and Dodge City never had their banks busted. Coffeyville was different. Everybody knew that. They thought they knew that. Word was that the people there were sheep waiting patiently to be shorn. It hadn't worked out that way. Up jumped a bunch of storekeepers, odd-jobs boys, one lame telegrapher and shot the Daltons to hell and gone.

Joe's boys talked about Coffeyville and other bank jobs. They were in the bank robbing business, so they talked about it the way barbers talked about some new brand of shaving soap. Most of the older men, if they had their druthers, would have stayed away from Fort Smith, and it wasn't just the size of the town, it was Judge Isaac Parker, the hangman with the soft voice and the silky beard. For the older men Parker's name tolled like a bell in their heads. If it went wrong and if they got caught, even if they hadn't harmed a soul, they would hang a quick as Christmas. Not wanting to seem edgy, some of the older men sided with the young ones. The younger men were all for Fort Smith, couldn't wait to spend the money from its banks. They were already planning what they would tell the whores in the crossroad saloons beyond the law's long arm. If they pulled it off they would brag about it, and if they didn't they would still brag about it, allowing as how they had nearly succeeded. That a woman was to be the means of busting the banks didn't mean a thing. She was just a figurehead, they were the men behind the guns.

Anna had her trunk open and was laying out dresses on the bed. She fussed with the dresses, trying to shake out the wrinkles. She put them all back except for two, one dark green, one dark blue. She decided on the dark green one. There was a perky little hat with a long hat-pin to hold the hat on her head.

"It won't kill you," she said when Joe announced that he was going to take a bath in the pool between the rocks where water leaked in from the river. The pool was shallow and the water was warmed by the sun.

"All this shaving and hair-cutting and laying out clothes makes me want to pretty up," Joe said. He took a bar of strong yellow soap and a towel and went out.

Anna went to the mouth of the cave to make sure he wasn't listening. Holding the green dress she turned. "I don't care what you're up to, Sundance. Just don't get me more mixed up in it than you have to. You think Joe will let me go, keep his word to let me go?"

Sundance said he didn't know. "You've been around Joe. What do you think?"

"I think I'd like to know what you're up to."

125

"A minute ago you didn't want to know."

"I swear I'll kill him if he doesn't let me. I don't care what happens, I'll kill him."

Sundance said, "You'll be out of it. I'll see that you're out of it. Joe won't be coming after you."

Anna said carefully, "You sound so sure."

"Sure as I can be," Sundance said. "The law won't be after you either."

"You're taking a big chance telling me all this. Maybe you're not. I don't want to remember anything about this place. It's got nothing to do with me."

Down in the pool Joe was singing; Anna looked toward the sound.

"You don't hate him as much as you say," Sundance said. "You want to get out, but I'm still taking a chance. You have to decide how it's going to go."

"I won't stay here."

"I think you want to go and you want to stay. Nothing so strange about that. I think Joe is the kind of man you never met before. You saw men like Joe, but you never got up close. With Joe you didn't have a choice. The question is, how much of a chance am I taking?"

Anna hung the green dress on a nail driven into a crack in the wall. She wet a towel in a bucket of water and began to dab at the wrinkles, and when she finished she snapped the damp cloth between her fingers.

"No chance," she said, turning to look at him. "Forget about that. I said it has nothing to do with me. You're going to kill Joe, aren't you? I didn't say that. It's none of my business."

One of the hooks on the back of the dress had come loose and she began to sew it back, biting off the loose thread with strong white teeth. She looked like she wanted to keep busy with anything she could find to do.

126

Joe was still singing by the river. In the gorge his voice sounded hollow, like a man singing in an empty church.

"You can't have it both ways," Sundance said at last. "If you want to stay with Joe all you have to do is tell him what I told you. That'll be the finish of it. I can't fight seventeen men. You can do it. Just remember, you'll never get another chance to go free."

"Because you'd be dead."

"I'm your way out."

Anna's face was defiant, not wanting any favors. "What you planned could still go on without you. It's a good plan, it will work. You planned it so well you're not even needed now. I could still go through with it, still get the money, my share, maybe your share, and go free."

"Why would you want to do it that way?"

"No reason. I just wanted you to know the world won't stop if you die."

"It will for you unless you really want to stay with Joe. Joe won't keep his word if I'm not around."

"You think a lot of yourself, don't you?"

"Nobody else will argue with Joe about you."

Anna said, "You'd do that for me. Why?"

"It was my plan. I got you mixed in it. Joe would never have thought of it. I got you in, so I have to get you out. I wouldn't like it if I didn't. Now what's it going to be?"

Joe was whistling as he came up from the river.

"Make up your mind," Sundance said. "It might as well be now."

Joe stood in the door of the cave with his boots and clothes in one hand, his gunbelt in the other. Old knife cuts and bullet wounds showed white against the dark skin of his wet, muscular body. "And it isn't even Saturday night," he roared, missing the quick look bet-

127

ween Sundance and Anna.

Anna's eyes went back to Joe. "My God!" she said.

Grinning, Joe threw his clothes under the bed, but kept his gunbelt in his hand. There was a bottle of lilac water on a shelf over the bed and he slopped some of it into his hand and rubbed it into his wiry, black hair. He sniffed like a dog. "Don't I smell sweet though. You want a splash of this stuff, Sundance?"

"You'll do for both of us," Sundance said.

Anna grabbed the half-empty bottle away from Joe. "You're disgusting," she said.

"I am not," Joe said. "I smell good and I feel good." He tried to grab Anna, but she pulled away from him yelling, "I'll cut you with this bottle. Leave me alone, you big, dumb bastard."

Joe winked at Sundance. "I'll get her later." He pulled on a clean pair of Levis and stomped on his boots. He shouldered his way into a shirt without tucking it in. He buckled on the gunbelt and sat down at the table.

Now Anna was sulking on the bed with her long legs drawn up, her head against two punched-up pillows, rattling the pages of an old newspaper. Suddenly her anger cut loose and she crumpled the paper into a ball and threw it away from her.

"You said you were going to bring back something to read," she said. "Didn't they have any books in that town?"

Joe took a bottle of whiskey from the shelf and set it down in front of him. "You don't like the paper because there's nothing in it about you. It's all about me. Why don't you read the *Farmer's Almanac* I got you?"

Joe picked up the newspaper, smoothed it out on the table and cut out the front page story about him with a knife. "IDABEL BANK ROBBED BY NOTORIOUS

OUTLAW," he read proudly. He scowled at his picture. It had been copied from his wanted poster. It was a crude rendering of his face and smudged with ink.

"You'd think they could do better than that," Joe said. "You think they'll write about me in the eastern papers after Fort Smith? I wouldn't mind that."

"They'll have the story," Sundance said. "Who else is there to write about. Jesse's dead, Frank's in jail, the rest scattered. You'll be king of the hill, Joe."

"I like 'mountain' better," Joe said.

"Jesus Christ!" Anna said, turning on her side to stare at the far wall of the cave.

"Hark to the game-hen," Joe said. "It's like you don't want nothing good for me. You and your airs. I don't know you, missy. Who are you anyhow? You act so goddamned independent but I got you going good a couple of times. Don't tell me I didn't."

Joe raised his growly voice to a falsetto that didn't sound anything like Anna. "Oh no, please, Mr. Buck, don't do that awful thing to me! What is that horrible thing you have there, Mr. Buck!"

Anna didn't turn to speak. "You horse's ass. I never said anything like that."

The glass in Joe's hand was clean, everything in the cave was clean, but he blew in it, a habit from a lifetime of blowing dust out of glasses. "You didn't have to say it," he said. "The times you got drunk you liked it all right. You ought to drink more. I like you better when you drink. You want a drink now?"

Anna yelled back, "Yes, Mr. Buck, I want a goddamned drink!" She filled a glass spilling-full and took it back to the bed.

Joe smelled of soap and lilac water. His hair, wet with lilac water, was plastered down on both sides of his face and tucked back behind his ears. He knocked back a glass of whiskey and smiled with contentment.

"Even this one can't get me too mad today. I always been lucky. Now more so. Sitting there in the pool I pondered on your plan. Not a hole in it. You don't mind if I take some of the credit, do you?"

"Take it all," Sundance said, knowing that Joe would do it anyway. He looked at Joe, grinning like a fool, and felt bad about what he had to do. It had to be done: there was no use thinking about it.

"I can't take all the credit," Joe said. "it wasn't all me. More like you and me putting our heads together to figure out the right plan. I couldn't have planned it without you, Sundance. The boys like it too, not that they have anything to say about it. Be that as it may, I'm going to have me a time, so are the boys. Where the hell is that Brindar?"

Joe yelled and Brindar came in. "Pass out whiskey to the boys," Joe said. "Only no gunplay. You tell them that. Fun or not, no gunplay. These walls throw sound for miles. Kill the first man that fires off a gun. Do it with a knife. Tell Sugarboy to get in here."

"Set a while," Joe said when the black Indian came in. "I was just telling Sundance it's good to have you back."

Joe hadn't said anything about Sugar. Sugar looked over at Sundance before he sat down and helped himself to whiskey. Anna was drinking by herself on the bed. Out on the sand by the river the sun was bright.

"You look all right," Joe said.

Sugar, sipping whiskey, said with a smile, "Parker doesn't beat you, he hangs you."

Joe said, "You get to ask for any last requests?"

"They didn't mention it, I asked anyway."

"What did you ask for Sugarboy?"

"I *did* ask for a rich fat woman. Word came back

they were fresh out of well-padded ladies." Sugar's laugh rumbled up from his wide chest.

"Why'd you ask for that, Sugarboy?"

"I wanted to die rich and comfortable."

Joe slapped his knee, laughing until he wheezed. "Sugarboy, you are a regular card, that's what you are. You see how he carries on, Sundance. I like that joke. How about the one where the old fella all crabs and shit goes into the bank. Tell that one, Sugarboy."

Sundance saw that Sugar had a big drink but was drinking it slowly.

"Well, sir," Sugar said, displaying square teeth. "This ragged old gentleman ventured into a bank. His shirt was frayed, his shoes had seen better days. Begging the lady's pardon, he stank! Yet for all his unfortunate appearance there was something about him that touched the banker's otherwise stony heart. 'What can I do for you, my good man?' asked the banker, whereupon the shabby old fellow asked if he might borrow five thousand dollars. No, he said, he could offer no security. He was, in short, a knight of the road, namely a bum. Nevertheless, the banker said a loan for that amount most certainly could be arranged. And saying this he proceeded to count out the five thousand dollars. He was about to hand it over with a friendly smile when the venerable gentleman said, 'Hold it right there, mister. I ain't so sure I wants to do business with a bank that will do business with the likes of me.'"

"Jesus Christ!" Anna Jacobson said and turned her face to the wall. Outside it was getting dark, but that was because the sun had moved over the western rim of the gorge, throwing it into shadow.

Another bottle stood on the table beside the empty

one and Joe was three inches into it. It would be dark in less than an hour. Joe got up heavily and turned up the lamp and when it glowed bright yellow Sundance saw that Sugar had poured a full glass of whiskey into the sand and was scuffing the damp place with his foot. He filled his glass while he was doing it.

"You're going to get drunk if you keep that up," Joe said. "I want you to get drunk, Sugarboy. That's an order, hear! Army regulations."

Joe said, "You were in the army, Sundance."

"Not in it. I was a scout."

"Then Sugarboy's got you all beat. Sugarboy was in the Buffalo Soldiers."

Sundance looked at Sugar. The Ninth Cavalry was a good outfit, all black except for the white officers. Even the Apaches were afraid of them. Sugar was more than he pretended to be.

"Why'd you leave, Sugarboy?" Joe said.

"I got tired of eating with a lot of buffaloes."

"Come on now, the reason, the real reason."

"I stuck a bayonet in a white man called me a buffalo. This happened in a town in Texas they don't like buffaloes. They were fixing to lynch me but you know how hard it is to lynch a buffalo."

Joe laughed hard. "Sugarboy makes a joke out of everything. Tell the one about the Irishman and the other Irishman."

Grinning, Sugar began another elaborately phrased story. Anna was asleep on the bed. There was a lot of hate in Sugar. They were all halfbreeds except the girl. Sugar was the only one who didn't like it. Sugar, the book reader and the fancy talker, was a very dangerous man, Sundance decided.

Sugar dragged on with the whiskery joke while Joe laughed, knowing every line of it by heart. Sundance thought about Joe and the plan to loot Fort Smith. It was a good plan; Judge Parker would have hated it. But the judge was there and he was here. The plan was the only way to keep a lot of people from being killed. Too bad he hadn't worked out a plan for Joe. A few came and went in his mind and he discarded them, one after another. But it had to end in Fort Smith. He couldn't see it going beyond there. He didn't look forward to turning Joe over to Parker and his hunchbacked hangman. The thought of it was like salt in a wound. Joe deserved to hang if any man ever did. How many men had he killed in his time? Probably Joe didn't know himself. He wasn't a gunman and didn't keep count. For a lot of years he had robbed and murdered. Sundance didn't agree with people who said hanging was too good for Joe. Hanging was just right for Joe. What he had to do was put Joe where he couldn't do any more harm, yet the ides went against the grain. Joe was a halfbreed who had been taught, had taught himself all the dirty white tricks. How to cheat and lie and to talk out of two sides of his mouth, but underneath all that he was still an Indian. The whites hated Joe, wanted Joe dead, because he had beaten them at their own dirty game. He had outrun the cavalry and outfoxed the law. What stuck in their craw was that Joe despised them, and not because he could never be one of them. Joe's contempt for the whites was real and that was no way for a halfbreed to be in a country ruled by whites. Sundance guessed Joe loved the Territory in his own strange way. The Territory was supposed to be different from other Indian land, all Indian land. Andy Jackson had given his word that the Indians could live there in peace as long as there was just one tribe. Andy said it was to be their land, not just another reservation bigger than all the others. Andy said the army would see there was no trespassing by the whites. But they came anyway. They always did. Sundance had seen it, fought it, all over the West, from one border to the other. They had done it in the Black Hills, the crazy white men looking for gold that there wasn't so much of after all the killing had been done, after Custer and more than two hundred men were dead, after the Indians were driven out, hunted and slaughtered and finally reduced to drunks and beggars. But even when they were destroying life in the Black Hills, some people still thought the Territory would be spared because it was unique. People, some people, argued that the government would never break old Andy's word, the word of a President. They broke it anyway and maybe Andy always knew they would. In the end, Andy was a politician like the others, and when a politician broke his word he always found a good and pressing reason for doing it. Politicians always broke their word with what they called "profound regret." But there was usually a good side to the breaking of promises. Politicians were like that. A politician could turn over a rock and where another man saw maggots the politician saw a fine new life for the people he was stabbing in the back. Oklahoma, The Territory, was the promised land, but every day more and more of it belonged to the land speculators, the crooked politicians, the men who smelled money at the same time they smelled oil. No matter: there was no help for it. He had to turn Joe over to the hangman. In the future, if he lived through this, there would be times when he would think about Rufus "Joe" Buck.

Joe was drunk now, smiling and happy. A drunk, happy killer—and the world would be safer when they were able to tear down his Wanted posters. Joe had no way of knowing that his life was already over; that he had run is course. He had fought the whites before the

134

fighting turned him into a killer, and after he was gone the whites would grab a little more land, always in the name of progress. Even now in Washington they were talking about throwing the Territory wide open. When and if that happened the Indian land claims wouldn't be worth much. The Indian would become a red nigger, which was what the whites called him now, a stranger in his own land. Of less importance than a good watchdog.

Joe was finally asleep, his head on the table, his long wiry hair hanging over his eyes. On the bed Anna lay asleep with her hands clenched by her sides. Sugar drooped in his chair with his eyes closed, a peaceful look on his shining black face.

Sundance went out into the moonlight.

CHAPTER 12

The men in the other cave had bedded down or were sleeping where they had fallen. A dull yellow glow came from the mouth of the cave and the moonlight gave the bottom of the gorge the look of being underwater. A cold wind blew through the gorge and made a sad, whistling sound in crevices in rocks, and far below the falls rumbled.

The fire in the cookstove had gone out and, still in flood, the river ran fast and the air smelled of rain and the fast-flowing river looked like oil.

His feet made no sound as he walked past the pool and the rocks to the edge of the river. The wind died suddenly but it was very cold and even when he was close to the river it still looked black and oily, and where it curved downward toward the drops in the riverbed that led to the falls it looked like a sheet of black glass. The reflection of the moon was pulled out of shape by the movement of the water and night seemed to soften the sound of the falls.

Sugar stepped from the shadows of the rocks on the far side of the pool. The moonlight glinted on the barrel of the gun in his hand.

"You won't get out of this as easy as jail," he said quietly.

"Joe won't like you leaving the party," Sundance said.

Sugar's voice remained quiet. "The party's over except for you and me. Joe's drunk asleep with his white bitch. So are the boys. Everything quiet, nobody to butt in."

"Doolin let you go," Sundance said.

"Oh yes," Sugar said. "That's what that white man did. Same as the judge let you go. I ought to be grateful to you. If it wasn't for you I'd be fizzing in a lime pit with the other hanged men. I should be beholden but I can't work up to it. The way of it is, I was ready enough to die. Nothing to be done about it so I was ready. Then Doolin showed me how ready I wasn't. You were the cause of that, friend. Doolin wanted you gone so he let me stay. What he did shook me all to pieces, gave me a bad feeling about myself. And for that I have you to thank. You notice I'm not taking your gun. You want to try for it you can."

"You'd like me to try that."

"I'm going to kill you anyway, but the gun stays in your holster. Wouldn't want it to look like I killed an unarmed man. Why don't you try for the gun? Do me the favor: try for it. I got a hate for you, Sundance. It's nice I can tell you about it. Doolin doesn't hate you, but he wants you gone. That bad white man is mad because if you brought Joe in it wouldn't be so good for him. Parker told him if any man could bring Joe in you could. The judge has a lot of confidence in you. Doolin thinks the judge is right and he doesn't like it. No telling what the judge is likely to do next."

"There's more to it than that," Sundance said.

Sugar was a little drunk, but the gun was steady enough. "Always guessing, aren't you? But you're right. A lot of people aren't happy with the way Parker has been running things. Respectable people that just happen to have a hand in whiskey running and cow stealing. The judge has been cutting down on the flow of their money, wrecking stills, hanging their distillers and cow thieves, not to mention what he's been doing to the elections. With the judge around there's no way to make a dishonest dollar any more."

"They think they'd like a new federal judge."

"Nothing but," Sugar said. "There's money behind this. Parker thinks he knows who his enemies are. Some of them he does. Some want him out for reasons of money and profit. Others just don't like him. The way Doolin sees it, letting you go was a big mistake for the judge. He turned you loose with the idea of bringing in Joe. Not a bad idea but how it's going to sound is something else. Instead of bringing Joe in, first thing you did was plan the bank robbing at Idabel. Doolin is putting out word that you planned both jobs, the first one before Doolin locked you up for murder, the second after the judge let you go. It's said you killed that constable in Idabel. All this is going into the petition they're getting up to get Parker removed. That state senator—Parker hung his son—is taking it to the President himself. The Governor is on the fence right now. He'll jump in too when Parker is down."

Sundance said, "Besides the reward, what are you getting, hoping to get out of this?"

"A full pardon. A full pardon plus the reward money on you. No more running for me. That's all done. This is the last time I'm going to put myself in the way of danger. I'm going to take my reward money and go someplace far I never been before. I could have said no to Doolin. That didn't seem like such a good idea the night they took me from my cell and stood me on the gallows. Right in the middle of the night he did it. First off, he gagged me and roped me, then walked me across that little park to the hanging place. He didn't explain

138

why he was coming to hang me in the dead of the night. There I was standing with my arms and ankles roped. But I was still ready to go because I thought I was going. I don't know what I thought when Doolin left me on the trap and walked over to the big lever, told a grip on it and called out, 'Down you go, nigger!' Only I didn't go an inch. I heard the pull of the lever, the hum of the springs, but he'd fixed it so the trap wasn't sprung. That's when I went all soft inside. You ever had that feeling? Not you. Then Doolin talked to me through the hood. Quiet, matter of fact. He explained this and that. I was to nod to this and that. I nodded—and I meant it. I feel good being able to tell you this. In a minute you'll be dead and I'll be alive. How scared are you?''

Sundance didn't answer.

"I wish I had time to make you scared," Sugar said.

Sundance smelled lilac water. It was faint but it was there. He raised his voice angrily. "Joe will smell you out. He'll get you and Doolin."

Sugar was startled by Sundance abrupt change of mood. Then he smiled. "You are scared. I don't worry about Joe. I caught you making for the ledge and stopped you," Sugar started to level the pistol.

"Ease down the hammer," Joe Buck said. "Don't turn. Ease it down and drop it."

Joe came out from behind the rocks.

Sugar dropped the gun. "You got it wrong, Joe. He was making for the ledge."

Joe kicked Sugar's gun out of the way and slapped him in the face with his left hand. Sugar went down in the sand.

"Stay down," Joe said. "Sundance was making for the ledge. Go on from there, you lying bastard."

Sundance cut in. "He was going to kill me for the ten thousand Parker has on me. Doolin and his pals want to get rid of Parker. They're using my jail break to make

139

Parker look bad. Doolin sent Sugar to kill me."

Joe pointed the gun in Sugar's face and he stayed down. "He's lying," Sugar said. "Parker- sent Sundance to kill you. That's the truth."

"You know a lot about the truth, Sugarboy," Joe said. "You rode in here, said you broke out. You said Sundance broke out. That's what you said. Fort Smith jail must be a regular tin can, all you fellas breaking out. The hard thing for you is this. A reliable man says Sundance did break out the way he said. Held a knife on Doolin. I got nobody to vouch for you except you. Like the old fella wanted to bank loan, you got no security."

"Doolin backed up the story about Sundance because he hadn't decided to go against Parker. You'd get a different story now."

"Would I? You're a smooth talker, Sugarboy. "You got an answer for everything."

It was bitter cold but Sugar was sweating; shivering and sweating at the same time.

"You should have told this story the first time you came back," Joe said. "Why didn't you do that?"

"I wanted to see what he was up to. You wouldn't believe me if I told you he didn't break jail."

"You didn't ask me, Sugarboy. Who told you Sundance was let go?"

"I heard it," Sugar said. "Rumors go round in a jail, you know that."

"Never been in a jail," Joe said. "Who told you? I can shoot off a finger at a time. Hold up your trigger finger."

"A prisoner told me," Sugar said. "A man called Jimson."

"Sure," Joe said amiably. "This Jimson told you the story in the prison restaurant. Only you didn't get it too straight because the waitress was listening. Jimson got the story from Ike, the judge himself. Ike went down to

140

the cells so he could tell Jimson personal. That must be how it happened."

"I don't know who told him. He told me. He said Parker took Sundance up to his office, showed him a hanging, made a deal with him. The deal was—get Joe Buck. Parker said he'd find him if he ran when he got out."

Sundance cut in again. "He'd keep after me but he wouldn't find me. You think he'd find me?"

"Not if you didn't want him," Joe said. "Even so, Ike would make a lifetime enemy."

"You're a lifetime enemy, Joe."

"True," Joe said. "But I don't mind that. I like being what I am. If you had to keep running you wouldn't be much good to your Indians."

Sugar sensed that Joe was coming back over to his side. "That's what I heard, Joe, what you just said. That's how Parker said it. You skip on me and you'll be hunted the rest of your life. Get Joe Buck for me and I'll up the reward money on him. Double it."

"Sounds reasonable," Joe said, smiling now. "It wasn't fear of Ike that made him do it. It was the money."

"Both reasons," Sugar said, sensing that he had made a mistake. "He didn't want to be hunted. The money was for his Indians."

"So you think the money came first."

"It had to be a big part of it. That makes sense, Joe." Sugar's hands were caked with sand mixed with sweat. It began to rain. Nobody took any heed to it.

"To you it makes sense, you too-smart son of a bitch. I always said that oily tongue was going to get our killed. A good liar tells his story one way, then sticks to it. You keep on embroidering like a fussy old woman. If Sundance wanted to make dirty money for his Indians he'd find an easier way to do it. An easier way, a lot more money."

The rain beat down harder, cold and heavy. It came down the rock walls as if through a sluice and hissed in the black, smooth river.

Sugar kept on trying. "I'm just telling you what I heard. Whose word you going to take, Joe? The years I been with you! You're not going to believe him over me."

"Years don't mean a thing, Sugarboy. Bob Ford was with Jesse longer than you with me. Bob shot Jesse in the back."

"I swear I'm telling the truth."

"And when Preacher's beard grows back he'll be Santy Claus. Too bad about you, Sugarboy. I'll grant you were with me a long time. So you can die with your ears and your other parts still attached to you."

Sugar tried to crawl away from Joe's gun, but the rocks and the pool were behind him. He knew that nothing he said would do any good, but he kept on talking. Talking for his life.

"Give me a chance, Joe. I'm trying to remember what happened."

"I'll bet you are."

"It was like I got out too easy," Sugar said, running his words together. He sucked in breath and started again. "That bothered me."

"You were about to be hung. You escaped and that bothered you."

"It was like somebody wanted me to get out so I could tell you about Sundance. Doolin must've been behind it. That's right—Doolin. It had to be Doolin."

Joe smiled. "Doolin hates Sundance that much?"

"Not Sundance, the judge. Doolin hates Parker."

"Doolin tell you that?"

"Why would Doolin tell me anything? It was the other prisoner, Jimson."

142

"You couldn't tell me about Sundance. It wouldn't be so good for you."

"That's it, Joe. You got it now. I didn't know how you'd take it. I figured the best way was to take care of it myself. That's why I made up the story about him making for the ledge. I had to have something to say after I killed him. I'd be in the clear and he'd be dead. I knew the Fort Smith bank plan was some kind of a trap. We can still do it without him."

Joe looked quickly at Sundance. "This trap, Sugarboy, how was he going to arrange that?"

Once again Sugar saw hope that wasn't there. "I don't know, Joe. Maybe he was going to use the woman. Get her to put a note in with the money when she went to the banks. It could be done that way. I seen them talking together. They been up to something behind your back . . ."

Joe turned away. "So long, Sugarboy," he said. "You do it, Sundance."

Sugar began to scream, "Wait, Joe! I'll tell you the truth!"

The straight-handled throwing hatchet flashed from Sundance's hand while Sugar was still screaming. Thrown sideways, the long, narrow blade buried itself in Sugar's neck. He jumped and died. His fingers kept on clawing at the sand after he was dead. Then the muscles and the sinews died too.

Anna came out of the cave rubbing her eyes. She stopped and raised the back of her hand to her mouth when she heard the terrible sound, and saw the dead man.

"Send him over the falls," Joe said.

There was gray light showing at the top of the gorge and Joe was eating steak and eggs. The rain had stopped hours before, but the sand was still wet. A spring wind blowing down from the mountain still had the chill of snow in it. In the river broken branches whipped past in the current and at the top of the gorge mist was mixed with light. The rain had washed away Joe's stink of lilac water.

Chewing on a hard-fried egg, Joe said, "Lucky for you I showed up when I did. He'd have shot you sure. Which reminds me you didn't say thanks."

"Thanks, Joe. Will that hold you?" Anna made good coffee and now she sat huddled in a blanket drinking it. It was damp and cold at the bottom of the gorge.

Joe held out his cup and Anna filled it, looking sullen, saying nothing. "You don't sound too thankful," Joe said. "I heard more thanks from a man borrowing a match." Joe grinned and there was egg yolk on his chin. He used his first mouthful of coffee as a mouth rinse before he swallowed. He knew Anna hated that. "You figured you could draw and kill him before he got off a shot."

"He was a little drunk," Sundance said.

"You led him into it?"

"It was a thought."

"You knew he wasn't on the square and you led him into it."

"It came out all right."

"Not for Sugarboy. There was an easier way to get him to talk, if you thought he was double-dealing. Hold a cigar to a man's rocks and he'll talk your ear off."

"Would my word be enough that Sugar was double-dealing?"

"I took your word when you said you broke out."

"After you had the story checked back."

"No cause to be sore. What did you expect me to do?"

"What you did. It's what I'd do."

144

Joe drank the rest of his coffee and told Anna to sling another couple of steaks on the skillet. "I like a man that agrees with me," he said. "That business with Sugarboy was dumb, you dumb halfbreed. Suppose you got killed. You'd be dead and I'd have a spy in my camp."

"You'd have caught him, Joe."

Joe's eyes narrowed. "Probably I would. Let me tell you something. It's hard being a spy, a dirty lying sneak. Sure, for some it comes easy. Most real men don't cotton to it. Suppose you're a spy and you got no special reason to hate the man you're fixing to betray when you get the chance. I can see a man doing it for revenge. I see doing anything for revenge. A few years back I caught one of Ike's spies here in camp. Didn't take any Pinkerton work to do it. One of the boys used to be a shotgun guard over by the town of Norman. Fed me some good hold-up information that man. The minute this spy joined up with us this fella pegged him right off as the brother of a girl got crippled in a stage robbery we done."

Joe said, "Would have caught him anyhow. The usual way I deal with Ike's spies isn't how I did this fella. This fella I just shot quick and merciful after I heard about the sister. A shame that had to happen. I went easy on him cause I could see his point of view. He wasn't doing it for money so I wasn't mad at him."

Sundance wondered if Joe knew himself what he was leading up to. Joe was a smart man in his way, but it was the animal in him that had kept him alive for so long, not brains. Sundance knew that Joe sensed danger, even if he didn't know what it was.

"I wouldn't be that merciful to a real spy," Joe said. "A man comes into my camp, eats my food, swaps stories with me, I expect something from a man like that. Any decent man would know what I'm talking about. A man who'd turn on another man for money is no better than a snake. I'd say a man like that just had to have a dirty whore for a mother and his father liked sheep when he couldn't mess with a young boy."

Joe looked carefully at Sundance.

"Most likely," Sundance said.

"I'd say his mother was a greasy pig . . ."

"You're getting worked up, Joe," Sundance said. "I get your meaning."

Joe blew on his coffee. "I know you do, Sundance. A sneak is the worst thing a man has to face. Or not have to face. Let the sons of bitches throw all the lead you like at me. Me, I just throw it back faster and straighter. That's how the game ought to be played, fair and square, the give and take of two men trying to kill each other. For the life, I don't know what turned old Sugarboy into a sneak. I guess it was in him all the time. I sort of knew it was there, but he was with me a long time, so I let it go thinking there wasn't a whole lot he could do. Lord! Did that nigger ever talk! He could tell stories a whole winter night and never repeat himself."

Joe laughed, thinking of Sugar. "Right now I'll bet he's halfway to convincing the devil couldn't he find him a cooler spot than he's in. Him and the devil sitting down to a big feed of water melon or a pitcher of buttermilk chilled in the well. Sugarboy always said the devil was a nigger. Always treat the colored man right, Sugar always said, or the devil'll get you sure. You think he was right?"

"He's got a good chance to find out," Sundance said.

Joe's eyes narrowed. "Any man that turns on me will get the same chance."

After Joe went to look at his horse, Sundance and

146

Anna were alone in the cave.

"How are you going to do it?"

She didn't have to explain what she meant. It was in her eyes. It had been there for days. It came and went, but it was always there.

"Joe and the others won't make it back across the ferry. I'm going to fix it so the ferry won't be waiting at the dock."

Anna looked startled. "But Joe is leaving a man?"

"I'm going to get word to the ferry man. As soon as we're across to Fort Smith Joe's man will have guns staring down his throat. There won't be any ferry. The only way back to the Territory is swimming."

Anna looked away. "Then they'll all die?"

"They'll die then or later. Makes no difference. You still bothered?"

"I never said it bothered me."

"You didn't have to."

"All right, you cold blooded bastard. It bothers me. Not enough. I want to get out. If this is the only way, then all right."

"You get going soon as you get the money," Sundance said. "Take it and be gone. They won't be looking to get the money back. They'll count up what was stolen and they'll be a little ahead. They can't accuse you of stealing what you deposited. That's your money, you get to keep it. Like I said, I'll fix the bank robbing charge with Parker. You were made to do it at gunpoint, so there is no charge. But get out fast. No more talk with Joe. You know where you're going to go?"

Anna got angry again. "None of your goddamned business where I go."

Sundance said, "Just go there."

"Where will you go?"

"Texas. Where I was going when this thing got

147

started."

Anna stared at the floor. "I don't know where I'm going to go."

"You don't have to tell me anything." Sundance didn't want to know.

"My husband is still alive. I can't go back to him. It wasn't his fault. It was me. I like men and I don't like them. I know the reason I don't like men, but I don't want to think about it. I thought if I got married I'd like men better. Not my husband though. I liked to think if I had a real man it would make me different."

She began to cry. "God help me, I can't stay with Joe." She looked at the walls of the cave as if she had never seen them before. "How can I stay in this place? You can see why I can't stay here."

Sundance had no answer for anything.

"If I stay I'll hate myself. Then it will be too late. You said I can't have it every way, you bloodless bastard. I guess I can't. I wish I could. I hate it here. Mostly I hate it. When I don't think about it I don't hate it so much. You don't understand anything I'm saying, do you?"

"Some of it. There's no help for some of it. You'll have to face that."

"I don't want to face it. The hell with you! I don't know why I'm even talking to you. Keep away from me, that's all I want from you."

By the time Joe came back, Anna had dried her eyes. "I'm about ready," she said.

Joe rubbed his hands together and let out a whoop. "Then let's be moving, brothers and sisters. Before you know it, we'll be rich—or we'll be dead."

148

CHAPTER 13

They went out the way they came in, clinging to the rope for safety as they crossed the river, and only one man was left behind. Everyone else was going on the big raid they had talked about for so long. Outside the steep walls of the gorge, the sun seemed to have a different light. The sky was a cold pale blue swept clear of clouds; new grass was coming up underneath last year's grass, now a soggy brown. The sky was limitless and empty except for fights of blackbirds, and higher up on the wind were soaring hawks, and higher still were the huge sandhill cranes, so far up in the sky that they were just specs against the faded blue. At times they were invisible and their lonesome cries seemed to come from nowhere.

Anna crossed the river with the others, and when she reached the other shore she turned for one last look, then she kicked her horse into motion and rode up the wet, clay-slick bank of the river. The clothes she was going to wear when she went to the banks were folded and wrapped in a rain slicker. Her hair was like white gold in the sun, and when she reached the top of the riverbank she raised up in the stirrups and looked at the country stretching down and away from the foothills.

At the river crossing they were still high in the hills; the hills went down from there in swells and breaks and sudden drops. In the hills there was sun but far out on the prairie it was still raining. They were moving out when the sun broke through far below and for a while there was sunshine and rain at the same time; a rainbow arced down from the sky as if one end were buried in the earth. The new leaves were bright green and Indian-apple blossoms and maple flowers were everywhere; the hazel clumps were alive with birds.

Four days' ride would take them close to Fort Smith; when they got there they would go over the plan again, and if nothing was found wrong with it, Anna, Preacher and Newley would cross the river early on Saturday morning and look the town over carefully before they went to the banks. Most important was to how many soldiers were in town. Fort Smith, in spite of its name, was no longer an army town; the closest military post was at Roundsville, fifty miles away, but soldiers did pass through the town, mostly cavalry but sometimes infantry, on their way to the ferry and from there to the Territory and beyond.

If they saw many soldiers in town or heard of soldiers on the move, Newley would go down to the ferry dock and stand there for a while. There was no need for Newley to make the crossing, because the dock would be watched with binoculars through all the daylight hours. If there were soldiers around, they were to do nothing but wait; to stay in the hotel until it was safe to try for the banks. If they had to wait, they would do it on the following Saturday.

On the way down the mountain the men were in high spirits; only Joe was in a bad humor, and this puzzled the men, who knew nothing about Anna's leaving. Joe, usually full of bad jokes and loud talk, rode by himself, slouching in his saddle, sour-faced and silent. An hour after they left there was a sun shower, but when it passed the day was warm and bright and it was cold only in the shadows of the stands of trees that dotted the lower mountain meadows.

After eight hours in the saddle, they made camp and ate a quick meal while the horses grazed on the new grass. Then they moved on again. Joe kept away from Anna and his mood changed and became boisterous. Now he rode with the men, talking to men he never talked to except to give orders. He told jokes they had heard many times, and they all laughed dutifully.

It wasn't a good plan, Sundance thought. It would have to do. If it worked, all the men he was with now would be dead. They would fight hard and die hard because they knew what was waiting if they gave up. No money they had, or promised to get, would make any difference. No lawyer was loud enough, smart enough to get them off; and though they didn't talk about it, since it was bad luck to talk about their own deaths, Sundance knew that they took pride in facing an implacable enemy like Isaac Parker. Mercy was as foreign to them as kindness. If they ever had families their memories were dim now; they had gone beyond everything other men clung too, and they took pride in that too. And even as he thought about how they would die, Sundance felt a sort of kinship with these doomed men; whatever else they were, they were not cowards. What was going to happen to them was inevitable; it had been waiting since they had stolen their first horses, killed their first men.

The wind died and clouds gathered on the horizon; clouds, black and threatening, gathered and moved across the sky. The lightning flashed and banged and the sky split and the rain came in torrents. The horses

151

hung their heads and plodded on; the men hunched their shoulders and their clothes underneath the slickers were heavy and damp. The first violence of the storm passed as quickly as it had come. The rain still fell and the horses slid in the mud and sometimes they fell. Then yellow light showed again on the far horizon and sun like bars of gold appeared in the sky and a rainbow arced again. The rain stopped suddenly and they rode on under the dripping trees and across wet, rain-flattened meadows. In another two hours it was dark and they made camp for the night.

They made camp by a high-flooding creek that ran down through a grove of trees. After the storm was gone a wind blew up and they were wet and cold. Under the trees it was dry, or fairly dry, and they gathered dead wood to make a fire. There was no more rain and when the fires burned bright they took off their slickers and stood close to the heat and steamed themselves dry.

Anna made coffee and they sat and drank it waiting for the meat to fry. The coffee smelled good in the cold, damp air, and when the meat was ready to eat Anna cooked more coffee and they ate and drank in silence, tired and shivery after the long day and wanting nothing more than to be dry and to get some sleep.

Joe drank whiskey by the fire after the men except for the lookouts were rolled in their blankets, dark shadows in the firelight. He stared into the fire while he drank the whiskey. He didn't share the bottle and he didn't talk, and when Sundance finished his watch and came back from the hill, Joe was still huddled by the fire with the empty bottle in his hand, morose and silent.

In the morning he was different, as if the black mood had passed. Sundance knew it hadn't. Joe was losing his woman and he was taking it hard; it showed in the dangerous glitter that never left his eyes. It was even more dangerous when he forced himself to be loud and hearty with the men, carrying on about Preacher's store teeth or repeating one of the dead black man's stories. He talked a lot about all the money they were going to steal, boasting of the record for robbery they would set.

"We'll be rich, boys," Joe said, "and this is just the start of it."

To Joe, the Fort Smith job was over already; he was looking forward to bigger robberies, daring raids that would astonish the world and make him the greatest outlaw who ever lived. The men listened slack-jawed to his wild schemes. In far off New York a man named Jimmy West and his gang had robbed two and a half million dollars from a bank without firing a shot. It was the greatest single bank job of all time, but Joe swore he would top it.

"There's nothing that can't be done if you have enough nerve. Nerve and brains, and I got both. No bank in the world can't be broke if you set your mind to it. With enough money in your kick you can do anything, be anything. You snap your fingers and the boot-lickers come a-crawling. All it takes is money to be a big man provided you're man enough to take it and keep it."

And while he talked Joe looked at Anna; there was a change in her attitude and he didn't like it. Though he kept away from her most of the time, now and then he snapped at her, waiting for her to give as good as she got. If she answered at all it was to agree with him, in a word or a silent shrug. The tension between them seemed to twang like a bowstring and only the thought of the money kept Joe from exploding into a murderous rage. Sundance hadn't decided what he would do if Joe started in on the girl with his fists and his boots. He guessed he would kill him before the others shot him down.

Joe wanted to kill someone and he did. It happened so fast and was over so fast that if it hadn't been for the dead man lying in the mud it might never have taken place. It happened on the second day when they were well down the mountain and making good time. Gates had to die because Joe wanted to kill and Gates fell down in a fit. They were crossing a shallow creek and Gates made a sound and fell off his horse and rolled around in the water. It had happened before, the men were used to it, and they waited for Gates to come out of it or drown. In the water, Gates twitched and jerked as the spasms twisted his muscles out of shape. Suddenly, Joe pulled the gun and shot him in the head. He kept on firing after Gates was dead. Then he stared down at the body as if he had never known a man named Gates. He reloaded his gun and moved on without a word, his back hard and rigid. The men exchanged glances and rode after him, glad they hadn't been Gates but not sure that they wouldn't be next.

That night Joe got drunk and made jokes about the epileptic, and even the men, hardened though they were, had to work hard to laugh. Sundance expected Joe to call the murder an act of mercy, but he didn't. Gates was too big a risk, Joe said. The bank job came first, Joe said. "No way you can depend on a cripple if something should go wrong," Joe said. "This is a fighting outfit, boys, and there's no place in it for cripples or quitters. Now take that tow-headed woman over yonder on the far side of the fire. That woman thinks I done a bad thing shooting down old Gates-boy."

Joe raised his voice. "I didn't hear your answer, woman."

Anna looked at him through the leaping flames of the fire. "What difference does it make?"

"No difference to me," Joe said. "Nothing you say makes any difference to me. I'm Joe Buck, that's who I am. I do what I like, go where I like. I take these lard-assed boys with me so's they can get an education in what's what. You know what's what, little missy?"

Anna stared into the fire.

"She thinks she so smart, only she ain't," Joe said, pulling at the bottle. "I took pity on her and took her in. Now I'm throwing her out. I'd like to keep her but what the hell. Being with a woman you take pity on ain't the same as being with a real woman. I tell you, boys, I'm going to catch me a solid gold woman real soon. A little bit younger than this one. Once a woman gets over the twenty mark she's well on her way to being dried up. One thing I hate is a dry woman. You fellas ever have any experience with a dry woman? It hurts something awful."

The men laughed uneasily, not because they had respect for the woman. Anna didn't seem to care. She fell asleep by the fire. Sundance looked at her. She was a long way from the place she started. But in the end, that was none of his business. He knew that nothing would ever be right for Anna Jacobson, and though she fought against it, she knew it too. All he could do was set her free; after that she was on her own.

Later, Joe sat by the fire by himself and Sundance was in his blankets but wasn't asleep. From where he was, he could see Joe and the woman asleep on the other side of the fire. Joe stared at her for a long time. Then he got up and put a blanket around her shoulders. Sundance hadn't moved but Joe turned feeling eyes on him. "Can't let the bitch get sick," he said in a whiskey-slurred voice. "Soon as it's over I don't give a damn she

155

dies in the street."

A killer in love, Sundance thought. Another few days would cure him of that.

The prairie-warmed wind blew in their faces now; the mountains were far behind. Out on the prairie there were reed-edged ponds ruffled by the wind; birds fluttered in the grass, alarmed by the passing of men and horses. Still too far away to see from where they were was the river, dark and wide and heavy with mud. There were roads now, but they kept away from them, riding by night and sleeping during the day. Among the men there was less talk. No talk was needed: they had been together so long that a word or a grunt or even a shrug was enough. They ate and slept and worked on their weapons. The horses were all right: none lamed or sickened by the rain. Now there was a sense of waiting in the camp.

They rode far into the night and it was Friday when they woke and they could see the river and Fort Smith on the other side. The grove of trees they were in was on a high hill above the river and while they watched the first ferry of the day came over from the eastern shore and nobody got off. Joe looked at his fat silver watch and after ten minutes the ferry went back with only one passenger, a man on a mule. The current was strong and the ferry was slow; a weak sun fought to break through the mist and rain on the river. Across the river the town was quiet. Joe passed the brass-framed army binoculars to Sundance. Joe seemed to be more in control of himself. Sundance glassed the ferry landing and the street that went up from the river to the start of the town. So far nothing moved but the ferry, then the town began to come to life. Cookfires curled up from chimneys and while he watched a short train came in from the east trailing smoke. The sound of metal beating on metal was carried from a blacksmith shop on the wind. Two men in a wagon came down the hill from the town and unloaded boxes on the dock. At one end of the dock there was a shack with a sign that said it belonged to the New Orleans & Southern Steamship Company.

"It looks good," Sundance said, handing the binoculars back to Joe.

Joe nodded. "Looks good to me. I wonder what Ike is doing this gray morning? Probably getting ready to hang another batch of men. I wonder what Ike would say if he knew we were up here getting ready to loot his town. Look at that goddamned town over there. So fat and safe-looking. Got nothing to worry about, the town thinks. I wouldn't mind burning that goddamned fat-gutted town. I'd like to see it go up in flames, all the nice little houses."

"No profit in that," Sundance.

"Who the hell is talking about profit? I'd be profit and a pleasure to me just to do it. I guess you're right though the idea gnaws at me like a rat. What time you figure they should start across?"

"Not too early," Sundance said. "A few hours. Banks open at eight. Maybe two hours after that. They have the whole day to do it."

"I'd still like to burn that town," Joe said.

They ate jerked meat and drank water from their canteens while a man watched the town with the glasses. It rained again and it was cold without a fire. Anna took the town clothes and went into the trees to get ready. She took a hairbrush and mirror and stayed in there for

157

a long time. The men grinned while Preacher stripped down to his woolies and worked his bony body into the new black suit. One of the men fixed his white rubber collar after he wiped it clean with a wet neckerchief. Then he tied Preacher's black ribbon tie and said some rich widow ought to marry him before he got away.

"Don't go near any undertaking parlors or they'll bury you," Joe said.

Newley took less fixing up and what fixing up there was he didn't like. Preacher wanted to know why he had to shave and Newley didn't. Joe looked at him and Preacher decided that shaving was a good idea, after all.

The money Anna was to deposit had been counted and wrapped. Joe did it again. Sundance didn't offer to help and Joe didn't ask him. The count came out right and Joe tied up the money again. Still, he hated to let it go.

"It's an investment," Sundance said.

"What in hell is taking her so long?" Joe said with sudden anger. "You'd think she was going to meet a man."

Preacher dared to make a joke about it. "Three men, Joe."

Joe turned on him and Preacher got away fast.

It was quiet there while Anna got dressed and Sundance was reminded of a theater before the curtain rolled up for the first act of the play. They were all part of it, but for now Anna, with her golden hair and green dress, had everybody's attention. Isaac Parker was part of it too. Sometimes Joe mentioned Parker's name, always calling him Ike, but the men never did. To these men, Parker was the devil and twice as real.

Joe stood up when Anna came out of the trees. The men gaped. Anna smiled nervously. Joe didn't smile. Preacher had the buggy hitched and was sitting on the seat holding the whip. The buggy was new and shiny where it wasn't splashed with mud. Newley, quiet as ever, was waiting to get on his horse.

Joe talked to Anna in front of the men. Sundance didn't expect him to do that.

"You won't change your mind?" Joe said.

Anna shook her head. "I have to get away," she said.

"Then go," Joe said, turning away from her.

When there was no one on the road below, Preacher drove the buggy out of the trees. Newley rode beside the buggy. When they got down to the road Preacher flicked the whip and the buggy went away. Sundance watched it, then picked up the binoculars and watched it all the way to the ferry. The ferry was waiting and in a few minutes it started across the river.

Sundance watched Anna leaning into the river wind as the ferry plowed through the choppy water until it got to the other side. Then the buggy climbed the long hill to the town, and disappeared. It was started now and nothing could stop it. The hand had been dealt and they had to play it out, win, lose—or die.

CHAPTER 14

The day passed slowly and there was nothing to do but wait. Newley didn't come back to the dock, so there were no soldiers in town. Sundance spent most of the day observing the town. Two trains arrived and departed during the day; Fort Smith was the end of the line for the railroad. Two hundred miles upriver there was a bridge; here, the ferry was the only way to cross.

Just before noon a steamboat hooter echoed on the river. The big paddleboat rounded a bend to the south and made its way to the dock. Steamboat business was dying on the big river; after the sternwheeler put cargo and a few passengers ashore, it was the only boat that passed for the rest of the day. In a few minutes the dock was deserted again; the ferry made its trips from shore to shore. Two boys came to fish off the dock, but didn't stay long. They took their poles and walked along the edge of the river in the reeds.

It was Saturday, a big day in town, and the ferry was busy with farm wagons with families in them. People who had gone over in the morning began to come back. Newley didn't come down to the dock. The wind blew hard on the river and for hours there was no sun. On both banks of the river reeds waved in the wind. No more trains arrived at the depot at the far end of town. No trains departed. A drunk crawled out from under a wagon halfway up the hill and went up slowly and into the town. The men played cards in the green light under the trees. No one paid much attention to the game; there was none of the usual bickering. Joe sat by himself with his back against a tree. He kept easing back the hammer and spinning the cylinder of his gun. Except for the soft slap on the cards on a slicker the clicking of the turning cylinder was the only sound.

Joe came up to where Sundance was with the binoculars. The wind bent the wide brim of his hat.

"How is it?" he said.

"Same as it was."

"I'm glad Newley didn't show," Joe said. "I'd hate to have to wait up here for a week."

"He could still show."

"Goddamn him if he does. I'd like to be gone from here. I guess she's doing all right though. You have to give her that—nerve. Most women don't have it. Maybe I'll grab another woman when I'm in that town. This time I'm going to catch a woman that won't give me such hardship as that other one over there. One time Sugar said to me why didn't I get a woman I didn't have to catch. Guess he didn't see the right side of it. I like a woman you have to break. That's half of what being with a woman is, the breaking of her. You have to do it right. You have to break them enough, not all the way. I never could be sure about that woman over there. Times I thought I had her just right, fairly right anyhow. Then she's 'round on me like a wildcat. You ever notice she looks like a cat?"

"Can't say that I have," Sundance said.

"Just like a big cat," Joe said. "Something strange about her I never could figure. Just as well she won't be around. I got boys to look out for, business to 'tend to. If she stayed on I'd probably end up killing her. Bound to happen some night. She ever tell you where he comes from?"

"Why would she tell me, Joe?"

"I guess she didn't then. I saw you looking at her a few times."

"I was just looking, Joe."

"I don't fault you for that. She's something to look at all right. Well, what the hell! No point talking about it."

It began to get dark on the river and the first lights showed in the town. So many wagons came down the hill to the ferry, that some had to wait for the ones in front to get across. There was no light left by the time the ferry took the last wagon to the western shore. The ferry had lanterns at both ends, and there was light on the dock. After it got dark the ferry stopped running; on the western landing there was a bell on a crossbeam that could be rung if someone wanted to cross over. The clapper of the bell was tied down to keep it from clanging in the wind. It rang once about an hour later and the ferry man went over. After that it was quiet except for the wind.

Everybody was up and ready to move when first light turned the river into a crooked ribbon of dull silver. They ate jerky and beans from the can and drank water. No one said anything, but the strain of waiting was in their faces. Sundance took over from the last man on guard. He turned the binoculars screw and brought the town into focus. At five-thirty the ferry man came down the hill from the town, scratching and yawning. Lights still burned on the tied-up ferry and he blew them out when he went on board and looked around. The drunk Sundance had seen the day before was sleeping on the ferry; the ferry man kicked him off and shook his fist at him. The drunk took a long time to get up the hill.

Joe snapped his silver watch shut. "Time to move in," he said.

A squall of rain blew down the river as they rode down to the ferry. In the river the wind blew the water into waves, white-topped and choppy before the force of the wind. They were all huddled in their yellow slickers, with hat brims pulled low over their eyes. On the other side of the river, Fort Smith looked gray in the rain. Church bells had been clanging for the past half hour.

The ferry came in and tied up before they got down to the dock. Two Indians in a wagon got off and drove away.

The ferry man, an old man with white chin whiskers, shielded his face to light a pipe before he looked up at them. All he saw were men in hats and slickers. He took out a watch that looked like Joe's. "Take you across in zackly seven minutes," he said.

"Take us over now," Joe said, pointing a gun at the old man's head. The others climbed down and led their horses aboard. The hoofs made a hollow sound on the planking of the flat-bottomed boat.

"Don't kill me, Mr. Buck," the ferry man said. "You ain't got no quarrel with me."

Joe winked at Sundance. "Smoke your pipe, friend. Nobody's going to kill you. Move fast now."

They left a man behind with the ferry man and started up the slope from the river, into the town. On the dock were stacks of boxes waiting to be picked up by the steamboat when it came downriver. The cobblestoned street that went up from the dock to the town was slick with rain and mud. The last church bell clanged and the town was quiet again. Joe looked at his watch again. "Ten o'clock on the dot," he said. "They're starting to sing the first hymn."

They passed a church; inside the congregation was singing, and Joe smiled again. "Nothing like working by the clock," he said. "You made a good plan, Sundance."

Sundance nodded.

They went along a street lined on both sides with warehouses with wagons and drays out front. A drunk without shoes lay under a wagon with an empty bottle in his hand. Everything in town was closed: saloons, stores, eating placles, everything. The rain beat down on the silent town, clouding windows, dripping from roofs. Except for the drunk under the wagon there wasn't a man in sight.

"Too bad this won't work but the one time," Joe said. "Makes me feel more like a businessman than a bandit. Anna should be finished by the first bank by now. Hell, this is so easy I feel kind of shamed."

The town square was at the end of the main street and at the far side of it was the federal courthouse, the ten-man gallows wet in the rain, and because of the trees they could see only the top of the courthouse looming up in the mist, solid and gray. Joe spat.

Now they were starting down the main street toward the banks. Anna's buggy was coming up from the other side, still half-hidden by the rain and mist.

"Easy," Sundance said. "That's the last bank. She's doing fine."

"That she is," Joe said. "Looks like there won't be any trouble, after all." His eyes glittered. "The little lady is about to get her wish."

They had reached the last bank before Anna and the

164

others came out. Newley still looked glum but Preacher was smiling with his ill-fitting teeth. "Got them tied tight as a drum, Joe," he said. "I'll just lock up now. I always wanted to lock up a bank." Preacher was having a good time.

Newley heaved the money sacks over the back of Joe's horse, then unloaded the others from the buggy. Joe watched carefully, keeping his eyes away from Anna. She climbed into the buggy and sat waiting, wet and cold. Her face had a pinched look and she was shaking. Sundance looked down the street. It was empty. Rain was still falling and the wind blew hard, carrying organ music from some church. Sundance threw his blanket roll to Anna, but she didn't try to catch it. It fell in the mud of the street; nobody looked at it.

"What do you think?" Joe asked Preacher, who was getting up on his horse.

"A rough count, going by the tags and what the bankers said—more than two hundred thousand," Preacher said.

"Pretty good," Joe said. Sundance didn't like the glitter in Joe's eyes. Something was going wrong.

"Joe!" Anna cried out suddenly. "Joe! It's a trap!"

Joe whirled with his gun out and shot her in the breast. The bullet knocked her back, then she fell forward without a sound. Sundance drew and fired at the same time. As he fired the buggy horse jumped forward. he missed and Joe fired back and missed. Sundance sprang behind a wagon. Brindar rode straight at him and Sundance killed him with a shot in the head. Bullets splintered the wagon and Sundance heard Joe yelling at them to get out. Sundance jumped up and shot Dancer in the back as they rode back toward the ferry. Joe turned and fired, yelling like a madman. Then he kicked his horse into a gallop. Men were coming at a run.

165

Anna opened her eyes when Sundance lifted her and carried her under the porch of the bank. She was wet with blood and rain. He held her against him so she wouldn't die in the mud. She didn't have long to live.

Sundance waved the men away. "Joe Buck down by the ferry. He can't get away."

"Just let go," Sundance said, holding her. "Don't fight it—just let go."

"I tried to warn him," she whispered. "I tried to warn him, and he shot me. The big dumb son of a . . ." She smiled.

"He didn't know," Sundance said.

"He wasn't so bad," she whispered. "A few times it wasn't so bad. I always wondered what it would be like with you. You saw me as a woman, didn't you?"

Sundance wanted her to die. He wanted her to be gone. There was nothing to be said. "How else would I see you?" he said.

She tried to nod. "Good," she whispered. "I like to hear that." Her hands clutched at him. "Don't hang him, Sundance. Kill him, don't hang him. Promise you won't hang him."

"Like hell I won't," Sundance said, but she could no longer hear him. She shuddered and died.

He left her where she was; somebody would look after her. It didn't matter. Down by the river there was shooting. It got heavier as he galloped toward the sound of the guns. It was time and past time to take care of Joe. Anna was dead because he hadn't done it sooner. That didn't matter either. They all had a hand in her death, no one more than herself.

The heaviest fire was coming from down by the ferry dock. Some of Joe's men were shooting back from behind the stacked crates, but from all over town men were coming with rifles. Sundance ran down the hill and

166

dived under a wagon. A man with a beard snapped the lever of his rifle and pointed it at his head. "You're one of them," he said.

"Judge is coming from the hill," another man yelled. The bearded man held the gun on Sundance while Parker came down the hill with bullets kicking up on all sides of him. A dozen men yelled at the judge to get down, but he kept coming, holding his rifle under his arm like a man out hunting.

"Give him cover!" Sundance yelled. The men under the wagon and all along the street facing the dock opened fire again, laying down a storm of lead. One of Joe's men staggered back to the end of the dock and fell into the river. The firing picked up again, getting heavier as more men arrived. There was no sign of Joe. Upriver there was more firing. It stopped after a while.

Judge Parker got behind the wagon, squinted down the barrel of his rifle and killed a man. He jacked another shell. "You brought him in. Not the way I wanted. He's here. Close enough."

Sundance was looking for Joe and then he saw him, firing back from the side of the steamship company shack. Dead men lay on the dock. Joe and his boys had fought their way through the trap. Now they had their backs to the river, and that was as far as they could go. On the other side of the muddy river was freedom; country where they knew every tree and gully and cave. They fought fiercely, men with absolutely nothing to lose; the deadly accuracy of their fire sent the attackers ducking and running for cover. Some of them yelled defiance, others fought in silence. Sundance leveled his rifle and shot the quiet killer called Newley. He got him in the neck, then in the chest while he was falling. Other bullets whacked into him after he was dead. The attackers had numbers on their side and they poured lead with the ferocity of ordinary men worked up to a killing rage.

Sundance fired at Joe as he dived from the side of the shack and rolled behind the stacked crates. Sundance readied the rifle for when Joe would show his head again. He guessed wrong and Joe ducked down and came up again and fired. Joe spotted Sundance and yelled. Sundance fired at his head, all he could see. Another head showed and Sundance blew it to bits. It might have been Murphy or Horn. They looked alike. He reloaded and looked again for Joe. Beside him, Parker was firing steadily. He killed a man and grunted. There were lulls in the firing. The firing was like a wind that came and went. It built up and slacked off until it built up again.

Joe was yelling and suddenly they were trying to break out of the trap. Three men ran out in front of the others with guns blazing in their hands. From behind another wagon a goose gun roared for the first time. The big-bore gun was loaded with chunks of lead and the blast killed the three men at the same time. It swept them off their feet as if a big wind that knocked them over. Another man's arm was shredded and it hung from his shoulder on threads of torn muscle. He was screaming and kept on screaming. A dozen rifles blew him to bits.

More than half of Joe's men were dead or dying. A man hit in the face stood up with his hands over his eyes and died that way. Some of the attackers had circled out and were coming along the bank of the river from both sides. The firing picked up again.

"Madness!" Judge Parker said. "It's all madness!"

Sundance fired and ducked down. "You don't like it, Judge?" He killed a man with his next shot and ducked down again. Bullets tore into the top of the wagon, showering them with bits of wood.

168

Parker snapped the lever of his Winchester. "I don't like it. I . . ."

Gunfire drowned out his words. Joe's men were running out of ammunition; the fire from the dock was weaker. It would be over in minutes. Sundance shoved a handful of rifle shells at the judge, and he reloaded with the same deliberate calm.

"Why don't they surrender?" Parker said. The judge took a white handkerchief from the sleeve of his muddied coat and tied it to the barrel of his rifle. He pushed up the rifle and a bullet smacked into the top of the barrel, tearing the rifle from his hands. The broken rifle clattered on the cobblestones. Parker crawled over to a dead man and got another rifle.

"They're fools," he said. "They could repent and die in the grace of God. It would be better than this."

Sundance wanted to shoot the judge in his pious face.

The fire from the dock began to weaken under the hail of bullets poured in by dozens of men converging from all sides. Soon the attackers numbered more than a hundred. At first, some of them didn't know whom they were shooting at, then word spread that Joe Buck and what was left of his gang were down there. But it wasn't yet time to move in.

"Doolin's out to get you," Sundance told the judge while he reloaded his rifle, his back against the side of the wagon.

"Not for long," Parker said, firing until his rifle was empty again. There was no gratitude in Parker's eyes, just he same flat look of the fanatic.

"They're done for," the man with the beard called out. "Let's finish this up." The last man behind the crates shot him dead as he moved out before the others. A hail of bullets and buckshot blew the shooter to bits.

They moved in, guns ready, but there was nothing

more to shoot at. A wounded man was shot before the judge pushed his way through to prevent it. "No more!" he said. He turned to Sundance. "I don't see Buck."

"There he is, the dirty red nigger," a big man yelled. "In the river. The red nigger's trying to get over in a boat!"

Parker knocked his rifle aside and ordered the others to hold their fire. "I said no more shooting."

Another man raised both hands above his head. "Listen to the judge, men! A bullet's too good for that red nigger bastard. Let the judge hang the son of a bitch."

"You're real popular today," Sundance said bitterly. They all wanted to hang the red nigger in the boat. He looked out at the boat, a little thing with oars, no match for the powerful current that was carrying it back to shore no matter how hard Joe rowed. Joe didn't know a damn thing about boats. It wouldn't have made any difference. The current and the wind from upriver carried him back toward the men lined all along the dock and down by the water. They were all yelling now, pointing their guns at Joe, yelling at the dirty red nigger to pull harder. The boat began to twist in the current and Joe's face had an astonished look, as if he couldn't believe what was happening to him. After all the long years of living free he was trapped and jeered at like something in a circus—a sideshow freak.

When the boat twisted again and Joe's back was to him, Sundance jerked the rifle to his shoulder and shot Joe through the head. He rose up in the boat as if something had pulled him to his feet for an instant. Then he pitched over the side and went under. A dozen men with gun turned to kill, but Parker raised his hand and his whispery voice reached out to the last man there.

"Go to your homes," he ordered. "My men will handle the rest. Go on now. Do what I say."

The crowd broke up and began to drift away and four of Parker's deputies gathered, waiting for orders.

"Find Doolin," the judge said.

Sundance and the judge walked up the hill toward town. The rain had stopped but clouds were rolling in again from the east. "What about it?" Sundance said. He knew he wasn't going back in any cell, no matter what the judge's answer was.

"I could still hang you," Judge Parker said calmly. "We made a deal but you didn't live up to it. You came this far and then you killed him. Why?"

"He killed a woman I liked."

"You're lying. You don't want to tell me. I think I know why you killed him."

"You're not going to hang me," Sundance said. "I still have my guns."

Parker looked at him. "And you'll go on using them, if I let you go."

"That's what I'm going to do, Judge. You do it your way, I do it mine. I suppose it gets done."

Parker resumed his stride. "You're wrong. My way is the only way this country is ever going to be civilized. Everything I ever learned tells me to hang you, Mr. Sundance. I'm not going to. You're free to ride out any time you like, provided you do it within the next hour. Be gone by then, Mr. Sundance. Be gone—or be dead. Don't ever come back to Arkansas."

It was all over now. Joe was dead. They were all dead—and so was Anna. Anna, with her wild temper and her long legs and yellow cat's eyes. All dead. It didn't feel so great to be alive still, but he knew he would get over that after a while. There was no way to tell how long it would take. He guessed a long time. If it didn't take a long time, then he'd know there was something wrong with him. Maybe there was. Maybe there was something wrong with every man who lived by the gun. But there was no helping that. It was what he did for a living. He saddled Eagle and rode out of Fort Smith feeling as gray as the sky. The big stallion sensed his mood and whinnied softly. He patted the great animal's neck.

"Let's go to Texas, boy," he said.

SUNDANCE

One

"The general is expecting you," the sergeant of the guard told Sundance. "I'll show you how to get there."

Sundance nodded. As they walked across the parade ground early in the morning, the sergeant, a big Irish bruiser, looked sideways at the tall, copper-skinned halfbreed with the shoulder-length yellow hair. The sergeant had fought in many campaigns, but he had never seen a man like Sundance. Few men had, but even to those who had never heard much more than his name he was a legend. And General George Crook, known to the Indians as "Three Stars," was his closest friend. Now Crook wanted something—and Sundance came without question.

The door closed and they shook hands. "This is a dadblasted way to say hello," Crook said. "It's my nephew. Maybe you've heard me speak of the boy. Son of Everett Randolph. Senator Randolph, God help us."

"I know your nephew's in the army," Sundance said.

"The same army I'm in," Crook said. "And if I don't do something about him there's going to be an awful lot of trouble. You won't like what you're going to hear."

"I'll let you know," Sundance said.

Crook lit a cigar and sent pungent blue smoke spiraling toward the ceiling. Three Stars was getting old, Sundance thought. He was still ramrod straight but the years of hard fighting and even harder command were etched in the lines of his face.

"I'm caught between a rock and a hard place," Crook said. "I'm not saying the boy, if you can still call him a boy at twenty-eight, shouldn't be in the army. I think he has the makings of a good soldier. That father of his is mostly to blame. Randolph was a politician before the Civil War made him a hero and he's never stopped being one. Hero my foot! Randolph was there with his volunteers when the Rebels were retreating. Half starved without food, shoes, ammunition. They'd probably have surrendered if he'd given them a chance. They were outnumbered five to one and Randolph cut them down. Claimed later they were massing for a counterattack and he saved the day. That's how the newspapers wrote it, that's what the history books say now.

"But getting back to the boy. I don't know that he ever wanted to be a soldier. Maybe he did. Maybe he liked the glory part of it, being a boy. So his father got one of his paid-for Congressmen to get the boy into West Point. It was none of my business; I kept out of it. Nothing I could have done anyway, not without everybody getting mad at me. At the Point that boy got into one scrape after another."

"I've heard some talk of him," Sundance said.

"Some is right," Crook growled. "Not the half of it though. Young Ethan played hob with all the rules. Drinking, gambling, absent without leave. The funny thing, he was pretty good at soldiering when he put his mind to it. That was his trouble. He wanted to be a great

178

soldier without following the rules. Admired George Custer, that mad fool. Studied German war manuals when he was supposed to be boning up on the French. Showed good sense there—in a few years those Prussians are going to trample Europe underfoot—but it's not for a cadet to buck the rules. You do that after you graduate."

Sundance smiled. "Like you, Three Stars."

"I buck the rules just so far," Crook said. "After that I follow orders. That's how it works, how it's supposed to. That's something the Point didn't teach Ethan. Anybody else, they'd have booted him clear out the front gate. It's happened to better soldiers than he'll ever be. It never happened because Randolph was always there to let them know what a big man he was in Washington. High up in the Democrat Party, chairman of the Military Appropriations Committee. The closest Ethan ever got to the gate was when he wounded some woman's husband in a duel. It took all the wires Randolph could pull to get the boy out of that one. The husband got a wad of money and told the commandant he got drunk and thought the boy was another officer."

"That story still gets told in the army posts," Sundance said. "I heard it two different ways but it's the same story."

"Like his hero, Ethan squeezed through," Crook said. "I didn't attend the graduation. The boy's mother —that's my sister Lizzie—was good and mad at me for not showing up. I couldn't be a party to it. Besides, I was busy fighting Indians on the North Platte. You'd know about that."

Sundance remembered the North Platte, one of the toughest campaigns the Indian-fighting army ever went through. He had been Crook's chief scout then, as he was to be in several other wars on the frontier.

179

"Well, sir, I thought maybe he'd find his way after he left the Point," Crook went on. "No such thing. If I had anything to say about it, which I didn't, I would have sent Ethan to some quiet garrison in settled country. Nebraska. Oregon. But not the South and not the West. What did they do? They went him to Georgia. Got into trouble there and Randolph got him transferred to the War Department as an aide to General MacPherson. I don't exactly know what he was supposed to do there. Guess he didn't either. There he was, still wet behind the ears, going to parties and balls, mixing with all the high mucky-mucks. The next trouble he got into Randolph couldn't fix that easy. Another duel, this time with a foreigner, some Frenchman, a French major attached to their embassy."

"That one got into the papers," Sundance said.

"You're dadblasted right it did," Crook said. "Ethan and the Frenchman got into a row at some party and Ethan threw the Franco-Prussian War in the foreigner's face. Said the Prussians taught them what real soldiering meant. The Frenchman slapped his face or some such nonsense and they had it out at dawn by the river. The Frenchman put a hole in Ethan with his rapier. The Republican papers got a hold of it, and after Ethan got out of the hospital he was posted to Nevada. This time Randolph had enough sense to hold his tongue, in public anyway. There was hell at home, a fierce fight between son and father. Randolph warned the boy to behave or he was through with him. He said he was going to make a general out of the boy if he had to kill him to do it.

"For a while there wasn't much heard of Ethan. I knew where he was, but that's all. It looked like he was trying hard. In his own way though, not the army's. There was some Indian trouble out where he was, nothing very big. Ethan saw it as a major campaign. He went against orders, fought Indians when he didn't have to, talked back to the garrison commander. He was most of the way to a court-martial when he got lucky. Major Bradshaw, he was in command, confined Ethan to the post while he went out to try to make peace with the renegades. Their leader was Running Charlie, the halfbreed, as treacherous a man as ever lived, told the Major, 'All right, we'll sit down to a peace talk.' ''

Sundance remembered part of it. ''Was Ethan the young first lieutenant who saved the peace party from being massacred?''

''Lucky like his father,'' Crook said sourly. ''Bradshaw was a good man but too trusting. Maybe he knew Charlie for the sneak he was but wanted to end the war. What he didn't know was that Charlie and his peace-talkers were all carrying hidden guns. Small pistols. In walked Bradshaw armed with nothing but an empty holster and a lot of good faith. If Ethan hadn't disobeyed orders and led men out to the peace talk they would all have been dead. Bradshaw got killed as it was. Charlie shot him. Ethan and his men were creeping up on them when the first shot was fired. Bradshaw. Ethan wounded Charlie and scattered his men. The army hanged Charlie and Ethan became a hero. Bradshaw was dead and nothing was said about the boy being confined to post. That's how he got to be captain.''

''At least he killed Running Charlie,'' Sundance said.

''Charlie was just a thief and a murderer,'' Crook said. ''The newspapers carried on as if Ethan had captured Geronimo singlehanded. Army men knew the truth of it but kept quiet about it. Randolph makes a bad enemy, especially for an army man. After he got to be captain, pushed to the top of the list and promoted to captain, Ethan started behaving like a real soldier. His

181

idea of a real soldier. You'd think he never took a drink or played a game of poker in his life. I guess that's what's wrong with Ethan. He never does anything by halves. After he got to be captain he made a complete about-face. Maybe he knew that he wasn't any kind of a real hero—Running Charlie was a mangy dog—so he decided he was going to square things with himself. I'm all for that if a man does it right. Takes stock of what he is and doesn't like it and goes on from there.

"They transferred him to the Dakotas," Crook said, "and managed to get a nice little Indian war going. After the whipping the Sioux got for killing Custer they'd been keeping quiet for years. Some trouble, not much. Horse-stealing, a few killings. A sensible officer would have handled it with a few men. Now don't you forget that Ethan was still just a new captain. He had plenty of officers over him. That didn't stop him. The usual insubordination, with Randolph backing him up, not that Ethan would ever admit to such a thing. He was his own man now, so he thought. But luck stayed with him. He got a war started, then stopped it. The Sioux had some of their land taken, and that suited the politicians fine."

Sundance nodded. To the politicians an Indian war didn't mean a damn thing if it meant more stolen land, more money in their pockets. Every time the Indians lost a war started by the whites they were boxed in tighter. And then there was another war, and so it went.

"It doesn't take much to beat the Sioux these days," Sundance said. "A few companies of volunteers wouldn't find it that hard. I don't see much glory in it."

"What about Victorio? You think he'd be hard to beat?"

Suddenly Sundance knew what Crook was getting at. "I didn't know the Apaches were at war."

"They will be if Ethan has anything to do with it. That's right, he's been promoted to major and is being posted to Fort McHenry. He'll be in command there. The garrison there doesn't rate a colonel, so Ethan will be top dog. He's a few years older now, but I don't see that he's changed. I know what you're thinking. You're wrong. I have no say outside my own department of the army. The way some people see it, some of them officers, Ethan has proved himself to be a good soldier. If killing Indians is all it takes, then I guess he's a good soldier."

Sundance said quietly, "Victorio will play hell if a war gets started. He's tougher than Geronimo and smarter and when he says he wants peace he means it. He wants it because he knows he can't win in the end. He'd wash Arizona Territory in blood if he thought he had a chance of winning."

Crook nodded. "Or if he had no other choice. Victorio isn't like the others. Years back, before Custer finally got what he was asking for, there was big talk of uniting all the tribes to fight one great war. All the tribes from Canada clear into Mexico would band together and rise up. That's nonsense talk. Some tribes hate other tribes worse than they do the whites. But some chiefs believed it could be done, so the medicine men went from tribe to tribe talking war. Some of them got as far as Arizona and talked their big medicine to Victorio. You know what he said? Of course you know what he said."

"More or less," Sundance said. "He said the Indians could never win, not even if they had all the men, horses and guns on earth."

"What else did he say?"

"He said he had made peace with the whites and would keep the peace as long as they did. Nothing small

183

would break it, he said. He said he would hang his own men if they broke it, if they were in the wrong when they broke. But he also said if he had to go to war it would be for the last time. This would be the last Apache war and there would be no surrender until every Apache was dead."

Crook bit the end off another cigar and put a match to it. He threw the match in an empty tomato can. "That's what I'm talking about. A war the likes of which the Southwest has never seen. Doesn't seem likely that one young officer could be the cause of a war like that. That's the pity of it, that's all it takes—one man. If I were in command of that department I'd ship Ethan back to Washington to fight duels with more Frenchmen. But there's not a blamed thing I can do. The men you can talk to in Washington are mostly gone. Sherman's gone. If they had Sherman still running the army I'd say, 'Now look here, Bill,' and you bet he'd listen. Even Phil Sheridan, hard as he hated the Indians, would listen. Phil's gone too."

"I can't think how much worse it could be," Sundance said. "Victorio means what he says. He always has."

"The Apaches are the worst of all," Crook said, "meaning they're the best. The bravest and the meanest. They don't fight like other Indians, think like other Indians. They've been fighting the Spanish and later the Mexicans for hundreds of years. No better fighting man ever lived than the Apache. You'll see real bloodshed if Victorio tears loose."

"He never did give up all his guns when he came in and made the peace," Sundance said. "You know that as well as I do. He's got them safe in caves in Mexico. That's where he'll fight from, the Mexican mountains. The Mexicans won't be able to handle it. The last time

Victorio fought a war he made peace with the Mexicans, something no other Apache leader ever thought to do. No more raiding and killing south of the border. Victorio kept his word and the Mexicans let him be."

Crook got up and paced the floor with his hands clasped behind his back. "The Mexicans, some of them, would be tickled to death to see Victorio making war on our side of the border. Provided they aren't mixed up in it. Could be they'll even give him some guns to make it that much hotter for Uncle Sam. They won't think that someday he might use their own guns against them. My God! I'm thinking of all those people down there who don't know what they're facing if . . ."

Sundance knew that his old friend was holding back from the main question. So he made it easy for Crook.

"What do you want me to do, Three Stars?" he asked.

"I hardly got the right to ask you," Crook said. "Ethan's part of my own family, my only sister's only son. It should be for me to straighten this out."

"You don't usually beat about the bush, Three Stars," Sundance said, smiling.

Crook threw away his half-smoked cigar. "I want you to go down there," he said. "Say no if you want and I won't blame you. I don't know what you can do. The officer Ethan's taking over from is retiring. Major Haskell. He's taking his chief scout with him."

"You mean Ike Greenwood?"

"That's the one. Old Ike. Haskell's going back home to Ohio. Ike's going to work for him. So they'll be needing a new chief scout. I can't do anything about Ethan but I can get you hired on as top scout. Ethan won't know that you've talked to me. I don't rightly know what you can do. But something has to be done. Do what you can, Jim, short of killing him."

Crook stopped to look at Sundance. "You've done a lot of things for me. Now I'm asking you to do something that no man can do—stop an Indian war!"

Two

Sundance knew he was being watched. The feeling was unmistakable, as strong and as solid as the big stallion under him. In front of him, as far as the eye could reach, was the desert dotted with mesquite, sage and greasewood, and beyond the desert were mountain ranges, and on the far side of the mountains the desert went on again.

There was nothing to see, but he knew they were there. The day before he had made good time between Sacatone and Bluewater Wells. A few hours of night travel took him to the Pecacho River, now dry, and a little past there he made dry camp until morning. The forty-five miles between the Pecacho and the Gila was hard country, gravelly desert covered with scrubby mesquite and cactus.

He knew they were there as soon as morning light pushed back the purple of the night sky. The feeling came suddenly and with no explanation, as it always did. It hadn't been there the night before, but now it was. It wasn't an animal because there was nothing in the desert strong enough to attack a man. In the mountains a man might come to be attacked by a hunger-crazed or rabid cougar; here in the desert the only enemy, apart from death by thirst, was another man.

This was the hottest time of the year and a furnace

wind swept across the desert. Now and then he saw the bones of man or animal, polished by the ever-blowing sand, bleached by the relentless sun. In the dry river-beds there was no water and along the dry banks grew cottonwoods and greasewood and far ahead was a mirage, a long silver lake with big birds rising from it. Beyond the lake was a mountain with spires and towers like a castle and as he rode closer the lake and the castle disappeared.

It could be anything: Indians, renegades, bandits from below the border. The feeling told him they were there, and that was all he knew. They knew what they were doing, for there was no movement in all the vast silence of the desert except wind-stirred sand, and kites sailing high in the sky. A lizard ran away and the sun was very hot and the sky was a clear, bitter blue; so blue that it looked cold in spite of the sun.

They hadn't come at him in the night, but they knew he was there, or they wouldn't have been there in the morning. He guessed Indians but it had to remain a guess for now. They could be men of any kind, for this country was a haven for killers and scavengers from as far away as Montana. But still he figured Indians.

A man with a good rifle could knock him out of the saddle at any time; a good rifle and a good eye and the luck you always needed to make a long shot. Few Indians had the rifles or the skill. He looked without seeming to; there was nothing to see. It went on like that for hours and he kept going because there was nothing else to do. Another day would take him to Fort McHenry, if he stayed alive.

Late in the afternoon he crossed a dry creek at the bottom of a mesa and went through a dense thicket of mesquite and ocochilla, and there they were. Right in front of him and on both sides, maybe eighteen or twenty Apaches, silent, waiting. He kept coming until one of them held up his hand. This Indian was dressed in a faded blue shirt, with a strip of cloth wound around his hips and between his legs and tied behind. Around his fierce black eyes were circles of yellow paint, and blue streaks ran down his face. Like the others, and like Sundance, he was coated with the fine gypsum dust of the desert. The stock of the long-barreled Winchester rifle in his hand was decorated with copper studs. They all had rifles of one kind or another. A few carried pistols. Sundance heard other Apaches coming in behind him.

He greeted the leader with the formality of a man who is not an enemy and not a friend.

"*Yo quiero que usted hable Americano*," the Apache said. "I want you to speak American. You have come into our country, but we do not know you."

Sundance remained formal even in English. The Apaches weren't at war. He had Crook's word on that, but it had been a week since he had seen Crook. A lot could happen in a week, and even if the Apaches were at peace, there were renegade braves always ready to do a little killing and stealing on the sly.

The smell of the Apaches was strong on the wind. Hair grease, sweat, glistening paint. They were light and wiry like their ponies. "I am on my way to Fort McHenry," Sundance. "I would go there in peace."

The Apache's black eyes took in Sundance's weapons belt, the long-barreled Colt. 44, the thick-bladed Bowie knife, the straight-handled throwing hatchet. He grunted. "You are what?"

Sundance told the Apache who he was and when the Apache repeated "You are what?" he said that his mother had been of the Cheyenne, his father a white man. "I am what you see," he said. "A halfbreed."

Sundance knew the Cheyenne meant nothing to the Apache. The Cheyenne were too far north: Indians so unknown to the Apaches that they might have lived on another continent. A man with a Pima or a Maricopa mother would have been killed without mercy.

"You are the new chief scout," the Apache said. "The old one has gone with the old major and you have come to take his place."

It was polite to show surprise, though Sundance felt none. The Apaches had eyes and ears everywhere and few things happened in a military post that they didn't know about. Every Indian was a spy, from the Hooker girls who sold themselves to the enlisted men to the old women who washed their dirty undershirts.

"You know many things . . ." Sundance said, waiting for the Apache to say who he was.

"I am Domingo," the Apache said as if someone were listening, though he kept his eyes fixed on Sundance. Sundance's heel touched Eagle and the big horse turned slightly. A tall figure stood high on a rock, outlined against the darkening sky, and even at a distance Sundance sensed the power and dignity of the man. In an instant the figure was gone. It didn't move away or duck out of sight. One moment it was there, the next it wasn't. Victorio! It had to be.

There was sudden anger in Domingo's wide, brown face. He was an arrogant man, and maybe a stupid one as well, and he was angry because he wasn't talking for himself. Sundance hastened to assure him of his importance, for Apaches were as touchy as women. He would be just as arrogant if he had to be; first he would try it the easy way; once an Apache felt insulted he would carry the grudge to the end of his life—or yours.

"I have heard many things of you," Sundance said gravely. "Who has not heard of Domingo? Domingo

190

killed many men at the Battle of Maricopa Wells when the Yumas sought to break the power of the Apache."

Domingo nodded. "Two hundred Yumas died that day. It was a great victory for the Apache."

Sundance nodded too. The number of dead Yumas was more like seventy-five. The so-called Battle of Maricopa was one of the strangest fights in the history of all the tribal wars. The Yumas and the Apaches had fought it out in front of a stagecoach station with the white agent and his family looking on. No one fired a shot at the whites.

"Indeed a great victory," Sundance said. "It is getting dark and I still have a long way to go. You would like me to bring your words to the fort?"

Domingo spoke slowly. "There is a message—a warning—but it is for you. Your name is Sundance and you are known to my people. You fought us in Diablo Canyon in Sonora. General Three Stars would not have found the caves there if it had not been for you. Because of you our people were driven out with cannon fire. Those who would not surrender were hunted and killed like animals. You think I do not speak the truth?"

"There was a fight and the Apache lost," Sundance said. It was time to stop being so polite. Talking to Apaches was like walking a tightrope. You couldn't go too fast or too slow. But it didn't matter much if they decided to kill you.

"You say it was a fight?" Domingo said, eyes glittering with sudden rage. The horses stirred as Domingo's anger spread among the braves.

Sundance knew a wrong word could get him killed. It didn't have to be a hard word. It just had to be wrong. "Does a man whine when another man beats him at war?" Sundance said, balancing caution against plain speaking. "Three Stars did what the Apache did to the

191

Yumas at Maricopa Wells. He caught you in a trap. You think I do not speak the truth?"

Domingo's eyes were bright with remembered hate. "Some day we may talk of this again. But now is now. It has been said that you come to this country because the whites plan to make war on the Apache. It has been said that the new major has sent for you because you are a killer of Apaches and know their country and their ways. We have kept the peace but how long can it last. The whites will not keep their word. What white man has ever kept his word?"

"Has Three Stars kept his word?" Sundance asked.

"When he was in this country he kept it," Domingo said, not wanting to say it but having to say it because he knew it was the truth. "Now he is not here and his word means nothing. If the whites break the peace, will Three Stars not come again to kill us with his cannon? Right or wring, will he not kill us? Try to kill us."

"Three Stars isn't here. There is no war."

"You bring war. Killing is how you live. You take the white man's money and you kill for him. You kill for him or help him to kill. It is all one."

Sundance said quietly, "The only money I'm going to get will be as chief scout. You are the one who talks of war. Does Victorio talk of war as you do?"

"You will go back," Domingo said. "You will not stay in this country to betray the Apache. Turn your horse and go back. I see nothing but death if you go to Fort McHenry. Go now!"

Sundance looked into the muzzle of Domingo's rifle; all around him other rifles were cocked. The wind blew sand against the legs of the horses. If he turned they might still shoot him to bits in a sudden wild outburst of hate. They had so many reasons for their hate. Women and children had died in the caves at Diablo Canyon.

Some had died of starvation, entombed behind thousands of tons of rockslides brought down by the cannon fire.

"Go back!" Domingo repeated. "Go back or die!"

"No," Sundance said. He didn't tell Domingo that he could kill him before the others got off a shot. It wouldn't buy him a thing. Domingo might not be ready to die but he would have to die because his life as an Apache would end if he didn't throw back the challenge.

"I am going to Fort McHenry," Sundance said. "You know you can kill me anytime you want. Then I'll be dead and the peace will be broken. If you break it, it will be broken for a long time. You will be dead. All the men with you now will be dead. In all your villages there will be nothing but starvation and death. You have the rifle. Kill me. Kill me and you will be a great and famous man. Not because you killed me but because you broke the peace. You will be great and famous for a time. A very short time. Then men will spit when they hear your name."

Domingo moved the rifle so the muzzle was pointing directly at Sundance's heart. "You are a talking dead man," he said. Suddenly he looked up and so did Sundance, but there was nothing to see. Then he lowered the rifle, wanting to kill more than he wanted to live, and he had to fight hard to overcome the madness in his eyes. Sundance knew that he had made an enemy for life. The other braves muttered angrily; the Apaches had been killing for so long that it came as naturally as breathing. Sundance spoke to Eagle and the big stallion started through the wall of men and animals. The Indian ponies were uneasy with the big stallion so close and they moved restlessly under their riders. Rifles were cocked and pointing.

193

Domingo gave the order to let him through and they obeyed, but they jeered and spat at him, poking at him without touching him. He knew he wasn't out of it yet. If one brave let a hammer slip, even by accident, every rifle there would cut loose. Some of the braves followed him, still jeering and spitting, until an order from Domingo brought them back. Sundance didn't look up at the rock, but he knew Victorio was watching. He had been tested and he had come through it without giving anything away. At least one thing had been established and that was that Victorio still had his warriors under control. But there was anger in them that went beyond the usual sullen hatred for the whites. If trouble came, Domingo would be the one to make it. Domingo and Major Ethan Randolph were the ones to start a war. Maybe not. It could start with a jittery, desert-crazy trooper or an Apache boy with a head sick from rotgut whiskey. A new game they had in Mexico could be the cause of it. On some of the ranchos they had pits into which they threw captured Apaches and half-starved Boston Bull terriers. The Indians were starved too. If they lived through the fight, armed only with a short club, they got to eat a dead dog. If they didn't, the dogs ate them. It was said that the Mexican sportsmen were running out of Apaches. Always it had to be an Apache: other Indians didn't fight half so well.

It was dark by the time he reached the end of a long high mesa and made camp in a scatter of rocks. The feeling of being watched was no longer there. After it got dark the night creatures of the desert came out, no longer threatened by the sun. Dead wood crackled and sparked on the fire, the tiny explosions brightening the darkness for an instant. He built up the fire before he rolled up in his blankets.

Three

Sundance reached Fort McHenry early in the morning and from far out he heard a bugle brassing and saw the flag going up in the wind still cold at that hour. The fort stood on a rock bluff high above a river that had water in it at certain times of the year. There was no water now and wouldn't be for many months; maybe there never would be again or at least for a very long time, because the course of the river was less predictable than the wind. And when there was water it flowed into the Ninety Mile Desert and disappeared in the sand.

This was Fort McHenry, the end of the line. This was where civilization absolutely and finally came to a stop. To the west was the Ninety Mile Desert, a blistering hell where the wind blew sand even at night and enough men had died to muster an army of ghosts. South of it lay the mountains and Mexico, dry as hardtack, where men lived who had never seen rain; where the idea of mercy was so impractical that the word for it had almost no meaning. To The People, the Apaches' name for themselves, the area was familiar as a cramped forty-acre farm was to a Yankee farmer.

A scatter of houses along the bank of the dry river looked listless in the sun and a road went past the houses and up to the fort. There was a trading post and a saloon; the other houses were adobe, the newer ones unpainted wood. Dogs barked and smoke curled up from the chimneys of the houses. A boy was driving goats and got splashed by a pail of water thrown from a door by a fat Mexican woman.

Sundance rode up the hill to the fort. There were guard towers on the four corners of the fort and a watch tower, higher than anything else, set back from the main gate. The watch tower was reached by a long ladder bolted to the criss-crossed timbers that supported it. Inside the fort assembly was over and the men had been dismissed. Sundance told the guard corporal that he had business with Major Randolph and was passed on through.

It looked like any other frontier post, dry and dusty, waiting for an attack that might never come. The officers' quarters lay to one side of the gate, a long, low building, two-storeyed with wide verandahs. An enlisted man in canvas stable clothes was watering a row of wilted flowers in front of it. A little girl with yellow curls and a blue dress came out onto the top gallery and stared at Sundance. The enlisted man drank from the watering can and went back to his work. A strong smell of horses and manure came from the stables.

The duty room was in a new frame building with a wide porch and steps in front. Behind a scrubbed table on iron trestles the company sergeant sat writing laboriously with a short steel pen. A very young lieutenant was drinking coffee behind another table. The lieutenant's light skin was badly sunburned and white sun blisters sprouted at the corners of his mouth. He looked as though he needed more sleep.

Sundance stated his business and the sergeant grunted and knocked on a door behind him. He went in and came out. "The Major will see you," he said. As Sundance went in, he heard the young lieutenant saying to the sergeant, "Well I'll be damned. Is that what he looks like?"

Major Ethan Randolph knew Sundance was there, but he kept on writing. His pen raced over a long sheet of foolscap as if he had to finish the page in so many minutes or get shot. For a while the only sound in the bare, clean room was the steel nib scratching its way to the bottom of the page. There was a chair and Sundance sat in it without waiting to be asked. Major Randolph frowned but kept on writing.

Sundance looked at an engraving of Abe Lincoln. Three Stars always said Honest Abe was the foxiest politician of them all. Three Stars hadn't liked Abe because he liked dirty stories and laughed at them in a high-pitched giggle. Three Stars always said that Abe did as much as any man to start the Civil War . . . .

Major Randolph signed his name with a flourish and waved the paper dry. Without looking up, he said, "You will stand at attention, Sundance!"

Sundance didn't move. He had seen newspaper pictures of Major Randolph's father. The Major looked just like his father, thinner than his father and thirty years younger, but somehow the same. He had the same heavy jaw and bulldog mouth and when he looked up his eyes were blank and cold like the old man's.

"I'm not in the army, Major," Sundance said quietly. Major Randolph was the kind of man who pushed other men when he didn't have to; kept on testing them when there was no need, and maybe he had been reading too many books about the Prussians and the force of will. Here and now was the time to set him straight.

"You're in my army," Major Randolph said. "You're not working for the War Department. You're working for me. I know the regulations better than you do. You're a civilian employee of the army and I can't force you to stand at attention if you don't want to. I thought you might do it out of respect for my rank."

"Yes sir," Sundance said, standing up, coming to attention. He knew how to do it and felt like a fool. The Major snapped a salute at him and told him to sit down. He handed over his papers and the Major pretended to read them.

"I see you were recommended by my uncle, General Crook," Randolph said.

"When I applied for the job I gave his name," Sundance lied. "I also gave the names of Colonel McKenzie and Colonel Brady."

Randolph held the ninety-day contract while Sundance signed it. He was in the army now, sort of, for three months. They couldn't shoot him for desertion but a Territorial court could send him to the hellhole prison at Yuma. They could send him there if the army wanted to be formal about it. Army scouts who gave too much trouble had been known to catch a stray bullet in the back of the head.

"How is the General?" Randolph asked, signing the contract as agent for the War Department.

"Everybody says he's looking very well, sir," Sundance answered. "I served with him in Mexico, earlier on the Platte."

Randolph gave one copy of the service contract to Sundance. "I know that," he said. "I know all about you and what I don't know I am going to find out. You should have come to attention when ordered. It would have been so easy to do that, but you didn't."

"Yes sir," Sundance said. Randolph was a big man and when he got older he would be heavy like his father. Now, just under thrity, he was as big as an Irish city-policeman and though his blue tunic was well tailored the cloth strained across the chest and shoulders when he moved in his chair. His big hard red hands were tufted with hair and the calluses on his knuckles hadn't been put there by hard work. The Major looked like one of those sporting Eastern-bred officers who liked to punch sacks of sand and run around in crew-neck sweaters before breakfast. Sundance was ready to bet that the Major knew a few things about the art of fisti-cuffs and the Marquis of Queensberry Rules. The only trouble was, the Apaches didn't fight fair.

"You're not in the army but I am going to repeat what I have already told my officers," Randolph said. "The officer before me had his own way of running this garrison and I have mine. My way will be different, very different. To me, the army is always at war. To me, peace simply means that the shooting has stopped for a time. War will come again. It always does."

"But there is a peace," Sundance said.

"Peace doesn't always mean the same thing, Sundance. To a soldier peace must mean complete con-quest of the enemy. The enemy must be broken and disarmed. This has not happened here. The Apaches have kept their weapons. They are as warlike as ever, more so, I am certain. All peace means to them is time to get more rifles, more time to play their next war. And while I say that, I respect them for their intelligence, their cunning, if you like. Above all, their bravery. All of which makes them deadly enemies."

Sundance knew that the Major wanted the Apaches to be all he said they were. For there was no glory in winning victories over mere breechclouted savages. Dog-eating aborigines who screamed at their likeness in a mirror.

"I agree, sir," Sundance said. "You have just given all the reasons why the peace must be kept at any cost.

Victorio is chief of the Apaches now. He is different from the others."

Major Randolph gave Sundance a thin, tolerant smile, the smile of an experienced man talking to a fool. "The only difference is he's smarter, and that makes him even more dangerous. Be that as it may, this post is going to remain on a war footing at all times. The men have grown careless in attitude and appearance. There is no fighting spirit here, sir, and by God I am going to change all that. There will be drill and then more drill. I don't give a Goddamn if a man has been a soldier for ten days or ten years. One and all, they will make themselves into what I think a soldier should be. They will do it or by the Great Harry, sir, I will do it. Do I make myself clear?"

"Very clear, sir," Sundance said, knowing that the Major was talking to hear himself talk. Drilling and such matters had nothing to do with a chief scout. A scout scouted and hunted for meat, among other things. As long as he did his job he could dress in rags and wear a beard down to his belly button, and some of the best ones did.

The Major picked up a book and slammed it down so hard a trickle of ink ran down the side of the inkwell. "That's Casey's *Infantry Tactics*, sir. That, sir, is my Good Book, my Bible, and this, sir, is Mr. Hardee's manual of arms."

Major Randolph threw down the third book, Cooper's *Instructions and Regulations*. "Those three books, sir, contain more than any enlisted man or junior officer needs to know. Do you want me to read you what Cooper says about the duties of chief scouts?"

"I know what he says, sir," Sundance said. He was getting sick of the Major and his lecture. He wanted to look around the fort.

Major Randolph bristled. "Do you now? No matter. You will take your orders from me. You will hold yourself available at all times, but first you will scout for signs of the Apaches. Not the ones we see, the ones we don't."

"I've already seen them, sir," Sundance said. "I ran into a subchief called Domingo and a bunch of braves on my way here. I just said hello and rode on through. They looked friendly enough."

"But they stopped you? They interfered with an employee of the United States War Department? I take that as provocation, sir."

"Nothing like that," Sundance lied. "Nothing much happened. I was a stranger and they were curious. Anyway, I wasn't working for the army at the time. I just signed on."

"A technicality," the Major said, wanting to make more out of it and not knowing how. "What did this Domingo have to say?"

"He warned me to keep the peace."

"You mean he warned me? You have no authority to do anything."

"In a manner of speaking that's what he did, Major. He said he hoped you would see the peace wasn't broken."

"The insolent bastard! It's just as I was saying. These Goddamned civilians are responsible for letting the Apaches run wild when they should be disarmed and put away on some island. That's what General Miles wants to do with the heathens and I agree completely. General Miles can't do it or he'd have those blasted Boston women after his scalp."

"Nothing happened, Major," Sundance said. "Nobody threatened me."

"I still take it as an affront," the Major said. "You

can take it any way you like. Before I get through with the Apaches they won't even dare to speak to a white . . . to an American citizen."

"I guess I'm a citizen," Sundance said, thinking he'd like to give the Major a chance to show how good he was with his fists. "I was born in Wyoming. Does that make me a citizen, sir?"

Major Randolph's face got very red. "Damn your impertinence! I didn't ask for you but you're here. I know who you are and what you've done in the past. Try your tricks here and you'll find yourself in Yuma Prison. You wouldn't like it there. You can go in for five years and end up spending the rest of your life."

Sundance stood up. No man, red or white or any color, talked to him like that. Then he thought of Three Stars and the good friend he had been for so many years. After the murder of his parents, grief and hate and whiskey had driven him so close to death that it hardly made any difference. All that lay ahead of him was a life as a killer and an outlaw. Three Stars had changed that, bullied and threatened him back to sanity. And so he didn't beat Crook's nephew until he bled.

"Yes, sir," Sundance said. "Will that be all, sir?"

"That will not be all," the Major said. "You will scout this entire area for a radius of fifty miles and report back to me. If you have reason to believe the Apaches are preparing for war do not pursue them. Report your findings to me. Is that clear?"

"Yes, sir," Sundance said.

"Very well." The Major nodded. "That's all. Sergeant Comiskey will show you your quarters."

The duty sergeant told Sundance where he could find Comiskey and the young lieutenant followed him out.

"My name is Gates," he said, holding out his hand.

Sundance took Gates's hand and let it drop. "Nice to know you," he said.

"Everybody's heard of you," Gates said.

Sundance didn't much like the man, but he wasn't there to make enemies. "Don't start that," he said.

Gates laughed. "Don't bother with Sergeant Comiskey. I know where you're supposed to go. I'll walk along with you."

"Obliged to you," Sundance said. Men on work details stared at them. Up on the bluff there was more wind than on the flat; it was just as hot. The flag that had fluttered earlier now drooped between puffs of wind.

"Did you really do all those things?" Gates said, still West Point straight in his blue uniform.

"If I say yes will you drop it?" Sundance asked.

"I guess you did at that," Gates said. He asked Sundance how he liked the new major.

"All right," Sundance answered, his dislike of the lieutenant growing stronger. It wasn't his place to bad-mouth the Major; taking sides in an isolated army post was the worst thing a man could do. Anyway, he had nothing personal against the Major, and maybe he wasn't as much of a fool as he seemed to be. He talked like a fool; still, there was something straight behind the bluster. Three Stars had sensed it, and now so did he. With Gates it was different; as the man said, he saw nothing behind the front he presented to the world. He smiled too much and it didn't come from good nature.

"You don't have to be so careful with me," Gates said. "I won't run and tell the Major. I don't tell the Major any more than I have to. You served with his uncle, didn't you?"

"On and off I did."

203

"Now there's a real soldier. No drill books and saluting for Old George. I once saw a picture of Old George on one of his Indian campaigns," Gates said. "Wearing an old round hat and a miner's coat. Is it true he always uses a shotgun instead of a pistol?"

"The General favors a 10-gauge Greener," Sundance said.

"You mean a sawed-off?"

"A medium-length barrel. Short enough to carry but long enough to carry a distance."

"I'll be damned," Gates said, full of admiration for a man he didn't know. "You'll never see the young Napoleon in there carrying anything but the regulation forty-five."

"It kills just as well," Sundance said. "Maybe he doesn't like shotguns."

Gates said, "There's nothing he likes much but the thought of being the youngest general in the United States Army."

Sundance said, "Custer beat him there. He got to be a brigadier at twenty-three."

Gates laughed. "That doesn't count. That was in the war and they broke Custer back to colonel when it was over. You ever hear of a peacetime officer making brigadier before thirty-five?"

"Never have," Sundance. "Never heard of one less than forty, more than forty, most cases."

"Young Napoleon swears he's going to make general before he's thirty-five," Gates said. "Maybe I ought to stop calling him young Napoleon. Young Bismarck is what he wants to be. I guess it's hard wanting to be a great warrior when you have nothing better to fight than Apaches."

They reached the chief scout's quarters, a small frame house set by itself not far from the stables. The smell of the stables suited Sundance fine. The stables beat the row of latrines behind the enlisted men's diggings. Somebody had left the door open and the floor inside the first of two small rooms was inches deep in fine sand; on a table stood an empty whiskey bottle and a deck of greasy cards.

"Home Sweet Home," Gates said, smiling at nothing. "The man before you wasn't much of a house-keeper, it looks like. Or maybe he figured you'd want to fix it up your own way."

Sundance wished to hell Gates would go away; there was no easy way to tell him. There wasn't much to fix up. The skillet on the cookstove was dusty but clean and there were rows of canned goods on a shelf. An old rifle crate was filled with stove-length chunks of seasoned wood. In the other room an iron bed was pushed against the rough-planed boards of the walls. A new mattress and army blankets were on the floor. It was all right.

Gates was careful not to get any dust on his uniform. "There's a saloon below in the town, so-called," he said. "Young Bismarck hasn't closed it down yet. Maybe we can have a few drinks in the back room tonight, one of these nights."

"Maybe," Sundance said agreeably. He picked up a worn broom and started to raise a cloud of dust and Gates got out fast. When he was gone Sundance threw away the broom and took Eagle to the stables, then grained and watered the big animal. The big stallion whinnied at the confinement of the stables, the presence of so many horses. "Don't fret, boy," Sundance said. "We won't be around here all that much."

When he got back to the house a big man was playing solitaire at the table.

"Step right in," he said. "I'm Sergeant Comiskey."

Four

"That's my true name," Comiskey said in a city accent that Sundance guessed to be New York. "And I'll tell you something else that's just as true. Which is that I'm the toughest mug that ever come out of the Five Points. No man ever stood up to me that didn't get stomped."

"Except officers," Sundance said.

That puzzled Comiskey for a moment. "We wasn't talking about officers," he said. "Don't be putting me off my train of thought, if you don't mind. Course you don't. I'd mind it if you minded, get me?"

"What am I supposed to get?" Sundance said.

Comiskey was wide as a door and just as hard; his little blue eyes were pig's eyes, even to the color, and they glared out at the world with goodnatured hostility. He was about forty, and Sundance guessed that more than half his life had been spent in the army. Even sitting down he swaggered, a born bully, his fists his only defense against ridicule. There was more animal than man in Comiskey. It showed in his eyes and the ferocious thrust of his heavy jaw. He was all face and no brain: stupid and dangerous, but with the cunning of an animal.

"Take the wax out of your ears and listen to what I'm saying," he said, sweeping the cards off the heavy with a hairy paw. "You're new here so you don't know who I am. So I'll tell you the one more time. My name, mister, is Sergeant Jake Comiskey, and I run this post like I run every post I ever been in. I'm new here too, but I've made my mark, and not in a manner of speaking. For your information, mister, I come here with the new Major. The Major and me is pals, if you know what I mean."

"You're pals with the Major," Sundance said. He would have to decide what to do with Comiskey. He would give it a few more minutes.

"You got it right. Good boy!" Comiskey said. "I like a man that's quick on the uptake. To continue now. Me and the Major has been all over, up north, the Dakotas, all kind of places. We get along just fine. Nobody bothers the Major and nobody bothers me, get me? I run a nice post for the Major, see that everything is just so, if you get my drift. Course you do. Didn't I say you was bright?"

"Thanks," Sundance said.

"Don't mention it," Comiskey acknowledged. "There's talk has come my way that you have the name of being a hard nut. For you that's not so good cause I don't like it, get me? Why, sonny boy, I ate hard nuts for breakfast. Never had any trouble eating nor digesting, get me? I was just as big when I was seventeen. What I'm trying to say is this, don't try to be a hard nut with my Major. Major Ethan's been good to me and I won't have it. First day I come here no more than three weeks ago there was this corporal thought he was something special. How was the poor mug to know I was in the prize ring afore I killed a man and had to light out and join the army? Of course it's agen all army regulations for enlisted men to fight on or off the post. But you know how it is. Us fellas managed to get together down there below in the riverbed behind the saloon. I won't say the Major knew about it and I won't say he

207

didn't. To make a long story short, I just about killed him. He's out of the infirmary now and we're the best of friends. So good he runs every time he sees me."

"You think I'm going to make trouble for the Major?" Sundance asked, thinking that he hadn't ever fought a prizefighter, even one who hadn't been in the ring for twenty years. Comiskey looked as though he got plenty of practice.

"I just know you wouldn't do that," Comiskey said. "But I have to be sure, you understand."

Sundance said, "What do you have in mind?" He knew Comiskey wouldn't attack him on the post.

"We're going to have to have it out, mister," Comiskey said. "I don't see any other way. You think you see another way? I don't, maybe you do."

"You're right," Sundance said. He might as well get it over. There were few men he couldn't beat; maybe he had met one of them at last. A man who bragged about his fists was just as dangerous, in some ways, as a man who carried a fast gun.

"Course I'm right," Comiskey said. "You'll just have to take your beating like the rest of them. It's a fact of life, something you have to face. Soon as it's over the post can settle down again. Maybe I'll even let you stay on. There's nothing personal, is what I mean."

"How did you work it with that corporal?" Sundance asked. "I don't see that we have to provide entertainment."

Comiskey pushed his cap back and scratched his close-cropped head. "My friend the corporal thought he'd put on a show and I didn't see the harm of it. You don't want that?"

"If you beat me you can tell people about it," Sundance said.

"I'll say this for you," Comiskey said. "You got

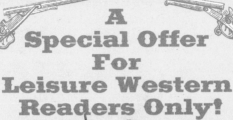

plenty of nerve. Won't do you a bit of good. We'll do it any way you like. Down along the river as good a place as any. Just you and me in the pale moonlight, as the fella sang in the beer garden. Ten o'clock tonight suit you?''

Sundance nodded. "Downriver. Round the bend from the saloon."

Comiskey was a heavy man but he stood up without effort. He was smilng and filled with wonder at the other man's foolishness. "Mister," he said, and after twenty years in the West his voice still had the true snarl of the New York slums. "Mister, you're going to wish you'd never heard my name."

All through the day the sun was like a brass bowl in the sky. The wind blew hot and out of the shade anything metal blistered the fingers. Down below, stretching away from the fort, the desert shimmered in the heat. Sundance didn't see the Major for the rest of the day. He cleared everything out of the house except for the bed, tables and chairs, and threw it into the deep trash pit behind the latrines. A trooper on latrine duty, carrying a bucket of lime, stared at him.

Sundance's orders were to ride out in the morning and he wondered how well he'd be able to sit a saddle. If he didn't beat the Major's tame thug he'd be wasting his time staying on at the fort. The men would know it and so would the Major; they would know about it in the straggle of houses down by the dead river. Word would get to the Apaches and maybe that was worst of all. It was bad all around. Comiskey had the weight on him, a few inches as well. Comiskey didn't have the look of a boozer; a rumpot, even one that had been a prizefighter, would be easier to beat. Comiskey was still light enough on his feet; it showed in the way he moved. He was about thirty-eight or -nine, and in the ring that might have worked against him. Still, even a man of fifty who had once been a prizefighter, and not a specially good one, could hammer most ordinary men into the ground. The only real chance he had of beating Comiskey was to wear him down, make him go beyond his usual distance. That would be the big man's weak point: it figured that no man had made him go the distance for a very long time.

Sundance smiled to himself. It was too late to start training for the fight, to start jumping up and down, or punching sandbags. He knew he was in good, hard shape without any of that; the way he lived was all the training he needed. There was no way to walk away from the fight. Comiskey would force it no matter what he did. The fight itself wasn't important; even the thought of a beating didn't bother him; a man had to be prepared to take a few beatings, or find another line of work. It wouldn't stop if Comiskey won; there wouldn't be a day when he wouldn't throw it in his face. If Comiskey did that, the other men would do it. He couldn't fight the whole garrison, one at a time or in a bunch. So he had to beat Comiskey—not just fight him to a standstill, for that would mean more fighting. He wondered if he would have to kill the sergeant. There was no way to tell until the fight was over. He'd know then for sure. Sundance smiled again. He was getting way ahead of himself: by the time the fight was done with, he might be lying in the dirt coughing blood.

The sun sloped and the air cooled as the afternoon wore on and in the fort the shouting and the bustle of meaningless activity began to slacken and men looked forward to doing nothing until the bugle blew bunk call. A few men with money would straggle down to the saloon by the river if the Major hadn't declared it off limits by now, or closed it altogether. It hardly mattered: few enlisted men had money by the middle of the month. Usually the only enlisted man who could drink all through the month was the fort moneylender, and because of his dirty business he had to drink by himself.

Sundance had pushed himself to get to Fort McHenry, and he slept for four hours when it got cool in the house. He owned the old key-wound silver watch that had belonged to his father, but he seldom had to use it, for when he had to wake up at a certain time, that was what he did. He did it now, with the fort quiet and the breeze from the open window getting colder, and when he went outside the sky was a deep blue and alive with stars. There were lights in the duty office and in some of the windows of the officers' quarters, and a lantern hung from a hook above the door of the guard-house. On the firing platform inside the wall sentries paced their allotted number of paces. A trooper passed on his way to the latrines.

The main gate was closed and barred and the sentry passed him through the postern. He stared at Sundance without saying anything and the man in the tower was watching too. In the starlight the desert looked cold and in the far distance the mountains seemed to have no depth, just edges. Shale crunched under Sundance's moccasined feet as he went down the hill from the fort. Two horses were hitched in front of the saloon and there were lights there and in the trading post. The other houses were dark, and there was no sound except the fretting of the horses and men talking in the saloon.

He walked down to the bend in the river and Comiskey was waiting, bulking big against the white sand of the riverbed and the banks behind him. At that part of the river there was a wide sandy place in the center, and hardly any rocks, and the noise from the saloon didn't carry that far. Comiskey's army blouse was turned inside out and folded neatly.

"You come armed, you wasn't supposed to do that," Comiskey said, looking at the long-barreled Colt .44.

Sundance had left his other weapons at the fort. Now he unbuckled his gunbelt. "It won't get in the way," he said.

Comiskey grinned, a man in no hurry. "I seen you looking about as you came in. Don't be so mistrustful. There's nobody here but me. Me is all it'll take. You should have took the opportunity I give you this morning. Now it's too late!"

Comiskey edged forward, without seeming to, as he talked. Sundance was ready for him. "What opportunity?" Sundance said.

"Don't talk dumb even if you are," Comiskey said. "You had a day and an evening to get yourself gone. That was the idea. I thought you'd have better sense than to go up against me. You should be halfway back to the Gila River by this time. But you're not, are you?"

"Any time you're ready," Sundance said.

"I'm ready, sonny boy," Comiskey said. He didn't try any tricks. He thought he didn't have to. There was no sudden swing in the middle of a sentence intended to take the other man off guard. There was no swing of any kind. He danced in like a prizefighter with his left poking the air, his right a few inches in front of his chin. The right hardly moved at all while the left reached out. He had reach as well as height and he knew how to use both. Sundance moved back and to the side and Comiskey followed, moving the right now and putting force behind his jabs. Grinning, he dropped his guard

212

and moved his shoulders, crouching more than he had been, advancing steadily with his left leg.

A straight-armed left rocked Sundance's head. It came out straight from the shoulder and rocked his head again. Sundance spat blood and blocked the next left. Comiskey led again with his left, still holding the right back for when he got closer. But his left was the probe, the feeler for the soft places in the other man's defense. He dropped a hard left to the body and tried to follow with the right. Sundance took the left and blocked the right hook, but even blocking it he felt the power behind it. Comiskey, still grinning, dropped his guard again and Sundance hit him because the other man didn't expect him to fall for it. Sundance threw a left to Comiskey's face and got him in the throat. Comiskey came in hard and Sundance had to take body punishment to save his face. Comiskey's wood-hard fists hammered on his ribs before he drove him back with a left hook to the face. He got him again in the same place, but this time he had to reach too far and when it landed light Comiskey already had his chin tucked in.

They circled and now Comiskey was more careful. There was no talking, no spewing out of insults. Comiskey was a loudmouth but not in a fight. Sundance had hoped that he would be. He thought he had Sundance's measure now; he seemed to relax and yet to speed up his attack. His left jabs came faster and his shoulders moved as his fists moved. Comiskey blocked a left to the face with the side of his right fist. Sundance knocked his left aside and punched him in the belly. Comiskey grunted and brought up the left again. Sundance took two lefts that forced him back. The two punches came out of nowhere and Comiskey hardly moved. The fight had started slowly but now Comiskey seemed to be working up to his pace, like a machine building to full power. Sundance had seen that before in boxers who hadn't been in the ring for a long time. All the old moves were coming back as he bored in, moving the right now but still not as much as the left. Sundance knew the left, thought he knew what to expect from it, and he watched the right more than the left. Comiskey attacked harder with the left, trying to force Sundance's attention away from the right. There was anger in his face when he wasn't able to do it. He started using the right as well as the left, no longer holding it in reserve for the right moment. Comiskey punched harder, no longer as sure as he had been, and the professional boxer's contempt for the amateur was replaced by determination. He knew that, after all the years of easy victories, he had met his match, at last. Or if not his match, then a man it would take all his skill and strength to beat. They circled and circled again, giving and taking blows, and as the fight went on, skill began to be less important than strength. Sundance began to put real weight behind his blows, punching hard at the body instead of the head. He was not as skillful as Comiskey but he was faster. The other man was better in the way he put his punches together and he varied the combinations as they became familiar to Sundance. He rocked Sundance with a left and followed it with another shorter left and then a right cross. Sometimes he hooked with a left and followed with a right. But the left always came first. He tried to reverse the combination and wasn't fast enough and Sundance drove him back with rights and lefts. Both men were bleeding from the mouth and glistening with sweat. Sundance's breath was coming easier than Comiskey's.

Their feet scuffed in the sand. Sundance came in too fast and a left knocked him down. He rolled away, thinking that Comiskey would use his boots now. It didn't happen. Sundance jumped up and the right uppercut that came at his face would have finished the fight if it hadn't missed. He felt the wind of the blow and for a moment Comiskey's belly was unprotected. Comiskey's belly was banded with muscle but there was fat on it too. The first belly blow didn't seem to have any effect, but Comiskey grunted aloud when Sundance hit him again. He shot his left out and dropped his right to protect his belly. Sundance took a long left and got Comiskey in the side of the neck. Comiskey drove him back with a flurry of blows. Sundance retreated and led him on. Comiskey was starting to break his own rules and he was using the right as much as the left. The real strength was in his right and he was using it instead of saving it. A light flashed in Sundance's head as Comiskey's left hit him in the right eye and three more blows landed, two in the face, one in the body, before he stopped trying to see with the injured eye and fought back as best he could using the other. Comiskey hit him again, breaking through his defense with strength rather than skill. He felt anger for the first time. He counter-attacked with sudden anger and was driven back and almost knocked down. He fought back the anger and punched hard at Comiskey's belly. For an instant, they got in close and traded blows one for one, until Sundance knocked Comiskey back with a short left and then another left. The second left didn't do any damage. Sundance's right eye was closing fast and Comiskey was going after the other, taking punishment, jabbing with the joint of the second finger stuck out in a point, always going for the eye. If he got the eye he would have the fight. He could play with Sundance, take his time, punch at will, hit any way he liked. Anger flared again and Sundance set his teeth against it. He blocked with his right and hit with the same hand. There was a snapping sound and Comiskey's nose spurted blood. His hand came up to shield his nose, then moved down again before Sundance could get under his guard.

Blood dripped from Comiskey's chin, but if he felt pain from the broken nose it didn't show. Blood ran into his mouth and he spat it out and came on again as if nothing had happened. He tucked in his chin and took punishment as he moved in. Sundance got him in the nose again and he kept coming. His punches came shorter but with more power. Sundance was beginning to tire. The feeling started in his wrists and traveled up his arms to his shoulder. His heart hammered at his ribs and his lungs were on fire, but he knew Comiskey was weakening faster than he was. It showed for a moment, then it was gone again, and Comiskey was forcing him back with a sudden burst of energy. There was strength left still, but it was the strength of desperation. He knew it was there. Sensed it, felt it, the desperation of a brute who was trying to think his way out of a place he had never been before. He hit harder. The desperation, the growing panic was still there. Comiskey couldn't understand what was happening because it had never happened before, not outside the ring.

Sundance, tiring fast but fighting well, knew this was the time he had to watch himself. He had to watch the right! He had to watch for the right! The weight in his arms was spreading to his head. They closed again, exchanging body blows, and when he wrenched himself loose his arms and chest were slick with blood. The muscles were quivering in his legs and then they moved apart, sucking in air, and then they joined the battle again knowing that it couldn't last much longer, each wanting to finish the other man so he could fall down himself.

Comiskey kept on coming. Sundance stopped him and tried to follow with a right that didn't land. He found his mind wandering and he fought it as he had fought the anger. His whole body was hot with pain. Then into his mind flashed the scnes from his initiation into Cheyenne manhood and the memory of the agony he had suffered gave him strength. The long-ago image was gone in an instant, but he felt a surge of new power to his arms and fists. Something of the feeling seemed to communicate itself to Comiskey and he fell back with a wordless sound of surprise. Then he recovered and began to fight back. It was no use. His fists hammered at Sundance, and still it was no use. Sundance drove him back, breaking down his defense, beating him into bewilderment. The scarred flesh over Comiskey's eyes broke open as neatly as if it had been cut with a knife and Sundance felt the spat of blood under his driving fists. All anger was gone, all feeling was gone. Now it was all Comiskey could do to use his fists. Sundance knocked them aside and punished the belly and the head. Comiskey's face was a mask of bloody meat; his jaw was slack and his eyes were starting to die. He started to fall. Sundance didn't let him fall. He planted his feet firmly and swung his right fist like a club. It came up with such force that Comiskey, big as he was, was lifted and thrown, and Sundance knew it was over.

Unable to move, Comiskey lay dribbling blood. Swaying on his feet, Sundance bent over him. Comiskey's mouth was moving; he was trying to talk through the blood.

"You wanted it, you got it," Sundance said. "You lost."

"I . . . kill you," Comiskey mumbled, then his eyes clouded and he lay still.

Sundance turned away in disgust. It wasn't over.

Nothing much had been settled. The next time Comiskey came at him would be with a gun or a knife. Now he knew what to expect.

Five

Even by first light news of the fight had spread through
the fort. It was in the duty sergeant's face when he
banged on Sundance's door as the sky sickened, the
Apache way of describing the grey color of the sky
before the sun came up. It was in his "Looks like it's
going to be a nice day. Yes sir, a nice day."

"Sure," Sundance said. It wasn't going to be a nice
day; the only nice days in the desert were in winter. This
day was going to be like all the other sun-blasted days of
the year.

The duty sergeant tried hard not to stare at
Sundance's face, swollen and battered, the damaged eye
still closed. "The Major wants you to report before you
leave," the sergeant said. "Right now, on the double.
That's what he said." The sergeant grinned. "I got
coffee going when you want it."

"I'll be along," Sundance said, closing the door in
the noncom's face. It looked as though he had become
popular overnight. He could do without that. He looked
at his reflection in a dusty window. Then he rubbed off
the dust with his sleeve and looked again. The night
before he had washed away the blood before he lay
down, trembling in utter exhaustion. During the night it
was bitter cold but he sweated under a blanket and his
mouth bled, and when he woke up there was pain. It
would be days before he'd be able to move without

pain, but he'd recover faster in the desert than in cold country. Sun would bake out the pain and sleep would give him back his strength. The mouth wasn't too bad; there was nothing he could do about the eye. His ribs were sore, splotched with bruises, but nothing was broken. He boiled up coffee until it was black and bubbling and the tear in his lip burned with pain when he forced himself to drink it. It was, he thought, one hell of a way to start his first day's work.

Men who had ignored him the day before waved as he crossed the parade ground to the Major's office. The sun wasn't full up yet but he was sweating and he longed to be gone from the fort, with nothing but his horse to keep him company. A morning breeze, still cool at that hour, spun dust into spirals on the parade ground, and while he was still crossing the bugle blew and the rest of the men turned out.

In front of the Major's office a dusty chestnut horse on a loose hitch was drinking from a bucket. The horse looked as though it had been ridden hard. It had bony flanks as if it had been fed too much corn and not enough hay. Inside, the door of the Major's office was open and the duty sergeant, back behind his desk, waved him through without getting permission.

Sundance went in and there was a barrel-bodied man with a bushy beard pacing the floor with a cigar in his mouth and an angry look on his face. Loose, crepy skin circled his hard blue eyes, and the rest of the skin on his face was loose and sagging. Words rumbled up from under his shaggy beard in a string of complaints. He talked around the cigar, taking it out now and then to make some special point, then put it back and mumbled again. He carried a new-looking Colt in a fancy Mexican gunbelt heavy with hammered silver and worked with silver wire stitching. He took the cigar from his mouth and gaped when Sundance came in.

"What happened to you?" Major Randolph said.

"Took a bad fall, sir," Sundance said, knowing that the question might not have been asked if the bearded man hadn't been there.

The bearded man wheezed with nervous laughter. "Must have been a well to mark you like that."

Sundance ignored him. "You wanted to see me, Major."

The bearded man gave Sundance a doubtful look. "Is this him?" It was plain that the bearded man wasn't too impressed by Sundance's battered appearance. Sundance felt like grinning in spite of the pain in his ribs, the dull throbbing of his swollen eye. He couldn't fault the man on that score. He wasn't too impressed himself.

Major Randolph made the introductions and they shook hands warily. The bearded man was Lafe Jackman and he ran the trading post in the town and owned a ranch five miles to the south. Sundance didn't like anything about him; he had the look of crooked trader stamped all over him. Sundance sat down while Jackman continued to pace, silent for the moment.

Sundance looked at Honest Abe and wondered what kind of Indian trouble Jackman was having. Whenever a trader had trouble, always it was Indians.

It was Indian trouble. "Mr. Jackman says the Apaches have been watching his ranch these past few days," the Major said. "At first he thought it was nothing so he did nothing. But when they were still there the next day he took his men—three men—and went out looking. They weren't there. He made a wide sweep around his ranch and there was nothing."

Jackman interrupted angrily. "I didn't say there was nothing. I said they weren't there. Not so's I could see them, but they were out there watching me. I called in the men and set a watch. Soon as I did there they were again, showing themselves and ducking out of sight. This went on all day. I'd see them for a minute, then I wouldn't. I know most of the Apaches in this country, but they stayed too far out to get a good look. So then I yelled what did they want. Come on in and we'd talk, I said. I got to thinking they were some bunch from Mexico. I still think maybe that's who they are."

"You fire at them?" Sundance asked.

"I told you I just yelled out at them. Hell no, I didn't fire any shots. I don't trade bullets with the Apaches, I trade goods, whatever is to be traded."

Sure you do, you son of a bitch, Sundance thought. He had a good idea of the rubbish Jackman sold or traded to the Apaches. These vultures were all the same, from the Canadian border to the Rio. One hundred percent profit wasn't nearly enough. No amount was enough if a little more could be squeezed out. They dealt in cotton blankets that wouldn't keep a dog warm on a cold night. One trader started a smallpox epidemic in Colorado by selling a wagonload of blankets a city hospital had set aside to be burned.

"You think they're hostile then?" Major Randolph said, prompting Jackman to answer the way he wanted him to answer.

"It doesn't have to be that," Sundance cut in. "They may be just waiting their chance to steal a horse."

The Major made a big show of looking surprised. "Steal a horse! What would you call that?"

"Stealing a horse," Sundance said. "You know some stealing always goes on, peace or no peace. Peace to the Indians means no shooting, no killing. Come to think of it, they may not even be Apaches. Could be a wandering band of half-starved Yumas or Pimas."

"Are they Apaches or not?" the Major asked Jackman.

"They're no Yumas," Jackman said. "Apaches is what they are. I said I don't know which ones. I don't know what they want. I know Apaches so it can't be good. Now are you going to give me some protection? I got a wife and kids out there."

"You left your wife and kids to come in here?" Sundance said.

Jackman shrugged. "I had to get in here fast. It's only five miles. I'm not saying it's bad trouble. It's some kind of trouble."

Sundance looked at Jackman. "You have any idea why the Apaches would want to bother you? They been stalking any of the other ranchers?" One thing was sure: the Apaches weren't watching Jackman's place for no reason. It could be a bunch of wandering thieves, outcasts from their tribes, or it could go a lot deeper. Ten to one, it had something to do with something Jackman had sold or traded to the Indians. Rotten meat maybe, too rotten even for Indians to eat. It could be something as small as brown sugar with sand in it, or as dangerous as a rifle that didn't work. Selling guns to the Indians was a hanging offense, but in spite of that it was one of the liveliest businesses in the Southwest.

"All I know is I want protection," Jackman said.

"You want me to ride out with him?" Sundance asked.

"Do that," Major Randolph said. "See what they're up to, then report back here. This may be the start of it. What do you think, Mr. Jackman?"

It was good to see a man like Jackman in a tight place. He didn't look like a rich man, but all traders got rich off the Indians. Dealing with Indians, if they didn't kill you for double-dealing, was as good as picking gold

223

nuggets off the ground. Jackman put both hands in his dirty beard and scratched.

"I don't know what it's the start of," he muttered, thinking of the money he was going to lose if an Indian war broke out. But Sundance knew that the trader would find other ways of making it back. An Apache war wouldn't remain local. It would spread and that would mean more troops, infantry as well as cavalry, and the army had to be fed. Men like Jackman would feed it, and if the money got big enough, they would do their best to keep the war going. Sundance had seen it before.

"I want you to give Mr. Jackman every cooperation," Major Randolph said.

To Sundance that sounded as if Jackman had some connections in Washington. Not directly, of course. The greedy politicians and businessmen who made up the Indian Ring were too high and mighty to have any direct dealings with an unwashed crook like Jackman, who was just a lowly noncom in the great army of graft and corruption that had its men in every crossroads settlement and far-flung army post. These men gathered in the money, kept their share, and passed the rest of it along. A trader who sold diseased meat instead of good sound beef was helping to bribe a congressman or a senator thousands of miles away. But they all got a cut depending on how important they were; the dirty money passed through many hands before it got to the end of the line.

The Major had been staring at Sundance. Now he turned to Jackman. "Please wait outside. My chief scout will be with you in a minute."

Jackman grunted and left the door open when he went out. The duty sergeant closed it. A hot wind rattled the oiled-paper window shades and there was shouting on the parade ground. Sundance waited for the Major to get on with it.

"You took a bad fall, is that your story?" Major Randolph said, tapping on the table with an empty coffee cup.

Sundance nodded. "That's what happened, Major."

"You look to me as if you've been fighting."

"No, sir. No fight."

"That's your story and you're going to stick to it?"

"Yes, Major."

"I won't permit brawling on this post," the Major said. "If you were provoked into fighting I want to know the man's name. Tell me who he is because I won't ask you again. What you say now will have to stand as it is. It will stand, do you understand?"

"There was no fight, Major," Sundance said. "No one provoked me. I took a bad fall."

Major Randolph looked relieved though he tried not to show it, and Sundance wondered how sure of himself he really was. Not every commanding officer had a pet noncom who did his dirty work, like spying on the officers, but many of them did. Comiskey was the Major's tame brute and it had worked fine until now, and if a report of the fight got back to the War Department it could find its way into his service file. In effect, the Major was telling Sundance to keep quiet about it. A tougher officer, one more self-assured, would have brazened it out, warned what would happen if he talked.

From force of habit, the Major snapped a salute at Sundance, then busied himself with his papers when it wasn't returned.

There was no sign of Sergeant Comiskey as Sundance and Jackman rode out.

They heard the shooting when they were about a mile from the ranch. A few scattered shots grew into the rattle of gunfire. In the great silence of the desert rifle fire sounded small, like firecrackers popping. Bulky in the saddle, Jackman cursed and raked his horse with cruel Mexican spurs. Sundance touched Eagle's flanks with his heels and outdistanced the other man in seconds. He pulled the Winchester from the boot as he rode, ready to kill if the Apaches rode out to attack. The firing went on as he covered the mile of ground to where the ranch began.

The main house was long and low and Mexican, with cottonwoods shading a spring and lime trees growing in a row. Down and through and up again from a dip in the road, he saw Apaches running from the house. They turned and fired when they saw him coming and he returned their fire, but shooting from the back of a galloping horse was no good. Jackman was yelling and firing and not hitting anything. Sundance jerked the rifle to his shoulder and followed a running Apache with the sights. The front sight bobbed with the motion of the galloping horse. Sundance put the sight in front of the running Apache and brought it back to meet him. He squeezed the trigger and the Apache ran a few steps before he fell and died. Sundance fired at another man and missed, then the Apaches were mounted and scattering south. Sundance and Jackman chased them with bullets until there was nothing to see but dust moving away rapidly in a long trail and suddenly it was quiet again.

Only the hot desert wind broke the silence; in the trees by the spring the dusty leaves made a dry clacking noise. The gate of the corral was open and the horses were gone. Sundance jumped down and ran to the dead Apache and turned him over with his foot, and even though he was smeared heavily with warpaint, Sundance recognized him as one of the braves who had stopped him on the way to the fort.

Sundance spun around when a rifle bullet smacked into the painted face of the dead Apache. Wild-eyed and cursing, Jackman was jacking another shell when Sundance shoved the man and the rifle away from him.

"Don't be a fool," he said, shoving Jackman again. The dust left by the Apaches was gone now.

Jackman jerked himself loose and started for the house. He stopped when he saw the dead woman lying on the other side of the low stone wall built around the spring. An attempt had been made to scalp her; the skin along the top of her forehead had been slashed with a knife; blood still trickled from her face. There were three bullet holes in her that Sundance could see. Maybe there were more. She was a young Mexican and she hadn't been raped. The Apaches didn't abuse dead women, though white men who killed Indians had been known to do it. It was all right to do it if they were still warm.

Jackman's grief was real, however hard he found to express it. It showed in the slump of his heavy shoulders, the way he mumbled, finding no words to express what he felt. He didn't touch the body. For a while, all he did was look at it. "She never did learn to speak American," he said, as if that had some meaning. "I gave her father ten dollars and a horse. It wasn't a bad bargain."

There was nothing to be said and Sundance followed Jackman into the house to look for the children. For Sundance this was the worst part of war on the frontier. Grown men and women knew what they faced when they came to this country; the children had no say in it. They were caught up in things they didn't understand; if they were young enough they didn't. The dead woman hadn't been more than a few years into her twenties, so these children had to be very young.

Jackman turned in the darkness of the low-roofed house. "They're gone," he said. "They got my kids."

"Then they're alive," Sundance said, then wished he hadn't said it because he didn't know if the children were boys or girls. They look of horror on Jackman's face told him they were girls. He asked how old.

Jackman knew what he was thinking. "Too old," he said. "One ten, one eleven. Dear God, I wish they were dead with my woman."

Sundance had nothing to say because Jackman was right. The children would have been better off dead. They were old enough to be raped, and they would be raped while they screamed and bled, understanding none of it. If they were lucky they would die of it, or the squaws would beat them to death with sticks and rocks. The squaws hated white women, even children, because they knew their men secretly desired them, and the taking of white women had been the real cause of many a war. Even if they survived, it would never get better for the girls; the Apaches weren't like other tribes, where a white woman could find some safety if some brave strong enough to fight all the others took her for his woman. The Apaches were the great haters of all the tribes, and they would abuse and torment the girls until the day when they were lucky enough to die. Until then, day and night, they would be worked like dogs and beaten until their bodies were scarred and broken. Or if some smiling Mexican had a good rifle to trade they would be sold into the rat-running whorehouses below the border.

Sundance watered the horses while Jackman buried his woman. Jackman made it plain that it had nothing

228

to do with him. Now, when he looked at Sundance, he saw an Indian. For some reason, Sundance hadn't expected him to take it so hard. Men like Jackman used up Mexican and Indian women, poor whites too, and turned them out when too much work turned them old too soon. He had been wrong about Jackman, but he knew he wasn't wrong about the other things. This was the start of the trouble and it could only get worse if something wasn't done about it. Right then, waiting for Jackman to get finished, he had no idea what could be done. The Major would see it as an act of war, be glad to see it that way, and who was to say he was wrong? Another officer, one less eager for glory, might have tried to contain the situation. Even in times of peace there was always random killing on both sides. As long as men carried guns somebody had to get killed. It could even be that the Major was right about Victorio for the wrong reasons. The fact that the Major wanted a war didn't mean that Victorio wasn't planning a war.

He watched while Jackman carved his woman's name on a board and he wondered how many other women would die or be taken captive before it was over. In a week the dead woman would be forgotten, but the killing would go on. Doubt nagged at Sundance. Somehow, it didn't make sense for Victorio to start a war in this fashion. Whatever else he was, Victorio was a bold strategist, a daring, ruthless commander who saw war in larger terms. In the past he had beaten the best men the army had thrown against him, until finally he had been overwhelmed by force of numbers and, as Three Stars often said, by the power of supplies. Three Stars, the most able commander in the U.S. Army, recognized Victorio as his equal; had stated flatly that he was the most dangerous Indian leader in the West, for he was the one man who could unite all the Apaches of both sides of the border. Like Three Stars, Sundance knew that Victorio would strike at the lines of supply and communication. Stage lines and way stations would be destroyed; where telegraph lines existed they would be cut. Wells would be poisoned, outlying settlements burned. Above all, Victorio would fight his war according to a plan, so where did the murder of a woman and the kidnapping of the children fit in?

Jackman dug a hole for the grave marker and firmed the dirt around it with a shovel. He took his hat off and put it back on, his final gesture of respect. Then he picked up his rifle and started for his horse without looking at Sundance. The two men didn't speak as they got on their horses and rode away.

Six

Major Randolph ordered Sundance to be silent.

"I have listened to your argument and I'm not impressed," he said angrily. "Mr. Jackman's wife has been murdered, his children stolen, and the Apaches did it. The Apaches did it and Victorio is their leader and by God, sir, I am holding him responsible. What do you want me to do? Wait until the whole frontier is in flames? There is no need to answer. It was not a question."

Jackman stood staring out the window at the parade ground bustling with men and shouting officers. Tension crackled through Fort McHenry like lightning. Men who had done nothing but drag their feet through the dead days of summer now ran in every direction. Horses, catching the excitement, plunged and whinnied as they were led from the stables.

"It's not a war yet, Major," Sundance said, making a desperate effort to keep the Major from starting a bloodbath. "With all respect, Major, let me go and find Victorio. Let me talk to him. He knows who I am. I fought him hard enough in Mexico."

"No. The answer is no," Major Randolph said, pointing at Jackman. "Save your talk for that man there. He knows what has to be done and so do I.

Anyway, why would Victorio listen to you? If he knows who you are, all the more reason to kill you."

Sundance turned toward the door. "then I'll do it without your permission. I'm not in your army, *sir*!"

Major Randolph drew his service revolver and Sundance let him do it. He hadn't come to Arizona Territory to kill Crook's nephew. Besides, it was a long run to the gate, and he knew he would never make it, after the first shot was fired.

"Like hell you're not," the Major said, cocking the Army .45. Jackman turned away from the window and stood watching. "You signed on for ninety days so you'll do what I tell you. The only way you can quit is to run away. Why don't you try that? I'd like to see you try that. There will be no talking with the Apaches, not now. Any talking to be done, I'll do it. No one else, is that clear? And when I do talk, if there is a talk, it will be done from the muzzle of a gun."

"You won't get Victorio to talk peace that way," Sundance said. "You may start this war but you'll wish you hadn't."

The Major talked with the .45 in his hand. "I don't have to tell you this, but I'll tell you anway. I won't be sorry for anything. You know why? A simple reason. This war had to come. There was no way to avoid it. The peace, so-called, was a mistake that I am going to set right, once and for all. The Apaches have to learn that it's all over for them."

"I can't think of a better reason for fighting," Sundance said.

The Major waved his gun. "This is all they understand," he said. "The gun, the rifle, the whip. You say the Apache spirit can't be broken. Rubbish. No man is so strong that he can't be broken. You just have to know how to do it. I think I know how to do it. I am going to shame the Apaches, take away their guns. Most important of all, I am going to take away their women and children. That's right! I'm going to take their women and children as hostages. You think that won't break them?"

Jackman came into the center of the room and there was a mad look in his eyes that hadn't been there before. "That's never been done, Major," he said. "By the living Christ! That's never been done. The Apaches treasure their squaws and bastard brats like they were human. It could work, I could get my girls back. Do it, Major. Don't let nobody stop you."

Major Randolph smiled, listening with half his mind to the preparation for war. "Nobody's going to stop me, Mr. Jackman. We're all alone out here in the desert. You think the white settlers are going to object, Mr. Jackman?"

"They'll kiss your hand if you finish the Apaches," Jackman said. "Do it, sir, and I'll follow you to hell. I had a few differences with the army in my time. That's all done with. Help me get my girls back and I'll put my hand in the fire for you. I know this country as good as any man, white or Indian. Ought to, Major. I been traveling it for twenty-three years. If there's killing to be done, sir, I'm the man to do it."

Sundance didn't want to fight with Jackman; his wife was dead, his children captives. Instead, he went at the Major again though he knew he was wasting his time. "You won't be able to keep it a secret," he argued, playing his last card. "What you're planning to do is against army policy, always has been. Even Custer never went that far, making prisoners of women and children. Where are you going to keep them, how are they going to be fed? You put enough of them together, disease is going to break out. What then?"

"Then some of them will die," Major Randolph said calmly, as if discussing an outbreak of hoof and mouth disease. "When you start a war you can't complain if some of your people die. That's what goes with starting a war."

Sundance looked at the Major with cold eyes. "You'll be remembered if you do this. If it goes wrong you'll be finished in the army. You won't just break you for this."

The Major called in the duty sergeant and pointed to Sundance. "You see this man?"

"Yes sir, I see him." The Sergeant looked uncertain.

"He is to be shot if he tries to leave the post," the Major said. "He is not to leave without permission. From me, in writing. Those are my orders."

The sergeant snapped to attention and went out. "Now we can talk plainly," the Major said. "I think you forget how the army works. It works like that. I tell the sergeant to shoot you, have you shot, and all he says is yes sir. He says yes sir and salutes. The sergeant doesn't ask why. I gave the order so he is not responsible. So you see I'm not finished, nor likely to be. If I don't do it right, as you say, I'll be finished, but not before. I'm willing to take the risk because in the army winning is all that counts. If I can crush the Apaches, put a final end to their menace, it won't matter much how I do it. Old ladies in Boston will tut-tut about the poor Apaches and no doubt General Miles will give me a stern lecture . . . before he promotes me to brigadier general."

"You figure to jump right over colonel?" Sundance said.

"I'll be a colonel before I finish the Apaches," Major Randolph said. "Then I'll be a brigadier and after that who knows?"

234

"Who will you fight then?" Sundance said, hoping the Major would catch a bullet the first day in the field. And maybe he would fire that bullet himself. Later, if he did it, had to do it, he would have to lie to Three Stars for the first time in his life.

The Major was so pleased with himself that he brought out a box of cigars and gave one to Jackman. "Take them all," he said. "We're going to be gone for a while. You ask me who will be left to fight after the Apaches are subdued. The answer is—somebody. There will always be somebody left to fight, always a war."

Jackman lit a cigar and blew smoke, fully in control of himself for the first time. "About my girls," he said.

"We'll get them back, Mr. Jackman," the Major said. "We'll get them back or we'll wipe the Apaches off the face of the earth. That's a promise, sir, one you can bank on. Get used to it, Sundance. Get used to it, or get shot. There's no third way. We move out at first light. Tomorrow."

The Major looked at the calendar on the wall, as if marking the date for posterity. "That's all, gentlemen," he said.

The garrison had been placed on full alert, the sentries doubled, all men confined to the post, and though the men had settled down to wait for morning, there was uneasiness in the air. After long hot months of inactivity, after plodding through the routine of make-work, the men were tense with anticipation. Below the fort the town was dark except for the saloon. Inside the fort, supply wagons were ready to move at dawn, and in the barracks men were snoring and some lay awake wondering if they would ever see Nebraska or Georgia or Vermont again.

It was dark when Sundance left the Major's office. The night was starry and cold and empty. The men in the guardhouse had been released, all but one man who was due to be hanged. Walking back to the chief scout's house, Sundance saw Comiskey for the first time since the fight. The guardhouse door was open and Comiskey was standing in the light of the lantern, and even at a distance his face looked bad, blotched and swollen, hardly human. For once Comiskey wasn't yelling and when Sundance passed he looked up only once. That one furtive look was all it took to convince Sundance that he would have to kill this man. There was no help for it, no turning away from the hard truth. If he didn't kill Comiskey, then Comiskey would kill him. It wouldn't happen in the fort, or while they were on the move. It would come in the noise and confusion of a fight, with bullets flying every which way and men too scared ever to recall clearly what they saw. That was how a smart noncom, an old stager, would do it. Comiskey wasn't intelligent but he was smart; one didn't have to go with the other.

Sundance fried a steak and made coffee and sat at the table thinking. He could get out of the fort, if he had to. Probably he could. He figured the Major had set men to watching him. Even so, he could get out, and then what? The column would be on the move long before he found Victorio, and by then it would be too late, for when the Major rode out he would be riding to war. The hell of it was that the Major could be right about Victorio. The Mexicans weren't above arming the Apaches if they got Victorio's word that there would be no war fought south of the border. It was possible, as the Major said, that Victorio had been biding his time, waiting until he had enough men, enough guns. Victorio had sworn that he would never go to war, but times changed and men changed. Victorio was getting old and maybe he wanted to die on his feet like a man.

There was nothing to do but ride with the Major; whatever happened, he was part of it now. Like it or not, the Major—the men—needed him. Of the Major's courage there was no question; at that moment he would have settled for a coward. One thing was certain: the Major was in for one hell of a surprise. He hadn't fought Apaches before; he'd be sorry when he did. The only word for the Apaches was . . . different. That explained nothing and everything. Other tribes fought when they had to; the real truth was that the Apaches loved to fight. A thousand years of warfare, fifty generations of fighting, had taught them to love killing for the sake of killing, so it was hard to figure what the end of the Apaches would be. The Major wanted to kill off the Apaches, and as a soldier he was right. If men were to live by textbooks then the Major was right. Beef and blankets wouldn't buy the Apaches, not even good beef and warm blankets. All they wanted was freedom, to live in their beloved, pitiless land without interference. And that was, of course, something they could never have. It was too late for that. In the mountains there were gold, silver, copper; and all the land needed, though worthless to the eye, was water. So every day more whites would come until finally there was no more land, no more freedom.

Sundance slept as much as he wanted to sleep, then sat at the table in the lamplight and worked on his weapons. It relaxed him to work on the tools of his trade, the things he lived by. All his weapons from the long-barreled Colt .44 to the great ash bow were in perfect killing order. Soon he would use them to kill men he didn't know, had nothing against. It was a fact, nothing more, and he didn't think much about it, and

237

when the killing started there would be no right or wrong. A man tried to kill you, you killed him first. Or he got to kill you. How well a man's weapons worked usually decided the outcome. Not all the time, just most of it. But in the end there was no way to guard against death. Death seemed to have a special fondness for men who were too careful to avoid it. But, cautious or careless, it came to claim its own.

A few hours were left until first light. Sundance put more wood in the stove and waited. The fort was quiet but there was restlessness in the very silence of the air. Sundance thought about the two Jackman girls. It was a hell of a thing.

Another hour passed and the fort began to stir. Men were up and moving about though reveille still was a long way to go. The men who were up would be looking to their weapons. They were cavalry so they carried the long-barreled Winchester repeater instead of the Springfield or the Winchester carbine. Sundance smiled. If he knew cavalrymen, they carried a lot of other weapons the regulations said they couldn't have. They all carried the single-action Army .45, but there would be other pistols: Derringers, .32's and .38's, maybe even some old Navy .41's. A man who got used to a hideaway or spare gun felt naked without it. It was a way of shaving the odds, and when a man thought he could do that he felt lucky; a soldier who felt lucky made a better soldier than one who saw nothing ahead but a blanket-wrapped burial. But lots of lucky men got killed; the optimists and the pessimists were all buried together.

Reveille blew like Gabriel's Horn, telling the men it was time to get ready to die. This was what Uncle Sam had been paying them for; ten weeks or ten years, it made no difference now. The infirmary had been emptied too, and there were men who would die in the

238

desert before they even saw an Indian.

Sundance saw the Major walking from his quarters to his office. There was just enough light to make out the Major's stiff stride, the straight-backed shoulders. The Major stepped lively for so early in the morning; already he had started down the Glory Road that would take him to his first star, the bullheaded son of a bitch. Turning away, Sundance felt sorry for the men who had to die.

He was buckling on his weapons belt when yelling came from the watchtower. The man in the tower fired off his rifle and kept on yelling. Sundance saw Major Randolph hurrying from his office, too dignified to run. Other men were running. The yelling went on.

Comiskey, already up on the firing platform, shouted down to the Major. "Five men out there hanging on posts. Look like crosses. That's what it looks like from here."

"Crosses!" Major Randolph allowed himself one single oath, then went back to being the stern commander. Sundance was close to him. "What do you make of it?" A frown creased the Major's sun-reddened face.

"Nothing else out there I can see, sir," Comiskey reported, shading his eyes with his hat.

"Crucifixion," Sundance said. "The Apaches do it. I've never seen it."

The Major told Comiskey to cover them while they went out. "You stay here," he ordered Lieutenant Gates. "If it's a trick, open fire. Don't wait for my order."

A trooper opened the postern and slammed it behind them. The desert was red in the morning sun and less than two hundred yards from the wall of the fort were the five crosses. With the sun coming from behind they made long shadows on the ground. Men watched them across rifle barrels as they went down the hill.

If the five Apaches weren't dead they were giving a good imitation of death. At first it was hard to see in the red glare of the sun. Then they got closer and saw that the bodies of the five dead men were riddled with arrows, but that wasn't all that had been done to them. Their eyes were gone and hadn't been picked out by birds; the feet and hands had been cut off, and hours after death their faces were contorted with the agony of the final moments. Their long crow-black hair blew in the wind and flies were gathering around the wounds.

"They've been castrated," the Major said calmly, trying to sound as if he'd seen it before.

Sundance knew he hadn't. He hadn't either though he knew Apache country better than most men. "They learned crucifixion from the Spaniards," he said. "It came to be the death the Apaches feared most, so the Spanish saved it for special occasions. Victorio did the same."

"Victorio did this?"

"For attacking the Jackman ranch, killing the woman. It's his way of keeping the peace."

The Major didn't want to believe what he saw. "What about the children?"

Sundance saw a movement at the bottom of the hill. A piece of cloth fluttered in a gust of wind, then nothing else moved. The wind blew again and the Major saw it too. He started to bring up his revolver. "They're down there, they're watching us."

"Easy with the gun," Sundance said, turning sideways to speak to the Major. "They're watching but not from down there. Put up the pistol. Do it, Major. I figure the children are down there. You want to take a look?"

"You're forgetting your place." But the Major holstered his revolver. "Let's go."

The Major had nerve but there was nothing remarkable in that. Most soldiers had nerve, or had it trained into them. "We'll go down easy," Sundance said. "We'll be all right as long as nobody fires a shot."

They might have been two men out for a morning stroll. "I'll hang the man that fires it," the Major said.

Sundance didn't tell the Major that he wouldn't hang anybody if just one rifle went off. The Major would die and so would he; guns they couldn't see were trained on them with every step they took. A few Apaches were crack shots; those would be the ones with the best rifles.

The two girls lay bound and gagged behind a bump in the ground and their eyes still fluttered with terror even when Sundance and the Major got close. Their faded cotton dresses were torn and bloody, and Sundance knew the blood hadn't come from wounds, not the kind of wounds the Major would understand. They were alive and young and the memory wouldn't last forever. Maybe it wouldn't.

The Major started to pick up one of the girls. "No," Sundance said, holding his arm in front of him. "Don't carry them. It will make you look bad if you carry them. No Indian carries a woman, not even a child. Do as I say, Major."

The Major bristled with anger, forgetting that death was just a few pounds of pressure on the trigger of a rifle. But he said nothing while Sundance knelt and cut the ropes with the Bowie. The girls were rigid with fear and he shook them gently, spoke to them before he loosened the gags in their mouths.

"Don't cry out when I take off the gags," he said. "Don't scream, don't do anything. Listen to what I'm saying. Do you understand what I'm saying? All right.

241

I'm going to let you up now. Walk ahead of us when we start back. Don't run. You're going to be all right, but don't run."

Sundance set the girls on their feet and started them toward the gate of the fort. The younger girl was moving too fast; the other girl grabbed at her arm to restrain her. Major Randolph walked more easily now, thinking the danger was past. Sundance ·knew better. Bullets could still cut them down before they reached the gate. The only sure thing about an Apache was that you could never be sure of what he was going to do. At the gate the Major turned, though Sundance had warned him not to.

"They're leaving," the Major said, framed for a moment in the postern. "The bastards are running away."

The last Apache to ride off was a man taller than the rest. Before he turned his pony he raised his rifle above his head, a greeting and a warning at the same time. Then he was gone.

Sundance followed the Major through the gate. "There goes your Indian war," he said.

Seven

He said much the same thing in the Major's office.

"Nothing has changed," the Major said, raising his voice, releasing his tension in sudden anger. "I don't give a damn if that savage crucified half his men. What about Mrs. Jackman? How is Victorio going to bring her back to life? What about the two children? You saw what they did to them. But that doesn't mean anything to you, does it?"

Meaning that Sundance was just a dirty half-Indian. "The men who killed the woman and abused the children are dead," Sundance said quietly. "One of them was Domingo, the subchief I told you about. Jackman says Domingo was Victorio's half brother. He killed him to make it right."

Major Randolph sat behind his desk and placed his hands on it as if the feel of the scrubbed wood gave him assurance, reminded him of what he was, the commander who gave orders that could not be questioned. "He can crucify his mother for all I care," the Major said. "His men committed an act of war and the killing of five savages can't make it right. What do five lives mean to an Apache? The way he killed them should tell you that."

So it wasn't over. Sundance said, "He killed them that way because it was the worst way he knew how. He

243

reached back into the past for a means of execution so terrible that word of it would spread far beyond this country. You know what it's cost him to do that? To torture, castrate and crucify his own flesh and blood? His enemies will use it against him. He could already be a dead man."

The major waved the argument away like a mosquito. "That's what he is," the Major said. "If the Apaches don't kill him I will. Maybe he'd be better off with me. I'll just hang him. It won't be like Geronimo, no train ride to Florida. I'm going to catch him and I'm going to hang him. Not behind a horse, not from some lone tree, but out there where that man in the guardhouse is going to hang. Let the Boston ladies cry at his funeral if they care to make the trip. They won't and neither will the Boston preachers. They'll stay home and eat their fish chowder and write letters, the way they always do."

It wasn't the thing to say but Sundance said it. "You'll have to catch him before you hang him."

The Major was full of dramatic poses. Now he struck one: a man coming to an inescapable conclusion. "I knew you were going to say that. You work for the army but you're not on the army's side in this. Your real sympathy is out there"—the Major waved—"out there with them. Go on, tell me you don't feel sorry for them."

Sundance thought of the men he had killed for not much more than the Major's accusation of disloyalty. "That's got nothing to do with it," he said. "I'll still do my job."

"But your heart won't be in it, is that it?"

Sundance forced himself to see the uniform instead of the man wearing it. It was time to lay it out for the Major. Nothing else had worked. This wouldn't work either but it had to be said and something in Sundance's eyes compelled the Major to listen.

"You better know this, Major. If I come through this I'm going to make a full report to the War Department. I'm going to go all the way with this, *sir*. I'm no Boston lady, *sir*, and I won't just write a letter, then sit back and feel I've done my duty. I'll follow it up, *sir*, and if that doesn't work I'll come back and kill you. One way or another, I'll finish you, *sir*."

For a moment Major Randolph didn't move. Then he said quietly, "I could have you shot for what you just said."

"Where's your witness, *sir*?"

"I don't need a witness." The Major snapped his fingers. "Like that. I could have you shot like that."

"It would be easier if you had a witness," Sundance said. "Why don't you send for Sergeant Comiskey?"

"I could do that," the Major said, trying to regain control of the situation.

Sundance decided to kill the Major if he called for Comiskey. "You're the dealer—so deal!" he said in a dead cold voice.

Seconds limped by and the tension built between them, and maybe the Major knew that he was closer to death than he had been with the Apaches. But Sundance knew the Major wasn't a coward, whatever else he was. He was weighing death against loss of self-respect. A knock on the door brought everything to a halt. The Major eased up, so did Sundance. The moment had passed. For now. But it hadn't gone far.

Looking at Sundance with something close to a smile, the Major said, "Come in."

Captain MacCrae, the post surgeon, came in; a middle-aged man with an unmilitary bearing and a doctor's white coat speckled with blood. Whiskey veins made a map of his tired face. Whiskey and too long in the desert had taken the life out of him; he looked like a man to whom smiling was as strange as a war dance. Either he hadn't shaved for two weeks or wore a very short beard. His beard was white like his hair and his thick black eyebrows didn't seem to belong with either.

"What about the Jackman girls?" the Major asked.

MacCrae seemed to know the Major held him in contempt, but it didn't bother him. The Major didn't like doctors who drank. Sundance didn't either. It went against the grain to be on the same side as the Major.

"They were raped and beaten, no need to tell you that," MacCrae said wearily. "The older girl got more of it. She was still bleeding when you brought them in. I think I've got that stopped. I hope I have. The vaginal area is badly lacerated. At her age and size—she's a small child—that's to be expected. I'm more concerned about blood poisoning from the bites."

Major Randolph was shocked out of his disinterested military pose. "Jesus Christ! What did you say?"

It was the first time Sundance had seen the man display real emotion. Everything else he said was hedged and guarded, done for effect most of the time.

"Human bites, the marks of teeth," the doctor said, unable to share the Major's outrage. "The girl was severely bitten in the vaginal area. I've seen it before, sir . . ."

"Oh you have, have you! Please disregard that, Captain. Go on with your report."

"She should be all right if infection doesn't set in," MacCrae said. "I've done what I can for her and her sister. They're sleeping now. I gave them laudanum. I'll watch the older girl carefully for the next day or two."

Major Randolph got up and walked to the window. MacCrae looked nervously at Sundance, unsettled by how the Major was taking it. "Your orderly will have to

246

look after the girls," the Major said without turning. "We're moving out in an hour."

MacCrae hesitated before he spoke. "She'll die if the infection takes hold."

The Major turned so abruptly, and with such a fierce look on his face, that the doctor took a backward step. "Then she'll die, Captain MacCrae. She may die anyway, with or without you, isn't that true?"

MacCrae nodded, wanting to be gone from the Major's anger. "That's true, sir. We aren't equipped to do much out here. Is that all, sir?"

Major Randolph began to gather up his papers and put them away. The only sound was papers thrown together carelessly, angrily. Suddenly the Major got impatient with his attempt at control and he slammed a book on top of the pile of letters and reports, his anchor of authority.

"I've listened to you, Sundance. Now you listen to me," the Major said. "I don't know what those two girls mean to you. Probably nothing. I know they don't mean anything to our drunken doctor. But by Almighty God, sir, they mean something to me. I say that though I know one of them may die and I'll be responsible for it. Me and Victorio. We'll both have a hand in her death, but I'll make her death count for something. I will do what hasn't been done and should be done and will be done. I will remove the Apache threat from this country. I don't care who was here first. Let the historians argue about that. The Apaches have outlived their time and their place. Like it or not, *Mister* Sundance, this is a white man's country."

Sundance didn't answer. He was thinking of the days ahead, out there in the pitiless land that nobody loved but the Apaches. Maybe the whites, some of them, loved it too, in their own way, but it wasn't the same.

How could it be the same? To the Apaches there was no sense of property, of ownership; they lived on the land as tenants of their ancestors and of their children. Even their graves were unmarked, as if they wanted, without thinking, to return to the bitter ground that had given them birth.

"You say you're going to report me, then do it," the Major was saying now.

Sundance looked up. He hadn't been listening to the Major's speech to himself.

"You're so sure you're going to come through this," the Major said. "What makes you think you will?"

Sundance was past anger. "I'm going to try hard, Major. I hope you make it too."

He was at the door when the Major's voice stopped him for an instant. He didn't turn. "A lot can happen out there in the desert," the Major said.

The men were in formation waiting to see a man die. It was not the way to send men off to war, Sundance thought, but then the Major had his own ideas about everything. A rough gallows had been nailed together in a hurry: nothing more than a platform with a crosstree and a rope. No trapdoor, just a wide plank supported by a thick section of lumber. It was just something to kill a man without taking too much trouble about how it was done.

The condemned man had killed another trooper with a knife after a card game had gone sour. It happened three days after the Major arrived at the fort. The only defense the accused could offer was that the dead man had been cheating. There was no proof of that; the cards were scattered; everyone, including the killer and the killed, was drunk.

Another commanding officer might have sent the killer to prison for life. But the Major rejected all pleas for clemency; before passing sentence he said the murderer, the Major's word, must die as an example to all the others. There would be no more killing on the post; if it had to be done then he would do it.

Now he was about to give them the other half of the lesson. There was no need for it; the presence of the condemned man in the guardhouse had thrown a pall over the entire fort. Astride their horses, sweating in the sun, the men waited for the Major to appear.

Mounted on Eagle, Sundance waited too. Sergeant Comiskey had been selected to do the hanging, or perhaps he had volunteered. He wore his battered face like a badge of defiance, daring anyone to stare at him. Jackman came out of the infirmary and got on his horse, showing no more interest than if he were there to witness the slaughter of a hog. Captain MacCrae, in the same dirty white coat, stood coiling and uncoiling his stethoscope. While they waited the Major appeared, brisky and soldierly in his clean blue uniform. He got on his horse and the spirited black Arabian pranced and stepped his way, like a show horse, to the foot of the gallows.

"Bring the prisoner out," he ordered, and the order was relayed as if he hadn't spoken in a loud, clear voice.

Horses stirred in the heat and the padre came out with the prisoner and escort. The prisoner was just a kid with the mark of a farmboy still on him. Supported by the padre, a lanky man of forty or so, he walked across the parade ground talking all the way. Sundance was too far away to hear what he was saying. There was no need to hear; the walking dead man was trying to explain his side of the story. His version of what really happened. Some men went to their deaths in stony silence; some went kicking and screaming and fouling their pants; others explained and kept on explaining right up to the moment when the rope cut off their words.

Sundance saw the need for the hanging, but didn't like the Major's reasons for doing it this way. Seeing a comrade legally strangled wasn't going to make them any braver; the Major, no fool in many ways, must have known that. What he wanted to do was to instill fear of death in men who were already facing death. That was like telling a man that you would shoot him if he didn't climb the gallows under his own power. Sundance wondered how the Major would take it when it came time for his own death. He dismissed the thought as having no importance at the moment.

The Major wore a silk neckerchief and it fluttered in the hot wind like a tiny pennant. Under the gallows Comiskey stood holding a heavy carpenter's mallet with both hands. Sundance looked at him and Comiskey looked back, taking a tighter grip on the handle as he did so. When the order was given, Comiskey would knock the wooden support out of place and the still living body would fall. Sundance looked at the noose swinging in the wind. Comiskey had tied it himself before going below to take his place. It looked professional enough; it would get the job done.

Two troopers without sidearms began to hurry the condemned man up the steps. The padre, a captain with twin crosses instead of bars of rank, stood aside clutching his Bible, still muttering prayers or advice on how to cross over to the other side. Then the prisoner balked, came to a halt, and matched his skinny body against the weight of the two older men who held him. He was talking rapidly now, finally convinced that it was going to happen if he didn't do something about it. At first he spoke to the Major, spouting words, repeating what he had said a moment before; when the Major didn't seem to hear, he twisted and almost broke loose. Feeling the tension, bothered by the girlish pitch of his voice, the horses fretted and pawed, digging at the rammed dirt under their feet. The men moved too, wanting to curse and slap at their mounts but unable to do anything but maintain eyes right. Sundance had seen other military executions; the soldiers who were forced to watch were always more embarrassed than frightened. The man to be hanged was no longer a part of them; they were alive and he was, though still talking, already dead.

"Put him up," Major Randolph said. No one relayed the order; maybe it wasn't intended to be relayed. He fought them all the way; he collapsed before they got him up and they had to lift and drag him the rest of the way. The boy was screaming now, still trying to break loose, and he snapped like a vicious dog at the men holding him. Angered, forced to go through it in silence, they began to treat him roughly, glad about the anger because now they could hate him for not accepting his death like a man; because the man who once had been their comrade was now a quivering, screaming, disgusting mass of fear. And because, ready to vomit, they wanted to get it done.

"Hang him—quickly!" Major Randolph had raised his voice to a shout of command. There was sweat on the Major's face and on the backs of his hands.

They got him under the noose and got it over his head. One man had to use all his strength to hold him while the other man pulled the knot up under his left ear. He fought his way off the wide plank at the edge of the gallows and they dragged him back. Foam flecked his lips and his eyes rolled in his head. Sweating, cursing silently, they dragged him and held him. The boy was cursing the Major; obscenities spattered from his mouth like bile. Then the cursing stopped and his head jerked back. Sundance couldn't be sure if one of the executioners had hit him in the small of the back. It looked as though he had. One of them, a corporal, nodded and they both stepped back, leaving the boy swaying on the plank. His knees buckled and he was starting to fall when the Major nodded quickly and Comiskey swung the mallet with both hands. He hit the support so hard that it flew past the end of the gallows. The gunlike sound of the mallet was followed by the crash of the hinged plank. But the plan didn't go down fast enough and the hanged man slid off the end of it like a child going down a chute into sawdust. The plank bounced back and struck him in the legs and he began to swing, choking and kicking at the end of the rope.

Sundance's head jerked away from the gallows at the sound of the shot. The Major's face was calm, almost immobile, as he pushed out the spent cartridge with the ejector and reloaded. Under the gallows the body was still spinning on the rope, a hole above the heart. It had been a fast shot, straight and deadly. A gesture of compassion, or bravado.

Major Randolph, reholstering his pistol with a gloved hand, called Lieutenant Gates to his side.

"Move them out," he said.

Eight

They made a brave show as they rode out, regimental
flag flying, the Stars and Stripes snapping in the wind
that seemed to come from some great furnace on the far
side of the distant mountains. Sixty-five men and officers, three wagons, a five-pound cannon and a Gatling
gun. Major Randolph set great store by the Gatling.
Leaving his four rapid-fire guns behind because they
were too heavy had cost Custer his life and the lives of
his men at the Little Big Horn. Everybody said Custer
would have cut the Sioux to ribbons if he had brought
along the Gatlings. Major Randolph wasn't about to
make the same mistake.

Sundance had nothing against Gatlings; they worked
fine when the enemy charged at you head-on. The Sioux
fought like that, so Custer should have brought along
his rolling thunder, as the Plains Indians called it.
Sundance doubted that four rapid-fire guns would have
stopped five thousand Sioux and their allies. Still, it was
a good story, and men still argued about it over camp-
fires and saloon tables fifteen years later. Major
Randolph thought he was going to profit by Custer's
mistake. *Not so*, Sundance thought. They weren't going
out to face the Sioux; the Apaches fought in their own
way, and the Major wasn't going to like it. The Apaches
broke all the rules; there would be no pitched battles;
for one thing the Apaches didn't have the numbers, but

even if they did they would still fight in the same way. They had been fighting since before history; by the time the Spanish came with their cannon and muskets, the Apaches had centuries of experience behind them, and so they were the only Indians the conquistadores had never subdued. In their way, the Plains Indians were closer to the whites; they fought with massed armies when it was possible to unite the tribes, and they prepared for battle with much oratory and long deliberation.

The Apaches did none of that. They fought with no fixed plan of battle. They did what had to be done; they improvised from one moment to the next. Three Stars said they were masters of retreat. Three Stars said that more men were killed chasing Apaches than facing them. All true. Except the Major didn't know it—or didn't want to believe it.

Sundance watched the Major riding at the head of the column. He rode well, but he didn't have the grace of the natural horseman. *The desert will loosen you up,* Sundance thought. *It will teach you things that you never knew existed.*

They rode in the hot blowing sand; far away the bare mountains gleamed in the sun. The colors of the desert were the red of mesas, the white of dunes, but most of all the desert was gray, dun-colored and dead. It was a country of shifting sand, baked clay and splintered rock. There were dunes of blue clay hardened by the sun, baked so hard that the horses' hoofs rang as if crossing smooth rock. It seemed to grow hotter though the sun had reached its hottest point an hour before, and the men sweated until they dripped. In this desert men sweated out water almost as fast as they could take it in. Here men fought to maintain the balance of water in the body, but somehow it was always a losing battle.

In the end, there never was enough water for man or animal. No matter how much water you brought along, it had a way of going faster than you expected.

They had been on the move for more than six hours when the major halted the column. Quick camp was made in the bottom of a yellow canyon with a pool of doubtful-looking water covered with green scum in its center. Sundance scooped up a handful of water, smelled it, tasted it, and said it was all right for the horses. He didn't say they might all be drinking worse before long. If they were lucky they'd have something to drink. The rivers in this country were wet or dry, depending on the whim of nature, and a waterhole that had sustained life for years would suddenly quit, or a sandstorm would bury it.

Major Randolph called a meeting of his officers while the men boiled up coffee or made a soup of hardtack and dried meat. Sundance, as scout, was part of it. The officers were Captain Danforth, a man Sundance hadn't seen much of, Lieutenant Gates, and a very young second lieutenant named O'Hara. Sergeant Comiskey was the only noncom present.

Major Randolph took a rolled-up map from a leather case, spread it out and used small rocks to anchor the corners against the tug of the wind.

"Here's where we are," he said, tracing the route from the fort with a pencil. "Deemer's Canyon. So far it's been easy travel. Soon it won't be so easy. You've been here longer than anyone, Captain Danforth. Suppose you tell us what we can expect."

Danforth was a good ten years older than the Major, and now, past forty, he was still a captain and unlikely to go any higher. He was a lean, dark man with red hair already grizzled over the ears, and he had a quirky, sourly humorous mouth. His habitual expression was that of a man enjoying some private joke that no one else could possibly understand. His Southern birth—Georgia—had held him back in an army still dominated by colonels and generals who had fought against the Confederacy.

He always had a long thin cigar in his mouth but was never seen smoking. Now he took it out and used it as a pointer. "Like the Major said, from here on it's going to be broken country. Hill country slashed across by arroyos and canyons. Between here and the mountains there is one river that always has water. Water and quicksands. So we're going to have to watch the wagons when we cross. The trial we've been following is what's left of an old Spanish military road. It crosses the desert, goes up into the mountains and down into Sonora."

"The Apache villages," Major Randolph prompted him. Danforth's laconic Southern voice seemed to annoy him. It didn't have enough military bark in it.

Danforth said, "The ones we know about, the main ones, are here and here and here." He tapped the map with the dry end of the cigar. "Country there is marked as desert on the map. A matter of some argument, I guess. Semi-arid is more accurate. Anyway, the Apaches can live off it. There, where the desert meets the mountains, they graze their flocks, sheep and goats, and grow what they can. Mostly corn, a few other things. There are three small villages instead of one big one because it takes a lot of country just to support a few people. As it is, they're half starved most of the time."

Major Randolph broke in to remind Danforth that they weren't concerned with the welfare of the Apaches. "Never mind how well fed they are." The Major's tone was sarcastic, his manner bullying.

"That last part was meant as an explanation of the enemy's physical condition," Danforth said calmly. The Major had made few friends at the fort; Danforth wasn't one of them.

Major Randolph ignored the Southerner's irony and scraped at the waterproof map with his pencil. "This village here. Twin Peaks. You're sure that's the biggest?"

Sand had collected on the map. Danforth brushed it away. "Twin Peaks is the closest name on the map. Yes, sir, that's the biggest village. The peaks are above the village. The village itself is backed up against a wall of the mountain, in a small canyon. It's got water, enough water, some grass. That's why the village is there."

"How much of a village, Captain?"

"Women and children, sir?"

Sundance could see that the Southern captain didn't have much enthusiasm for the Major's hostage-taking plan of operation. Some military men would have considered it a good plan, but this military man didn't like it.

"I mean everybody," Major Randolph said, knowing that Danforth had understood what he meant in the first place. The sarcasm in the Southerner's voice was muted but real: as real as the unstated hostility that had grown up between the two men.

"I'd say about a hundred people all told," Danforth said. "Make that about a hundred and twenty, sir. My estimate is sixty women and children. No way to tell how many old people in that number. To the Apaches old men are counted as women. They let them live if times aren't too bad."

"How many fighting men?"

"Thirty or so, Major. Some of them may be there now. Mostly they're away, hunting whatever they can find. The women tend to the crops, look after the flocks. How many men? No way to tell. Game is scarce and getting scarcer. They wander pretty far afield."

"Then it shouldn't be too hard," Major Randolph said.

Sundance looked at the Major. "You mind if I talk?"

"Fire away, if it has to do with scouting, that is." Major Randolph sounded almost agreeable.

A trooper brought two pots of coffee for the officers; woodsmoke and food smells drifted over from the fire; the enlisted men ate their food with the stolidity of men who had given up thinking for themselves.

Sundance said, "If they haven't got us spotted by now they soon will. Any advantage we have is this. Victorio has gone back to his people thinking his execution of the renegades, Domingo and the others, has restored the peace. He didn't just kill them. He went far beyond that, as you saw, sir."

"Get on with it," the Major said.

"If Victorio didn't think everything was all right, there would have been Apaches watching us from the time we left the fort. Maybe they have been."

The Major allowed himself a thin smile; the smile was like a slit in his face. "You can't seem to make up your mind. Would you have known if they were watching us?"

"Maybe not," Sundance answered. "Whatever they're doing now they'll have us bagged long before we get where we're going. The minute Victorio gets word he'll call in every man. No matter how far they've gone, here, in Mexico, he'll get them back. The fastest runners will find them."

"Why?" The Major didn't want to hear the hard facts. "The Apaches can't know what I . . . we . . . plan to do. All right, I grant you there's no point pretending to be a patrol. Too many men. Besides, the guns. My guess is Victorio will think we're just showing the flat. A display of Uncle Sam's might. The army's way of warning him that no further outrages will be tolerated.''

Sundance said, ''What Victorio thinks has to be guesswork. What he'll do is pretty definite. There has been peace for a long time, so it's true that many of his men will be gone from their villages. They favor Mexico because they aren't at peace with the Mexicans. When there is game to hunt, they hunt. The rest of the time they run off horses and cows in Sonora.''

''The peace-loving Apaches,'' Major Randolph sneered.

This wasn't the time to speak up for the Apaches. It was as the Southern captain said. They were half starved most of the time, and in the good years they were just hungry and could manage to stay alive. There was never enough food; foraging took up most of their waking moments.

''If what you say is true we'll have to move all the faster,'' Major Randolph said. ''Let the men sleep in their saddles if they have to. You, Mr. Danforth, will circle the village and block the pass at Twin Peaks. This will prevent any escape from the village. If Apaches are coming from the south you are to hold them while we round up the hostages. Then you will pull back and rejoin the column. What are the chances of Victorio attacking the column after we take the hostages?''

The question was addressed to Danforth, but he let Sundance answer.

''He won't attack,'' Sundance said. ''The young women and children are all the Apaches have. Without them they're finished in every way. So are you if you lose them along the way. Because of the women and children this won't be just another fight between cavalry and Indians. Once you start it you better hold on to the hostages. Even if none of them die—and some will die—this Indian war will be different from all the others."

Captain Danforth spoke up. "After we get the hostages, what then, sir?"

"Then I will call on Victorio to surrender," Major Randolph said, pretending to be surprised by the question. "Did you think I was going to use the hostages to pick cotton, Mr. Danforth?"

Major Randolph laughed and Gates joined in. Comiskey couldn't laugh because he was just a noncom. O'Hara didn't laugh and that brought a sharp look from the Major.

"Not just Victorio," Major Randolph said. "Every Apache male capable of bearing arms will surrender, at which time he will be disarmed and made prisoner. Then and only then will the women and children be released. I know what you're thinking, Mr. Danforth, and the answer is no, I haven't changed my mind about hanging Victorio. But there will be no trickery, sir. He will know that he is going to hang. We'll see how much of a man he really is."

"What will you do if he doesn't surrender, sir?"

Major Randolph hadn't expected such a hard question to come from Second Lieutenant O'Hara, a too-tall youngster with sandy hair and blinking blue eyes and a wide mouth that he tried to make soldierly by pressing his lips together. Sometimes he forgot and his mouth gaped.

"I'll get them shipped to Florida," Major Randolph answered. "I can get it done if I have to. That's where they belong anyway. That's where all the Indians ought to be. There's nothing there worth having, so let the

Indians have it. Round them up and ship them there, seal off the border and let them fight it out. I guarantee in a few years they'd kill each other off, Indians being Indians. It's not an original idea, Lieutenant, but it's a good one."

Major Randolph rolled up the map and put it away. "You think the threat of exile in Florida will be enough to make Victorio come in?"

Sundance stared into the Major's satisfied smile. "It would, if it got that far. First he'll try everything else. Don't expect any gallant gestures from an Apache, Major. Bravery, yes. Gallantry, no. If there is nothing else, Victorio will trade for the women and children."

Major Randolph stood up and dusted sand from his uniform. "Then let's get to it, gentlemen."

They wound their way through the maze of canyons, the horses' hooves crunching in black volcanic sand, and on the last day before they broke through to the last stretch of desert that went from there to the mountains on the border, Sundance saw the first Apache scout. It didn't take much spotting; the scout wanted to be seen. He knew they wanted to be seen, or they would not have been seen.

"Makes no difference," Major Randolph said. "They want to see if we'll fire on them." Then he gave orders that the first man to fire a shot, except to save his life, would be killed on the spot. If the Apaches opened fire their fire was to be returned, but there would be no pursuit, no splitting of the force until it came time for Captain Danforth to ride ahead and to seal off the pass at Twin Peaks.

Pushed by the Major, the officers and noncoms pushed the men even harder; the stops to rest men and animals were shorter, and they moved on well after sundown and were on the move again before it was light. The Major pushed himself harder than he pushed the men, but Sundance saw nothing to admire in that. Major Randolph might have been alone for all he cared about the others; indeed, he would have done it by himself, if it could be done that way. He slept short hours, but it didn't seem to bother him; the Major was in a hurry and the conquest of the Apaches was just a way station in his career.

Sundance thought about killing him. Captain Danforth would take command, but a question remained. Danforth's orders were to proceed with the operation, as planned, in the event that Randolph was wounded badly or killed. As the new commander, Danforth could reassess the situation and decide to turn back. Or he could carry out his orders in the hope that a successful campaign might mean final advancement to major. It was hard to decide what Danforth would do. No doubt the Southern captain was a capable soldier; what he didn't have was Major Randolph's boldness and determination. At the moment, the Major's very boldness—ambition and boldness—had set him on the wrong road. Even so, if it came to a fight, and Sundance knew it had to, the Major's ruthlessness would be more vulnerable than the Southerner's routine capability. So Sundance decided to stay with the devil he knew—sort of knew—and even while he made his decision he knew it might be a wrong one.

The men grumbled but kept going. The operation had not been explained to them, and as usual with enlisted men rumors spread and were distorted and embellished in the telling and retelling. They cooked their food and ate it quickly and slept when they got a chance; when the Major called a halt, many of them sank to the ground to sleep with the reins in their hands; slept in the glare of the sun with their caps pulled over their eyes until roared awake or kicked awake.

They had not been fired on and the Major grew more confident. One night, the last night on the desert, the Apaches crept in close and ran off a few remounts, but there was no shooting when they stole the horses, and no pursuit.

"We've got them confused," Major Randolph said, not as sure as he sounded but wanting to be sure. "They don't know what we're up to and we'll be on top of them before they can make up their minds. Do the unexpected, gentlemen. That's what Stonewall Jackson always said, Mr. Danforth, as no doubt you know."

They were sitting by the fire and the Major for once was in a relaxed, almost genial mood, so Danforth dared to show more sarcasm than usual.

"That's what General Jackson used to say," Danforth agreed. "I guess he carried it too far. He got shot by one of his own men."

"But that was an accident, Captain."

Danforth smiled too; the two men traded smiles like gentlemanly duellists about to pace off. "Well, they cried a lot, sir," Captain Danforth said.

That night, the last night before the attack on the village, Major Randolph doubled the guard. It got late and only Sundance and the Major were left at the fire. Comiskey was there to, surly and silent. Not a word had been exchanged between Sundance and Comiskey all the way from the fort. In fact, their most recent words had been spoken at the bottom of the dead river. The Apache village was about five miles ahead in the canyon that ran into the wall of the mountain. In the darkness the men slept heavily, uneasily, in full gear. Out past the camp the sentries moved between their stations and a cold wind blew down from the pass.

The Major was reading his favorite book, a small, leather-covered volume with scraps of paper stuck between the pages to mark the passages he liked best. Now he closed the book and thanked Comiskey for the fresh pot of coffee. To Sundance, Comiskey looked like a big, clumsy, vicious dog that answered only to one master, someone who treated him kindly. Comiskey sat by the fire and began to whittle on a chunk of soft pine that he had been working on for days. His battered face was getting back to its normal lumpy ugliness.

Major Randolph looked at Sundance, still affected by what he had been reading. "You mind telling me something?"

"What is it?" Sundance asked.

"A matter of interest, nothing more," Major Randolph said. "From what I hear you've been fighting men all your life. How long would you say you've been at it?"

"Since I was a boy. The best part of twenty years."

"And you're telling me you don't like it?"

"I didn't tell you anything, Major. You're right though. I don't like it. What's there to like about killing men?"

Major Randolph smiled to show he didn't intend to give offense. "You're a liar, Mr. Sundance. You just don't know you are. The truth is, you like it better than you know. You have a great reputation for honesty, they tell me. Come on now, sir, be honest with me. Admit there are times when you like killing pretty good."

Sundance knew the Major was speaking the truth, some of the truth.

"Come on now," Major Randolph said, still smiling. "Fess up."

"Not the way you mean," Sundance said slowly, explaining it to himself more than to the Major. "When I have to do it, I do it. I know how to do it, so I guess there's some pride in that. Not the kind you mean. It's just the knowing how to do it better than the other man. I don't force it. If it comes up I deal with it the best I know how."

"Ah yes," the Major said, enjoying himself. "But you're always there so it happens. You're there so you have to kill somebody. A man, men, whatever the number. If you don't like it, why aren't you somewhere else? Why don't you raise chickens in New Jersey? Nobody's going to shoot at you in New Jersey."

"This is where I am, Major."

"And so am I. That's how it works, sir. You haven't bothered to think about it. I have. You think you're here by accident. Not so. You're here because you want to be here. You put yourself in the way of having to kill men because you want to kill them. That's what soldiering is all about. A soldier's purpose is to kill, as a gun is meant to kill. But we're no barbarians so there has to be a balance. A soldier kills when he has to kill because that's his job. My point is—there is no reason why he shouldn't enjoy it. Maybe enjoy is the wrong word. Satisfaction is the word I'm searching for. That's it. Satisfaction in his work."

Sundance didn't answer.

Nine

Captain Danforth and his men rode out first and the others, standing in formation in the first hard light of morning, watched them go. Everybody had risen early, on the Major's orders; the Major wanted everything to look military. Sullen as the men, the noncoms moved among them, growling and cursing. Everybody had to look neat, the Major said. It was a waste of time, but they tried, scraping dirt from their uniforms, from their horses. There was nothing anybody could do about the stink of old sweat; and when the sun came up they stank even worse, from the Major to the youngest recruit.

Danforth was gone now, heading for the pass, but still they waited. Lieutenant O'Hara mentioned the word "attack" and the Major snapped at him. "This is not an attack, not unless they turn it into one. I have the right to move Indians wherever I please. Therefore, I am removing the women and children from here to Fort McHenry. If there is resistance, then you may call it by any name you choose."

Sundance rode his horse close to the Major and spoke quietly. "There's still time for me to ride ahead. You could be riding into a trap."

"Nonsense," the Major said impatiently. "If they wanted to attack, why didn't they do it in the hills? They've had plenty of chances, better chances than they have here."

266

"Maybe Victorio is going to do the unexpected, Major."

Major Randolph pulled on his oil-softened leather gloves and patted his holster. "No more talk," he said. "We go forward as planned. Nothing changes unless they attack Danforth."

"Then it wasn't the pass after all," Sundance said.

"It was the pass, sir. Why are you looking so angry? If they attack Danforth then you'll be right. Now take your position. It's time to move out."

Four miles lay between them and the start of the canyon, a lot of ground to cover in daylight. They started at a walk, listening for gunfire to come down from the pass called Twin Peaks. The mountains were dead ahead, with no foothills between the desert and the pass, and no sound came except the hot wind and the creak of leather. At the head of the column, the Major raised his hand and the line spread out, moving faster now, and when they reached the canyon the outer ends of the line would close around the rim of the canyon while the center rode in from the front. When they reached the canyon the Gatling gun and the five-pounder would be set up, the Gatling closer than the cannon. Up in the pass, Danforth's men were to hold until the main force rounded up the hostages and pulled back. Then they were to follow and rejoin.

At a word they kicked their horses into a gallop and the guidons that had fluttered feebly now grew taut with the increased speed. Sun flashed on sabers, and the tails of the horses straightened out as their necks extended with the force of the gallop. Men sullen and grumbling and afraid moments before, were now part of the great moving machine. It was only a small force but it seemed as if nothing could stop it, and it swept closer to the mouth of the canyon.

Sundance yelled when a line of rifles opened fire from the rim of an arroyo to the left. Only five or six rifles were firing from there but the men behind them were firing fast and without taking proper aim. Only two troopers were knocked off their horses by the first volley and then there were no more volleys, just fast, random shooting. A horse went down in front of Sundance and he jumped Eagle over the dying, kicking animal. Shooting started on the right, not from an arroyo but from behind anything that afforded cover. The bugler blasted the charge and the line divided to attack on the right and left, on both flanks, and while it did Sundance heard the Major yelling at the men to ride straight into the canyon. At that moment, Sundance knew what was going to happen. He yelled at the Major but his words were drowned in the crash of rifle fire. The Indians firing on both flanks were driven back and were pursued, running, until they were hacked down or shot down. Up ahead, the Major was still yelling, ordering the line to close up and head for the canyon. Sundance fired at a running Apache and brought him down and killed another man wounded badly but still moving. The Major rounded his horse and rode back, urging the men with the Gatling to close up the gap. The wheels of the Gatling bounded over the broken ground as the horses ran wild-eyed, straining to shake off the weight behind them.

The line had reformed and was pouring into the canyon; the Gatling and the cannon brought up the rear. Then, moving too fast, one of the wheels broke under the Gatling and the gun crashed to one side, the barrel battered on rock as the team flogged the horses down into the canyon. It went into the canyon with both wheels broken, with the rotating barrels battered out of shape, the firing handle torn away. The small five-pounder got down without suffering any damage, but the Gatling would never fire again. It didn't make any difference. There was nothing to fire at in the canyon. Lodges still stood but they were empty. Sundance looked up at the rim of the canyon and saw what he expected to see: men spaced out along its length. A moment later they opened fire, raining down bullets from both sides. Between the breaks in the firing Sundance heard gunfire coming from up in the pass. Danforth and his men were under attack.

The canyon was small but wide and there was no cover except a stand of trees where it ended at the wall of the mountain. A cliff began at the end of the canyon and went up without a break for several hundred feet. They were heading for the trees when rifles opened up from the top of the cliff. The firing that came from up there was spaced and deliberate. In the center of the canyon the Gatling, now cut loose, lay twisted and broken. A dead horse lay close to it, and beyond it, two dead troopers. Other dead or dying troopers lay along the middle of the canyon. One man with his face half shot away screamed at Sundance as he rode past. The man had his hands out, as if in prayer, and Sundance shot him in the head and didn't wait to see him fall. A bullet creased Eagle's flank and the big stallion screamed with pain. Sundance caught up with a running man, grabbed him by the collar and dragged him toward the trees. A bullet killed the man before they got there.

Sundance rode in and jumped down. Under the trees there was good protection except from the Apaches on the cliff. By the spring that came from the base of the cliff the Major stood cursing. The spring had been covered with rocks so big that they couldn't have been carried there. The Apaches had used ropes and horses and all their strength to move rocks of that size. Fire

269

from the canyon rim slacked off, but the sniping from the cliff continued as the troopers settled into their shooting positions. The stand of pin oak gave some protection; there would have been better cover if the Apaches hadn't cleared away all the rocks and deadwood. For the moment they had water and food wouldn't be important for a while. There was plenty of dead horsemeat; a lot of men would be on foot, if they got out of there.

None of the officers there had been killed. O'Hara had a gash in his head but that was from a fall and not a bullet. Gates and the surgeon were all right. Dead troopers lay in the open and there were dead and wounded under the trees. For a drunk, MacCrae was cool under fire, moving wounded men into the middle of the trees, doing what he could for them, which wasn't much. One man's arm had been all but severed by a heavy caliber bullet. Now and then a big rifle boomed from the clifftop and it sounded more like a big old Hawken than the biggest Sharps. A trooper shot through the guts sat with his back against a tree, his pants unbuttoned, his shirt pulled up, examining the hole in his belly, moaning to himself, "You don't have to die of this. This doesn't have to kill you." No pain showed in his young face, just an awful fear of death. He seemed to be two men: one mortally wounded and knowing he was going to die, the other a kind friend giving him words of comfort. And, still talking to himself, he died.

Sundance looked at the Major and wanted to kill him. Instead, he held his rifle steady and waited for an Apache high on the cliff to show his face. The man fired and jerked back out of sight. Sundance waited and killed the Apache when he pushed out the rifle and tried to line up a shot. He fell forward but before he did another Apache grabbed the rifle. The body sailed down the cliff and bounced at the bottom. Sundance waited for another good shot but didn't get it. The Apaches had them boxed in and were saving their ammunition now that the first fierce attack had broken the back of the cavalry force. Protected from the wind, the high-walled canyon baked in the sun while the sniping went on. Soon bodies would begin to smell in the sun.

No more gunfire came from the twin peaks where the old Spanish road went through to Mexico. It wasn't likely that any of Danforth's small force had survived. More than half the main force had been killed or wounded; and any wound that wouldn't respond to Captain MacCrae's rough doctoring meant the man who had it would die. MacCrae moved among the men looking at their wounds, leaving those who would die no matter what he did, and except for a few who cried out and clawed at him, they took it well. Those with flesh wounds had the best chance; anyone with bullet-shattered bones was already dead. First came the swelling, then the gangrene. After the gangrene set in there would be no more pain. They would stink, but there would be no more pain. A compensation, Sundance thought, turning away from a man who was missing the lower half of his jaw, crying quietly, praying for death.

After warning Comiskey to watch for a sudden attack, Major Randolph waved Gates and O'Hara to where the best cover was. Bullets still came from the cliff, thocking into tree trunks, showering leaves when a branch was broken, but where the trees were thickest there was little danger of being killed except by a stray bullet. Under the trees it would have been peaceful if there hadn't been a battle going on. As it was, the occasional shot from the cliff didn't seem to disturb the silence very much.

Major Randolph was talking about a frontal assault and what they would do about it if it came.

"They won't attack like that," Sundance said, levering a round, still wanting to kill the Major. "They don't have to so they won't. Before they rocked up the spring they took all the water they needed. No way to tell how much ammunition they have. Enough. Major, they don't have to do anything but wait."

Gates hated the Major and dared to show some of it. "What are you going to do, sir?"

"We're going to hold," Major Randolph said.

"Then what, sir?"

Major Randolph spoke to Sundance instead of answering Gates. "What do you think?"

The Major seemed to know that he would get a straight, hard answer; there would be no anger, no recriminations.

"It's very bad," Sundance answered. "About as bad as it can get. All we can do is try to break out when it gets dark. I don't know what good that will do. Maybe no good. But there's nothing else left but that. At least half the men are dead or can't fight. You're going to lose a lot more when we make the break."

Jackman had been chewing on a blade of grass. He spat it out. "Sundance is right, Major. It can only get worse. My guess is all Victorio's men aren't here yet. The ones far to the south will be coming in soon. He's lost some men but that will make up for it. If we don't break out at night we're dead. We may be dead either way."

Sundance knew they were all thinking the same thing. They all knew so there was no need to talk about it. There would be no reinforcements from the fort, no relief column. The garrison was shorthanded as it was,

272

and the men they had were all they were going to get.

"Then that's what we'll do," Major Randolph said, as if he had a choice. "We'll break out tonight."

Jackman looked at Sundance. "Victorio will figure that's what we'll do."

"That's what he'll figure, what he's counting on. That's why he rocked off the spring, led us in here. Moving those rocks would be a job even without the sniping. If we try to use horses they'll be shooting at the horses. Anyway, the water could be poisoned."

Jackman spat. "I thought of that. You think we got any chance at all?"

"Not much if we try to go out the way we came in."

Jackman was tough enough to grin at the idea. "Seems to me that's the only way out. Suppose we make it, what happens then? Most likely Victorio has already set up a surprise for us. Sure, we'll get fire from the rimrock, but that'll be just to help us on our way. We'll have to go straight at them when we get out of the canyon. They'll fire the brush and knock us down at will. You think I'm wrong?"

"Not if we do it like that."

Jackman grinned again, finding sour humor in the hopeless situation. "But you know a better way?"

"Another way," Sundance said, waiting for the Major's reaction. "Another way and maybe a worse way."

"You're crazy," Jackman said. "You fell and hit your head. That's what you must have done. What you're saying is crazy."

"Is it?" Sundance said, knowing it was the only chance they had.

Major Randolph frowned impatiently. "What in blazes are you talking about?"

Jackman said, "Sundance wants to break out into the

Ninety Mile Desert." He waved. "Out there. West. That's where it is. Country so hot your blood boils in your veins. If you could spit, which you can't, it would dry up before it hit the ground. It's on the maps, Major, but that's about all we know. It's been crossed though I don't know by who. The Spanish crossed it. The Spanish did everything. Take my word for it, Major, it's the closest you'll come to hell on this earth."

For a moment fire from the cliff picked up and bullets spattered through the leaves over their heads. Gates ducked in spite of himself; the others didn't do anything. The last bullets from the cliff wounded a horse. Then a dying trooper shot the horse before he shot himself.

"It's as bad as he says," Sundance said. "The Spanish crossed it, so have other men. The Spanish moved in large numbers and had guns. The Apaches didn't. The Spanish always carried plenty of water, no matter what else had to be left behind."

"But to cross it—to where? On the map there is nothing but mountains." Major Randolph didn't reach for his map case.

Sundance said, "I don't mean to cross it. The Apaches aren't afraid of much but they fear the Ninety Mile. Good reason to. My plan, if you can call it a plan, is to head out across the desert, then head north till we meet the dry river and follow it back to the fort."

Gates didn't look so good. "But the Apaches will follow us into the desert."

"We may not even make it to the desert," Sundance said. "We'll be lucky if we do."

Jackman spat. "Some luck."

"What you say means going over the west rim of the canyon," Major Randolph said. "If you're wrong about Victorio moving most of the men to block the

274

mouth we'll be slaughtered. I'm not arguing, just making a point."

The Major is backing down some, Sundance thought. A bit late, but anything was better than the way he had been.

"If I'm wrong then we'll be dead. Some of us will anyway. I'm just going by what I know about Victorio, about all Apaches. It could be that he has already figured on a break through the desert. If so, there's nothing else to talk about. Trying to go out the third way, over the pass and down into Mexico, won't work. First we'd have to go up the east rim. Even if we made it up we'd still have to get through the pass. It has to be the desert, Major. That way—or nothing. Your decision to make."

Major Randolph stared at Sundance, trying to see past the words. Then, finding nothing, he nodded. "The desert it is. Lieutenant Gates?"

"Yes, sir."

"Get started on it now. All canteens are to be collected. Those partly empty are to be filled from others. Keep some of the empty canteens in case, God willing, we find a waterhole out there. As soon as it gets dark get the canteens of the men in the open."

"I'll do that," Sundance said, knowing there would be noise if he didn't collect the canteens himself.

Jackman said he'd help with the canteens and the Major nodded. Then he went on: "Tell the men to get rid of everything but what they need. Make them turn out their pockets if you have to. Nothing that can drag them down. Not by as much as a pound. That goes for pistols. They keep their knives. Let them know what they're in for, Gates. Work you way over to the left. O'Hara, you take the right."

Jackman went with the junior officers and bullets

sang at them when they had to cross a clearing in the trees. They made it to safety and the Apache fire died down.

Major Randolph looked at Sundance. "What about the horses? It's a long climb to the top."

Sundance had studied the west rim of the canyon. Most of it was too steep to climb, but there was a place not far from the cliff where it was broken and sandy and it might be possible to get out with a few of the horses.

"The horses are going to buy us a little time," Sundance said. "If the Apaches fall for it, they will. As soon as we're ready to make a break for it we'll send the horses out through the mouth of the canyon. We'll tie the wounded in their saddles, use dead men too. That way when the Apaches fire the brush they'll see more than just runaway horses. It's going to be tough on the wounded, but they'll die anyway."

The Major fairly bristled with anger and Sundance waited for him to let it out. "You would do that to wounded men?"

"I'd go myself but I'm not wounded," Sundance said slowly, hating to think of what had to be done. Not all the wounded would be killed; those not so lucky would be captured by the Apaches. They would die by inches, given over to the women and the old men who knew all the ways to make a man suffer. "There's no point talking about it," Sundance said. "I know what you're going to say. Leave the wounded, those that can to hold the Apaches for a while, fight a rearguard action while we break out of the canyon. It just won't work. Like it or not, we have to send the horses out with men on their backs. But you do what you like, Major."

"I'm glad you said that," Major Randolph said. "You were beginning to sound like you were in command. You've been thinking about that, haven't you? Nobody's listening. Say what you want to say."

"I've thought about it," Sundance said. "I've got nothing to say about anything but getting out. You led us in here, Major, and you're going to lead us out."

"You mean you are?"

"All right, you want to force it, here it is. You better lead us out, Major. I'll do it if you don't do it right. If that means taking your gun or killing you, that's what I'll do. This may be your army but I won't see any more men killed for nothing. I've been watching them today and they're all right. Given a chance they're all right. I mean to give them a chance. And don't go telling me you can have me shot for such talk. It wouldn't take much to kill you, the way I feel. Pull a gun on me, sir, and I'll blow your head off."

Major Randolph's hand moved away from the holster. "This isn't over, Sundance. You just talked to me like no man ever did, in or out of the army. So it can't be over between us."

"It may be over already," Sundance said.

"Over or not, I won't forget this," Major Randolph said. "But we're here so we have to make the best of it."

"Suits me."

"How many horses you think we should try to take over the rim?" Major Randolph asked. "Why try to take any horses? They won't be any good in the desert."

If the Major had done any fighting in real desert he would not have found it necessary to ask about the horses.

"The horses have blood in them," Sundance said. "That goes for my horse too. We have to stay alive any way we can, even if it comes to drinking horse blood."

The thought of drinking horse blood didn't sit too well on the Major's stomach. "If we have to," he said curtly. "At least you didn't say anything about dying men."

It was good to take some of the starch out of the Major. "That's been done too," he said.

Ten

The day dragged on as if the sun would never set again. In the canyon there wasn't a breath of air and the bodies lying in the sun began to bloat. Blue flies crawled on the faces of the dead. Far out a man they thought was dead began to cry for help, and not getting any, began to scream, trapped in his agony by the dead horse that had crushed his legs. The dead horse was between the crippled trooper and the stand of trees, so there was no way to kill him, to put him out of his misery. The Apaches would have killed him from where they were, but they let him live, savoring his pain, wanting him to live as long as he could.

Only the badly wounded took no heed of his cries; the faces of the other men twitched as the screaming went on. Soon it dwindled down to sobbing and cursing, but he kept it up, and in the still, hot canyon it sounded very loud. It didn't bother Sundance any more than it should have; he knew it was getting to some of the men; it wasn't a good way to prepare for the fight ahead.

He crawled out past the forward firing positions, ignoring the Major's order to come back. In his dun-colored buckskins he was able to crawl to the last of the trees before the Apaches on the rim opened fire. No fire came from the cliff because they couldn't see him from there with the trees blocking their view. Now he was as far forward as he could go without being chewed by bullets. Bullets came at him as he ran from one tree to another without being hit. Then he got to the biggest tree, one that had been split by lightning, and swung up into the lower branches, while bullets sang through the leaves. The firing continued as he climbed higher into the tree. The Apaches kept on shooting, and missing, and then he braced his back against the trunk of the tree and parted the leaves with his hand. Braced that way, he lined up the Winchester, but all he saw over the sights was the middle of the dead horse. He could see the crippled man's legs, but not the rest of him. He would have to go higher to get a shot at the head because that was all he would see. Then he heard the Major yell out the order to return the Apache's fire. A volley rang out from the trees and the Apache fire slacked off, then resumed, and now he was about as high as he could go. On all sides, below and around him, the firing went on.

All he could see was the crippled man's head; the dead horse lay squarely on top of him, pinning him to the ground. It was a long shot and there wouldn't be time to fire many shots. Once he fired the first time the Apaches on the rim, those closest to the tree, would be able to fix his position. They would be shooting at branches and leaves instead of a clear target, but if enough of them shot at the same place one bullet would be sure to find its mark.

From where he was it was well over three hundred yards from the muzzle of his rifle to the man's head, a small target at such distance. He had to shoot without a rest, bracing himself as best he could against the bole of the tree. He moved up the rifle and sighted along the barrel. The trooper still had his cap on, the leather tight under the chin, and the head moved and the screaming went on while he sighted again. Sundance didn't know who the man was; there was no way to know what he looked like. It was time to get it done. Sundance made one last sighting, just below the bottom of the cap, and squeezed the trigger. The head exploded under the impact of the heavy bullet and he slid his body over the side of a branch and dropped to the ground, landing easily and going over in a handspring as bullets chased him away from the tree and behind another. They waited and opened fire again, but this time he went the other way and, running and weaving, he made his way back to safety. Then all firing ceased for an instant and when some of the troopers opened up again the Major ordered them to stop. It was quiet in the bright sunlight, and from the trees to the mouth of the canyon nothing moved.

The sun began to die.

Sundance moved over to where MacCrae was talking softly to a wounded man.

"What is it?" the doctor asked when Sundance motioned him to one side.

"Save any liquor you got till we move out," Sundance said.

The doctor had whiskey on his breath. "Some of them need it now. There's nothing left but liquor and not much of that. What do you expect me to do?"

"Just what I tell you," Sundance said. "I want them lively when we send them out. That means you save the liquor for the last."

MacCrae was turning away when Sundance stopped him with a sharp command.

"I heard what you said," MacCrae snapped, rubbing at his booze-reddened eyes. "You don't have to repeat it."

"I mean all the liquor," Sundance said. "That goes for your own supply. Everything goes to the wounded, you understand. Don't let me catch you with liquor after we leave here."

MacCrae made a feeble effort to assert himself. "I'm the doctor here. I'll decide how much alcohol is to be kept."

Sundance liked the way the doctor called it alcohol now that his private supply was threatened. "No," Sundance said. "You won't decide, not about that. It goes to the wounded. They're going to need it. You, Captain, are going to have to sober up."

"What does Major Randolph have to say about this?" MacCrae argued.

"Nothing," Sundance said. "Suppose you ask him. You problem is—I don't give a damn what the Major says. Don't let me catch you with liquor."

The sky had been red for a long time and still it wasn't dark. Under the trees it was dark, but in the open there was light enough to shoot by. Cookfires smoked beyond the rim of the canyon and now that the wind was down some smoke drifted down to the flat. The men huddled in the gathering darkness, chewing patiently on jerked meat, talking quietly or not at all, waiting for orders. Some of the wounded had died and lay stiffening with men they had known chewing meat close by. In an hour or so the bodies would lose their stiffness and by then they would be supple enough to rope onto the backs of horses. Then the others would be doped with whiskey and medical alcohol and readied for their last ride.

Major Randolph was very quiet as he spun the cylinder of his Army .45. Now and then a shot rang out from the cliff; mostly it was quiet. The Major looked up as Sundance came close. Looking out at the red-hued canyon, he said, "I don't know there's much left to do."

Sundance nodded. "Not a lot. Once it gets dark we'll move the wounded out to the edge of the trees, make enough noise to be heard. Not so much they'll catch on some of us are going the other way. I'll touch off the cannon when we're set. But we don't go until the wounded are in the mouth of the canyon and the Apaches open fire. That'll draw the others down from the rim. That's the idea, Major. If Victorio outguesses us we'll be walking into it.''

Major Randolph put his revolver away. The dying sun was throwing long shadows across the canyon and it was quiet. "Wouldn't it be better to wait until late?''

Sundance said no. "They have us bottled, but some of them will try to come in. They don't have to come in the dark, so maybe Victorio will order a night attack. We go in less than an hour or we don't go at all.''

The last light was thick with dust motes swirling in places where there were breaks in the overhanging branches. Horses were lined up and held and wounded men were loaded on like sacks of meal. The doctor moved along the line with a bottle in his hand, followed by his orderly carrying another bottle. Some men, well mannered even in their last few minutes on earth, drank no more than they were offered. Others grabbed at the bottle until it had to be pulled away. Some of the doomed men took it well enough and some didn't, but no matter how they took it, the others held him firmly in their saddles, executioners who themselves had to face their own deaths in a few minutes.

One young trooper, drunk on the small amount of whiskey the doctor had given him, began to sing. The doctor ordered him to be quiet but he laughed instead. "What'll you do, Doc? Send me to the guardhouse?'' And he laughed again, and kept on laughing.''

Two men were pulling the five-pounder into the firing position.

"All right,'' Major Randolph said and Jackman took

the cigar from his mouth and touched it to the cannon. The five-pounder bucked under the explosion and the shot whistled into the darkness. For an instant their eyes were blinded by belching flame. A trooper cut loose with the bugle and they whipped the horses away from the trees, yelling them out into the canyon mouth which seemed to burst into flame from one side to the other. They drove the horses out, flogging them, goading them with sharp sticks until the animals were frantic with pain and terror. Ahead of them the bone-dry brush heaped up by the Apaches crackled and flamed, lighting the darkness like a nightmare. The horses ran wildly into the wall of fire, some trying to break through it, some trying to turn back.

"Not yet," Sundance cautioned. "Go when they open fire."

The firing following his words, and from behind the wall of flame and on both sides of it the Apaches loosed the first volley as the dead and dying and wounded bore down on them. Some of the wounded yelled their last defiance as the hail of Apache bullets swept them from their saddles, and the screaming of the Indians mingled with the screaming of the horses. It would be over in minutes.

Sundance made for the break in the canyon wall with Eagle moving swiftly behind him. Some of the troopers were on the slope, digging their boots into the sliding sand, trying to find a way up. Some were taking the horses up too fast. One horse fell over backward close to the top and buried two men on the way down. One was killed, the other was all right. The survivor grabbed his sand-fouled rifle and started up again. Major Randolph was still at the foot of the slope, holding his horse with one hand, urging the men forward with the other. No shooting had come from the top, but now it came, ragged but fierce. The brush fire had petered out and the fight there was over except for an occasional shot. Apaches had come through the fire and were pouring into the canyon, running through the center, trying to catch them between the floor of the canyon and the other Indians coming along the rim.

Some of the horses couldn't make it to the top, and had to be left. Yelling now, the troopers clawed their way up and over the top, killing the Apaches there, driving the rest back. Firing steadily with his .45, Major Randolph ordered the men to hold on the rim. Sundance yelled at Randolph to get the men away from there. They could hold for a few minutes, but by then they would have Apaches coming at them from three sides. Sundance grabbed Randolph's arm and was shaken off, then Randolph ordered the men to fall back. Jackman was killed as he ran.

The far side of the canyon ran downhill through dry yellow grass; there was a level stretch of rock and sand, then it dropped again. Fire from the canyon glowed weakly as they ran. By now the Apaches had gained the rim and were firing after them, shooting into the gathering darkness. In the darkness the rifles spat red and yellow and for a while the Apaches pursued them until repeated commands brought them back. For now, Victorio was calling off the attack, unwilling to risk his men in a night ambush, a sudden about-face by the troopers. Victorio was in no hurry, not now. He knew where they were going and, as soon as first light came, he would start after them.

Lieutenant O'Hara and six enlisted men had been killed during the breakout. There was no time to take stock of the others. They were alive and they were moving. At first they ran, sobbing for breath after seven or eight hundred yards. Some were ready to collapse by the time a command from the Major slowed them up. Back in the canyon the Apaches were yelling, then there was no yelling and no light in the sky. It was as if no battle had taken place. Out of the canyon there was wind, gritty and cold as it blew down from the twin peaks they couldn't see in the dark.

There was no moon and the darkness was so deep it almost had texture. They moved keeping close together in spite of the Major's order to spread out. Three horses were left. Sundance's and two cavalry mounts. As they moved forward the men called out their names. Sundance listened for Sergeant Comiskey's name. It came, hoarse and confident. Gates was alive and so was the surgeon. Two miles from the canyon they rested for a few minutes, then moved on.

The desert began with surprising suddenness. Stars pinpointed the sky and when the light grew stronger they could see the desert in front of them, and even in the washed-out light it seemed to go on forever. Barrel cactus stood up in the half-light; the arms of the cactus seemed to point them toward—nothing. Signposts to nowhere.

After telling the Major what he was going to do, Sundance stayed behind to check their back trail while the others moved ahead. The sound of boots crunching in sand went away and it was quiet. Sundance crouched in the shadow of a cactus and waited. Under his moccasined feet the sand was cooling fast; soon, in the immense basin of the Ninety Mile Desert, it would be very cold. The middle of the desert was below sea level, and while they weren't going that far out, during the day it would get so hot that it wouldn't make any difference. Arizona was the land of extremes, blistering days and freezing nights, but men could get used to that if they followed certain rules. Out in the Ninety Mile there was no way to get used to anything. Out there the desert made the rules, but once a man tried to follow one rule it changed, and so did the one after that, and soon instinct replaced thought; heat and cold and thirst and hunger gave way to a great loneliness. In the desert men banded together as a way of survival, but there was no comradeship as death drew near.

Sundance waited for thirty minutes, silent in the shadows, listening for sounds—anything. Nothing came on the wind and he knew he would have smelled the Apaches if they had been close. A night-hunting sidewinder, out of its nest after the heat of the day, made tracks in the sand a few feet away. The snake swam out of sight in the sand, and nothing moved after that.

He caught them up without any difficulty; they weren't making such good time. Coming up on them he made plenty of noise, and though they knew he'd be coming back, some of the jittery ones dropped into a firing position. Then he heard Major Randolph telling them to put up their rifles.

"Nothing to report," Sundance told the Major while the men took a five-minute rest, making the most of the water Comiskey doled out to them. "If they're out there I didn't see them. That doesn't mean they aren't there. My guess, they won't come at us in the dark. Not this first night. We still have enough men, enough rifles, to inflict heavy casualties. They won't come at night until they wear us down. The desert will do most of the work."

Major Randolph said, "There's something you aren't saying."

"No use laying it all out at once," Sundance said. "They may have started out—some of them—right after we did."

"Then where are they?"

"They could be in front of us by now. I'm not saying they are. They could be. An Apache can travel faster on less than any man here."

"Except you, of course."

Sundance bypassed the Major's tired sneer. "If they have circled out wide and got in front of us they'll set up an ambush. Try to. That's one of the things we have to watch for. The Apaches behind will try to see that we don't. If they make a full scale attack from the rear, forget about the ambush. But if they hang back and snipe at us, that's when we have to tread carefully."

"How do you propose to do that?"

"Best way we can. A couple of men on point won't do it. They won't see the Apaches and they'll just walk on through. Single file is just as bad when we get to places that look good for an ambush. They'll try to break the line, divide the force."

Major Randolph stood up and set his hat straight on his head. "Single file is how it's done."

"The Apaches would agree with you, Major. They've been studying the army so long they know every move, every tactic."

"Don't be so modest. You're thinking you showed them some new one back at the canyon."

"A spaced-out line is better than single file," Sundance said. "We should spread out in a wide line when we come to ambush spots. No desert is all sand. This one is mostly flats and dunes, but we'll come to places. Broken rock, old dry rivers."

"But you're not sure?"

"No way to be sure about the Apaches. I'd sure as hell rather be fighting somebody besides Victorio."

"You think he's that good?"

"They're all good or they wouldn't be chiefs. Geronimo is tougher than Victorio, tougher than any man white or red, but he isn't as smart as Victorio. Geronimo had a style of fighting that worked well enough for a time. With Victorio it has to be different. Sometimes he'll do his thinking in reverse, figuring that if we're smart we'll be doing the same. Other times he'll keep it simple and fight like Geronimo, wear us down, attack and withdraw, then do it again. Like I said, there's no way to be sure."

Major Randolph looked up at the sky. "The men need sleep. It's been over a day and a half since we left the fort and they've been in two fights since then. Some look ready to fall down."

"They better not fall down here. We'll move on till the sun is full up. Traveling by day is no good. Somewhere else, all right, not out here. We'll do some day walking when we have to. Don't see how we can avoid it. You'd best pass the word, sir."

Major Randolph stiffened but knew he had to listen. All his so-called Indian fighting in the Dakotas wasn't worth a damn in this country. A murmur of protest ran through the men as the order was relayed by way of Gates and Comiskey. But that's all it was. *This is the easy part*, Sundance thought. *They think they've had it bad, but they haven't started on the main course yet.* Soon the muttering would grow louder and then, close to despair, they would look at the Major and fester with the thought that he had led them into this. The greenest recruit would grumble about tactics and what the Major shouldn't have done and what he ought to do now. And then the Major would become the enemy because he was real, had a shape and a voice, and every order he gave, right or wrong, would be further proof that he was trying to get them killed, and they would hate him as much as the knowledge that they couldn't throw away their rifles and surrender. Knowing what the Apaches would do would keep them in line—for a while.

As they moved on into the night, shuddering with cold, Sundance knew there would be trouble with the men. They were good enough men, good enough for men who had run away from wives or the law or enlisted while drunk or for just about any reason, but the long peace with the Apaches had spoiled them, and it wasn't their fault or the army's. Those who came through this would be better soldiers and, though they hated it now, later they would brag about how tough they were. Those who survived would have a kinship they didn't have now. And what they didn't have now was a real fighting spirit. Maybe they would find that spirit, and maybe they wouldn't.

Starlight filled the sky and it got colder; their breath was white in the cold air. They pushed on, urged by Sergeant Comiskey, himself moving without effort, an old campaigner at his best in the thick of trouble. For what he was, Comiskey was the best of the enlisted men, and better, in his way, than Lieutenant Gates. It was too bad that O'Hara had been killed instead of Gates. There had been a quietness about him that suggested reserves of strength. Gates wasn't that kind of man, which wasn't to say that he wouldn't do a good enough job. That was the trouble with Gates: he was just good enough.

The surgeon, MacCrae, didn't matter much, and there was a better than even chance that his booze-soaked body wouldn't be able to take it. Anyway, his doctoring skills wouldn't count for anything where they were going. From here on in he was just another man who could shoot a rifle.

Comiskey would hold up. Sundance guessed the Major would too. His pride would keep him going when his body wanted to call it quits, and Sundance decided that he would side the Major as long as he was worth siding. It was an agreement but nothing that couldn't be changed with a bullet.

Slowly, as they moved on, the desert turned red.

Eleven

At first it glowed red as if the door of some great, distant blast furnace had been opened for a moment. Then the light came up white and strong and blinding, as if the furnace door had been opened all the way. There was no wind and the motionless air seemed frozen in the first harsh light of morning, and the desert was washed with colors of many hues: red, purple and brown. Cactuses threw long black shadows against the white glare of the sand; in the distance were white dunes that rolled away like billows on the sea. Then as the sun flooded up to full light, the wind came up too, lifting the sand on top of dunes like froth on top of waves.

The passing of darkness seemed to lighten the spirits of the men; to give back some of the energy that had been weakened by fear and the fading of hope. Sundance knew that before an hour had passed they would look back on the night with longing; the bitter cold would seem like a lost dream that could never be recaptured.

But for the moment they seemed almost cheerful; they knew where they were; they could see it. The sullen aloneness of each man gave way to nervous banter, an attempt at reassurance.

Soon the sun that had warmed them tried to kill them. It beat down with silent hammer blows, silent force echoing in silence. The sound of voices died in the vast emptiness of the desert. Light on the dunes hurt their eyes like sun-glare on snow, and the wind-blown sand gritted in their teeth, filling their ears and noses.

They crossed the sandy ocean of dunes with their heads bent against the wind, sucking in air so hot it seemed to blister their lungs. The two cavalry mounts kicked feebly as they were kicked and pulled through the knee-deep sand. Atop the highest dune, Sundance scouted the country behind. Nothing moved in the hot silence; high above, buzzards sailed lazily in the pitiless blue sky. The desert ran away in front of them until it was lost in the shimmer of heatwaves.

Major Randolph looked at Sundance. "How long?"

"Not till noon, when it's hottest. Maybe a little before if we find shade."

"And if we don't?"

"Then the men will have to bundle up best they can. There's no other way."

The sun climbed up into the sky like a great ball of polished brass; the whole world seemed to vibrate with its force. Past the dunes they rested and drank, wetting their cracked lips with drops of water, grunting angrily as Comiskey forced them to give back the canteens. Now and then, Sundance found Comiskey looking at him, daring him with a glance, silently betting that he wasn't going to make it. All their faces were white with alkali, like masks, with only the eyes alive, staring out from their private fears, unable to say what they wanted to say.

The hours were slow as a man running in a nightmare. Here, in the sun, the nightmare was real; there was a gray sameness to the landscape that made it seem as if they were standing still, the ground under their feet a treadmill. Only to Sundance was the desert as varied as farmland or mountain. It looked desolate and empty, but there was life here, lizards, birds, snakes, even animals; man was the only creature that didn't belong.

Sometime after eleven he saw a rise in the ground about a mile away, an ancient riverbed that ran from north to south, cutting into the floor of the desert as far as the eye could follow. Nothing grew along the waterless banks, but the long bump in the land said a river had been there unnumbered years before.

"That's where we'll sleep," Sundance said, pointing. "It's best to make the approach we talked about. Break the line, Major."

Major Randolph nodded and gave the order and this time he didn't relay it through an officer and a noncom. "Go in steady," he ordered. "A steady pace as we move it. If they're in there we'll have to take it."

Rifles ready, they spread out in a line and started for the riverbed. Now that they knew where they were going, had an objective after all the brain-numbing miles, there was more purpose in their movements. Comiskey called out to a trooper who was moving too fast.

They still had more than four hundred yards to go, and the shooting, if it came, wouldn't start until they had gone well over half the distance. The only sound as they moved was the creak of leather, the dull clack of metal.

Major Randolph unholstered his .45 and blew dust from the barrel. He spun the cylinder and cursed the grating sound it made. "You're the chief scout," he said. "Are they there or not?"

"As soon as I count off two hundred yards I'll let you know," Sundance said. "I'd say yes if the river ran the same way we're going. That way they could hope to catch us from the side."

Walking beside the Major, Sundance didn't have to count the distance. He knew where it would come;

Victorio wouldn't bend the rules that far. If he let them get too close they might overrun his position; to open fire when they were still far out would be just as big a mistake.

"They aren't there," Sundance said. "We're past the point where they would have opened fire."

"You sure of that?"

"Sure as I can be. We'll know when we get there."

They went in slowly, some of the men tottering with fatigue, ready to drop because they knew they could drop. For a while, they could. The banks of the river were still high after centuries of wind, and they had to slide down, some falling and tumbling and not caring, trembling with eagerness to sleep. At first they sprawled all over the riverbed, heedless of the sun, now close to the noon position. Comiskey walked over them dragging the sentries to their feet, kicking men who wouldn't get up. Comiskey never drew his revolver. Instead, he used his fists and his boots. One by one, he dragged and pushed them to their posts, threatening what would happen if they fell asleep.

The men who were allowed to sleep burrowed into the sandy banks of the river, digging with their hands, cursing when sand collapsed on the holes they had made. A few kept at it while the others, too tired to go on, pulled their hats over their eyes and slept like stones. The sleeping men twitched as they slept, as if they were cold. Sundance guessed the temperature was at least a hundred and twenty. He watered Eagle and made do with a single mouthful himself. The two other horses looked bad, drooping in the heat, their legs unsteady. One horse was in worse shape than the other, and Sundance killed it with a powerful thrust of the long-bladed Bowie. Struck behind the left ear, the horse died instantly, kicked twice and crashed to the ground.

Sundance looked at Comiskey. Comiskey was smiling. Up on the banks the sentries turned at the sound, then went back to watching the desert.

Major Randolph stripped off his uniform coat and asked Sundance for his knife. Sundance passed it over without a word, and after the Major removed his insignia he slashed the coat to ribbons. Taking off the coat was something he should have done before they left the fort.

Major Randolph gave back the knife. "I don't want to see my coat on some Apache," he said. "Is it true that Victorio still wears the coat my uncle gave him? I always thought that was a peculiar thing to do."

Sundance said, "I never heard of him wearing it. I guess he's wearing it now. Your uncle gave him the coat, Victorio gave him a blanket. An exchange of gifts, one friend to another. Not exactly friends, enemies who saw the need for peace. You don't have to love the Apaches, Major. They wouldn't like it if you did."

Major Randolph tried to spit, but gave it up after the first try. "I sure as hell don't love them now. At least we know where we are."

"Where are we, Major?"

Oddly, the Major's smile seemed to be real. It was hardly the place for smiling, but the Major smiled. "We're carrying out an orderly retreat," he said. "You think we're doing something else?"

"I thought we were trying to get away with our lives," Sundance said. "I guess you could call that a retreat. The only thing is, my understanding of the word is something you do before you counterattack. You figure to attack the Apaches?"

Major Randolph smiled again. "Not right now. But the answer is yes. I'll tell you something else. I'm going to come through this and then we'll see about the

Apaches. When I hang Victorio he's going to be wearing my uncle's coat."

"Your uncle wouldn't like that, supposing you could do it."

"No suppose about it. I'll do it all right. I'm beginning to think all this talk about Victorio is just that. Look around you, sir. Do you see any Apaches?"

"I'd just as soon not, Major."

"How long ago did we break out of that canyon? I make it about eighteen hours. We lost men but so did they. My point—maybe they don't want to lose any more. If they're coming, then why haven't they come?"

"They'll be here. Depend on that, Major. You made your point, now I'll make mine. In eighteen hours the Apaches can be anywhere. Don't you think that Victorio has figured where we're going? Where else could we go but the river? Our only hope is to get there before he does. If he's already at the river I don't know what to say."

"I think you're wrong. If Victorio takes all his men into the desert, uses every man to hunt us down, then what about his villages? The villages will be left undefended."

"Nobody's going to attack the villages."

"How can Victorio know that reinforcements won't be coming from Camp Bain?"

"Because he makes it his business to know things like that. Anyway, if a column did come from Bain it wouldn't be to attack the villages. They'd be coming for us. No, Major, Victorio's business is with us, mainly you. The rest of us are just along for the walk. Victorio wants you."

For some reason, the Major seemed to like the idea. "He better be careful he doesn't find me. All right, I grant you we took a beating at the canyon. It's happened before in this man's army, so it'll happen again. Soldiers are paid to soldier, soldiers get killed. It goes with the job. Now if you don't mind I'm going to get some sleep."

Sundance slept for two hours and when he awoke the Major was still hunched over with his hands wrapped around his knees, his hat pulled over his eyes. His shirt was sweated through and he muttered in his sleep. His hands, clutching his knees, looked big and helpless. Dozing not far from the Major, Comiskey jerked awake when Sundance stood up. It was quiet except for the snoring, the muffled grunts of the men.

Comiskey hadn't spoken to Sundance since the fight. Under the white mask of dust, his face was lumpy but most of the swelling had gone down. Comiskey was sweating like the others, but it was just sweat, not fear coming out through his pores.

"Where are you going?" he asked. "I'm just interested, bucko. No need to get your back up."

Sundance looked at the man he had beaten so badly. "I'm going to take a look around. Along the river a ways."

"I thought about that," Comiskey said. "Mind if I walk along?"

"Do what suits you," Sundance said.

They walked north along the riverbed and it was just slightly less of a furnace than it had been. It was three hours past noon, but the sun hadn't lost any of its force. A lizard skittered across sand and hid under a rock. Here and there were ancient trees now turned to stone.

Comiskey picked up a pebble and sucked on it. Sundance wondered if the New York hooligan planned to come at him with a knife when they were out of sight. Maybe it would be just as well if he did. It would finish the feud that was none of his making. He would kill

298

Comiskey before his hand moved an inch. There was no reason not to use the Colt; the shot wouldn't give them away; the Apaches knew where they were.

It was at that moment that Sundance knew what Victorio was going to do. Hit them the moment it got dark, just as they were preparing to move out for the night march.

If Comiskey had any plans to murder him they were quickly forgotten. "Sure, that's what they're going to do. We'll be getting ourselves together and they'll come along the riverbed, both sides, north and south. They can't get close by day, so that has to be it. And all the time I was thinking it would come later tonight. Late at night, with the men tired. The sleep they're getting won't do much good."

"Then you agree?"

"Didn't I just tell you I did? The thing is now, how are we going to stop them? I guess we can beat them off, but I'd like to do more than that. Like kill a lot of them, is what I mean."

Sundance nodded. Comiskey was right. Beating off an Apache attack wasn't enough; it had to be more decisive than that. What they had to do was give them such a pasting that Victorio would have to think about changing his plans. Fifteen men were left, troopers and officers. A small force but everone was armed with .45-70 caliber Winchesters, the 8-shooter the army was trying out in the Southwest. In the big caliber it took half as many bullets as some carbines, but once a man was knocked down by a .45-70 he stayed down. Sundance always thought the .45-70 could have used a longer barrel, but they had fixed it at twenty-six inches, and that's what they had. It was plenty in the hands of men who knew how to use it.

"Stage an ambush, that's how we're going to do it,"

Sundance said. "We have to figure they'll come by the riverbed. You think it will work any other way?"

"Not a chance of it. If they attack from both sides of the river instead of down the middle, we're done for. Maybe not done for. We could hold for a while. The only other thought I have, is we can pull out now while it's still light. I'd say that would just be putting it off. You think that?"

"That's what I think," Sundance said. "Once it got dark they could come at us late like you said, when the men are falling over their feet. They didn't attack last night because the men were still fresh. Fairly fresh, anyway, able to fight better. We have to bet on the river."

Comiskey rubbed at his sweat- and alkali-smeared face. "Sure," he said, "but how are we to draw them in close? We can draw them in just by standing around. The next minute we won't know what hit us. But somebody has to be there when they come sneaking down that river. I'll tell you what. I'll pick out the men should be moving around when the Apaches come. A few men I got a special feeling for, if you get my meaning."

They turned a bend in the river and there was a straight stretch that went for a mile. "That wouldn't work," Sundance said. "You'd have to put the fear of God in them to make them stand there as bait."

"That could be done. I could do it," Comiskey said. "It's face me or the Indians. I'd be just as bad, believe you me."

Sundance said, "You could make them stand there, but the Apaches would know something was wrong. One of them might bolt and give it away. I don't think we're going to get another chance as good."

"I'll do it," Comiskey said.

"That makes two of us. Three would be enough if we

rigged up a few dummies."

"They're all dummies for my money," Comiskey said.

A trooper named Cranley volunteered to stand with them, and while the guards watched for Apaches the others cut cactus limbs and used rocks to prop them up in the center of the riverbed. The Major's knife-slashed coat got a place of honor. Men stripped to their undershirts and used the outer shirts to outfit the dummies when they were in place.

Major Randolph looked doubtful. "You'd have to be blind to be fooled by those. Maybe they'll look better after dark. I still don't like you and Sergeant Comiskey using yourselves as bait. If they come you'll be right in the middle."

"That's where you come in," Sundance said. "Whether we live depends on how heavy a fire you lay down. The first ten or fifteen seconds are going to decide it. You have to give us time to find cover."

"You'll get it," Major Randolph said. "The force will be split, half the men on one side, half on the other. Men on both banks. There and there."

"Not so close together," Sundance said. "Move them out a bit. Tell the men to wait until the last Apache passes, then they open fire. It's best they check their rifles again. Then one last check before it gets dark. One or two sand-fouled rifles could cost us the whole shooting match. Tell the men to watch for an Apache with a big rifle. That's the old Hawken they were using up on the cliff. A long range gun could give us plenty of trouble if we don't get it. They'll know the sound when they hear it. Loud as a Big Fifty Sharps, maybe louder. If we don't get the Hawken the man that carries it can just lay back and knock us down at will."

Major Randolph frowned at his coat flapping in the

301

hot wind. "What happens if we get spotted? If they're as smart as you say?"

"Then you open fire, kill as many as you can. You're not supposed to get spotted, Major. So no ducking up and down. Nobody wears a hat. The minute it gets dark the men climb up the bank and crawl to their positions. Just one man raising his head can ruin this. When they reach their positions they lie there. Not right at the edge of the bank, back from it. Absolutely nothing is to stick out over the bank."

"He's right, sir," Comiskey said. "Cough, a sneeze, a rivet scratching on a rock—and it's goodbye Apaches."

"You'll hear them coming so you don't have to look," Sundance said. "You won't hear much but you'll hear something. Then nobody raises up but you. Let's just hope you're ready to open fire before they are. If we win this we'll be a lot closer to Fort McHenry than we are now."

Major Randolph seemed to be fascinated by his ruined coat, as if he regretted having destroyed it. "You think Victorio will lead them?"

"Not likely," Sundance answered. "It's possible. Victorio is the general, but maybe he'll want to take a part in it. Maybe he sees this as the end of us. He's the one to get, Major, if there is any getting to be done. He's tall for an Indian, even tall for a white man."

Major Randolph smiled through his mask of dust. "And he'll be wearing my uncle's coat. Does it have the three stars?"

Sundance said it did. "The General took it right off his back and gave it to Victorio. That old coat has saved a lot of lives over the years."

Anger showed in the Major's eyes. "Meaning that I'm responsible for a lot of deaths. Tell me this then. If I was so wrong about the Apaches planning a war, why are they so well armed? You saw the fire they laid down at the canyon. No let-up in the firing except when there was nothing to shoot at. You think they were using muskets and old trade guns?''

The Major had a point, not that it mattered much. ''They were using Winchesters. Except for the Hawken the other rifles sounded like Winchesters. I thought about that. You could even be right about Victorio planning a war. Look at it the other way. Victorio could have been waiting for the whites—the army, somebody —to wage a war against him.''

''But he had the guns ready?''

''That's the best way to have guns, Major. Clean and loaded and ready to shoot. You say war and I say maybe. A war plan doesn't fit with the way he killed Domingo and the others. What does it matter what he was planning to do? He's doing it now.''

Major Randolph held up his hand, worrying the idea like a dog shaking a rat. ''Isn't it possible that Domingo jumped the gun on Victorio's war plan? A man who did that would be executed in any army. Domingo was a risk to Victorio so he had to be killed. Killing him bought Victorio some time. In my view, we saved lives by attacking the Apaches when we did.''

Sundance refused to allow himself to be angry; now was not the time to show anger. ''A lot of dead troopers would disagree with you, Major.''

Major Randolph liked the hero's role he had talked himself into. ''I was talking about civilian lives,'' he said calmly. ''That's what the army is here for, to protect civilian lives. While Victorio is busy with us he can't do any raiding or killing.''

''That's true enough,'' Sundance said patiently. As soon as they were overdue at the fort the officer in command would send a rider to Camp Bain fifty miles away. As soon as he got there a force would start for Fort McHenry, so there was time, some time, to give protection to the settlers between the fort and Apache country.

"Good," Major Randolph said. "Don't forget to put that in your report to the War Department."

Sundance cleaned his rifle and put it back in the fringed scabbard. He worked on the Colt .44, getting out the grit, then oiling it. When he finished he wrapped the cylinder and hammer in his bandanna and stuck it inside his belt under his shirt. That would keep out the dust until he was ready to use it. Some dust would seep in—desert dust got through anything—but not enough to foul the action. There wasn't a whole lot more to be done. Soon it would be dark. The sky was red and there were shadows in the riverbed and sand flew in the wind.

The young soldier named Cranley pointed at Sundance's middle. "The way you put your gun away, that reminds me how we used to do the same up in Montana. Only we did it to guard against the damp. Never thought of doing it in the desert."

Cranley was very young, maybe a year shy of twenty, a short man with that hammered-down cowpuncher look, spiky sandy hair clipped to about an inch. A knife and fork haircut, the troopers called it. His eyes weren't crossed, but they were close to it.

"You herded cows up that way?" Sundance asked to make talk, to keep the kid from tensing up. It happened. The young ones started out brave enough, and some of them stayed brave, but most got jittery. Cranley sure as hell was a long way from the rain-lashed cow country of Montana. His chances of ever getting back there weren't so good.

Cranley said, "Mister, I herded so many cows I got to

know every mucking cow in the state. Not just Montana. Wyoming and across the Canuck line in Alberta. Hell! That's no life for a human critter. You eat dust in summer, freeze your hind end off in winter. When you're afoot you walk in cowshit till you're ready to believe the whole world is floored with cowshit.''

"I've done some of it," Sundance said. "I didn't like it either. I guess it's better than sheep."

Cranley laughed. "Six of one. Depends the kind of shit you hate most. It wasn't that bad when I started out. Hell, when I was a kid there was sull some freedom on a ranch. In them days the ramrod didn't give you the sack if he caught you with a bottle in the bunkhouse. Now it's right out the gate. Everything's changing in the cow business. On some of the real big spreads owned by these foreign Englishmen they don't even expect a rider to come with his own rig. Now I ask you, what kind of a damnfool outfit is that?''

Everything on the desert was washed in red, even their hands and faces, as the sun began to slide. A good time of the day if you were knocking off work, heading for the cookshack or fixing your own grub. Here and now, red was the color of fear.

Sensing the growing panic in the boy, Sundance hastened to answer him. It was best not to agree with the boy; an argument would keep him more interested.

"Sounds pretty efficient, the cow trade was always too careless," he said. "That was fine in the old days when there was plenty of open range. Now the farmers are coming in so it's so much land for so much cow. The foreigners know what they're doing."

Cranley objected to that. "That's a hell of a thing to say. Some of them Englishmen don't even sit an American saddle. One fool I worked for never even talked to the men. Did everything through the Scotch foreman. Damned if us men understand the half he was saying, that Scotch brogue and all.''

It was going all right. So far it was. "Least they got enough sense to get rid of the longhorns," Sundance went on, looking at the light on the back of his hands. A few more minutes. That's all it would take. "Those old rackheads hardly had enough meat on them to make it worthwhile. Nobody ever managed to breed the wildness out of them. They'd spook faster than a jittery horse and be twice as dangerous. You take these new Herefords. That's where the future of ranching is. Cow like that'll give you four times the meat and it's good tender meat. The old rackheads are done for and about time.''

"Well and good that may be," Cranley said. "On the other hand, there was nothing like the sight of a herd of old rackheads in full flow. Mister, they were like a river on the move . . .''

Cranley's face tightened as Major Randolph spoke softly to the men, telling them to move out. The sun died but there was enough light to see the shirt-draped dummies if you walked away from them. On both sides the men climbed the banks, then crawled on their bellies in the dark. Sundance stood up and kept talking. Comiskey was walking around talking to himself. Sundance was close enough to Cranley to see the amazement in his face. The boy was surprised to find himself where he was. There was nothing new in that; Sundance had seen it before. A lot of heroes were born like that—by accident. Cranley wanted to show the others that he was still a fire-eating cowpoke from up Montana way.

Sundance moved around and Cranley followed him. Comiskey was talking to one of the dummies. "You mean to say you never saw me fight? Aw, you can't mean that. Why, man, I fought all over the place. Mostly it wasn't legal but we did it anyway. One time I fought Jemmy Sykes the English Dandy on a barge in Boston Harbor. Then this boatload of coppers comes alongside and tells us to give it over, we're all under arrest according to the laws of Massachusshits. They was too much money riding on the fight so the beadle boat got sunk. But that was nothing compared to the time we was down in Havana. Now there's a real town for you. Them senoritas there is something fierce."

Cranley didn't want to talk about longhorns versus the new breed of range stock, but Sundance kept at him, prodding him to answer. It was a good thing that Comiskey was such a bigmouth. He was making enough talk for three men, asking questions and answering them himself, playing the fool for all it was worth. Comiskey was a heartless thug, but he wasn't a coward.

"Look, kid, I don't believe you ever were a cow-puncher. A runaway store clerk is what you look like to me." The men were in position now. "Go on, tell me I'm a Goddamned liar," Sundance said.

Cranley spun around.

Twelve

The arrow struck him in the throat at the same instant, choking off his angry words. It came with such force that it penetrated both sides of his neck and the steel head of the arrow came out under his left ear for four or five inches. Cranley made a terrifying sound, clawed at the arrow, and died.

He was still falling when the riverbed erupted in gunfire, blazing up and down on both sides. Screams shattered the silence that had been absolute a moment before. Sundance kicked over one of the cactus limbs and threw himself behind it, the only cover he had. Fifteen feet away, Comiskey was hugging the bank, throwing lead as fast as he could jack shells. There was plenty to fire at, plenty of fire coming back. Yellow flashes with red cores split the darkness. Bullets spattered in the sand and whined off rocks. The last cavalry horse was hit and ran straight into the Apache fire. Apaches screamed as the crazed horse ran over them, plunging and kicking before it crashed down and died.

Sundance fired until his rifle was empty, then picked up the dead boy's rifle and fired every time he saw a flash. Bullets sang all around him. A bullet broke on a rock in front of him and nicked his face with lead splinters. Blood trickled into the corner of his eye and he wiped it away. All along the bank, on both sides, the men were firing fast and steady. They killed silently; killing was serious work and they were past yelling. The Hawken rifle boomed and a trooper yelled and pitched off the bank, tumbling in the shale and sand. Through the crash of the rifles Sundance heard the lighter crack-crack-crack of the Major's revolver. The Hawken boomed again and this time Sundance saw the big muzzle flash behind all the others. It fired again and he threw a bullet and missed.

Suddenly the men started acting like men instead of machines. It started when some trooper, mad with the joy of killing, let out a long wild Rebel Yell. The sound rose up from the battle like a clarion and then, as if rehearsed, as though the yell were a signal, the other men cut loose with a howling and screaming that was wilder than the wildest Apache. Sundance had heard it before, not often, and he might not hear it again, not from these men. But for the moment there it was, the mad exultant howl of victory that men gave when they knew they had a hated enemy on the run. The fire increased, grew heavier, and though the Apaches outnumbered their attackers, there was nothing they could do to match it.

Then the Apaches started to fight their way out, leaving their dead and wounded. Ignoring the Major's order, the men rose up from their positions, firing at will, still yelling their hate. The Apache fire began to weaken and Sundance heard Comiskey laughing as he moved away from the riverbank and into the center. The Hawken boomed and the Winchester was torn from Comiskey's hand. Sundance fired at the flash of the Hawken and killed the man behind it. Disobeying the Major, or not hearing him, men swarmed down the riverbank. A trooper screamed as a clogged rifle barrel exploded and split, blowing the fingers off his forward hand. Running toward where the Hawken should be, Sundance blasted an Apache who rose up in front of him. The Apache grunted and tried to bring him down. Sundance upended the rifle and smashed him in the face. He shot him when he fell, then ran on, jumping over dead men or men staggering toward death. Sundance heard Comiskey running behind him, still laughing, shooting everything that stood in his way. "Some fun, ha, bucko!" he yelled at Sundance.

The Apache attack had been broken and now they ran while the big .45-70's fired at their backs. At a bend in the river they tried to make a stand and were driven back again. Then the bugle and the Major's yelling forced the men to pull back, and when they did the Major wasn't the enemy any more. Once again they were part of the same army, and the Major was part of it too. But once the sun came up and the hellfire of the desert burned again, when the let-down from the fighting set in, they would hate the Major more than ever.

Sundance wrenched the Hawken from the dead Apache and ran his hands over it. Then he searched the corpse and came up with a handful of bullets. More bullets were in a deerskin bag. Close by he heard the Major kicking empty shells from his revolver with the ejector rod. If the Major hadn't been a major he would have whooped. Sundance could see the Major's bulk in the half-darkness. The Major was gloating like a man who had just proved himself with a woman hard to please.

"I guess that'll hold the red bastards for a while," the Major said, clicking shut the loading gate, spinning the cylinder more than he had to. He spun the cylinder against the flat of his left hand, then set down the trigger, holstered the revolver. "You did fine, Sundance. Comiskey! Where in hell is Comiskey?"

"Here, sir," Comiskey reported.

Major Randolph slapped Comiskey on the back. "They can't kill you, you ugly Irish bastard."

"Thank you, sir," Comiskey said.

"The trooper? What's his name?"

Comiskey said, "Private Cranley, sir."

"He got killed," Sundance said. "It's time we got started on the wounded Apaches."

Major Randolph had an idea, not a good one. "Why don't we leave them as they are? Maybe the others will come back and try to bring them out. If they do, that could be the finish of it. What do you think, Sergeant?"

Comiskey knew they wouldn't be back, but he didn't want to go against his superior. "Well, I don't know what to think, sir. It could be they'll come back."

Sundance cut in. "They won't be back. They try to get their wounded if they can. If they can't they mark them as dead. And they won't come back for the dead even when we pull out. They don't chant over them, don't even bury them. All they do is leave them where they die."

"Dispatch the wounded," Major Randolph said.

They used bullets to kill the six Apache wounded. A knife or a rock would have served as well, would have saved six bullets, but the shots would remind Victorio that six more of his people were dying.

"There you go, bucko," Comiskey said to the last Apache before he blew his head off.

Once again there was nothing but the absolute silence of the desert. Still keyed up, the men were inclined to boast, to tell one another what they had done, as if somehow they doubted it, were unsure of their victory, but their voices trailed off into nervous laughs, and then silence. The let-down was coming fast, Sundance

311

thought.

Five troopers had been killed in the fight; only one man was wounded and the wound he had was no more than a bullet burn in the shoulder. They buried their dead as best they could, doing it as a mark of respect, a ritual; once the coyotes had finished with the Apache dead they would start to uncover the graves. Already the coyotes were howling far out on the desert.

After the men drank, Major Randolph told Comiskey to move them out. Twenty-six Apaches had been killed in the ambush, six after it was over. The Major stated the figure as if someone doubted it. "Thirty-four dead Indians, not a bad night's work. Not bad at all. The way I look at it, they must have to out some of the wounded. Some will die, the others won't be worth much. So it's more than just thirty-four enemey dead. Forty is more like it."

"Likely enough," Sundance said.

"You don't sound too enthusastic, Sundance."

"No reason to be, Major. Even with their losses, they still have us outnumbered four to one. Could be five to one. And I wouldn't count on any more ambushes."

"Maybe there won't be any more attacks. Going by your figure, Victorio has lost half his men. If he's such a smart Injun"—the Major made the word a sneer— "he'd do well to call it off, take his ragged warriors and head for Mexico. Down there he won't have to face the United States Army."

"The Mexicans can kill Apaches pretty good," Sundance said. "He won't run to Mexico. Not yet. If the war goes on he'll have to. Right now we're the ones have to do the running. The fact to be faced is this. We didn't get Victorio."

"I think we'll get him sooner or later," Major Randolph said, and maybe he felt the confidence he expressed. "I watched for him in the riverbed and there wasn't a tall Indian there. He's going to lose face if he doesn't stop playing rear line general. He tried to box us up in the canyon and that didn't work. Neither did the riverbed. They're going to start calling him General McClellan instead of General Victorio."

"Victorio is more like Mosby," Sundance said, referring to the great Confederate irregular. "We'll feel his weight soon enough. But you're right, and I wish you weren't. Next time he'll lead them himself. It's not like he can call for reinforcements. What he has is what he'll fight with. Don't expect any more direct attacks."

The Major seemed disappointed. "If he things he can do it by just wearing us down, why did he risk his men at the riverbed?"

"He doesn't want to take his men through this desert any more than we want to go. An Apache fears the desert as much as any man. Nobody likes the desert except a few old rats who make their living by it. Crazy old desert rats and lung cases."

The Major was limping and trying not to show it. Unless he slit his boots he was going to be in trouble, but it wasn't Sundance's business to tell him. "What do you think we can expect?" Major Randolph said.

"Mostly sniping from as far out as they can stay and still get a shot. They'll hit and run, then do it again. We're going to lose men, no way we can't. From now on they won't just hit us from places that look good. We'll be watching those and we'll get some fire. Then we'll get fire from places we won't expect. An Apache will lie in the open for hours, take the full brunt of the sun just to get off one shot. When there is absolutely no cover, they will lie under a dirt-smeared blanket to get a shot. That, Major, is what you have to call dedication.'

The men were tired and the cold didn't revive them. It tired them even more, the tensing of their muscles to keep from shivering. Sundance didn't do it. Not tensing against the cold was something he had learned long before. You had to accept the cold as it was, not try to fight it but get used to it. If you did that, finally it wasn't so bad. The army had plenty to learn about men and cold, men and heat, men and everything. The way to prepare men for hardship was to make them go through it, as close as you could, when there wasn't any fighting going on.

Sundance guessed the men wouldn't like his ideas. He watched them slogging onward in the dark; overhead the stars were so bright they looked like painted cardboard stars in a theater. Background for the fake-looking stars was a deep dark blue close to black. Night on the desert could be peaceful or terrible; for these men it was terrible. The Major was limping worse than he had been; only Sundance and Comiskey were able to take the pace without faltering.

Nothing happened during the night, and Sundance guessed they could have slept without fear of an attack. It wasn't like the Apaches to suffer a defeat and then to make another attack right after it. Victorio would have to make new plans. The Major was right about the loss of face. A white leader could lose a battle and explain it away, and if he hadn't lost too many battles, he would get to keep his command. Excuses would be made for him by his supporters. Conditions weren't right or he was betrayed or forced into a fight he couldn't win. Something or many things that sounded right. An Apache leader didn't get off so easily; when a man was a chief he was expected to win battles. And he remained a chief only as long as he did. As in any fighting force, there would be ambitious subordinates wanting to be generals too. Victorio was far from young, and the sub-chiefs would argue that wisdom wasn't enough to defeat the white devils.

The Major had lapsed into silence, breaking it only when he ordered the men to rest. Otherwise, he plodded on like the rest of them. The short water ration was taking its toll of the men, and they were thirsty in spite of the cold; the air was just as dry when it was cold. As near as Sundance could tell, they were about sixty miles from the river. On the map, mostly blank except for a few whimsical names given by long-ago cartographers—Mussel Shoals, McGuire's Place, Spanish Arrow—a few waterholes were marked. The map had been made nearly thirty years before; some of the waterholes would be as dry as the men who made it. Some would be gone altogether, covered by decades of sand.

The Apaches let them march unmolested, then they killed a man first thing in the morning. Sundance had been waiting for the first rifle shot. They were still moving when it happened. A red sun was warming the desert, though the wind was still cold. To the right a long low brown ridge ran for about a mile, a broken spine of shale and sand. They had not been able to see it in the dark; they were moving away from it when the rifle shot cracked in the quiet of the morning. It killed one of the two men carrying the canteens and he fell over with the canteens clanking together. The rifle cracked again but by then the men were flat on their bellies, holding their fire because the light was red and thick and there was nothing to fire at.

Another rifle opened up some distance down the ridge from the first sniper. Sundance sighted along the long, heavy barrel of the Hawken. The old Hawken had a tube sight and it cut down on the glare of the sun. He moved the tiny circle of light along the ridge. The

315

snipers wouldn't stay in the same place. They would shoot and run along the safe side of the ridge, then find another place to shoot. So far there was nothing to see; he would have to guess where they were.

Moving the sight, he said, "Move the men out, Major. Tell them to crawl, you do the same. Keep on crawling till you're a hundred yards from here. After that you'll be out of effective range." He tapped the barrel of the Hawken with his finger. "Unless they got more of these."

Major Randolph said, "We could circle and clean them out. There's just that one ridge."

"You don't know what's behind it. One or two men or the whole force. They may be trying to draw us in. Do what I tell you, Major. Move the men. Once you're clear of the ridge it's all open country. I'll give you some cover."

"You're giving me orders again," Major Randolph said, watching the ridge. No shots had come since the first two.

"Call it advice," Sundance said. "Move the men."

A rifle bullet kicked up sand. Sundance held his fire. The Apaches wouldn't show themselves until the men started to move. Frowning, the Major barked out the order and the men went away on their bellies. Sundance knew the Apaches were watching unseen and he held the tube sight just below the top of the ridge. A rifle flamed red in the sun and a bullet nearly killed the Major. Sundance swung the big rifle but by then there was nothing to see but the ridge. Another bullet came right on top of the first one. It came from at least three hundred feet down the ridge, which meant that there were two men shooting. There were two, and maybe the whole force. The men were moving away as fast as they could crawl and, covered with dust, they looked like giant bugs.

Two shots came from the ridge at the same time and kicked up sand. A head showed and Sundance drove it out of sight with a bullet from the Hawken. He put down the Hawken and started blasting with the Winchester, hosing the ridge with bullets. No bullets came his way until he started to reload the Hawken. He did it quickly but the bullets came fast. He took a quick look before he put the tube sight back on the ridge. A few more minutes and the men would be safe enough except for a lucky shot.

One of the Apaches was more cautious and Sundance passed him up in favor of the other. His target fired and ducked out of sight. He moved the sight again and waited. Then the man's head and shoulders came up and Sundance squeezed the trigger. The Apache wasn't faking the yell he let out. He pitched forward and lay dying on the crest of the slope. It was easy to finish him off with the Winchester and he didn't move again after he was shot. Sundance rolled on his back again and reloaded the cumbersome old Hawken. It was a great big hunk of iron, but it threw a bullet like few other rifles. Now the men were out of range and the fight was between Sundance and the man on the ridge. It turned into a duel. Whoever he was, he was pretty good, and maybe he had been an army scout at one time. No more wild shooting came from the ridge. Sundance knew he couldn't leave his position because there was no one to give him cover. Besides, the man on the ridge had to be killed; he was too good at what he was doing. If he didn't die now he would turn up again to harass and snipe. The Apaches hadn't started this war, yet this man had to die.

The Apache had moved back along the ridge to shorten the range. He fired after he got set and Sundance felt the hot wind of a bullet close to his face. It

317

grazed the skin like a warm feather, didn't even break the skin. Sundance flattened out even more and held the Hawken steady. There was no way to know what the Apache was going to do, go down the far side of the ridge and disappear into the desert, or wait it out in the sun.

Minutes passed and nothing happened. By now Sundance had decided that the main Apache force was somewhere else. If they had been there, and failing in their attempt to encourage an attack, they would have come swarming over the ridge with blazing guns.

There hadn't been a shot for five minutes; still Sundance waited. He lay like a stone, blending into the colors of the desert, as much a part of the desert as the rock and sand that covered it. He heard yelling from far away and maybe the Major was telling him to hurry up and get himself killed.

Now, ten minutes of silence had dragged by. The sun climbed higher and grew hotter until the bare brown ridge seemed to tremble under its onslaught. Sundance blinked the sweat from his eyes, but remained perfectly still. As always when he had to kill, he felt a quiet confidence. It wasn't enough to be merely a good shot; that was only part of it. To kill efficiently a man had to draw on his reserves of experience and determination. But there was even more than that. A man had to decide he was going to do it, quickly and cleanly, before he did it.

He waited without impatience and then it happened. The Apache fired but he didn't duck down. He kept his position and continued to fire, risking his life to shoot slowly and carefully. Sundance looked along the barrel as bullets sang past his head. He fired and the Indian died, blown back by the heavy bullet. The rifle he had been firing stayed where it was after he rolled down the far side of the slope. There was no need to confirm his death; no Apache would ever leave a rifle. Lying in the sun, the rifle barrel glinted in the sun.

Sundance reloaded the Hawken and sighted on the fallen rifle, aiming for the stock because any other shot would have been impossible at that range. Then he touched the trigger and the rifle flew into the air, smashed by the bullet.

Two Apaches down, and how many more to go?

Thirteen

The water was just about gone when they stopped to sleep at noon. Muttering, dead on their feet, the men took what water they got and slumped into unconsciousness. Some fell down without bothering to cover themselves against the blaze of sun. Others, the older troopers, did the best they could before they pitched into exhausted sleep. There was a wildness, a madness about them that Sundance didn't like, and he knew the hate for the Major was festering inside them. At the best of times, enlisted men had no liking for officers, but they relied on the officers to pull them through. The army was a sort of deal between enlisted men and their commissioned superiors: blind obedience in exchange for good leadership. Now they felt betrayed; the Major's ambition had led them into a trap, and they felt they were still in it.

The surgeon wasn't doing too badly for a drunk. Sundance knew the hell MacCrae was going through, the wild craving for the drink he couldn't have, for he had been through it himself back in the days when Three Stars had bullied him away from the bottle. There was no easy way to do it; Three Stars hadn't offered him any. MacCrae looked like an old man as he stumbled among the sleeping men, trying to cover faces against the sun. His hands shook and his balance was off, yet he kept trying. When he finally gave up on it, he sat down heavily staring with red-rimmed sleepless eyes. The sand blew against the bodies of the sleeping men, finding a hold and drifting against them, and if they stayed there long enough it would cover them, and the buzzards that stayed with them all the time they were on the move were closer. There was nothing but sun and sand and silence.

The Major had the map out again, but there were no stones here to anchor it. Miles of white sand ran away to shimmering dunes in the distance. The map flapped in the burning wind.

"There's the river," Major Randolph was saying, "and there's the only waterhole between us and river. If there is water there we won't be too bad off. If there isn't maybe we'll find another."

Comiskey said, "We have some water, sir. If we made some changes we'd maybe have enough to get us to that river. There's no way we can count on the waterhole. You catch the drift of what I'm saying, sir?"

Major Randolph looked up from the map. Alkali dust and sweat had hardened in the stubble on his face giving it the appearance of plaster that hadn't completely dried. "What're you saying?"

Comiskey fidgeted with his battered hands and jerked his head toward the sleeping troopers. "There's too many of us and too little water."

The Major grunted, stupefied by fatigue. "Tell me something I don't know, Sergeant."

"He means kill some of the men, the weaker ones," Sundance said, watching Comiskey. He looked at Lieutenant Gates crawling over to join them.

"I heard you talking," Gates said.

For the moment it was between Comiskey and the Major. "You can't mean what you're saying," the Major said. "I don't want to hear any more talk like

321

that. We'll get through somehow. If we don't, at least we'll die like civilized men."

"Begging your pardon, sir, you're right about the dying part," Comiskey said. "We don't look that civilized right now. When it comes to the last few swallows of water there's going to be killing. I don't figure to get killed, sir."

Gates joined in so quickly that Sundance wondered if he had been talking with Comiskey. Since he was an officer and a gentleman, he couldn't put it as brutally as the noncom. "It's horrible, but it's realistic in this situation." He added, "sir."

"It hasn't come to that yet," Major Randolph said, looking at the troopers as if seeing them for the first time, but he seemed uneasy for a moment, finding opposition from an officer and his trusted sergeant. Then he sat up straight in spite of his fatigue. "We're all in this together. There will be no more talk of killing."

Comiskey dared to go on. "I wasn't talking about the able men, sir. There's some that'll die quicker than the rest. Look at them, sir, there's some there that even water won't help. They're dying but while they're doing it they're using up water. Water that could be used by the living instead of the dead."

Sundance sensed that something had gone wrong between the Major and Comiskey. He had noticed it for several days, but hadn't thought much about it. The desert did strange things to men, even to friends. Now he knew that there was something else behind Comiskey's defiance of the Major.

"I told you to shut up, Sergeant," Major Randolph snapped. "We've been together a long time so I'm going to disregard it. If I hear any more of it, it won't go well for you. Is that understood?"

"Yes, sir," Comiskey said, silent for the moment but

waiting for Gates to back him.

"Excuse me, Major," Gates started off again, "but I agree with the Sergeant. It's all right to say we need every man we have to fight off the Apaches. If they were all in fighting condition I'd be the first to agree. But they aren't, sir. Some of them, it's all they can do to keep up with us. Worse, sir, they're slowing us down. Why don't you say something, Sundance? You know what I'm saying is true."

Sundance looked at Gates and wondered why good men like Danforth and O'Hara had to be dead. The boy Cranley who hated cowpunching. The trooper who had been killed that morning.

"I'm with the Major this time," he said. "I don't see that true or false has anything to do with it. Like the Major said, we're in this together. You don't kill another man just so you can steal his water. A man is a man or he isn't."

"But you don't deny the truth of it?" Gates was more afraid of Sundance than he was of the Major.

With good cause, Sundance thought. It wouldn't take a moment's thought to put a bullet between the foxy lieutenant's eyes, and he found himself close to anger. "I just said truth has nothing to do with it. And if that doesn't mean anything to you, think about this. I don't know how many men you have in mind. Say it's two. All right, that gives us enough water to get through tonight. Then what? Do we kill another two men in the morning? How much water will that give us, and how long will it last? Don't forget some of it will be gone by then."

"I'm talking about now, Sundance. You think I want to kill those men?"

Sundance restrained his impulse to make Gates the first man to die for his water supply. "What men?" he said. "Who's going to do the choosing. You, Gates? You want to start with Doctor MacCrae over there? I forgot. You can't start with a fellow officer. Tell you what, Gates. I'll give up my water if you do the same. Here's your chance."

Gates blinked as Sundance's Colt came out almost too fast for the eye to see. The hammer was back and pointing at his face. None of them moved.

"We can do it like this," Sundance said. "Unholster your pistol and we'll kill each other at the same time. If you don't like it in the head you can have it in the heart. Me, I don't care. Do what I tell you, Gates."

Gates mumbled behind the mask of dust, appealing to the Major, who just stared at him. Comiskey sat still, knowing that Sundance could kill him in a wink.

"Do it," Sundance said. "Here's your chance to be noble. Bring out your gun, then cock it and aim it at me. Now, Gates!"

Gates's hand was shaking as he unholstered the big army .45 and brought it up to point at Sundance. He forgot to cock the trigger of the single-action until Sundance reminded him.

"This is madness," he said, trying to hold the gun steady. "I don't want to kill you."

Major Randolph spoke up. "Put the gun away, Gates. The point has been made. Nobody gets killed unless the Apaches kill them."

Sundance set down the hammer of the Colt but kept it in his hand. "Maybe the whole point hasn't been made, Major. Comiskey ought to get a chance to sacrifice himself. I think every man deserves that chance. How about it, Comiskey? You started this killing talk."

"You'll get yours, bucko," Comiskey said, knowing better than Gates that Sundance had no intention of letting another man kill him. He had been called and didn't like having to fold. "You'd shoot me before I got my gun in my hand. You won't get me that way."

"Then let the Major hand out the guns," Sundance said.

Major Randolph wanted no part of it. "That's enough, both of you. Everybody's going crazy in this heat, that's what it is. Everybody get some sleep or you'll be no good for anything. That's an order. Forget it ever happened, that's my advice."

"Yes, sir," Comiskey said, and in his bitter silence there was more than words.

Lieutenant Gates tried to say something else to the Major, but was waved away.

Major Randolph closed his eyes and opened them when he felt Sundance was looking at him. "That order includes you," he said. "That was a stupid thing you did just now."

"You better watch them," Sundance said. "They didn't just come up with the idea at the time. You mind telling me why Comiskey is turning against you?"

Major Randolph tried to pass it off. "Is that what Comiskey was doing? Anyway, that's army business, not yours. What happened was nothing more than men talking crazy."

"I'd say it was more than that, Major. I think they mean to do it. The rotten thing about it, they're right. Extra water would make a lot of difference. You know it, too."

Turning away, Major Randolph said, "Maybe I had you wrong, Sundance. Sure I know what the water means. I thought you'd be the one to start about killing the men who aren't going to get through this. I mean, what I mean is the kind of man you are."

Suddenly the Major's voice turned irritable, not wanting to go on about it. "Too much talk in this heat.

Do what you like, I'm getting some sleep."

The guards were changed and the men slept on through the hottest part of the day. Sundance stood a two-hour watch and slept again. The men sprawled in the hot sand, the water seeping out of them under the force of the sun. They were getting the look of men who were beginning to die, for death came close and waited when the water ran out. No matter how sparingly it was doled out, it would be gone within twenty-four hours. As the last of the water was handed around, the men who hadn't drunk yet would wait with angry eyes, sure they were being cheated of their rightful share, and there would be curses and accusations, even feeble fights. And then, hating each other, they would wait to die.

Sundance woke when he heard a shout. A rifle shot followed. Then he was on his feet before any of the others. One of the guards, the one who fired the rifle, was yelling and pointing. He jacked a round and tried to steady the rifle for another shot. Sundance grabbed the trigger guard before he could shoot again. Far out on the desert a single figure was moving in the heatwaves. The figure was distorted as if bent out of shape by moving water. It appeared and took shape for an instant, then seemed to vanish again.

The guard, crazed by heat, fought for the rifle. Sundance took it away from him and punched him to the ground. Other men muttered angrily and there was the clack-clack of rifle levers.

"Somebody's coming in with a white flag," Sundance told the Major. "He's alone so it must be real enough. Tell the men not to shoot."

They watched while the figure got closer and it was hard to see the white flag of truce because of the sun-glare. It flapped white in the wind.

"What do you make of it?" Major Randolph said.

"They want to talk. That's all I make of it."

"You speak Spanish, you handle it," Major Randolph said. "You think they want us to surrender?"

Sundance said no. "Surrender isn't one of their words. It has to be something else."

"That's far enough," Sundance yelled when the flag bearer was a hundred yards away. The Apache with the flag, a strip of cloth tied to the top of a rifle barrel, wore the uniform coat of a Mexican officer. It was dirty and torn but the tarnished gold cloth of the epaulets glittered in the sun.

Nothing moved on the desert. Whatever it was, it wasn't a trick. From where they were the desert ran away flat and featureless, no broken ground to use as cover for a sneak attack.

"Come ahead," Sundance yelled.

Now he was close enough to be seen clearly, a young brave who looked white in spite of the sun-darkened skin and heavy war paint. He might have been a half-breed or a Mexican taken as a child. He didn't have the head shape or the wide nose of an Indian, and his hair, though black and dirty, had glints of brown. The rifle the flag was tied to was an old Springfield with a cracked stock. The Apaches didn't want to lose a good rifle if the boy got shot.

When he came in he spoke to Sundance in Spanish. They squatted n the sand and the boy looked at them without fear. "We have the white captain named Danforth," the Apache said.

Major Randolph started at the mention of Danforth's name. He knew what had been said before Sundance translated.

"He is not of great value to us, wounded as he is,"

Sundance said.

"He is not wounded," the Apache said. "He has been tortured but not to the point of death. He says you are the one who have been leading the white soldiers. He says you are in command here and not Major Randolph."

"What's he saying?" Major Randolph said, angry because he did not understand Spanish.

Sundance said, "He says Danforth says you are in command here." To repeat Danforth's words wouldn't do the Major any good, not in front of Comiskey and Gates. "Danforth is alive."

"What is there to talk about?" Sundance asked the Apache. "Who are you?"

"I am Alcazar and though Victorio is not of my blood he is my father. You are Sundance, the enemy of my people."

"I am not the enemy of your people. I would stop this if I could."

"Then why did you start this war?"

Sundance translated for the Major's benefit. "Tell him the Apaches started it," Major Randolph said angrily.

Instead, Sundance said, "This war can be stopped before the other soldiers come from the north. They will come and they will destroy the Apaches. They will burn the villages and hunt you in the mountains, as before. Tell your father to stop the war before it is too late."

Alcazar said, "My father has thought of that, but thinks it is too late now. You say you did not start this war, then you rode with the men who did. You are their scout. Your name is known to my father. If it had not been for you the soldiers would have been slaughtered at the canyon. At the river you killed many Apaches."

"We'll kill many more if the war goes on," Sundance

said. "You may kill us, but you will be dead men if you do."

"We are dead men now."

"Not so. It can be stopped. You came here to trade Captain Danforth for something. What is it?"

Alcazar pointed. "It is you."

"Wait a minute," Sundance said to the Major.

"I don't like that kind of trade," Sundance said. "I am no friend of Captain Danforth."

"My father says you are a man. You puzzle my father," Alcazar went on. "You have the name of a man of honor, yet you ride with the child-killers."

Sundance disregarded the insult; trading Danforth wasn't the only reason Victorio's adopted son was here. It had to be something more important or he would not have sent his own son knowing that he might be killed.

"I want a better trade," Sundance said. "If Danforth is all you can offer go back and tell your father the answer is no."

"What the hell is he saying? What are you saying?" Major Randolph said.

"Victorio wants to trade Danforth for me," Sundance said. "I said that isn't enough."

Comiskey was grinning like a madman, but he kept quiet. Gates was nervous and rubbed at his face.

"Tell him we're not trading anyone," Major Randolph said.

Alcazar had been watching Sundance's face while he spoke in English. "There can be a better trade," he said. "My father thought of that too. You will come and face my father. My father says there will be no peace while you live. You are the dangerous one, he says. More dangerous than all the others. You carry a hatchet and a knife. My father will fight you with those weapons. Either one."

"Maybe," Sundance said. "What happens if I kill your father? Will not the war go on under a new chief?"

"My father's word it will not," Alcazar answered. "The subchiefs have given their word. Even if you kill my father his word will be good. Nobody has ever doubted my father's word."

"Nobody's doubting it," Sundance said, knowing that the subchiefs would honor their pledge to let the others go. "What happens if I get killed? Does your father's word cover that too?"

"The soldiers will still go free," Alcazar said. "They will die in the desert, my father says. If some of them live maybe they will tell the truth of what happened. Even if they don't they will remember what happened here. They will not come back to attack the Apache so soon. If they are wise they will not come at all. If they do come we will give them what they got here. My father wants to make sure that if they do come you will not be alive to ride with them. What is your answer?"

Sundance told him to wait: it had to be talked about first.

"I won't allow it," Major Danforth said. "What's to stop them from killing you the minute you get into range? Why haven't they shown us Danforth?"

"They have him," Sundance said. "Two reasons. How else would they know his name? Reason number two is Victorio says they have him. I'm going to do it, Major."

Comiskey was grinning again. "That's the spirit, bucko."

Major Randolph roared at him; the sound came out as a croak. "Maybe you'd like to go."

Comiskey scowled and said, "No, sir, I wouldn't."

"What about you, Gates?" Major Randolph said.

"They don't want me, Major, they want Sundance."

"They're not going to get him," Major Randolph said. "You said we were in this together, Sundance. Then abide by your own rules. It can't be helped about Danforth. We aren't going to trade. Now tell this Indian to get away from here. He came with a flag of truce so he goes out the same way. This talk is over."

Sundance stood up and said to the Apache, "Where is this fight to take place?"

"Between our two forces," Alcazar answered. "My father says it must be at a distance so that no man can interfere no matter what happens. You will fight and one of you will die."

"All right," Sundance agreed. "But if your father thinks I'm so dangerous why is he willing to fight me?"

Alcazar smiled, but it was not a smile of friendship; he smiled in honor of his father. "Victorio knows he will win," he said.

The Major protested again, angry to the point of trying to shout. "You will obey my order or be placed under arrest," he said. "You'll be going to your death. Damn it to hell, I don't care what happens to you, it's not the way to do it."

Turning to Comiskey, the Major ordered him to place Sundance under arrest.

"No, sir," Comiskey said, unafraid of the Major's anger. "If he wants to do it let him go. It's a way out."

"Gates!"

The lieutenant shook his head, scared and defiant at the same time. "It's a chance, Major. Sundance wants to go."

Before Major Randolph could draw his gun Sundance had his own gun out. "Sorry, Major. Gates is right, it's a chance for you go get through this. How is this to be done, Alcazar?"

The Apache had been watching the three soldiers,

understanding only some of it. "My father will walk out with Captain Danforth as soon as you come with me. When we meet at midpoint Captain Danforth will keep on going. So will I. When it is time you will fight my father to the death."

"You're a fool, Sundance," the Major said, turning his back.

"Maybe I am," Sundance said. "Forget that and listen to me. I'm going to depend on you, Major. Victorio's word is good, but I don't know about our own people. I gave my word and that means I'm giving it for you. Whatever happens after the fight, take the men and keep going. There could be water in that hole. If there isn't then dig deep and maybe you'll find enough."

Major Randolph didn't want to look at Sundance, but he did. "You think you can do it? Kill Victorio?"

"A lot of men have tried it," Sundance said.

Fourteen

Sundance and the Apache walked out onto the blazing whiteness of the desert. Behind him the voices of the men died in the distance. Soon the only sound was the wind. The sun seemed to swirl in the sky, threatening the world with its power.

As he walked Sundance tried to remember everything he had ever heard about the great Apache chief. Some said he was greatest of all because he had learned the ways of the whites better than any chief who had gone before. That meant he was intelligent as well as cunning. No longer a young man—he had to be in his early forties —nevertheless, he would be a dangerous adversary. That he had lived more than four decades in a violent land was proof of that. He would be good with a knife.

A long way off two figures began to emerge from the heatwaves. They shimmered and took on substance and kept coming. Sundance had been counting off the distance he had come; there was no need to turn and look back. In a few minutes they would be out of range, and if some jittery trooper took a notion to shoot he wouldn't have much of a chance at that distance.

Alcazar said, "This is where we stop."

Victorio and Danforth got there and stopped. Danforth's uniform was in rags and the mass of blood on his face had been baked hard by the sun, and then

333

cracked. His eyes were wild, his fists knuckle-white by his sides; and the gash in his forehead bound with a bloody gray rag.

Danforth extended his hands and they were like claws. "Where is he? Is he dead?"

"He's with the men, go on now," Sundance said.

"I'm going," Danforth mumbled, clenchng his fists again.

They stood there until Danforth and Victorio's son had gone. Two men standing in the limitless desert, waiting to fight to the death. It didn't seem to make much sense.

The man facing Sundance was tall for an Indian, with wide shoulders tapering to a thin waist. His shoulders were banded with muscle and his arms were thick and strong and oiled now for close fighting. Maybe he was forty-two, hard as a rock, lithe in his movements, and the strange serenity of his face had been earned by great suffering. Except for the long gray hair, he looked like a man in his early thirties. It would not be easy to kill this man, Sundance knew.

They had to wait until Danforth and Alcazar got back to their own lines. Victorio said slowly, "How does a man like you come to be here? Killing my people for no reason?"

"To keep from being killed," Sundance answered. "I am their scout so I am here. It's my job."

"That is not a good enough reason, Sundance. Your friend Three Stars would be ashamed to claim you now. He fought me in the old days but he never attacked for no reason. When you discovered what the soldiers were going to do you should have warned us. If you could not bring yourself to do that you should have gone your own way. But you stayed and you helped them to kill."

"I could say a lot of things but it wouldn't make any

difference," Sundance said.

"Not now," Victorio. "We are here and it is time."

Sundance unbuckled his weapons belt and tossed it away; Victorio had come to fight armed with nothing but a thick-bladed Mexican knife about the same size as Sundance's Bowie. It had a wider, thicker guard; that was about the only difference.

They circled in the sun, each taking the measure of the other, watching for movements that told of weakness. Sundance didn't see much that he could use to his advantage. Victorio wasn't afraid to die, but didn't want to die because of his people. None of the subchiefs was his equal as a leader; without him the Apaches would be leaderless. So maybe that was an advantage, his not wanting to die.

Victorio tried for a wrist-turned inward thrust that came straight at Sundance's belly. Sundance jumped aside and knocked the blade down and away from him. Then he made an upward slash at Victorio's forearm. Their knives locked for an instant, their faces not far apart, and then they broke and fell back. Victorio came in again, slashing right and left, forcing Sundance back. Victorio's knife blade moved so fast, it was like a silver streak in the sun. Sundance came back, moving the Bowie in short arcs, with the point held high, ready to jab at the other man's throat. He feinted downward, then turned the blade and went for the throat. The up-curved point of the Bowie darted like a striking rattler and only a quick jerk of his head saved Victorio from instant death. The point of the Bowie drew a thin line of blood just an inch from the jugular and then Sundance was driven back again in a flurry of blows. Steel rang against steel as they gave ground and regained it. The years Victorio had on Sundance didn't seem to make any difference. They were about as evenly matched as two men could be, and if there was any difference between them it was because Sundance had learned more than one way of knife fighting.

The sweat on Victorio's oiled body looked like drops of rain as he bored in again, breathing easily. Oddly, there was no ferocity in his face; nothing but a determination to kill. He came with thrusts instead of slashes. Sundance could avoid the slashes or block them. Once again the knife blades locked as the sharp steel of Victorio's blade sawed into the thick, softer steel on the back of the Bowie. Sundance had to give way as his knife was forced downward. Tendons stuck out like cords on Victorio's neck as he put everything he had behind the attempt to force Sundance to his knees. The lock was broken when Sundance dragged his blade back, feeling Victorio's knife cutting even deeper. Then the Bowie was free and Sundance jumped in with a swordlike chop at Victorio's upper arm. Victorio jumped and blocked, but not fast enough. The blade of the Bowie chopped through to the bone without breaking it. Victorio's face showed no pain as he threw the knife to his other hand. Sundance didn't give him time to get set before he pressed his attack, going for the belly. Victorio moved back, throwing up a defense with the Mexican knife, holding it out from his chest, thrusting when Sundance got too close.

Sundance knew he had the fight; it was only a matter of time before he killed his man. As they felt their energy draining away, they fenced with the long, thick blades. Victorio jumped with his right leg forward, thrusting with his right hand at the same time. The point came in straight and true but Sundance was already moving back and the knife just pricked his stomach. He slashed down hard and cut Victorio across the back of the wrist. Victorio grunted but held on to the knife, and when Sundance slammed down the thick back of the Bowie, the knife dropped from Victorio's hand. He straightened up with blood dripping from his hands.

"Finish it," he said.

If Sundance hadn't moved at that instance the heavy bullet that creased his skull would have shattered it like a turnip. The boom of the heavy rifle echoed over the desert and by then Sundance had swept the wounded Apache to the ground. Their blood ran together as they burrowed into the sand, waiting for the big rifle to fire again. But there was nothing after that.

Sundance raised his head, and where the line of soldiers had been there was nothing. Somebody had fired the Hawken, then they had moved out as fast as they could go. Victorio was losing a lot of blood from the deep wound ih his right arm. Sundance ripped off his bandanna and wrapped it around the arm close to the armpit. He pulled it tight and made a knot when the flow of blood eased up. Then he heard the Apaches coming.

They came yelling their grief and anger and Sundance got ready to die. He was turning the point of the Bowie toward his heart when Victorio grabbed the haft with his left hand and turned it to one side, and he showed amazing strength, even with the wound.

"No," Victorio said, forcing the knife point away from Sundance's chest. "You do not have to die. I will not let you die."

The Apaches surrounded the two wounded men, poking at Sundance with rifle barrels, jabbing at him with knives, but they fell back at Victorio's command. "This man could have killed me and he did not," Victorio said. "He could have let me bleed to death and he did not. Listen to my words. He is not to be harmed. The man who harms him will die."

The Apaches muttered angrily until Victorio ordered them to be silent.

"I better fix that arm," Sundance said after he wrapped a strip of torn shirt around the crease in his head. Soon the rag was soaked but the bleeding stopped. The inside of his head throbbed like a drum.

Victorio's arm bled again when he loosened the tourniquet. At his order Apaches pried lead from cartridges and poured gunpowder into his hand. Then he told Victorio to bend his arm upward until the wound was almost closed; and when it was he poured the gunpowder along the top of the wound until it was covered by a thick line of black. He dug into his pocket for a sulphurhead match and lit it on the stock of a rifle. The creosote-soaked wood flared and he touched it to the gunpowder. The gunpowder hissed and popped as it burned along the top of the wound, sealing it completely, and when it stopped burning there was a thick scab of burned flesh.

"I don't know how good the arm is going to be, but you won't lose it," Sundance said, tearing a shirt to make a bandage and a sling. He knotted the sling over Victorio's shoulder and put his arm in it. The Apaches whispered and pointed. "You'll have to go easy with the arm," Sundance said. "Don't touch the scab till it falls off. It should heal."

Victorio used some of their precious water to wash the wound in Sundance's head. Then he bandaged it. "Why did they try to kill you?" he said. "They were not shooting at me. I was the dead man but they shot at you. Why?"

"I guess they thought your word wouldn't hold if I killed you. I don't know what it was. Something like that. I'd like to find out."

Victorio said, "Do you want the help of the Apaches?

338

I have already told my people that they are to go from this desert, with or without me. That was my word but there is no longer any need to keep it. We will go with you and we will destroy them."

Sundance shook his head. "No need to destroy all of them. I just want the man who fired that shot, the men who helped him. The others are just men crazed by the desert and afraid to die. Keep your word, Victorio. Take your people away from the desert. Too many have died. Take your people into the mountains and wait. You will be safe for a while."

"You will come back to fight us?"

"I won't fight you any more. I will do my best to see there is no more fighting. There will be a full report to the War Department. That should count for something. I will make the report and Three Stars will sign his name under mine. You're right. I should have stopped them any way I could. If they move against you again I will come and warn you. If they go that far I'll join you."

A thousand years of killing showed for an instant in Victorio's expressionless eyes. "The two of us together, that would be a war they would remember. I will not lie to you. One part of me wants such a war, longs for it. They have done so much to the Apaches. But they would kill us all in the end. I will do what you say, what part of me wants to do. We will go to the mountains and wait. If they move against us we will fight until we are all gone. I often think that is how it must end. But men must hope . . ."

Sundance started out in pursuit with three full canteens of water slung from his shoulder. The Apaches had just about run dry giving him the water. He had no way of knowing who had fired the shot at him with the

Hawken. He guessed it was Comiskey. But it could be Danforth. If Comiskey had fired the shot, then something had happened to the Major.

They had a start on him, but now he had water and they were running dry. They had more rifles; he had more bargaining power. Out there on the sea of sand he would find them again, and those who sided against him would find him a deadlier enemy than the Apaches. There was only one place they could go, and that was the waterhole. If there was water there he would lose some of his edge. But if they found nothing but dust, then he could call the terms.

A mile from where he was now he found the Major tied hand and foot but alive. His face was turned to the sun and it was burned almost black. His lips were purple and black, covered with oozing white blisters, and eyes were caked shut. Sundance let water trickle through the Major's lips, then wet the bandanna and wiped the gummy muck away from his eyes. They fluttered open, seeing nothing at first. The Major's hat had fallen off and blown away in the wind, then snagged in the sand. Sundance found it and brought it back. He put the hat on the Major's head and pulled it down over his eyes.

Finally the Major was able to talk. "Comiskey did it," he mumbled. As soon as you went with the Indian he jumped me. Comiskey and Gates. Comiskey killed MacCrae and another man. It got started when Danforth came through the line. He ran at me and we were grappling when Comiskey hit me on the head. MacCrae and the other man tried to . . . they killed them with a knife . . ."

"I see them," Sundance said looking at the two bodies now half-covered with sand. "You think you can travel?"

"Help me up. I can travel. Comiskey wanted to kill

340

me, but Danforth said let me die slowly. So they roped me and moved on."

Sundance gave the Major another small drink and helped him to his feet. He swayed against the hot wind, trying to spin the cylinder of the Colt Sundance gave him. He kept mumbling about what he was going to do to Comiskey and the officers.

"Shut up and listen." Sundance could have done without the Major. Still, if it came to shooting, he would be an extra gun. "There's still enough of them to finish us off if we get too close. What we'll try to do is go round and get ahead of them. Get to the waterhole before they do. If there is water there we'll hold them off and bargain for it. If there's no water we'll let them have it. You think you can move that fast? Say it now so we won't waste time. I'll give you water but I won't let you slow me up."

The Major said he could keep up.

In another hour, with the sun sinking fast, they spotted the dust kicked up by the men ahead. Sundance and the Major waited until they disappeared in their own dust, then they went out wide and quickened their pace, overcoming weariness with determination. In the desert there were few landmarks to guide them to the waterhole. According to the map there was an outcropping of red rock thrusting from the sand a mile from the waterhole. He guessed it was red: the place was called Red Man's Rock, one of those strange formations that occurred in the otherwise featureless wasteland. The waterhole was northwest of the rock; at least a waterhole had been there when the map was made.

They rested for five minutes and sipped water, feeling the power of possession that water gave men in the desert. Food was forgotten: in the desert water was food, water was everything.

"I should be dead but I'm not," Major Randolph said with a sort of wonder. "When they left me there I was ready for it. I've been shot at, plenty of times I have, and never thought much about it. When a bullet kills you there's no time to get ready."

"Are you ready now?" Sundance stoppered the canteen.

"You'd think I would be after what happened. You'd think the feeling of being ready would stay with a man."

"Doesn't work that way," Sundance said. "Some of the feeling stays and you don't know about it. A man that's too ready usually gets what he's ready for. What you have to do is always be ready, then fight like hell to stay alive."

Major Randolph got up and got ready to go on. "You still going to write that report to the War Department?"

"That's what I mean to do," Sundance said. "You think I shouldn't?"

Major Randolph said he wasn't asking because of that. "I don't know that I'd stop you if I could. It's been bad all the way because of me. Lying there waiting to die, I thought of the men who were dead and I killed them as much as the Apaches. Until now I was sure I had stopped a war by starting one. A quick campaign instead of a long war. You know for sure I was wrong?"

Sundance said, "Maybe not all the way. Victorio told me he longed for a great war that would drive out the Americans. It might have come when he felt ready for it. Now there won't be any war, not from Victorio's side. It will be a long time before he is ready again. Maybe never. Maybe you stopped a big war but you went about it the wrong way."

"But you're still going to write the report?"

"For what it's worth. There won't be anything that

342

isn't true. You think you can stand the truth?"

"I don't know," Major Randolph said. "I never had it put to me like that."

Looking out over the desert, Sundance said, "It may never get that far, Major. There isn't a sign of that rock."

Fifteen

They didn't find the rock until three hours later, and if it had been darker than it was, they would have missed it. Red light from the setting sun washed over the desert. At that hour there was no horizon, and the sun seemed to hover on the other side of the continent. In a few moments it would disappear leaving nothing but a lingering glow.

But there was the rock, so small that it hardly deserved a name, except that in this wasteland anything was something. Red Man's Rock wasn't even as high as a man and it was buried to half its height by sand. It threw a thin black shadow on the white sand around it. It didn't look like a man of any kind. It was just a rock.

Sundance pointed, squinting against the last glare of the sun. "That's where the water is, if it's there. If it is we're going to have to fight for it. They haven't been making good time but they will when they get closer."

"This is the first time I ever felt like praying," Major Randolph said.

"Won't do any good," Sundance said. "The water is there or it's not. Either way we've got some kind of jump on them. The hardest thing will be persuading those troopers they won't hang. You think they ought to hang?"

"Not the men. I have a feeling that nobody's going to hang, not even me. They'll just kick me out."

"That's the idea," Sundance said.

The waterhole was right where the map said it would be. First, there was a long stretch of shale and rock that seemed to be part of the same formation that had thrown up Red Man's Rock. Then it dipped down into a natural bowl and when they reached the rim wild excitement showed in the Major's wreck of a face. Sundance tried to stop him from running but he broke away with a mad cry, stumbled, fell, and rolled all the way down. Sobbing with anticipation, he crawled to the outline of the waterhole, and when he reached it he gave out with a wild howl of despair that echoed into the sky. He lifted handfuls of sand and flung them around him. He broke into a lunatic dance before Sundance could get close to him.

"It's dry, dry, dry!" the Major cried, stepping through his mad dance.

Sundance leaped on him and knocked him to the ground, clamping his hand over his mouth. "Be quiet, you fool, you want to let them know we're here? One more sound and I'll lay you out. You hear me? Nod your head if you know what I'm saying."

Sundance took his hand away and let the Major breathe. "There may be water underneath the sand," Sundance said. "Start digging and don't make another sound. They may be on top of us at any time. It won't be so easy if they heard you."

Darkness closed in like a doubled fist, shutting off the light in an instant. Lying beside the hollow place, they dug into the still hot sand with their hands, gasping in utter exhaustion. Sundance looked up when he thought he heard a sound. There was nothing. The pile of sand they had scooped out grew higher and still no trace of moisture. Now they were more than a foot down and they had to lean in to get at the sand.

The Major dragged himself out with a whispered

curse, and as he did Sundance felt the faint touch of wetness under his fingers. He took his hand away and wiped it on his shirt before he reached in again. It was too dark to see anything. He took his hand out and touched his eyelid with the tips of his fingers. Reaching out to hold the Major back, he said quietly, "There's some water in there. Keep back, I said. If it seeps in we'll be all right."

"How long?"

"No way to tell. Nobody's been by here for a long time. It may fill a few inches, maybe more. We better get up to the rim and keep watch. I'm betting they won't be able to find this place in the dark. First they have to find the rock or they'll wander for hours. Likely they'll sleep now that it's dark. I'll take the first watch. Don't count on there being much water down there. It may come down to what we have left."

The Major said he couldn't sleep, and while he was still saying it, his body slumped to one side. Sundance turned him on his side so his eyes and mouth wouldn't fill with sand. Then, watching, waiting in the darkness, while the hot day wind turned cold, he knew the end wasn't far off. All that had gone before would end here by a wet place at the bottom of a hole. He wondered what had become of his horse, the great stallion that had served him so well. They hadn't killed Eagle because he would have seen the buzzards. But for once he wished they had used a bullet on the big animal. Death by thirst was no less terrible for a horse than for a man.

He was sure they wouldn't come to the waterhole by night. They would dig in, sleep, wait for morning. Killing MacCrae and the trooper would not have done them much good; they would have drunk more than they should. When you counted Danforth, there were six men left. Danforth had survived the Apaches and would be well able to fight. So would Comiskey. Gates would fight if he had to. He guessed they would all be willing to fight for the water. Their thoughts would not go further than that. To hold them off, force them to surrender, he and the Major had a Colt and a Winchester and too little ammunition. The water, if there was anything in the hole, would be their ammunition, their best weapon. Or it could be their greatest danger, in a way, because the survivors would fight all the harder to get it.

Sundance heard Major Randolph coming up the slope behind him. On the desert coyotes were howling. "Get more sleep," Sundance said. "There's a long way to go till morning."

"How are we going to do it?" the Major asked, shapeless in the half-light. He rubbed his arms, stiff with tiredness and cold. "Some water is coming into the hole. So far only a few inches. It'll soak back if it stops coming."

"Maybe it will. We have to wait for everything. The only way we can handle it is to open up on them as they come in. If we can get two on the first try that'll give us more than a chance. That short gun won't be much use unless we get them in close. If we can kill Comiskey and Danforth the others will cave in. But we'll kill who we can."

"I guess you're still wondering about Comiskey?"

"He didn't turn on you for nothing."

"No, he had a pretty good reason. That's the hell of it. He wanted to do it for me."

"Such as?"

"Comiskey wanted to kill you all along. You know something? I wasn't that much against it. Comiskey figured with you dead there would be no report to the

347

War Department. I don't know how much he was doing it for me, how much for himself. If they kicked me out of the army he'd be left by himself. No more major's favorite noncom. It's no credit to me that I let him get away with so much."

"That's right. It's no credit."

"No need to repeat it. I just said it. Comiskey saw it all slipping away from him. He's got a bad name in the army. Once I was gone the other men wouldn't let him forget it. I told him not to talk about it. He did. I thought it was finished until you went out to fight Victorio. Danforth made the difference. If he hadn't come back Comiskey wouldn't have dared."

"They could have made a good case for relieving you of command," Sundance said. "I don't say that to rake up what's done. You're still going to be in trouble if we get through."

"Doesn't seem to matter that much," the Major said. "There's going to be a fight if we don't get the drop on them."

Sundance was tired of talking. "I'm going to look at the water," he said.

When he got down to the waterhole he walked carefully so as not to disturb the piled-up sand around it. He lay on his belly and reached into the hole. He touched the surface of the water. With his hand held straight down, the water came up to his thumb, enough to fill a canteen and maybe more. If the hole filled at the same rate it would be nearly full by morning.

He emptied one canteen into the other and laid the empty one at the bottom of the hole; when it was about half full much of the water in the hole was gone. He took the canteen out, holding it over his mouth so he could catch the drippings. It tasted good after the stale warm water he had been drinking ever since they left the fort. What was in the hole might be all the water they would see. It could stop coming and drain back into the earth.

He slept and there were no alarms during the night. The sky was carpeted with stars and the wind whistled cold over the top of the slope. The Apaches would be well on their way to the mountains. He went back and checked the waterhole again. It was filling again and he scooped water until the canteen was full. He drank deeply and then called the Major down to drink.

"If it stops coming we'll be all right," Sundance said. "We can still walk out of here with what we have."

After that no more was said. They were beginning to act like a team, though they had nothing in common besides a determination to remain alive. They put the canteens out of the way of bullets before they took up their positions. Light began to glimmer in the eastern sky. Comiskey and the others would be on the move by now. They still had the Hawken and that was going to count for a lot. The sun inched its way up, as if trying to take the world by surprise. Then the far rim of the desert flamed red and any small thing cast a shadow.

Sundance could see Red Man's Rock from where he was; with the sun behind it, it looked bigger than it was. Nothing showed on the far side of it. A kangaroo rat skipped across the sand, casting a blur of shadows before it disappeared. Far out a coyote howled defiance at the sun, and then it was quiet.

The Major's eyes were staring inward and Sundance had to tug at his sleeve. "They're coming," he said. "Out there." He pointed out past the rock to a line of men straggling across the sand. The sun rolled up in its fury and the desert was glaring bright.

Sundance said, "We'll hit them, then try to talk. You move to the far side if they start crawling. The longer they wait the worse off they'll be. But they have more guns."

Now they had reached the rock and were starting away from it, moving faster than they had been. Some yelled feebly as they came, trying to get their legs to move with the same urgency with which they longed for water. Sundance sighted the Winchester and waited for the first man to get into range. In the glare of the sun they were just figures, none distinguishable from the rest. Then someone shouted and there was another shout and they threw themselves flat. All but the man out in front. He kept running with his hands out in front of him. Sundance stopped him with a bullet and when he jacked a shell and sighted there was nothing good to shoot at.

"That was Comiskey yelling," Major Randolph said from over on the left. "He spotted something or sensed it."

A bullet flew wild and there was more shouting. Sundance sighted at a hump in the ground but held his fire. The hump in the sand began to move and he fired at it and it stopped moving. It moved again and he didn't fire. "Get over there," he told the Major. "They're going to come from both sides. So far they don't know who we are. They know there's one rifle in here. When they get around they're going to lay down fire to see what we've got. Hold off firing as long as you can. They'll know a handgun when they hear it."

Gripping the Colt, the Major skittered down the slope on his back and started across to the other rim. Two bullets kicked up sand on the rim where Sundance was, but he didn't return fire. He turned and the Major was in position, the barrel of the Colt resting on his left forearm.

The first fire came from the Major's side, three

bullets spaced close together. That made three riflemen on that side. The Major held his fire. Rifles opened up from the other side, whining across the hollow in the sand. More bullets came and it got quiet again. On the Major's side firing began again, heaving fire from one rifle. The Major yelled, "They're coming in," and opened fire with the Colt. He fired slowly and steadily and yelled again, "I got one."

The Major rolled on his back and reloaded the Colt. Out in front of Sundance's rifle they were crawling fast in the sand. Sundance shot a man in the hindquarters and killed him as he thrashed in pain. They dug in again, and the firing stopped. The attack on the Major's side started again. "Two men running!" the Major yelled, firing steadily. Fire came at Sundance and he returned it, then whirled when bullets came at him from the other side. A man was running over the top of the rim, firing wildly at the Major. The Major squeezed the trigger and the firing pin clicked on a spent shell. Sundance fired and dropped the man before he could fire again. He rolled down the slope and lay still. The firing stopped.

The silence lasted for a minute, then Comiskey began to yell. "You want to deal? That you in there, Sundance? It has to be you! You better deal. We can wait you out."

Sundance looked over at the Major. "You do the talking. That ought to shake them up."

The Major nodded. "This is Major Randolph!" he shouted. "You hear that, all of you? Comiskey, you hear that! Here's the deal. Put down your weapons and come in with your hands up. That's the only deal you'll get. You want water? All the water you can drink in here. Cold and clean."

"No deal, Major," Comiskey yelled back. "We got

enough water to last us. You want to deal? Here's a deal. We share the water and go our own way. If there's enough water it'll get us to Mexico. We don't aim to hang, Major. Give us water and we'll be on our way. Don't have to be no more killing. What's your answer?"

"It's one way to get out of it," Sundance said without turning. "We're a good way across right now. With water they could make it to the mountains. More fighting won't do them any good."

The Major spun the cylinder of the Colt against the flat of his hand. "Would you let them get away?"

Sundance said, "Not Comiskey. I don't care about the men. Comiskey and Gates should go down for this. Danforth's crazy. I don't count him. Don't talk to Comiskey, talk to the men."

When the Major finished shouting, Comiskey shouted back, "You have to deal with me, Major. I give the orders here. Any man tries to give up I'll shoot him like a dog. You hear that, you dog soldiers? I'm your general, you'll do what I tell you."

A man stood up and Sundance's finger began to tighten on the trigger. Then he eased the pressure as the man threw away his rifle and took a step forward. A rifle cracked and the man pitched forward on his face. "There's your answer," Comiskey yelled. "Give us the water and let us go. That's the only way you're going to get out of that hole. The deal is still good if you want to take it. Come nightfall no more deal. You can't keep us out in the dark. How much more ammunition you got?"

Major Randolph held out his left hand to Sundance. Four brass cartridges glistened in the sunlight. "That's it," he said. "How about you?"

Sundance patted the side of the Winchester. "Six in

here, nothing to spare. He's right about the bullets. They have what they took from the dead men. You can still change your mind, Major. The only thing, if they kill us they don't have to dodge to Mexico. Some of them will. Maybe not Comiskey; Gates if he's still alive. If they get back the report will show that you were killed by Apaches. There won't be a word about relieving you of your command. They'll be heroes, Major. You'll be dead so you'll be a hero too.''

Major Randolph's grin was painful. "I always wanted to be a hero,'' he said. "Not this way though. Everybody's been offering deals today. Here's one for you. We have three full canteens. Drink your fill at the hole, then we'll fill it in. You saw for yourself the water isn't coming in so good now. We fill in the hole and that should finish it for a while. Take the canteens and go out in the dark before they make a night attack.''

"And you'll stay and get yourself killed, is that it?''

"I don't see it as such a bad idea.''

"You want to be a hero after all?''

'I'm past that,'' Major Randolph said. "Way past it.''

"Then you want to make up for all the dead men?''

"Maybe that's it. Something like that.''

"Can't be done, Major. You rate yourself high if you think getting killed will make a difference to them. You just want to get killed, no two ways about it. Sorry I can't take your offer. What's between you and the Army and your conscience is your business. Comiskey broke my word for me, tried to kill me. And, Major, sir, that makes Comiskey my business.''

"Then there's no more to be said.''

"Not much,'' Sundance agreed. "Here we are and here we fight. After the sun works on them for a couple of hours they won't be so feisty. Right about noontime

I'm going to do something you won't like. I won't like it either but I'm going to do it."

"What would that be? What won't I like?"

"All that good water I'm going to waste. I'd say that will drive them crazy if nothing else will. Soon as that's done they'll know for sure how it's going to be."

Major Randolph's face set itself in grim lines. "You're right," he said. "I don't like it."

Sixteen

"It's time," Sundance said, squinting at the sun, now in the noon position. He picked up one of the canteens and told the Major to drink as much as he liked. "Not the whole thing. Then I'll drink and shoot a hole in what's left. I'd say a quarter-full canteen ought to impress them."

"This is crazy," the Major said before he drank greedily from the canteen.

Sundance took the canteen and shook it before he drank. It was good to be spendthrift with the water. When he had enough he stoppered the canteen and handed it to the Major.

"Sling that high and hard when I get through talking," he said. "I want them to see what they're missing. Make it good and high so they'll see the water spilling out on the way down. Could be one or two will make a run for it before it's all gone. Get a grip on the strap, then wind up for a long throw."

"I got such a good grip I hate to let go," the Major said.

"Comiskey!" Sundance shouted. "Pay attention out there. All you men listen!"

Comiskey shouted back. "You ready to trade?"

"No trade, not your way. You think we're just bluffing about the water. Not so. You want to wait till it's night. Wait all you like. You won't find us here—

and you won't find water. How are you going to keep us from slipping out when it's dark? You hear what I'm saying?''

Comiskey's shout came back. "Say the rest of it!"

Sundance shouted, "Before we go we'll fill in the waterhole. There's water there now. Won't be when we dump sand in it. You can dig but it'll be days before water starts again. Days if you're lucky."

A yell came back. "You're bluffing, halfbreed!"

"Then watch this!" Sundance nodded to the Major.

Swaying on his feet below the rim, the Major swung the canteen by the strap and let it go, falling as he did. The canteen sailed up into the air, black against the blue of the sky, and Sundance followed its flight with the sights of the rifle. It went up as high as it would go and began to fall. Sundance's rifle followed it down. He fired and the canteen broke and spattered water and a wild yell went up from the men watching it. It clunked in the sand, still dribbling water, and a man staggered to his feet and came toward it. Sundance shot him down. He let him get it and lift it to his mouth before he killed him.

"God!" Major Randolph said, turning his face away. "That was young Bannister."

Sundance had no time to mourn Bannister, whoever he had been. "That's one canteen gone," he shouted. "You want to see more shooting? Come in shooting or give up, that's the only way you're going to get water."

"Go to hell, halfbreed," Comiskey shouted back. "We'll take our chances where we are."

Major Randolph's eyes were bitter. "It didn't work," he said.

Suddenly a pistol shot rang out and they both looked up. The pistol fired again and again, but no bullets came their way. Sundance motioned the Major into silence.

"That's Gates," Major Randolph whispered when shouting started again. They inched up to the rim, but there was no one in sight.

"This is me, sir, Lieutenant Gates," the shout came. "I just shot Comiskey. Sir, I just shot Sergeant Comiskey. We're coming in, sir. You hear me, sir? This is Lieutenant Gates!"

"Come in, Gates," the Major yelled, adding in a whisper, "You dirty, crawling son of a bitch." He raised his voice. "Come in slow and pile the rifles when you're fifty yards from here. We'll cut you down if you try anything. Every man's hands high above his head. Bring in Comiskey when you come. Come in without him, we'll open fire. Got that, *Mr.* Gates?"

"Got it, sir," Gates yelled back.

"Notice all the 'sirs,' " the Major said. "*Mr.* Gates thinks it's going to be all right."

"Watch for Comiskey," Sundance warned, sighting the rifle. "He may not be dead."

One by one, the troopers showed themselves. Gates stood up. So did Danforth. Danforth's wrists were tied. Gates and another man lifted Comiskey's body from the ground, staggering under its weight. They started forward with it. The other men came forward with their rifles held above their heads, weaving in the sun. They reached the fifty-yard mark and dropped their rifles, one clattering on top of the other. Gates and the trooper moved on with Comiskey's body. It was time to shoot, Sundance decided. He shifted the front sight on Comiskey's chest and squeezed the trigger. The dead man screamed and pulled a .45 from the back of his belt. The revolver was coming up to fire when Sundance shot him again. Comiskey fell and Gates sprang away from him and stood trembling, begging Sundance not to shoot.

"Come ahead, *Mr.* Gates," the Major ordered.

The men came in, avoiding the Major's eyes, staggering down the slope toward the water. Sundance handed the Major the rifle. "Don't let them drink too much. I'll collect the rifles."

When he came back with the rifles the Major had the men lined up with their hands by their sides. Gates stood by himself. Danforth sat in the sand muttering. Gates was talking again and the Major told him to shut up. Sundance stood on the rim of the waterhole looking out over the desert. Then, far away, he saw a speck, something moving. It got bigger and his heart leaped in his chest. Ignoring the others, he grabbed a canteen and ran out, falling and getting up again as he ran. He yelled up into the hot empty sky.

The great stallion came on slowly, using up the last of its enormous strength. It tried to break into a run when it saw Sundance. Then it faltered and stopped and waited for him. It whinnied as water splashed into Sundance's hat. "It's all right, boy," Sundance said softly. "It's nearly over."

Sundance led the big stallion back to the waterhole. He wanted no more of it. "It's all yours, Major," he said. "You have some water, make your way back as best you can. I'm taking my horse and water for both of us. You do what you like. Get yourself another scout. I hope I never see you again, Major, sir."

"What about your report to the War Department? All my crimes?"

Sundance looked at the line of men, the ragged, swaying line. "The hell with the War Department, the hell with the army, the hell with you. A word of advice. Do what you can to help the Apaches when you get back. If I hear of you raiding them again, I'll be back. I told Victorio I'd join him if he needs me. Think about

358

that, Major. I don't know what you're going to turn out to be. Maybe you learned a few things out here."

"A few things," Major Randolph said quietly. "You don't have to bring charges against me. I'll report what happened here and I'll tell it straight, as you say. I'll give my side of it too. There is my side of it."

Sundance looked at the men. "That's fine for you; what about them? They'll get shut up for life. Knowing that they may turn on you again. It's time to bend your back, Major. Make a deal with them. Not in words. That wouldn't be any good, to say it, I mean. Without saying it, let them know they aren't going back to a court-martial. Damn yourself if you want to, leave them out. You're the Major again. It's time you all joined the same army again."

"How?"

"Give Gates a drumhead and shoot him," Sundance said. "But you do what you like, Major. That's what he faces anyway. Find him guilty, line up the men, shoot him. You might even make a little speech saying that Gates and Comiskey were the guilty ones. Now they're dead and that's the end of it. If you don't think that will work, my advice is to watch your back. So long, Major."

Sometime later, staring at the mountains that were beginning to appear on the far side of the Ninety Mile Desert, Sundance heard the quick crash of rifles coming on the wind. That was all, a single volley, and then there was silence.

"Goodbye, *Mr.* Gates," Sundance said. In less than a day the desert would be behind them. It was hard to believe that there was another world where things were green and water ran freely. In the days ahead they would rest until both were strong again. Maybe it was over. Only time would tell. Time and the United States

Army. He'd be back if the Apaches needed him, and that was a promise.

A promise he would keep.

DAN'L BOONE

DODGE TYLER

THE KAINTUCKS

The Natchez Trace is the trail of choice for frontiersmen heading north from New Orleans. But for Dan'l Boone and his small band of boatmen, the trail leads straight into danger. Lying in wait for the legendary guide is a band of French land pirates out for the payroll he is protecting. And with the cutthroats is a vicious war party of Chickasaw braves out for much more—Dan'l Boone's blood!

4466-8 $3.99 US/$4.99 CAN

KIT CARSON

KEELBOAT CARNAGE
DOUG HAWKINS

The untamed frontier is filled with dangers of all kinds—both natural and man-made—dangers that only the bravest can survive. And so far Kit Carson has survived them all. But when he sets out north along the Missouri River he has no idea what lies ahead. He can't know that the Blackfeet are out to turn the river red with blood. And when he hitches a ride on a riverboat, he can't know that keelboat pirates are waiting just around the bend!

___4411-0 $3.99 US/$4.99 CAN

BLOOD HUNT

David Thompson

With only his oldest friend and his trusty long rifle for company, Davy Crockett explores the wild frontier looking for adventure, and has the strength and cunning to face any enemy. But even he may have met his match when he gets caught between two warring tribes on one side and a dangerous band of white men on the other—all of them willing to die—and kill—for a group of stolen women. It is up to Crockett to save the women, his friend and his own hide if he wants to live to explore another day.

_4229-0 $3.99 US/$4.99 CAN

Dorchester Publishing Co., Inc.
P.O. Box 6640
Wayne, PA 19087-8640

Please add $1.75 for shipping and handling for the first book and $.50 for each book thereafter. NY, NYC, and PA residents, please add appropriate sales tax. No cash, stamps, or C.O.D.s. All orders shipped within 6 weeks via postal service book rate. Canadian orders require $2.00 extra postage and must be paid in U.S. dollars through a U.S. banking facility.

Name_____
Address_____
City_____State_____Zip_____
I have enclosed $_____ in payment for the checked book(s).
Payment <u>must</u> accompany all orders. ☐ Please send a free catalog.

MAX BRAND

SLUMBER MOUNTAIN

Here, for the first time in paperback, are three of Max Brand's best short novels, all restored to their original glory from Brand's own typescripts and presented just as he intended. "Outland Crew" is an exciting tale of gold fever and survival in a frontier mining town. In "The Coward," a man humiliated in a gunfight finds a fiendishly clever way of exacting revenge. And in "Slumber Mountain," Brand presents a harrowing story of man versus the wilderness as a trapper fights for his life against the mighty wolf known as Silver King.

___4442-0 $4.99 US/$5.99 CAN

The Lightning Warrior

The Indians call the great white wolf the Lightning Warrior because of the swiftness of his attack. But even the giant Colbolt isn't interested in the massive wolf until Sylvia Baird makes the beast's pelt the one condition for her hand in marriage. She thinks she is safe, but when he returns with not only the pelt, but the wolf itself, and demands his prize, Sylvia's only hope is a desperate flight for freedom. Colbolt sets out in determined pursuit, but he's forgotten Sylvia's newest ally. . .the Lightning Warrior.

___4420-X $4.50 US/$5.50 CAN

Dorchester Publishing Co., Inc.
P.O. Box 6640
Wayne, PA 19087-8640

Please add $1.75 for shipping and handling for the first book and $.50 for each book thereafter. NY, NYC, and PA residents, please add appropriate sales tax. No cash, stamps, or C.O.D.s. All orders shipped within 6 weeks via postal service book rate. Canadian orders require $2.00 extra postage and must be paid in U.S. dollars through a U.S. banking facility.

Name_____
Address_____
City_____ State_____ Zip_____
I have enclosed $_____ in payment for the checked book(s).
Payment <u>must</u> accompany all orders. ☐ Please send a free catalog.
  CHECK OUT OUR WEBSITE! www.dorchesterpub.com

OUTLAWS ALL

From Alaska to the Southwest, Max Brand, the master of the Western tale, brings the excitement of the frontier to life like no one else. His characters live, breathe, struggle and triumph in a world so real you can hear the creaking of the saddle leather. Gathered in this collection are three classic short novels by Brand, all filled with the adventure and heroism, the guts and the gunsmoke, that made the West what it was.

___4398-X $4.50 US/$5.50 CAN

Dorchester Publishing Co., Inc.
P.O. Box 6640
Wayne, PA 19087-8640

Please add $1.75 for shipping and handling for the first book and $.50 for each book thereafter. NY, NYC, and PA residents, please add appropriate sales tax. No cash, stamps, or C.O.D.s. All orders shipped within 6 weeks via postal service book rate. Canadian orders require $2.00 extra postage and must be paid in U.S. dollars through a U.S. banking facility.

Name_____
Address_____
City_____State_____Zip_____
I have enclosed $_____ in payment for the checked book(s).
Payment <u>must</u> accompany all orders. ❑ Please send a free catalog.
CHECK OUT OUR WEBSITE! www.dorchesterpub.com